to
Marilyn

May you
have the
strength and
courage to go
you may

Debbie

MW01598240

SPLIT SECOND
DECISION

VICKIE SWAN

authorHOUSE®

AuthorHouse™ LLC
1663 Liberty Drive
Bloomington, IN 47403
www.authorhouse.com
Phone: 1-800-839-8640

Published by AuthorHouse 06/24/2014

ISBN: 978-1-4685-8538-4 (sc)
ISBN: 978-1-4685-8539-1 (hc)
ISBN: 978-1-4685-8540-7 (e)

Library of Congress Control Number: 2012906884

I dedicate a special tribute to say thank-you to my "Angels" for helping me write and edit this extraordinary book.

CHAPTER ONE

Anita's eyes fluttered as she struggled to open them. Panic commanded her to move, but she soon became aware her body would not budge no matter how much she willed it to. Her closed eyes danced wildly back and forth and an uncontrollable burst of warm liquid flowed from them. A sinking feeling swept through her body as she acknowledged she was being prevented from performing the simple task of brushing her tears away.

Her stomach felt as though it housed a school of fish, and every muscle felt powerless to fight back. Distraught, Anita laid still, took several deep breaths, and concentrated on identifying her surroundings.

Forcing her eyes to open as wide open as they could, Anita found their lack of cooperation frustrating, as the only results she acquired were mere slits. As she peered through the narrow openings, she realized that her effort to open her eyes had been wasted; her surroundings were completely dark. She decided to remain calm and let her other senses tell her what she needed to know.

Anita strained her ears and heard a faint engine noise. Her body vibrated with subtle movements, and she calculated she was on a moving vessel. Twitching her nose back and forth brought her attention to the repugnant odor of urine, and she concluded that her constraints meant her toilet was right at her disposal; she was lying in it. The combination of the smell and the knowledge that she was lying in her own body fluid repulsed her, causing her to gag.

Quickly changing her thoughts, she was trying to see how else to put her other senses to use, when something furry brushed up against her leg. She closed her eyes, shuddering, and she resigned herself to the fact that she had no control. Anita silently prayed to go back to sleep; instead, flashbacks emerged, flooding her with memories and images of how she had arrived in such a situation.

1

CHAPTER TWO

It was an extraordinary night as high winds blew the trees with force, lightening bolts lit up the sky, and thunder could be heard as it rumbled and echoed through the valley. The rain pounded down as if someone had overturned buckets of water. Anita stood before the mirror, tied her hair back, and took a second look. Sighing, she looked out the window at the horrid scene Mother Nature was displaying, turned and headed downstairs. The lights flashed off one last time as Anita entered the kitchen and a silhouette appeared, causing her to gasp. She calmed down when she became aware that the figure was that of her bother, Jake, sitting in the shadows. The frequent flash of lightning, eerily lit the room for seconds at a time, but the power did not come back on.

A look of gloom was written on Jake's face, as he spoke, "Any idea where our wayward parents are?"

Anita grabbed a glass of water and sat across from him at the table. "No. Haven't heard a peep from them in several weeks and it's uncharacteristic of them not to check in. Think something may have happened to them?" Jake shrugged his shoulders indicating he had no way of knowing, and answered, "They say no news is good news. Although the mere thought of what any one of his clients could do to them frightens me."

Anita could feel coolness run through her veins. She rubbed her arms to bring back the warmth, and said, "Thanks for the grisly vision. You may be right. Dad does defend and counsel some of the most notorious criminals known to man. You think something may have happened to them, don't you?" Jake made no attempt to respond, so Anita changed the subject. "So what are you up to these days? You look like a man on a mission."

Testing his sister's integrity, Jake watched her reaction as he questioned her. "Suppose I were to throw a party. Would you join in with the festivities?"

Sliding forward on her chair and leaning back to get comfortable, Anita responded, "You know how much being a lawyer means to me, so stop the digs and hassles about my being too serious. Besides, it would depend on the night and the occasion. You do have a theme night planned, don't you?"

Planting a guilt trip on his lovely sister, Jake threw in a little extra bone. "Ever since our dear parents left, all you do is study. There is a life outside of books that you should explore, and, our parents aren't dead, merely misplaced. I hope anyway. You know, we never spend time together anymore, and I thought a party would be fun and we could get to know one another again. What do you think?"

Getting up from her chair, Anita searched around the kitchen for the emergency flashlight, retrieved it, and sat back down across from Jake. Shining her light in his direction so she could see his facial expressions better, Anita looked her brother squarely in the eyes, and retorted, "Like you really care. We've never seen eye to eye on anything. You would much rather spend time with your friends than with me. So, since when did you start taking an interest in what I do? What, no friends to talk to?"

Jake got up from his chair and towered over Anita as he looked down at her. His voice held concern. "I'm worried you've become a hermit, and too much like Dad. I thought you needed a little pick me up. Excuse me for caring." Knowing his sister was about to cave by the pout on her face, Jake added, "Oh and bring a date. You know, a member of the male species, unless you're gay."

Before Anita could blink, the words flew out of her mouth. "Where am I supposed to find a date?"

Jake laughed as he pinched Anita's cheek. His voice took on a sappy sound as he approached her with an idea for a date. "Jon would like to escort you."

Frowning at such a preposterous suggestion, Anita got up and stood face to face with her brother. She hissed, "Jon's a stud, or rather thinks he is. The least you could do is come up with a better plan than that. Never mind, I'll find one on my own and don't laugh. I can do this."

As Jake left the room, his laughter could be heard over the brewing storm. She shone the flashlight down the hallway and noticed that he walked like an old man. As quickly as the power had gone off, it was back on, again. Putting the flashlight away, Anita was now determined to meet Jake's challenge and made it her main goal.

3

CHAPTER THREE

Still flustered from her conversation with Jake, Anita entered her father's den. Looking around her at the books and resources the room housed, Anita despaired that she would never measure up to her father, a criminal lawyer known the world over for his work. Flopping down into the cozy leather chair behind the desk, Anita put her head down, neglecting her studies, and concentrated on where she was going to find a date; after all, she had to show Jake she wasn't a prude.

Contemplating her next move, Anita made a phone call to her best, and only friend, Carolyn. The word 'opposites' described them to a tee; Carolyn was bouncy, carefree, and outgoing. Nothing bothered her. Anita on the other hand, was studious, predicable, and had a conscious that drove her nuts. She was very much a Miss Prissy.

Learning of Anita's little dilemma, via their phone conversation, Carolyn burst out laughing. She congratulated her friend on getting out of her little box, and told her not to worry, that everything would be taken care of. Hanging up the phone, Anita felt queasy; she was no longer in control, having given Carolyn the task of finding her a date for the party. She looked around the intimidating room once more before closing its door behind her. Any thought of concentrating on her studies had gone out the window.

Taking refuge in her room, Anita was amazed when Carolyn called back, having already found her a date. Curious to see what kind of representative of the male species awaited her, Anita eagerly agreed to the meeting the following afternoon.

The next day, dressed in her usual attire and looking like a bookworm, Anita met with Carolyn, and the two friends caught up on each other's news while waiting for the man of the hour to arrive. When he did, his appearance blew Anita away. Jeremy was a well-built, handsome man, and she was elated. Jeremy, on the other hand, was flabbergasted by his date's appearance; she was clad in sneakers, jeans, and her hair tied back, and because of her paleness, she resembled a ghost. Studying the woman before him, Jeremy wandered what he was getting into, and wished he had seen her before agreeing to this meeting. The vision before him made him rethink his position and was about to leave, when he felt Carolyn's hand on his arm and he conceded the subtle gesture to join them. Catching a glimpse of this interaction, Anita's hopes for the impending date were crushed.

Attuned to the nervousness of both Anita and Jeremy, Carolyn began to drop details about each of them into the conversation, slowly putting the pair at ease. Anita learned Jeremy was going to school on a scholarship, and Jeremy learned Anita was attending law school, and preparing to write her bar exam. Eventually, both agreed to the date. Anita felt bubbly inside, while Jeremy was still uncertain what lie before him.

Days passed by quickly, and before Anita knew it, the party was upon her. Rarely did she see Jake, but on this day his smile was that of a rat, as he asked, "So sis, you really have a date?"

Smugly, Anita responded, "Didn't think I could pull it off did you? Why is it we can't be civil to each other? It seems we are always in competition."

Jake kissed her on the cheek. "It's a love hate relationship, but we both know we love each other. Just different than most siblings."

A darker side to Anita's mood began to show through. She put her hand on her brother's arm, and asked, "Jake, have you heard from Mom and Dad? I'm really worried."

Jake's eyes clouded over, as he spoke, "No. I'm too busy right now to worry about them. Tomorrow's another day."

The unsettled nagging in the back of Anita's mind screamed foul play. The fact their parents hadn't been heard from in such a long time made Anita believe their lives had come to an end, and she yelled at Jake. "Tomorrow we'll start looking for them." She watched Jake turn and wave his hand in the air as though to say he was in agreement, or at least that's how Anita read it.

Judging that she had some time to relax before the party, Anita drew a bath and let the aroma of the soft scented bubbles awaken her senses. She began thinking about her parents and, instead of thinking negatively about them; she surmised how they were going to get a scolding from her upon their return; mainly for their lack of phone calls. A smile appeared across her face. Finding this new way of thinking eased the tension that had built up inside her body, and she sighed. Sheepishly changing her thoughts, she now grinned at the prospect of maybe having a second date with Jeremy.

Feeling refreshed, she was heading down to the study to make a couple of adjustment to her project when the doorbell rang. Anita was stunned; there on the step stood the most handsomely dressed man she had ever set eyes on. Jeremy, for his part, was disappointed with his date's appearance; her attire hadn't changed since the day he first met her. His depleted expression conveyed his disappointment. Reading his emotionless demur, Anita placed her arm under his, and walked him to the party room.

While fixing him a drink, Anita took the time to explain her lack of readiness. "I thought I had more time to prepare. I was just about to make a few adjustments to my thesis for school."

Before they could take a sip of their drink, Jake walked by and, seeing the couple, joined them in the room. "Going to introduce us?" he asked his sister.

Embarrassed, Anita quickly made the introductions and downed her drink to calm her nerves. Grabbing Jeremy by the coat pocket, Anita was going to lead him to her sitting room, when Jake blocked her path. Teasing his dear sister, Jake commented, "Oh sis, a man in your room. What will the neighbors say?"

Feeling shy, Anita pushed her brother off to the side, and jeered, "Jake, not now."

Trying her best not to scare Jeremy away, Anita's fingers grasped the liquor bottle, mix, and ice cubes. She motioned for Jeremy to follow her and they hurriedly headed up the spiral stairs.

Reaching the top stair, both were out of breath and Jeremy took a few minutes to reflect on what just took place. He was confused about the body language between the siblings, but thought they may have been having a bad day. Anita had hoped her first drink would have taken the edge off her nervousness, but since it had failed to do so, she made two more drinks right there at the top of the stairs. Not knowing what to do, Jeremy looked over the edge of the stairwell and drank in the full richness of the house. Now focusing on Anita, Jeremy watched patiently as Anita downed her drink. He expected her to hand him the other one, but instead, she looked at it and then let it slide down her throat. She gave a shake as she wiped her mouth with the back of her hand.

Realizing their date was not shaping up well at all, Anita beckoned Jeremy to follow her to the sitting room, where she announced, "I'm not an alcoholic, but I'm also not a socialite. I had hoped a couple of drinks would help me relax." Placing the bottle, mix and ice on the table, she continued, "Help your self while I change. I promise you, you won't be disappointed."

True to her word, when Anita emerged from her bedroom, she was a knockout. Jeremy beamed at her, though acutely aware of his own pauper's status in the presence of his noble. Ready for the night's gala, Jeremy held onto a very unstable Anita and together they wobbled down the stairs.

Carolyn was waiting anxiously for Anita to make her entrance so she could introduce her best friend to the new man in her life. Seeing the couple enter the room, Carolyn rushed over to Anita and invited her to meet the man who put a glow in her heart. Jeremy escorted the two lovely ladies to meet the man of Carolyn's dream, but when Anita took one look at him, he reminded her of a hillbilly. He wore a faded clean shirt, his pants were torn and Anita expected to see a rope being used for a belt - but couldn't see one - and his hair was greasy looking, as though it hadn't been washed for a few days. Anita's heart sank because she was sure he was giving off evil vibes and she could feel goose bumps forming all over her body, marking him as a slime ball.

Anita's strict upbringing gave her the ability to be empathetic, and she quickly concealed her aversion by becoming cordial for Carolyn's sake. She shook Blake's hot sweaty hand. Feeling repulsed by the excessive moisture on her skin, Anita dove for the nearest chair, discretely wiping her hand on her dress as she sat down. Pleased with how well she handled the distasteful situation, she looked around and saw that the others had joined her. Blake almost sat on top of Carolyn and his nearness to her friend gave Anita the dry heave feeling. The men shook hands and Jeremy explained they were friends. A red flag went up inside Anita, and she sensed trouble was brewing.

The group began a conversation, which Anita tried to ignore, but her ears perked up when one of them mentioned there would be a valentine's cruise ship dance held the next evening, and that they would very much like to go as a foursome. Shyly, Anita declined, but was soon caught up in the moment when the others made a pact that Jeremy would be her puppet: all she had to do was yank his string. Not ever having control of a date before, it made Anita laugh and she readily agreed. Besides, for her it was a double celebration: she would be able to celebrate the fact she was one of the top five in her class and, she was getting her second date.

While mingling amongst his guests, Jake was approached by a woman who whispered in his ear, "He's a stripper."

Jake, unsure of what he'd heard, replied, "Excuse me?"

The woman spoke with certainty, "Jeremy strips at the club downtown. Believe me, I'd never forget a body like that."

Jake stroked his chin, and smiled. "Let's see how good he really is." He walked over to the D.J. and requested a song he thought might entice Jeremy to let loose with an exotic dance. At first Jeremy ignored the music, and then he began to sway to the music grabbing everyone's attention. Anita was intrigued with how well his body moved, and he thought she was enjoying his dance skills and began to dance a little more provocatively by removing his shirt. Embarrassment and shock ran through her veins, and before he knew what to do, she stormed out of the room. Jeremy, half naked, quickly picked up his clothes off the carpeted floor and raced after Anita apologizing for his actions. "I'm truly sorry," he insisted.

Anita was fast on her feet and was nearly at her bedroom door when he caught up to her. He grasped her arm, spinning her around to face him as she hurled her words at him, "Those moves. Why were you dancing like that?"

"Everyone was enjoying my dancing, including you, so I thought I would spice up the party a little. I'm an exotic dancer. That's how I make my extra money. I don't have rich parents like you," he shot back.

Anita spat back at his insinuation. "Don't put words in my mouth. I was proud of you for going to school on a scholarship. You and Carolyn could've told me when we first met."

Sensing he may be able to salvage their rocky start, Jeremy put his arm around her shoulder, and asked, "We could finish the evening off by having some fun and put this behind us, or we could end it. Which shall it be?"

Pulling away, Anita reached the bedroom door and opened it. "Consider it a night," she replied.

Furiously, Jeremy yelled out so she could hear. "You take life too seriously."

A crushing feeling swept over her, and she turned back to face the handsome man, who might've swept her off her feet, and spoke in an even tone, "Maybe so, but this kind of surprise I don't like. Had I been informed earlier, things might've been different. As it turns out, you shamed me and I don't take kindly to that."

"You'll regret this," Jeremy called back to her, over his shoulder.

"I already have," Anita retorted back. She made sure to close her door with force.

Jeremy finished his route to the main door and slammed it hard behind him, but the impact was muffled by the noise of the party, and his efforts to let everyone know his true feelings were squashed.

In the party room, amidst the revelers, Jake felt remorseful for his actions. He dodged Carolyn for the remainder of the evening, fearful of the repercussions of her wrath for how he had treated his sister. He knew Carolyn said exactly what she was thinking and could often be brutal.

Knowing how Anita's mind worked, Carolyn and Jake knew that Anita would readjust, but for now mamma bear was in her room, hibernating for the night.

CHAPTER FOUR

The next morning Carolyn thought Anita's ego would be intact, and took over a cup of latte coffee and sweet glazed donuts. At first Anita wouldn't let her in, but she was hungry and the temptation of such sweet succulent treats won her over. Carolyn began the conversation by asking Anita what she thought of Blake, and Anita had to scramble for an appropriate answer. She told Carolyn that she thought he was a down to earth kind of guy and didn't care what people thought of him, and that she admired that in a man. Carolyn was happy with her friend's evaluation of him, and then turned the subject around to Jeremy.

Anita shut down and sat still, so Carolyn continued talking, filling the room with noise. She apologized for not telling her about Jeremy's side job, but she didn't think he'd dance in such a manner, but had to admit he jazzed up the night. Carolyn could see a small smile forming in the corner of Anita's lips, and continued on with her quest to win her over and go to the dance.

"What time do we pick you up?" Carolyn asked.

"For what?" Anita asked.

"You know, the dance. You are still going aren't you?" Carolyn stated, more than questioned.

Anita's face became hot and sweaty, and she looked at her best friend in shame. "He'll never forgive me. I was mean."

"Yah, he was a little pissed, but would like to make amends and show you a good time: your way. What do you say?"

The vision of his appearance from the night before made Anita drool, and she lifted her coffee cup up and clinked it with Carolyn's. "I'll go, but he has to pick me up and we'll meet you at the dance. I have some apologizing to do. He was right. I need to loosen up a little," she admitted, to her best friend.

Carolyn changed the subject, yet again, and spoke, "Have you talked to Jake?"

"Not yet. I don't know where his mind goes at times. Sometimes he's cruel and other times he acts like a brother. I guess I have to accept him for who he is and not react to his strange tactics," Anita spieled, and then continued, "wow. I hadn't told anyone that and it feels good to release such vital inner thoughts."

. Carolyn agreed that Jeremy should pick her up alone, at seven o'clock, this evening. Anita scooted her best friend out the door so she could get ready for her date. She was so excited, and the minutes seemed to drag on.

Trying her best to find Jake and make amends got her nowhere as he could not be found anywhere. Sighing, Anita wrote a little note to say she had gotten over the nights fiasco, and first thing in the morning they should pair up and find their parents so they can rest easier.

The magic hour had approached and exactly on the hour of seven, the doorbell rang. Jeremy, well dressed and looking like a male model, was very pleased when he picked up Anita. She was clad in a stunning, low-cut red gown, and her neck and ears were adorned with jewels made of rubies. They arrived at their destination, walked up the plank, and stepped onto the lavishly decorated boat. Anita felt giddy. The vessel's deck was loaded with balloons filled with prizes, flowers arranged into heart shapes, complete with red and white lights that lit up the entire ship. Anita gave Jeremy's hand a quick squeeze, letting him know she was thrilled and had forgiven him completely.

The music, played by a live band, was soft rock and Jeremy did a slight bow and asked his lovely date if she would like to dance. Anita curtsied back and said she would love nothing better. While up on the dance floor, Anita's eyes diverted to the food table and off to the side was a bar, and found herself guiding Jeremy over for the scrumptious taste of a Mai Tai. Consuming a glass of the wonderful tasting drink, Anita asked Jeremy to join her in a bite to eat, to which he was very agreeable to and escorted her to the food bar. There, they shared in a conversation about their likes and dislikes in food, and Anita felt very much at ease and was enjoying the young man's company.

While at the food bar, Anita strained her neck to see if she could spot Carolyn, but she had no luck. Jeremy suggested they start a walk about, to which Anita was happy to do, and she ordered a couple a drinks for them to take on their journey. Coming across Carolyn and Blake, Anita was relieved to know they were aboard ship and hugged her best friend. Anita suggested that they all have a drink in their hand, which sparked a little curiosity, but Anita held her tongue until all were well armed with a drink. Raising her glass, Anita's words were full of not-so- humble, pride. "Thanks for being my friend and insisting I come out tonight. I have news I'd like to share with everyone. I am amongst the top five, in the graduating class, and my next step is to take the bar exam. I'm so excited to be able to share this news with you."

Anita warmly received hugs and congratulations, making her feel like she had just been crowned Miss Popularity and she downed her drink. The music filled their souls and all four advanced towards the band and began to dance. Feeling exhausted, Anita tapped Jeremy's shoulder and suggested they sit down. Noticing the time lapse, Anita began to search for Carolyn and became frantic when she didn't spot her anywhere in the immediate room. Jeremy suggested they may have gone on deck, and without warning, Anita whirled around and headed in that direction. Coming up empty handed, Anita became concerned that she couldn't find Carolyn, and red flags went up in her mind, indicating something was out of place.

A rush of adrenaline made Anita edgy. As she searched the entire vessel more thoroughly, Jeremy did his best to reassure her that everything was okay, but she shrugged off his intentions with a hiss. Needing to think, Anita sat down on a chair on the open deck. She was trying to recall the last time she had seen Carolyn, when a passing crewmember extended his hand and gave her a note. As she read the note, summarizing that Carolyn and Blake had been abducted. Their safe return would depend upon the successful exchange of an unspecified amount of cash, and other items. She whispered the final instruction aloud. 'Wait for further instructions at your home'. Anita's expression was like a calm night terrorized by a coming storm.

Anita's eyes were volatile. She stared long and hard at Jeremy, and when she spoke, it was with malice. "You and Blake cooked this up, didn't you?" she said.

Jeremy was taken aback at such a bold accusation. "How can you say that?" I've been with you the whole time, or did you not notice?"

Angry and irrational, Anita pursued the allegation. "I'm not stupid," she said. "You were getting even for our first date. Admit it."

Jeremy's hand quickly reached for Anita's arm and applied pressure, forcing her to look at him squarely in the eyes. His voice was full of rage. "Getting a little high on yourself, don't you think? I want you to listen and listen with both ears. You have no grounds to accuse me, and you have nothing to back up your statement, so I'd be very careful if I were you."

Yanking her arm away, Anita shot back, "Are you threatening me?"

Knowing enough to keep his temper in check, Jeremy walked to the end of the deck to keep his fist from connecting with a solid mass. "I'm making you aware of your allegations. That's all," he shouted.

Anger had filled Anita's body. It was as if ice formed on her words as she spoke. "Neither you nor Blake have a dime to your name. I was persuaded to join you all tonight. Need I say more?"

Jeremy stopped dead in his tracks and swung around to look at the woman before him. His eyes narrowed so it looked as if his eyebrows were joined. "Meaning what, exactly?" he queried.

The icicles of Anita's previous words melted as fireballs now hurled from her lips. "I have money, and neither of you do," she said. "What part of that don't you understand?"

Shaking his head at how someone could think so little of him, Jeremy lowered his voice, "You really think that? I thought we were passed that. You really do need to get out more in the real world."

Even though she realized she was out of control, Anita pursued her allegations. "I thought we were passed all this as well. But things have changed, and if its true, I'll prove it," she said. Before she could do any further damage to her relationship with her new acquaintance, Anita turned and walked away. Her next thought was to find the captain and see what was to happen next in the search for Carolyn.

CHAPTER FIVE

Finding the captain of the boat at the wheel, Anita approached him and inquired what the next step was in finding her best friend. The captain was shocked, because he had heard nothing, and asked Anita what she was talking about. Handing him the note she had received, prompted the captain to immediately sound the bells and had all crewmembers report on deck. Once they were all there, he instructed them to do a thorough search and report back to him immediately. Taking command of the situation, the captain then radioed the authorities explaining what had taken place. Their response was that they were short handed and he and his crew were to detain the guests, let no one off, take down statements, and they would be there as soon as possible. This he related to Anita in hopes of keeping her calmed down.

Confronted with having to wait for the search to begin, Anita's rage reached the boiling point. Adrenalin flowed through her body while she waited anxiously for the ship to dock. The crew reported back that there had been no sign of anyone taking a rescue dingy off the boat to get ashore. There was no space that had been overlooked as in the way of a hiding space. The captain then instructed the crew to begin talking to the other guests aboard the ship and see if anyone saw a boat approach, or if they saw something unusual like a person jumping overboard, or if they even saw the couple in question.

Sitting by the captain, Anita began to feel ignored by everyone around her and watched as the crewmembers started to interview the passengers on board. Not wanting to waste valuable time, she decided to take action.

Anita found Jeremy on the deck where she had last seen him, and whispered in his ear, "I'll see you in hell." Then she jumped overboard to make her escape in the freezing water, swam to shore, and started walking in the same direction as the traffic.

Walking backwards with her thumb out, in an attempt to hitch a ride, Anita- clad in sopping wet evening attire- received strange looks from drivers as they passed by. Finally a young man stopped to give her a lift. Anita did her utmost to pull her drenched hair off her face, but couldn't see how her makeup had run down her cheeks making her look like she had just come from a horror-themed costume party. Little was said in way of conversation, but his glances towards her indicated he was trying to figure out where she had come from; thus giving her an uncomfortable feeling in spite of this man's generosity. She declined to give him any explanations, except where he could drop her off. Thanking her Good Samaritan after he dropped her off at the Police Precinct, Anita hurriedly entered the establishment as the wetness from the lake water was beginning to numb her senses.

Having had the pleasures of seeing Anita with her father a few times over the years, but never actually meeting her, the Lieutenant watched her approach and could see she was shivering and in a state of shock. He took off his jacket, and placed it over her shoulders, and in an instant, the warmth calmed her down. Her tongue began flapping revealing all she knew of the events leading up to Carolyn's disappearance. The lieutenant let her finish telling her story, and was hoping Anita was in a good frame of mind. He took a chance and reprimanded her for not following instructions to stay on board the ship. Anita coolly responded that every second counted for her friend, and because they were short handed, drastic measures were needed to get a good head start: even if it meant not obeying orders.

The lieutenant sat back and looked at the young, frightened lady before him, and asked, "What are you suggesting here?"

Close to tears, Anita made a snorting sound to clear her nose so it wouldn't drip, and stated, "My father is a very powerful and influential man, with clients of the same nature. So, kidnapping comes to mind. Ransom money is another thought. Take your pick."

Handing her a tissue, the lieutenant feeling sorry for the damsel in distress, held back his irritability and explicated that the FBI would be involved by placing a wiretap on her phone. She was not to worry, he explained; everything that could be done was being done. Still not pleased with or trusting the lieutenant's smooth demeanor, Anita pulled a wet picture out of her purse and tried drying it on the jacket draped over her shoulders. She handed it to the lieutenant and in a sad tone, she said, "This is a picture of Carolyn. I'm trusting you will put an APB out for her.

As for Blake, you're on your own. I do know a friend of his, though; my date, Jeremy, who is still aboard the boat."

The cold dress clinging to her legs made her shiver and Anita's legs began to bounce up and down while she waited for the lieutenant to make his call to the ship. When the truth be known that Jeremy was nowhere to be seen, Anita was horrified and stood up like someone had set her on fire demanding she be taken home immediately. Surmising the case was going to be flubbed even more so than it had already, Anita decided a new strategy had to implemented.

The trip in the car with the officer was noiseless, as Anita sat deep in thought about her next move, and the officer concluded she was not in a talkative mood. The car hadn't come to a complete stop in front of her house, when Anita jumped out. She entered the house and ran up the stairs to her room. After a hot shower, she found the warmest clothes to dress in, and then headed down the stairs to look for Jake. Finding only a hot, crackling fire roaring in the study, Anita poured a drink and sat down to capture the fire's warmth. Contemplating on what had just taken place, Anita began to ponder on the possibility that this was, indeed, a kidnapping and she was sure one of her father's clients was behind it. 'Why Carolyn and not me?' kept repeating in her head.

Tears began rolling down her cheeks as memories of the good times they had flashed in her mind, and in that minute, Anita realized she had just lost her best and only friend. Wiping away her tears with her hands and rubbing them on her pants, she vowed she would find her friend, starting with her father's clients if need be.

Making a last attempt to call her dad on his cell proved to be a dead end; all she got was his voice mail. Distraught, Anita began to search the study to see if she could find a list of private phone numbers her father may have kept around, and was soon rewarded with a short list. Going through the list of names meant nothing to her, so she began to dial each of the numbers getting the same answer; they had not seen him for a long time.

Coming to the last name on the list, Anita hesitated before dialing, because she knew this was her last hope. Taken by surprise by the impatient voice, Anita was lost for words, and stammered. "Sorry to bother you, but I am looking for Douglas Jefferson. Have you, perhaps, seen him in the last few weeks?" she asked.

The man snapped back, "Who are you?"

"My name is Anita, and he is my father and it is very important I reach him as soon as possible. Have you seen him?"

"He was here about a month ago," the man said, and was about to hang up the phone.

Anita, anticipating he was done talking, quickly threw in, "And where am I calling? What part of the world are you in?"

"If you *don't* know who you are calling, and *don't* know where you are calling, you shouldn't be calling," he said, in a strained voice and hung up. Saddened by the reaction of the gentleman Anita dialed the number back, but it went to the answering machine, and she hung up. Deep down she was hoping that she had planted a seed, and that the man would contact her father passing on the information. The desire to know where this person lived, Anita got out the chart for phone prefixes, but was unable to find the one she wanted. Disheartened, she sat down before the fire, picked up her drink, sipped on the contents, while images filled her mind with tragedies happening to her parents and Carolyn.

Feeling a presence in the room, Anita looked up. There was Jake watching her every move. She motioned for him to sit and then told him about her misadventure, hoping to hear his views on what he thought may have transpired. Listening intently, Jake made no attempt to talk, but when she had finished her story, he told her he knew a little of the circumstances. He explained he had lit the fire for her; adding he knew she had jumped overboard and she would need a little warmth to keep her bones from freezing.

Thanking her brother for such a kind act, Anita patted his hands. "You surprise me. Thank you. I found some phone numbers in Dad's drawer hidden at the back, and called them. Only one answered and he had seen Dad about a month ago. He wouldn't tell me what country he was in and hung up. I'm hoping he makes a call to dad," Anita said.

Sitting by the fire and watching as it playfully danced around the wood, Anita and Jake knew that waiting for something to materialize could take awhile and concocted a plan. Jake would find Jeremy and note every move he made, while Anita would keep trying to reach their parents. Jake got up, made a drink, and toasted to the fact that this was their first time in alliance making Anita smile: for indeed, it was a very true statement.

They were startled when the phone rang and Jake immediately put it on speakerphone. Before they could say a word, a disguised voice could be heard as though reading from a paper. "In exchange for your friend, we want a million dollars, a new car filled with gas and non-perishables, and it is to be ready in forty-eight hours." Click. The phone went dead. Had there been a trace to pinpoint the origin of the call, it would've been futile. After the initial shock wore off the brother and sister team, Anita and Jake began to pool their resources; together they came up short of what was demanded. Although they are not religious, their ashen faces turned towards the ceiling as they prayed their parents would call very soon, and help them through this ordeal.

Not wasting another second, Jake disguised himself beyond recognition and sat outside Jeremy's apartment building following his movement and documenting every detail. At home, Anita grew impatient and began to go stir-crazy waiting for any news that would put her out of her misery. Growing increasingly restless, she finally violated her brother's instructions to stay put, and ventured downtown.

In her travels, Anita caught a glimpse of a person resembling Blake sauntering through the downtown core, and instincts told her it was indeed Blake. Admitting her stalking skills needed a little polishing, Anita did her best to follow, but soon lost her target. Like a hurricane picking up speed, Anita turned her vehicle in the direction of the police station. Pulling up in front of the building, she slammed on the brakes, parked, and walked into the station like she owned it. The lieutenant was very displeased with seeing her, and directed her to go home, stating that everything was being handled accordingly. Finding the nearest chair, Anita made sure she scraped it across the floor, noisily, and sat down.

Folding her arms in front of this obvious numb skull, according to Anita's thoughts, she spoke with a very authoritative voice. "I want a search warrant put out for Blake and Jeremy and I don't mean later, I mean right this minute. They're not figments of my imagination; they are on the run. So, I will wait here until I see the warrants."

Trying not to say the exact words that wanted to escape from his mouth, the lieutenant held his breath as he spoke, and did not exhale until he was done. "I need hard evidence to back up what you say, not intuition."

Anita's words cut the tense air like a hot knife being inserted into a brick of frozen ice cream. "Fine. You want evidence, you will get the evidence," she said, and stormed out of the room, leaving everyone in the precinct aware of the intensity of her anger.

Feeling as though he had handled her more like a child than an adult, Anita headed home and hoped there was some word about something good. Jake had arrived minutes before, and the two sat down watching the clock as it ticked on the wall; the minutes seemed to be doing double time and the two knew the time to fulfill the ransom was coming fast.

Jake got out his papers and showed Anita that Jeremy's comings and goings were that of a normal person with little to hide. He hadn't gone anywhere out of the ordinary, but he had made a few calls from a pay phone, and then went home.

Anita could see, in her mind, Blake and Jeremy had joined forces in the abduction, but something went wrong and now they were going their separate ways. Rather than sit there and wait for something to happen, Anita decided she *would* make something happen. She got up, ran up the stairs to her room, and packed a small bag, making sure she had everything needed for surveillance on Blake. About to leave, Jake's body blocked the entranceway, but Anita's determination to find her prey gave her the strength to push him off to one side. Her tone was that of a dictator. "You stay close to the phone. Anything could happen and time is crucial. I'll go see if I can find Blake, and I promise to check in every couple of hours."

Jake was unhappy he had to sit and wait and, with a harsh tone, he responded back, "Why do you get to call all the shots?"

"Because if I stay here, my mood could make a snake look more inviting," she retorted.

Resigning to the fact that his sister's mood could get ugly, he waved goodbye as she left and he went to the fireside, poured himself a drink and downed it in one, all the while keeping one eye on the clock.

It was easy to decide where to begin her search. She would start on the less affluent side of town, since neither Blake nor Jeremy had much in the way of funds, and she would then work her way into the upscale end of town and see where the trail leads. Showing pictures of Carolyn and a composite of Blake around town got her nowhere, though, and Anita became tired, frustrated, and hungry. She pulled up in front of a little diner, intending to go in and tame her hunger pains. However, as Anita was stepping out of her car, she spotted a moving vehicle out of the corner of her eye and swore it was Blake driving. She hopped back into her car and began following, hoping to get a location and phone it into the police.

As she tailed him through the dark streets, Blake made several little stops. Anita suspected that he knew she was onto him and was trying to foil her plans. Finally, Blake came to a complete stop, and Anita found herself parked in front of a sleazy motel. She watched and then followed as the man in question disappeared around the back of the building. Shrubs blocked her view of the motel's back wall, but tiptoeing around a bush, she saw a door close. She did not see, however, whether it was Blake who closed it.

Anita flipped a coin and decided to stay awhile longer and watch for activity, but as time passed, she became convinced that Blake was staying put. Anita called the police precinct and demanded they send a squad car over immediately to apprehend Blake. The desk Sargent, who answered the phone, politely indicated he would have a car go and check it out. Anita was so proud of having found Blake that she wanted to stay and see the fireworks. She wanted to watch him go down in flames.

Rejoicing in her accomplishment, Anita spotted the police car as it approached the motel, but was astounded when they just shone a spotlight on the cars parked outside and drove off. Sleep was not a possibility for Anita at this point, and she decided to wait for Blake to resurface. Looking at her watch, she realized she hadn't check in with Jake. Her conversation with her brother revealed that there had not been any calls, making them both feel destitute.

Anita's irritation regarding the police precinct was stronger than her respect for it, at the time, and she chose to drive to there and wait for lieutenant Giles to enter his office.

He was barely in the building when Anita made her appearance known, and her voice was loud, like someone had turned on the loudspeaker. "What kind of police force do you have?"

Turning sharply to look at the person speaking in such an obnoxious manner, the lieutenant motioned for her to go to the office. "I'd prefer we talk in the office, rather than out here," he said, matching her tone.

Not making any move towards the office, Anita continued with her sharp tone. "My father would be so ashamed if he knew how incompetent you are," she said.

The lieutenant's mouth was agape, and he stood holding his cup of coffee in his hand, and again gestured for her to step into the office. Complying, Anita's heavy steps could be heard echoing throughout the lobby. Once they were both in the office, the lieutenant closed the door and set his coffee cup down as he leaned in towards Anita. His words were clear and concise, as he spoke, "You will never barge in like that again. This is a professional building, and I expect a professional attitude from you, at all times. My respect is for your father. You have not earned any yet."

Feeling a little meek, Anita's face went crimson red. "I admit I was out of line and from now on, I will respect where I am with the appropriate attitude."

"Now," the lieutenant said, "What has you so riled up?"

Meekly, Anita described in detail everything that had occurred that evening and questioned him about what action he proposed to take. He knew no amount of apology would satisfy the young individual before him, so he candidly explained that the department was shorthanded, and that he thought her concerns could wait until morning.

The words, 'he thought' rang throughout her head causing her to show him how much she detested the remark. She leaned onto the desk and huffed like an enraged bull, as she peered at the lieutenant. "This case may not mean much to you, but it does to me, and I feel you are shirking your responsibilities. I'm hoping that was professional enough for you."

The lieutenant's face went flushed and let his own feelings be known. "Go home. I've said this before and I'll say it again, all is being done in the proper manner."

Taking heed his temperament, Anita became dyspeptic as she left the station. She got in her car and decided to make another trip around the motel, when an old beater truck went sailing past her in the opposite direction. A side glimpse told her it was Blake; she knew he was taunting her. Driving like a mad woman, Anita sped up to make a U-turn, giving him the extra edge he needed to vanish. Anita hit the steering wheel and swore. Her heart beat fast. Her hands shook as she phoned the station and gave a brief description of what just happened and the type of truck he was driving. She was appalled that they didn't show much concern. Glancing at her watch, Anita noticed it was time to check in with her brother. Her tears wanted to unleash themselves when Jake told her the news: there had been no word from anyone. After hanging up the phone, Anita vented her frustration by screaming as loud as she could. She hit the steering wheel releasing a portion of her pent-up anger, and became somewhat subdued.

With a tormented tear-stained face, Anita drove to her house and, as she pulled into her driveway, she saw the lieutenant pull up behind her. In a low voice, he asked her to stop and listen, and then explained that the FBI would be arriving at her house later in the day to attach wiretap equipment on the phone. The news hit her like someone was having a baby: extra guests and new rules. A loud distracting scream was heard coming from the house. Jake had opened the window, and bellowed, "Anita, get your ass in the study right now!"

Without hesitation, Anita and the lieutenant bolted into the house in record time. As they entered the study, they could hear heavy breathing over the speakerphone, and then words were spoken clearly and concisely. "Back off and stay put because pursuing us will only jeopardize your friend's safety." A click, and then silence ended the call.

The lieutenant's face turned a grayish white color, as if he were near death. He became edgy, as he faced the fact that Anita's parents were wealthy and held much clout in their community, but also in other parts of the world as well. What bothered him the most were the implications of what Anita had been saying about Carolyn: she had been kidnapped.

He patiently waited for Anita's blow-up, and was not disappointed. Her words penetrated the awkward silence. "Well, what do you say now?" she asked.

Not wanting to show remorse, the lieutenant stood firm on his decisions, and calmly responded, "I sent two officers back to investigate the motel, and the clerk could not verify that anyone resembling Blake had been in or around the grounds."

The room was warm, but it took on a chill that was felt as Anita let her reply flow from her mouth. "You didn't hear a word I said, did you?" she asked the lieutenant. "I said he went around the back and entered a room, not through the front office or the front of the building. If what I've seen in the past two days is classified as a 'misunderstanding', how do you explain the threat that just came over the phone? The ransom is due in about five hours."

"Do you have everything in place?" he asked.

"We are a little short. I'm hoping my dad calls, like right now," she responded, earnestly.

The lieutenant felt like he was in a tight corner: he either admitted he was wrong or complied with her whims. "I'll go back to my office and get some search warrants for both Jeremy's and Blake's apartments. As soon as they come through, I'll send a detective to carry out the searches," the lieutenant said, hoping it would appease her.

"I want to be a part of the search," Anita said, more demanding than asking.

"No. Having a civilian on a case is not protocol," the lieutenant quipped back.

"That wasn't exactly a question, nor is this a normal case. I have taken law, so I do know a few things about what is and what is not protocol. Besides, you say you have a small police force, to which I don't understand why you didn't call in more recruits from other areas. My going along will keep him honest. I know I'm involved with the case, but who better to tag along than someone with a little insight. I promise not to touch anything, just observe," Anita stated.

His eyes narrowed, like someone in deep thought, and he finally conceded to let her tag along, even though it went against his principles. "Just observe. If I hear you foiled the investigation even on the tiniest detail, I'll see to it you don't practice law: ever. Do you understand?" he said, making sure she knew he meant what he said.

Watching the lieutenant drive off, Anita's lack of patience became apparent and she started pacing around the room. Jake, who had remained behind the scene and witnessed how Anita had manipulated the lieutenant, spoke up. "Time is almost up, and you're going off to investigate?"

Stunned by her brother's insinuations, Anita retorted back, "I can't sit here and wait. There's about left. I have to be doing something constructive, because if I don't, well we both know how ugly I can get. I was there. Without Carolyn I feel like a lost soul and I need to do everything in my power to get her back. Can you understand?"

"Just remember, I too, care what happens to her. What are we going to do if we can't come up with the money, that is, if mom and dad don't call?" Jake asked.

"Like I said, there is about twelve hours left before the deadline. I know they will call," was all Anita could say in response to her brother's question.

Anita sat down and stared at the fireplace, that had kept her warm the day before, and every muscle in her body was tense. Jake left the room knowing that any conversation with his sister was now over, and he would wait for whatever happened first: a call from the parents, a call from the abductors, or a call from the police. He just knew he had to be patient and wait.

When the lieutenant arrived Jake let him in, but not before he let his thoughts be known. "Do you realize what you're doing by letting Anita tag along during the investigation?"

"Yes. I'm letting her work on her demons. I take it you don't approve," the lieutenant replied.

"We don't have the money. What happens then?" Jake asked.

"One step at a time. The FBI will be here within the hour and will set everything set up. We'll take it from there. Does that ease your mind at all?" the lieutenant asked.

"No," said Jake. "You just make sure Anita and the detective are here when the call comes in, do you hear me?" Jake said, with a shaky voice.

"Count on it," the lieutenant replied.

The lieutenant entered the study. Anita was sitting with very little life in her body, and he cleared his throat, making her thoughts disappear. "This really won't help you know," he said. "Sitting and staring I mean."

Anita glanced over at the lieutenant, and then turned back to resume her position. "Not physically, but emotionally perhaps," she responded. "Have you ever had someone snatched right before your eyes? Has it ever occurred to you that they wanted me and not her? What are you going to do about it?"

The lieutenant spoke softly, "We'll deal with things as they happen," he said. "We have to retrace the events of the night, find the culprit, and take it from there. The thought that you were the intended target had crossed my mind, actually. We've been going over the statements given by everyone on the boat, and I scratch my head because no one saw or heard anything out of the ordinary."

Before he could say another word, the detective entered the room, along with Jake. The lieutenant introduced Anita to Detective Christian. Against his better judgment, the lieutenant handed the warrants over to the young detective. Anita bounced out of her chair, grabbed Detective Christian, and ran out to the car. She was ready.

CHAPTER SIX

As they arrived at Blake's apartment doorstep, Anita couldn't wait to enter and see how the man, she loathed so much, lived and was not disappointed in what she saw. It was dingy, with dirty windows, and had very little in the way of furnishings; like someone who didn't hang around much. Gloving up, the detective gave Anita a little pep talk. "Remember, touch nothing and report anything out of the ordinary to me. This has to be by the book. Got it?"

Anita held her gloved hands in the air, and replied, "Got it. I'll start in the bathroom. I know Carolyn spent a few nights here." Detective Christian nodded for her to go ahead and he started in the living room.

Anita searched every inch of the bathroom, but found no sundries belonging to Carolyn, nor anything of Blake's. Detective Christian thoroughly searched every drawer inside, outside and underneath, every corner in each of the rooms, through books and magazines, under the couch, checked the couch cushions, and examined every pillow in the place; no clues were to be found.

Meeting in the bedroom, they went through all the closets and drawers, checked under the bed and a bewildered Anita sat on the bare mattress. Detective Christian joined her and was about to suggest they leave, when they felt a slight bump between them. They jumped up and turned over the surface they had been sitting on, discovering a couple of shirts. Anita and the detective each examined a shirt, and Detective Christian found bloodstains on a pocket. This discovery ended the trail of treasures. Placing their findings into a sealed evidence bag, Detective Christian then opened his police kit and produced equipment needed for fingerprint dusting. His work revealed only partial prints, however, and both he and Anita became dispirited.

Their plan of action was to take the evidence and fingerprints to the station for further testing, and then go for coffee, before beginning their next quest. Because time was dwindling away and they only had about hours before the call came in, it was agreed between them, that they would search Jeremy's apartment, take the evidence in, and if time permitted they would go for coffee.

Making their way to Jeremy's apartment, Anita and Detective Christian found it completely emptied and it offered no trace of having been inhabited. Anita mumbled under her breath that the police were incompetent. Overhearing the remark, Detective Christian defended his department, saying, "This is a small town with a small police force that can only do so much. Kidnapping is a matter for the FBI so; therefore, all is being handled appropriately. You may not like to hear that, but those are the facts."

The words spoken were not appealing to her, and Anita shot back, "Oh come on, they think I'm a shark with no insight, and they think I can be pushed out to sea. If they'd listened to me in the beginning, we would've had a much better shot at finding Carolyn. She could be anywhere right now."

Keeping his cool, Detective Christian dusted for fingerprints around the windows, doors, and doorknobs. "Granted," he replied. "But let's not cry over what was. Let's concentrate on pooling our ideas together. As I understand it, you are a lawyer, and now's the time to put your training into practice."

Admitting that she had been acting like an ass, Anita raised her eyes to meet the detective's. "Well, I'm not officially a lawyer yet," she responded, "but how about we start at the club where Jeremy performed? There is nothing here to search, so we have a little time left. We can grab a coffee while we scout out the area. What do you say?"

Watching him prepare to put his kit away, Anita inquired, "Get any good prints?"

Detective Christian nodded and showed her the sealed envelope with the telltale signs that Jeremy did exist. "We have only one hour, then we head back to your house. You need to be there."

Going to his favorite pastry shop, Detective Christian bought them each a coffee and a donut, and then drove towards the club. "Where are your parents?"

"I've been asking myself that for weeks and actually, I'm worried something has happened to them. Until recently, it's been their custom to check in with us, but lately we've had not even a whisper as to their whereabouts. My dad is a consultant for highly decorated lawyers and criminals alike around the world. I say that because, he seems to have a talent for helping criminals elude their charges. I, however, want to defend the people who truly need help. Enough about me, let's focus on getting my best friend back."

As he sipped his coffee, Anita watched him and realized how much he was like Carolyn: they were both positive people, took things in stride and didn't over react. Thinking of her best friend again, she began to cry and the tears fell like streams of water in a shower. Not sure what to do to comfort her, Detective Christian handed her a napkin to wipe away the tears.

Trying to ease her mind he spoke, softly, "I don't know if this will help, but I am to remain with you until the case is solved." Through her blinding tears, Anita sized up this detective's level of competence. Unsure of whether having him assigned to her case was a good or a bad thing; she concluded she could've done worse.

Enjoying Anita's company, Detective Christian took a small detour through downtown before heading to the club. As they pulled up to the nightclub, Anita saw Blake entering the bar. Detective Christian radioed for backup. Suddenly, her presence made him unsure as to how to proceed – whether to follow the suspect and leave Anita behind, or wait for backup to arrive. It was not an easy choice, but Anita urged him to go, specifying she would lock the doors. With reluctance, Detective Christian waited until the doors were locked and he entered the building alone. Not wanting to be totally exposed, Anita sank down into her seat so only part of her could be seen and waited, hoping Detective Christian would get their man.

A few minutes later, Anita was stunned when her window was smashed and the door swung open in one easy movement. A hand cupped her mouth to prevent any noise escaping from her throat, while another hit her on the back of the head. She was then carried to a nearby vehicle. Minutes later, the backup unit arrived only to find an empty unmarked police car. The officers waited for the detective to return. Christian arrived shortly after the backup squad car, and asked them where Anita was hiding out; but the smashed glass, blood on the back of the seat she had previously occupied, and her purse on the seat of the car, made it clear she had been abducted. Detective Christian was beside himself for leaving her alone, and now admitted that this case had become personal - for him.

Trying to keep the news of the abduction from hitting the streets, the officers decided they would do a quiet investigation in hopes of tracking down Anita, before the news of the disappearance became public. Less than an hour after the abduction, Jake received a call from the kidnapper, who demanded two million dollars, a car loaded with non-perishables, and a full tank of gas. The caller was adamant that, if his demands were not met in full, no one would hear from Anita or Carolyn again. Jake went into shock; they had his sister. He wondered why he hadn't been notified of her abduction from the police. Jake had just placed the handset into the cradle when the phone rang again, making him nearly jump out of his skin. He was relieved to hear his dad's voice, and he looked up, clasping his hand together in gratitude. "Thank you," he said, out loud. Because of the recent excitement, Jake was only partially coherent, but he did his best to explain how things had manifested into a nightmare for the family. Upon hearing the news that his parents were on the next flight home, Jake felt relieved. His folks were alive and well and coming home; he wished he knew that Anita and Carolyn were, too.

CHAPTER SEVEN

As Anita remember the events leading up to her abduction, she became terrified at the knowledge that from now on, her story would become known to her only as it unfolded, and that its final outcome was unknown. Fully conscious, the pain in Anita's pounding head far exceeded any she had ever had, including the pain caused by hangovers. Trying to move, she discovered that her arms and legs were tightly bound to her body; she was immobilized.

Her ears picked up a noise outside the door. In walked a dark, heavy-set man. His voice was high-pitched, as if he had been given a wedgie. "Oh, you're finally awake," he said. "This will be your new quarters for the next few days, and if you promise not to scream or act out, I'll untie you."

Trying to keep herself grounded, Anita nodded her head. She was grateful to be released from her bondage and was surprised when the man handed her a glass of water. She downed it in a matter of seconds and once again she was left in the dark.

From out of what Anita assumed to be the corner, came a shuffling noise. She thought the sound had to be that of a rat and shuttered. But she strained her ears when she thought she heard a whimpering. "Anita, is that you?" said the voice.

Thinking this was too good to be true Anita answered back, thinking that if it was just her imagination no one will know how stupid she felt, but if it was her, she would feel alive inside. "Yes, Carolyn, it's me," and then thought to herself, '*How did she know it was me? I hadn't spoken*'.

Before either of them could say another word, they heard what sounded like a foghorn blow twice. Carolyn spoke quickly, "Think we're on a ship?" she asked.

Anita's mind was working fast. She replied, "Yes. I've felt movement for some time now, and I'd really like to know where we're bound. This whole charade has been a nightmare." Then, changing the subject, Anita inquired, "Carolyn, how did you know it was me?"

Carolyn gave a short dry laugh. "Your body smell. We all have one and, in the dark you tend to rely on your senses."

Anita responded with a half laugh, "Never heard of that. Guess I'll have to try using that in a court case to see if it has any impact on evidence."

As Carolyn spoke, her words were a little shaky. "What do they want?" she asked. "I mean really, what do they want?"

Choosing her words carefully, Anita responded. "My guess would be the black market for white slavery, and because they think we come from wealth, we would bring a much higher price."

Carolyn got up on her knees, and told Anita to keep talking so she could navigate through the darkness towards her. Once they were side by side, they hugged one another, which almost made the whole scenario seem trivial.

"Did they make any demands after I was abducted?" Carolyn wanted to know.

Sugar coating it a bit to make it sound better, Anita revealed what she knew. "They wanted a million dollars, plus a car with a full tank of gas, and loaded with non-perishables. I'm sure the ante went up once they had both of us."

Deep in thought, Carolyn asked, "If you hadn't been abducted, would you have paid the ransom?"

Annoyed that her friend could doubt her in this way, she replied, "Of course. We were just waiting for the time and place for the drop. We even had the police and the FBI looking for you. Speaking of police, I have found the perfect match for you."

Carolyn managed a little laugh. "Hey, I'm the one that does the match making, remember?"

Getting her digs in, Anita replied, "Oh, you do a fine job. The one you chose set us up. I saw him in town and he did a good job of eluding me. Not only that, but while the police were searching a bar for Blake, I waited in the police car, and the enemy chloroformed me, hit me on the back of the head, and here I am. Nice picking."

Trying to make light of the situation, Carolyn added, "Well, you have to agree this is an experience neither of us will forget."

In a matter-of-fact tone, Anita reciprocated, "Carolyn, next time go with my instincts. You are far too trusting. Now that I have that off my chest, can you fill in the blanks of what happened to you?"

Getting comfortable, Carolyn recounted the events. "I remember dancing with Blake when I felt an arm wrap around me, and they covered my mouth with that stuff they use in the movies. When I woke up, I was in this small, dirty, dingy room with one free hand and the other handcuffed to the bed. With the free hand I was able to eat and drink, if that's what you called it. Should I have made any sound, well, that privilege was revoked.

Knowing my options were limited, I decided to bide my time and wait it out. The thought of being slapped, beaten, or raped didn't appeal to me. As for Blake, I don't know what happened to him. Come to think of it, I never saw him again."

Being inquisitive, Anita turned in the direction of where she her friend was sitting. "Now that you have time to reflect, did you see your abductors at the dance, prior to your kidnapping?"

Taking a few seconds to ponder the question, Carolyn finally responded, "My abductors wore masks the whole time, so I can't say one way or the other if they were at the dance."

The door opened, letting in light, and both women winced from the pain of the sudden glare. A man stood there watching them as they shielded their eyes for a few minutes, and then handed them each a glass of water. Food was not offered, and Anita guessed this was because it induced bowel movements and, their captors did not want to clean up after them. After drinking the small amount of water, they both became very weak. Anita assumed they were being drugged to keep them partially paralyzed and suppress their appetites. Their hearing became distorted and they could barely make out what the abductor said as he warned them there was no washroom and good luck with eliminating their body fluid waste.

When the intruder left them again in blackness, the two friends clasped hands and prayed to go into a long sleep until they reached their destination.

Anita heard Carolyn's quiet breathing and knew her friend was in a state of total relaxation. Anita's mind, on the other hand, bounced back and forth as though it was in a demolition derby. One thing was clear to her: things were only to get worse. But as little furry creatures scurried over their bodies, Anita wished that the journey would end, soon.

As no word regarding the ransom drop had materialized; Jake counted down the two days, and then the hours and the minutes until his parents

31

arrived at home. Happy to see his parents as they pulled up into the driveway, Jake knew his dad would now take charge of the situation. But in the back of his mind, he assumed all that had happened, had something to do with his dad's work. The FBI swarmed around the house like bees to honey as they set up their equipment. The police lieutenant was there to lend his expertise, as he was the only one with all the details, up to that point.

Jake's parents were barely settled in, when the ransom call came through. No one interrupted as the abductor spoke. "We want two million dollars, a car filled with gas and loaded with non-perishables. It is to be dropped off at the airport. There is to be no GPS tracking, cannot be a bait car that stops after a few minutes of driving, and no one is to follow us. Is that clear?"

Douglas's voice boomed on the other end of the phone. "Before I meet your demands, I want to talk to Carolyn and my daughter, Anita. I need to know they're still alive. They are to speak to me personally; no tape recorder is to be used. Is that clear?"

The voice on the other end of the line went silent, and then indicated they had to think about it. The line went dead. Anita's father, Douglas, looked over at the FBI in hopes that they had determined where the call had originated, but it had been too short, and everyone in the room was disappointed.

Anita could feel her senses returning. The dead calm in the background told her they had come to a complete stop. Carolyn reached out for her friend and the two huddled together, wondering what was in store for them. Two men came into the dark room and escorted them off the vessel. The sunlight beamed onto their faces, blinding them, and they tried shielding their eyes with their arms and hands. Their arms were rudely pulled away, however, and were forced down to their sides. They were then carried to a waiting vehicle, strapped down in their seats, and were transported to an undisclosed location. The vehicle jerked as its tires hit each pothole, forcing Anita and Carolyn's head to bob. They slumped down into their seats trying to avoid a head trauma. Coming to an abrupt halt, the vehicle created a dust storm. As the man on the passenger side got out of the car, the ladies could hear a unfamiliar voice outside the vehicle, but were not able to see who was speaking, as the newcomer had turned his back to them. Instantly, the two ladies knew they were up for sale: The black market.

The driver, a tall, heavy-set, bald man, jumped out of the vehicle, and opened Anita's door. With one quick thrust he pulled her off her seat by her hair, causing her to wince in pain. She struggled to stand up without losing her balance, and hoped to release the firm grip he had on her hair. Her eyes squinted to see her abuser, but all she could visualize was a big, fat, monster. Her legs were wobbly, so he put his arm around her waist and dragged her into the phone booth. She was forced to stand up, but when her legs gave way, she felt the bald man's body press against hers to stabilize her.

Her vision still wasn't clear, but she could hear as the man dial a number, and then spoke in a foreign language. After a slight pause, the man spoke directly to Anita in a no-nonsense tone and handed her a piece of paper. "Say what's on the paper and nothing else. If you attempt to give your location away, I will shoot you on the spot."

Anita laughed, sarcastically. "Oh like I could. I have no idea where we are. I can't even see you properly, yet. My eyes haven't adjusted to normal light. You'll have to coach me."

The tough little man had his hands firmly planted around Anita's throat, and squeezed. "Just do as you are told or your little friend will feel a lot of pain," he replied.

Cackling like a witch making her brew, Anita hurled her words back at him. "*Pain,*" she said. "Haven't we been through enough already?"

The man grabbed her hair and tugged hard, jerking her head backwards. His voice was impatient. "Keep it sweet and simple. Understand?"

Trying to keep her body in an upright position, without touching the volatile little man for support, Anita retaliated, "I would salute you, but I can't make my arms work."

Before she could blink, he had forcefully pushed her head forward and slammed it into the base of the phone, and Anita felt pain rip through her head. His words were harsh. "Do as you're told," he said.

Remaining silent, Anita stood helpless by the man's side as he spoke to someone, and then a minute later she found the phone shoved to her ear. Anita bore holes through her assailant with her eyes, as he coached her on what to say. When she strayed from his script, he cuffed her across the head and she yelled in pain, allowing her father to guess what was happening. The conversation was brief, and she could hear her father sigh when he learned she and Carolyn were together. But as quickly as the phone had been placed to her ear, it was taken away, and Anita listened as the man discussed the issue of ransom with her father. Then there was silence.

"What was the idea of a car with gas and food? Was it a ploy to throw the authorities off track?" Anita asked.

When the man didn't respond to her question, she threw another one at him. "There's no way in hell you're letting us go, is there?"

He looked her over and smirking, said, "Seems you're as smart as they say you are."

As he pulled her towards the vehicle Anita staggered, falling to the dusty, dry ground. He stood her up forcefully. "Your friend over there doesn't seem to be as bad as you. What gives?" he asked.

"I don't know what you're talking about," Anita hissed. "Are you talking about attitudes? Cause if you are, that's where we differ."

The fat little man felt her forehead. It was warm to his touch and he swore, "Damn, you're hot."

Trying her best to break his hold on her, Anita smartly responded, "Thanks for noticing."

Forced to stand up in the hot sun, even with help, Anita felt both her energy and her fighting spirit becoming depleted. She was near the point of passing out; her eyes were beginning to roll back into her head. Carolyn sat quietly in her seat, taking in what was happening outside the car. She grew fearful at the thought this was the end of the line for them both, and tears began to trickle down from the corner of her eyes. Anita teetered back and forth as she stood supported by the man holding her. Anita thought she was seeing a mirage as a dust storm was headed towards them, and an outline of a vehicle emerging from it. But she could hear the sound of the engine and within minutes, the vehicle stopped directly in front of Anita and her host, and in one sweep, Anita was thrown onto a seat in the dust-covered vehicle. A teary-eyed Carolyn waved goodbye to her friend, as each vehicle drove off in different directions.

Anita's red face and near-volcanic, hot flushes determined her destination; she needed to be nursed back to health. Carolyn's health was much better and she was on her way to a safe house, where her destination was to be determined at a later time.

CHAPTER EIGHT

When Anita opened her eyes, they wouldn't focus well, but she thought she saw a two-story cottage near a lake. Closing her eyes she gave her head a slight shake. Upon reopening them, it confirmed that it was as she had thought; a cottage in a beautiful setting, next to a lake surrounded with nicely kept grounds. Yet, somehow, the place reflected coldness.

A mysterious man was there to greet them. Anita couldn't help notice his rugged build, dark hair, and cold blue eyes. With the little energy she still possessed, Anita looked down at her attractive attire: dusty black boots, black skirt with holes in it, a torn white blouse with dirt spots on it, and dirty, unruly hair completed her well-groomed appearance. Her eyes felt puffy, dry, and droopy all at the same time. Her knees were knocking so loud she thought they were echoing into the trees, and she felt cold even though the hot sun was beating down.

As the man spoke, his deep voice caught Anita off guard. "What can I do for you?" he asked.

Anita's escort replied, "Can you keep her for a few days until her health improves? She is of no value to us in this shape."

The man looked her over and shook his head. "I think not," he said. "I don't want to get involved and, besides, she's very ill."

The escort pleaded with the man, hoping to change his mind. "Please, you are the only one we can trust."

The young man glanced Anita over with a sharp eye. "You say only a few days?" The escort nodded his head eagerly. "Okay. I'll expect to see you in a few days. You had better not leave me hanging," he said, in a tone letting them know he was not happy with this arrangement.

The escort shook the man's hand so hard that one would have thought it was a loose connection. He replied, "You'll be rewarded in the usual manner. Thank you."

Not happy about this agreement, Anita tried to jump from the vehicle and escape, but as she opened the door, her foot became caught and she

35

landed sprawled out with her face pointing downward. The escort left her there and sped off, leaving the other man to help her to her feet, making his expectations clear. "My name is Chris," he said. "And as long as you behave, no harm will come to you. Do you understand?"

Tears filled her dry, puffy eyes. She tried to wipe the dust off her hand before extending it. "My name is Anita and yes, I understand," she replied.

Chris, annoyed at having to nurse this newly acquired houseguest back to health, ignored her outstretched hand, and said, "Good. Let's get you settle down for the night. And believe me, it will be a long night. Your illness is just getting started."

Staggering down the long walkway, Anita's legs buckled and she fell. But she made her determination clear when she got back up and marched on. Chris, unsure as to how this woman would respond to his gesture of help, guided her to the room she would be occupying, found her a change of clothes, lead her to the bed so she could lie down, and locked her in, all the while she seemed to be compliant.

Having prepared a meal, Chris took a tray up to Anita and placed it on the nightstand so she could eat at her leisure. He left without saying a word. Later, he retrieved the dishes and was pleased to see the food gone. Anita had enough wits about her to fool Chris by making him think she had eaten; however, the truth was that she had hoarded the food and was planning her escape. Concerned, Chris later returned to her room to see how she was faring. He was displeased that the fever had gotten worse, and amazed that she hadn't complained. While he checked her over, Anita didn't move. Chris assumed she was resting, and quietly left the room. Anita's eyes popped open and she listened as his footsteps faded away, figuring this would be his last check until morning. Retrieving her stash of goodies from its hiding place, Anita placed it below the window. She propped a pillow up against the window to muffle the sound of glass breaking, and made her getaway.

Restless and worried about Anita's condition, Chris went to check on her and found the room empty. He immediately got a flashlight, and then went through the window in hopes of tracking down which direction she was headed. When he was certain which direction she had taken, he ran for his car, intending to find the very sick young lady.

Feeling fatigued, Anita found it tough to keep going, and eventually had to stop for the night. With the tiny amount of energy she had left, she gathered leaves for a bed and rested upon it, surrendering to the needs of her body. Being an excellent tracker, Chris would alternately get out of his car and follow her signs and drive on, which led him to her huddled form. He startled her by gently shaking her. The terror that ran through her whole body, made her cower and slither away from him like a scared animal.

Chris watched this for a few minutes and then said, softly, "Anita, I'm not going to hurt you. Please come with me."

Still slithering away from her tracker, Anita replied, "I must find my friend. She needs me now."

His voice was tender as he crouched beside her, and said, "Anita, you're very ill, and until you get better, you'll be of no help to your friend."

Ashamed of how she must look, Anita choked back the tears. "If I wait, you'll give me to those men and then I won't be able to find her. You're just being nice so I'll come peacefully." She paused, and then said weakly, "I guess it doesn't matter. You can pawn me off at your leisure."

Chris looked stunned. Here was a young city woman in a part of a country she knew nothing about, in a state of delirium, thinking only of her friend and not of her own condition. Meeting this unselfish person made Chris think carefully about the situation. He extended his hand down to her and spoke, calmly. "Come on," he said, "You have no idea what lurks about."

Getting off the ground with Chris's support, Anita tried to laugh. "What a choice. Either the big bad wolf will get me here or back at your place. Who cares anymore? I really don't feel well." She almost passed out. Chris caught her fall, picked her up and strapped her into the vehicle. No words were spoken in transit, but once they came to a stop in front of the house, Anita perked up and commented, "Gosh, if I made it this far weak, imagine how far I could've gotten healthy."

Chris studied her, noting every detail, and a faint smile spread to his lips. "You are determined to find your friend, aren't you?" he asked.

Anita avoided his eyes and instead looked towards the lake. "Chris, tell me. What will happen to me, us, I mean Carolyn and me when the time is right?" Chris dropped his eyes and fell silent. Anita tested him again, saying, "You know don't you? You won't admit it, but you know. Let's see, two white females assuming they're from wealthy families, kidnapped and taken to a foreign country. It can only mean one thing: the black market. I'm right aren't I?"

Chris's lips did not move, prompting Anita to speak out in sheer defiance. "If they hadn't drugged us, things would've been a lot different," and she said no more.

Picking her up, Chris carried her to her room. He gently placed her on the bed and covered her up. He felt her head. It was very warm, and beads of sweat glistened on her cheeks. He knew she had pneumonia, or worse. Her eyes were sealed shut and Chris knew she was going nowhere. He quietly closed the door behind him. Within a few minutes, he was standing on the porch with a drink in his hand, pondering over the day. A phone call disturbed his train of thought, and the caller inquired about Anita's health. Chris found that he did not wish to divulge any details about Anita's condition, but he then learned that she was worth more than two million dollars on the market, and if he played his cards right, he would become a very wealthy man. After the call, Chris was indecisive about which way to turn.

Guilt ridden over having locked Anita in her room earlier, Chris went up to see if she needed anything, not realizing how much time had passed by. It was about one in the morning. Walking over to Anita, he took one look at her, and he knew she was burning with fever, and shivering from chills at the same time.

Shaking Anita to rouse her, Chris's tone was agitated. "How long have you been like this?" he asked her.

Her lips moved, but the words didn't coincide. "All my life," she replied. "Now, walk away, close the door and let me die. The thought of being sold to serve some jerk doesn't appeal to me, and I know your job is to make me better. The better I am, the wealthier someone becomes. What am I worth now?"

Trying desperately to ignore Anita's comment, Chris's voice was stern as he asked again, "How long?"

Anita's teeth began to chatter and she found it difficult to speak. "I hear my teeth chattering, but the words don't sound right. Has this ever happened to you?"

Chris's impatience was apparent. "Answer my question," he demanded. "How long?"

Snuggling back into her warm blankets, Anita sighed, saying, "You're no fun. It really just started. Happy now?"

Chris's glare was like a magnifying glass with the sun beating through it. Anita felt the heat radiating from his look. "How do you feel?" he asked.

Flippantly, she retorted, "How do *you* feel? I feel with my fingers." Anita could tell she was pushing Chris's patience, and added, "If you could just take me to the bathroom, I think a cold shower would help me with the heat wave I've developed."

Chris scowled at her. "And go into convulsions. Not likely. I'll arrange for a doctor to make a house visit and you, you just stay put."

Her laugh was haunting and her voice held no enthusiasm. "Just where do you think I'm going?"

Against his own judgment, Chris had found himself in the middle of something he knew he had no right to be involved in. He arranged for a doctor to come over – a difficult task because he had to disclose part of the ailment and needed to be careful that no one saw her or learned of her existence.

When the doctor arrived, he and Chris entered Anita's room. The doctor checked her vitals and quickly set up an IV with antibiotics, and gave Chris a crash course on how to monitor the flow of the drip, change it, and sponge bath the patient with an alcohol solution to help reduce the fever. The doctor expressed his concern that the young woman should be in the hospital, but Chris explained that she was his fiancé, and that he would like to do the honors of caring for her. The doctor was still dissatisfied, but agreed to come back and check on the patient.

For three days and nights, Chris bathed Anita and watched for signs of improvement. True to his word, the doctor stopped in from time to time, and was pleased with Anita's recovery. He looked directly at Chris, and said, "She had pneumonia. How did she get so sick if she had all her shots?"

Chris replied quickly, and with confidence, "I assure you, she had all her shots, but I do recall her saying she was ill at the time she got them. That could've caused them to be less potent in time of need. Isn't that correct?"

"It could be one reason, or Hepatitis," the doctor said. "But, there's more to it than that, of that I'm certain. We'll let it go for now," he said, drawing a blood sample and making Chris feel uneasy.

CHAPTER NINE

Anita opened her eyes, glanced around the room, and swore loud enough for Chris to hear. "Damn, I'm still alive. You must be a sadist and like to see other people in despair."

Getting up from his chair, Chris leaned over to check her fever, which had finally broken. "Hmmm," he said. "I see you're on the mend."

He lifted her into a sitting position and tilted a glass of water to her lips. She let the moisture flow over her tongue, down her throat, and then she pushed Chris away. She tried to get out of bed, but her legs failed her and she fell to the floor. Chris stood and watched as she struggled to get up, but after a few minutes went by, he held out his hand for her to grasp, and assisted her back to bed. He encouraged Anita to drink more water, promising her a shower when she settled down.

Anita tried to get past Chris's cold exterior and looked at him from the tops of her eyes. "You probably poisoned the water to shut me up," she said. Studying his expression as it changed, Anita then asked, "So tell me, who was my nightingale?"

The corner of Chris's lips went up and Anita smiled back until he answered, "Me."

Anita pulled the covers up to hide her body. "How much of me did you see?" she demanded to know.

Chris's exterior was crumbling as his expression lit up his face. His voice was gentle as he replied, "I had to give you a sponge bath, and so I'd say there wasn't much I didn't see."

Anita's face turned bright red and she pulled the covers right over her head, hiding her entire body. Chris gently tugged at the blankets, releasing the hold she had on them and they were again face-to-face as Chris said, "I'm sorry if I embarrassed you, but why did you ask?"

Darting her eyes from the man before her didn't help subdue the heat that had been building up inside of her. She had a glow that made her look very attractive, despite her disheveled state, and she said, "I'm stripped down to nothing. Only one person has ever seen me that way and I'm very shy."

Anita noticed a twinkle in Chris's eye, but then just like a lightening strike, his eyes quickly diverted to their cold, steel blue color, and he barked, "Drink. Then you can shower." He left the room, leaving Anita bewildered.

Alone and sulking, Anita sat on the bed and drank the welcome liquid, waiting for Chris to return. He knocked before entering, and his tone had changed and he appeared contrite. He encouraged her to try walking to the shower on her own, but watching her uncooperative legs, Chris guided her there and she teetered while he ran the water. He assisted her into the bathtub, rather than the shower, thinking it was safer, and he waited outside the door just in case.

Hearing a thud and a whimpering coming from inside the room, Chris panicked. "Are you alright?" he asked.

Anita's voice was between crying and hysteria, as she replied, "No. I really need your help. Just hand me a towel for starters, please."

Obliging, Chris handed her a towel and turned his back. When she asked him to raise her to the edge of the tub so she could wrap herself better, he tried his best not to look at the vision before him. Having fulfilled her wishes, Chris quickly turned his back and she wrapped herself up in her towel, doing the best she could. When she was ready, Chris spun around and slipped one arm around her waist and the other under her knees and lifted her up, when the towel slid open.

Mortified by the whole episode, Anita broke the tension between them when she said, "It's nothing you haven't seen before," and tried to cover up what had been exposed. Chris tried pretending it was nothing – more for Anita's sake than his own. As Chris placed Anita upon the bed, he instructed her to remain there and take it easy until her strength returned. After Chris left the room, Anita put on the clothes Chris had out for her, and crawled to the chair in front of the window. Looking out, she took in the beauty beyond the grounds: the high hills and the different types of flowers, trees and vegetation that surrounded her, and she appreciated what Mother Nature had to offer.

CHAPTER TEN

Trying to decide about whether to hand her back to her abductors, Chris's mind was interrupted with a phone call from one of the captors. He told Chris he was coming back to pick up his prize. Thinking quickly, Chris explained that Anita was still in very poor health and was under a doctor's care. The man on the phone did not believe this news, however, and indicated that he was on his way as they spoke. Angry that the abductors mistrusted his judgment, Chris went up to Anita and quickly instructed her to look like someone who was not going to remain on this earth for much longer. After he had left the room, Anita wasn't sure exactly what Chris meant. Pondering over his statement, Anita clued in and staggered around the room, using the furniture for support, in search of something that would hold heat. Finding a hot water bottle under the sink, Anita filled it with very hot water, navigated to her bed, and laid on it.

Having dozed off, Anita awoke to the sounds of several different footsteps approaching her room. Her door opened with a thrust. The ugly man, who had escorted her to Chris's home, walked over to her. Anita held back a gag as he touched her forehead, feeling it for fever. Discovering that she was warm and clammy, he pulled the blankets back and scanned her from head to toe; she indeed had weak and frail written all over her. Chris was just as surprised as was his houseguest at Anita's appearance, and was grateful she had followed his instructions.

The men headed downstairs and Chris took the opportunity to find out the man's name. "Exactly what is your name?" Chris asked.

"Bruno," the man replied.

"Well Bruno," Chris began, "she is still unable to walk or eat. Leave her here until she is fully recovered," Chris said.

Bruno was furious his prize was so sickly looking, that a screaming match took place; Chris was accused of letting Anita get into such a state and spoiling all their plans of becoming millionaires. Chris countered that she had been brought over illegally, with no shots to prevent the disease from invading her body, and that he had to nurse her back to health, with the help of a doctor – a doctor, to whom he had lied to in order to get help. Chris stood in the middle of the den with his hands on his hips, and lowered his voice. "I will call you when the time is right and not before. Leave me your number," he said. "Do I make myself clear?" Bruno saluted him, wrote down his number, and left. Chris felt anger knocking on every sensitive organ in his body.

Anita, not knowing what was in store for her, managed to get herself back into the chair. She sat rocking back and forth; shedding tears as she realized this was a game for keeps. Chris was at the top of the stairs when he heard her sobbing, but chose to ignore her and headed outdoors to get a new perspective on the situation.

The days that followed were hard for Anita; just walking around the room was exhausting. A part from when he came in to monitor her recovery, Anita saw very little of the man who rescued her, and this added to her misery. Knowing she needed to get out of her room, Chris asked if she would like to join him for dinner and she accepted, since dining alone, to her, meant confinement not independence.

As they sat at the table, Chris looked at Anita with intensity, and his words carried little enthusiasm. "You're starting to look a lot healthier," he said.

Anita's reply was full of sarcasm. "Yah, I'm on the recovery to hell." Realizing this man was not at fault for her predicament, she apologized. "I'm sorry," she said. "You've been good to me."

Not responding to her last comment, Chris asked, "After dinner, would you like to go for a walk on the beach – if you promise not to escape?"

Trying to hold back her laughter, it was given away when her body started to shake. She answered, "Like I would get far. Thank you for the invite and I accept your generosity." Then, changing the subject, Anita asked, "So tell me, who does your cooking and cleaning?"

Chris's smile lit up his face and Anita was captivated by his physique. She focused on his body as he responded to her question. "Not me, if that's what you're thinking. I have a housekeeper, Delia, and she's been with me for a couple of years. I seem to have her around more often, now that I have a house guest."

Anita toyed with her food. "Why don't you just hand me over? I've been nothing but trouble for you and I seem to be on the mend."

Chris's tone held a little mystery in it. "Let me worry about that," he said. "Now eat up. It will give you strength."

After dinner was finished, Delia cleared the dishes. Chris stood behind Anita and encouraged her to walk as much as she could on her own to the beach. Happy to be free of her room, Anita did considerably well and only had to rely on Chris for support a couple of times. Small talk evolved as they sat watching the water gently caress the shore.

Chris threw a small pebble into the gentleness of the waves as it rippled towards the shore, and said, "Tell me a little about yourself."

Anita was surprised by the change of Chris's mood, and decided to join in the conversation. "There's little to say," she replied. "I wanted to follow in my dad's footsteps, and went to school to become a lawyer. Carolyn, my best and only friend, and I went on a cruise ship dance, with dates Carolyn had arranged, and the next thing I knew, she had been abducted. Now I suspect I will never see her again – *or* get to write my final bar exam. I had been involved with one man. My father is well known around the world, and I assume that's why I'm here: for ransom money he may or may not pay, because deep down he knows he may never see us again."

Chris's head turned sharply and he studied the woman before him. "Who is your father?" he demanded to know.

Feeling the urgency to answer, Anita replied, "Douglas Jefferson. You know him?"

Chris's eyes shot wide open with surprise. Anita felt like she had said something wrong and was relieved when Chris said, "Not personally, but I do know of him."

Avoiding the possibility of hearing any more bad news, Anita spoke as though she were in a fantasy world. "If I were to get married," she said, "I'd want my husband to be the opposite of my dad."

Jokingly, Chris asked, "Dirt poor and a nobody?"

Taken aback by his statement, Anita struggled to stand up and looked down on him. "No," she replied. "More like kind, considerate, loving, and with a good sense of humor. Money, fame, and all that glitters mean little to me. What I want right now is to find Carolyn, because she is more like my sister than my best friend – not that anyone gives a hoot."

Keeping her promise of not running away, Anita tried to run towards the house, but her legs gave way and she fell down. Pushing herself into a sitting position, she sat there crying. Chris felt awkward, not knowing what to do. Finally, he got up, pulled Anita to her feet, and supported her back to the house.

On the way back, Chris told Anita she could have free reign of the house, but stipulated that she couldn't venture outdoors alone. She readily agreed. With each passing day, Anita felt stronger and was grateful for Chris's kindness and generosity. Bored, and seeing very little of Chris, she would wander into the kitchen and help Delia prepare meals. She attempted to do housework, too, all the while laughing as these thoughts and actions had never once been on her list of things to accomplish in her lifetime. Each day she hoped to catch up with Chris, and was heartbroken that he kept his distance.

One day, the sun was shining brightly as Anita peered out of her bedroom window and caught a glimpse of a vehicle pulling up to the house. She knew the captors were back for their trophy. Watching the action from her window, Anita saw Chris approach the visitors. She opened the window and leaned out as far as she could to hear what Chris was saying, and was taken aback when she learned he was adamant she was still not well enough for their plans. The visitors accused Chris of having an affair with her, and said that they were not giving her up to him. This irked Chris immensely, but he kept a calm exterior as he described her slow progress. He told the captors that she had just begun her transition from weakness and fragility to being able to walk on wobbly legs. He told them that she collapsed from time to time, and that she had just started to eat full meals to regain the weight she had lost due to being undernourished. He told them that her illness would lower the price they would get for her, and that time was of the essence in her healing. Discouraged with the news, the captors vowed to be back in three days, whether she was ready or not. By the tone in their voices, Anita knew they meant it. She was stunned, and could see the next stage of her journey quickly approaching.

Chris watched as they drove away and then headed into the house and instructed Anita to get ready; they were going shopping. A huge grin spread across her lips. She was elated, and took only a few minutes to fulfill the request. Standing in Chris's baggy clothes, her tattered boots, and with her hair tied back, she reminded him of an orphan looking for a place to belong in the world, and had to force himself not to grin.

Chris pulled up in his vehicle and beckoned Anita to get in. Although little was said between them, Anita was amazed at how beautiful the scenery was, with hills covered in trees and blooming flowers circling their trunks. Waterfalls rippled down the mountainside and gorges were lined with a layered rock foundation. Anita fixed her eyes on the waves as they teasingly touched the shoreline and receded back, and the movement spellbound her, making her forget her own troubles.

Chris broke her train of thought when he spoke, "Beautiful isn't it?"

Not taking her eyes off the picturesque view, Anita replied, "Absolutely breath taking."

The trip seemed short to Anita, and driving into town was like going back in time. Shops were built of old brick, and many proprietors displayed their wares on the street. Some were sitting on a stoop watching the comings and goings of potential buyers, and some were peddling their wares on bikes. Awestruck, Anita couldn't wait to explore the little shops and find new treasures.

Chris had been speaking to her, but, lost in her own thoughts, Anita hadn't heard a word he said. He cleared his throat, bringing her back to reality. Satisfied he had her full attention, Chris handed her some currency. He instructed her to buy whatever she needed and to meet him in the little cantina down the street when she was done.

With excitement running through her veins, Anita ventured off into a world she had never experienced before. Watching her surrounding with a sharp eye, Anita observed other buyers and feeling brave, she tested her bartering skills. She found that dickering down prices was a hoot, but she still wasn't sure of the value of the currency she held in her hand. Elated with her purchases, Anita headed down towards the cantina. Once there, she ran into the bathroom and slipped into a subtle outfit, theorizing that she didn't want to humiliate her rescuer with her appearance; even though it would only be for a short time.

Trying to hide her enthusiasm, Anita rushed over to Chris's table. Her shopping bags hit everything in their way, knocking a few items off the table, and causing a slight disturbance, which amused Chris. Embarrassed, Anita slowed down and tried to act like a lady, but her bubbly mood outshone anything else, and she sat down at his table before her legs had a chance to collapse.

Babbling like water spiraling downstream, Anita showed Chris her wonderful bargains, speaking as if she didn't have a care in the world. Suddenly, she quit talking. She turned around and met the sharp shooting eyes of the approaching waitress. The waitress's eyes shifted to Chris, and

Anita felt a pang of jealousy. As Anita pushed back her chair to leave, Chris grabbed her arm, forcing her to remain, and ordered lunch. All through the meal Anita found it uncomfortable and hard to dodge the daggers shot at her from the waitress's eyes. Her excitement abated. Chris kept looking for an explanation of the mood change, but Anita chose to seal her mouth, giving Chris a sign something was wrong.

The meal was spent in silence and, on the drive home, Chris's curiosity go the better of him. "What happened back there?" he asked. "You were so bubbly when you first came in."

Anita could feel his eyes beaming upon her soul, and replied, "The waitress. That's what happened. If her eyes were lethal weapons, I'd be dead right now."

Chris knew better than to probe her and left the topic alone allowing silence to fill the air between them. Anita was grateful for the quiet; she had her own demons to contend with and wondered when she would be changing hands again.

The hush followed them into the house. Anita, restless and eager to show her gratitude, took advantage of the time before dinner by making herself look gorgeous, hoping to put a spark in Chris's eye. At dinner he silently noted how well she could transform into such beauty – but chose to ignore her, knowing she was dangerous-goods.

Unhappy with the silence, Anita broke the ice by asking if she could walk along the beach. Getting a "no" for an answer, she became upset. Not use to being in the hot seat, Chris clarified that he wasn't refusing, but that she would have to wait until he conducted a little business, and then the two of them would go walking along the shore. Chris immediately left the room, and a very bored Anita scoured the house for a drink. Finding a bottle of vodka and some orange juice, Anita poured herself a drink. But one quickly turned into several and, when Chris entered the living room, he found her sitting in the middle of the floor having a party for one. Anita handed Chris a drink and he readily accepted. They saluted each other and then he assisted her to her feet, noting she was a little unstable. She swayed as they strolled down to the beach. Holding onto Chris every so often for stability, Anita couldn't help marvel at how the brightness of the moon was lending its light down the path, hinting at her that after the calmness, a chaos was brewing.

Anita's voice was unintentionally audible. "This is so beautiful," she observed. "To be a prisoner and not able to enjoy the full beauty is a severe punishment."

Chris remained tight-lipped and the two sat on the shore, and watched the waves ripple in the moonlight; creating the appearance of diamonds sparkling on the waters ahead, playfully hinting they were fun to watch, but could be deadly at the same time.

Curiosity got the better of Anita. "How long have you been here?" she asked.

Chris answered nonchalantly. "About two years. It was my father's dream to retire here, but he passed away a year ago."

Anita, truly sorry for his loss, replied, "I'm sorry to hear that. I guess, in a way, I've lost my parents, too. Will I ever see them or Carolyn again?"

Chris diverted his eyes away from Anita and looked to the other side of the lake. "Please don't ask me that," he said.

Determined to get her feelings off her chest, Anita inquired. "I don't get it. You've had the opportunity to hand me over and haven't, which brings me to the conclusion that you have something horrible in mind for me."

Chris's wide eyes looked directly at Anita. "How could even think like that?"

Set back on her heels, Anita expressed herself freely. "Here I am," she said, "wherever *that* is. I've been nursed back to health by you, and shielded from harm by you. You've passed up a fortune for me, giving me no explanation, and your world has been turned upside down by my presence here. *And,* my best friend has been shuffled around, perhaps because of me. So what would *you* think? All that comes to mind is the worst."

It was as though Anita had been talking to herself. Chris changed the subject entirely, asking, "Do you have a decent outfit to wear?"

Upset by the change of subject, Anita's tone changed. "Yes," she replied, curtly.

Chris got up and grabbed Anita's hand, pulling her to a standing position. "Good. When we get back, I want you to put it on and wait for me," he said.

Confused, by the sudden mood swing, Anita replied, "I know I've had a few drinks, but I don't understand."

Chris's eyes became cold and hard as he spoke, "Just do as I say, got it?"

The walk back to house was brisk. Anita went immediately to her room and changed her attire to suit her mood. Her first outfit consisted of baggy clothes and messed-up hair, thinking that would teach him for annoying her. But her conscience kicked in and she redressed, this time making herself look irresistible. This way, she thought, when Chris made the exchange, he would know what he was giving up. Tears trickled down her cheeks as she realized she was infatuated with this man.

Finally ready, Anita entered the living room and found Chris sharply dressed. As he looked at his houseguest, he was pleased with what he saw and complimented her, but she tuned him out, scared as to what the future held.

CHAPTER ELEVEN

With Chris driving, Anita felt secure - until he veered towards an unfamiliar direction, leading her mind to wander fearfully. Every so often she glanced at Chris and he seemed to be preoccupied with his thoughts. This gave Anita a reality check; he was definitely planning to hand her over and become rich very soon. Her body broke out in a sweat. Panic overtook any emotions she had previously and she almost passed out.

Chris pulled up in front of an odd building that looked like an old church, and yet, had the features of an old, one-room schoolhouse. Chris led her inside, and Anita spotted rows of chairs laid out in the style of a lecture room, and a pedestal was strategically placed in front where a figurehead would stand. Out of the shadows a man emerged, wearing dark clothes. Anita fainted. Chris detected the motion as she began to fall, and caught her, laying her gently on the floor and tapping her lightly on her cheek to rouse her.

Dazed, Anita looked up, and smiled. "Well, I guess this is goodbye," she said. "I just wanted to say thanks for everything."

Bemused by Anita's statement, Chris laughed. "It's not what you think. Quick, get to your feet as we don't have much time."

Not wanting to postpose the inevitable any further, Anita struggled to stand erect. With blurred vision, she saw the darkly-dressed man was a preacher, and wondered if he was there to read her last rites or help her escape through an underground tunnel; she surmised that she had watched too many movies.

Regaining her focus, Anita heard the preacher tell them to repeat after him. Numbly, she murmured all the right words at the right time. After she had spoken, she heard Chris mutter the same words and, as if someone had slapped her across the head, she realized that they were married. With no pause in the ceremony, Chris kissed her forehead and slipped a ring on her finger. She was handed a ring to place on his, which triggered shock and fear to take turns running through her veins. She was in disbelief.

Chris recognized how she must feel, but his immediate concern was to get her to safety, not comfort.

It was dark when they left the church and Anita felt so alone. In the car, she closed her eyes and let the tears flow, hoping to drown in the pools they formed, but sleep was her ally and kept her afloat. Upon arriving at the house, Chris woke Anita and walked her to her room. Sleepily, she asked, "What no goodnight kiss?" Chris grinned, opened the door, and sent her in with no affection: just emptiness.

As the morning sun kissed her face, Anita pondered how to behave, what to say, and wondered if his intentions were honorable or not. Getting ready for the day ahead, Anita had an airy attitude. She bounced downstairs, noticing for the first time how beautifully and lavishly the house was furnished, while still keeping a farmhouse atmosphere. '*Yep,*' she thought, '*this man wasn't hurting for anything',* and she decided his intentions were honorable.

Finding Chris sitting at the dining room table sipping coffee, Anita sweetly smiled as she greeted him, but he made little effort to reciprocate, and breakfast was served with a code of silence. As she finished her wonderful meal and sipped on her coffee, Chris lifted his head, and pointed to the door. "Meet me on the porch," he said. "We have much to discuss."

As Delia cleared the morning dishes, she looked at them both and, in broken English, she asked Chris, "What you do to put smile on Anita?"

Without changing his facial expression, Chris simply stated, "I married her." Muttering in Spanish, Delia looked at one and then the other, and Chris kindly reminded her, he heard every word she said. Delia shuffled her feet with her head bobbing as she disappeared.

Anita was in shock, and stuttered as she spoke, "What is my last name?" she asked. "I don't recall that part."

"Preston," Chris barked. "And it's not what you think. Outside, now." Anita saluted him like a private would a general, and hightailed it out to the porch to prevent any further repercussions.

Anita sat on the porch like she was waiting for a beating - frightened, yet so innocent. Chris couldn't help but realize this was a delicate situation. He knew she had been through a lot and that the worst was yet to come.

Sitting beside her, Chris took her hand in his, and spoke tenderly, "My intentions are not to harm you," he said, "but, from now on you must be very careful where you go, and *never* go by yourself. When they find out we're married, all hell will break loose. If I seem angry at times, it's just the way it has to be. It's going to get rough. Do you trust me?" Her ears sharp and her vision clear, Anita kissed his cheek, and said, "I have to trust you, but I'm so scared and feel so alone."

Showing compassion was difficult for Chris, but he extended his arms and wrapped them around her to show he could be trusted. Then he let go and headed indoors. Anita was mystified by the recent events, and started walking away to clear her head. Finding herself beside a creek, she began to pick flowers, and then heard Chris's loud, harsh words. "Get back here. Did you even hear a word I said?"

She pulled back her hand like her fingers had been pricked, and jumped back apologizing, "I'm so sorry. I was so close to the house and I thought."

Chris cut her off. "Do not, I repeat, do not venture off on your own. Call me. They could grab you at anytime, anywhere, unless that's what you want."

Anita was furious and threw the flowers at him. "Of course it's not what I want. Flowers make me feel better. I assure you, it won't happen again."

Chris backed off. "This situation has me on edge, and I apologize for yelling. Now, pick up your flowers, and let's head back to the house."

Anita did as she was instructed and the usual silence fell between them, but she felt at peace knowing he was trying to protect her. When they got back to the house, Anita kept her promise and stayed in her room, and away from Chris, hoping to salvage the growing bond between them.

The next day, when Anita refused to leave her room, Chris inquired if she was all right, and her explanation of avoiding trouble settled his curiosity. Chris sat on her bed, while she sat in her chair, and he asked, "How would you like to go to town for a change of pace?"

Her mouth dropped open in surprise, and her eyes lit up like twinkling stars shining in the sky, and did a little dance filling the air with happiness. "I'd be delighted. Could you give me a few minutes to freshen up? I'll meet you in the living room, say in half an hour?" she asked, happily.

Nodding in agreement, Chris went downstairs and patiently waited for Anita, but when she came down the stairs looking gorgeous, he knew it was a big mistake.

The drive to town was calm and unwinding, compelling Anita's anxiety to get ready and let loose. An exhibition of joy written across her face was exonerating. Every time she peered over at Chris and looked away, it reminded him of someone possessing innocence and seduction at the same time. He felt good being in her company.

Inside the cantina, it was plain with small wooden tables and chairs, dimly lit, tiny bar, with music playing in the background, and a few patrons mulling around. Chris ordered a round, and before the drinks were placed on the table, Anita grabbed hers from the tray, and downed it, ordering another, all in one breath. Chris's eyebrows went up. "Go easy, or we'll be going home sooner than we need to," he said.

Anita smiled, and clinked glasses with him. "Aye, aye Captain," she said.

Maureen, the waitress, made a beeline over to the table, and put an accusation before Chris. "Is she the reason I haven't seen you in awhile?" she asked.

Anita stood up and brushed up against Maureen, making her presence known, and answered the question for Chris. "No. I'm not your rival, now if you'll excuse me, I'd like to sing a song with the band," she said, and began to walk past her.

Nearing the band, Anita took a deep breath and walked up to them, leaving Chris and Maureen alone. She could see Chris taking a side glance her way from time to time, making her feel like maybe he did care. The band spoke very little English, and Anita expressed her wishes to sing with them. The band strummed a few cords of music they thought she might know, and finally the right song was selected: La Bamba. Taking center stage, Anita wiped her brow, and silently thanked Carolyn for her persistence in teaching her a few songs and dance steps. Giving her best performance, it sent exuberant vibes throughout the cantina, as the patrons joined in to make it more fun. After a warm applause, Anita bowed, and then headed to her table. Seeing her drink on the table, Anita welcomed it as it moistened up her parched throat.

Chris's smile softened his persona. "I didn't know you could do that," he said.

Shyly, Anita bent her head down, and replied, "I hope I didn't embarrass you."

Chris sipped his drink and couldn't take his eyes off his partner. "You didn't," he said, with earnestness.

Maureen, waiting impatiently for an introduction, blurted out, "Just who the hell are you?"

Anita looked at Chris for a little guidance in what to say, but only received a blank look, and she calmly responded, "You might say a friend who dropped in without warning."

Maureen's smile was full of vengeance, and her tone was sharp. "Don't lay that crap on me. It seems since your untimely arrival, he hasn't been the same. So, here's the deal. Lay off my man."

Chris was about to say something when Anita's hand slipped up to Maureen's chest, found the opening to her blouse, and pulled it tightly together, forcing Maureen to enter her personal space. Her words were cold as she spoke, "Now you listen to me. No one owns anyone. To set the record straight, Chris has full reign to do as he pleases. It just so happens he's had his hands full, and has been kept very busy. I assure you, he hasn't spent time with me."

Maureen pulled back hard, ripping her blouse and exposing a very voluptuous chest. Her short breaths, made it noticeable as her chest rose and fell with each breath, and hotly retorted, "uh right."

Not skipping a beat, Anita's hands pushed against Maureen's chest, forcing her back into her chair. Her point was well emphasized as she spoke, "You believe what you will. I'm out for a good time. You may join us if you like. That's your decision."

Using good body mechanics, Anita turned Chris's chair towards the dance floor and dragged him away from the table. They began to dance, while Maureen sat waiting; like a witch casting a spell. On the dance floor, Chris thanked Anita for not divulging their marriage, but Anita let it ride, thinking it would be her ace should it ever be needed to play at a later time. They boogied across the dance floor, having a good relaxing time. Making her point to Maureen neither of them owned him, Anita led Chris back to the table. After a few drinks, Anita was cracking jokes and trying her best, with universal sign language, to communicate with other patrons. Chris watched Anita as she went from table to table and he soon became consumed by his own thoughts. Maureen was in a state of turmoil because she wanted to be with the man who sat across from her. Knowing Chris as well as she did, she knew he was in his own space that didn't involve a woman.

After being the last patrons to leave, Anita decided they would not have the usual silence. They had just gotten out of town when she began to sing and to her amazement, Chris joined in and they both felt more relaxed than they had in a long time. Parking the car in the driveway,

Chris assisted Anita's tipsy body to the house, but when they opened the door, they found it had been ransacked. Anita could feel prickles being poked into her skin and she made sure she was as close to Chris as she could possible get. Chris wrapped his arm around Anita, giving her a rare comfort feeling, and after surveying the message through the damage, Chris told Anita to pack quickly; they had to leave immediately. Within minutes, Anita was ready and they hopped into the jeep and drove off.

Chris knew Anita was terrified, and tenderly spoke, "Are you alright?"

Barely able to move her tense shoulders and head, Anita answered the question. "Yes."

Chris showed emotions he didn't quite understand himself. He reached out for Anita's hand as he spoke, "You can sit next to me, if it'll make you feel better." Not needing a second invite, Anita slid over and made sure his body was touching hers. She felt him slide his arm around her shoulders, and his hand rested on her arm demonstrating a warm embrace. To keep the tension aloof, Anita talked about her family, but mostly about Carolyn. Chris listened and made mental notes, in case it was needed later down the road. After a lengthy drive, the vehicle seemed to stop in the middle of nowhere. Out from the bushes came a strange little man clad in dress pants and a white shirt, and as Anita tried to see his face in the dim light, her eyes were directed to his shoes. They stood out like a spotlight – they were black and white saddle shoes. The men spoke for a few brief moments and then the man hopped in the back of the jeep, and Chris drove a little further down the road, into a secluded area; to keep the vehicle from being detected by passersby any time of the day.

Once parked, Chris introduced Gappy, known for the gaps in between his teeth, to Anita and explained the situation to the eccentric man. The man looked over at Anita, and commented, "She must be someone special to risk everything."

Chris's answer was short. "Yes."

Handing the precious gem over to Gappy, Chris got back into the vehicle when he felt a hand on his. He looked up to see Anita's saddened eyes, and she asked, "Are you leaving me here?"

Patting her hand, Chris spoke reassuringly, "I trust Gappy, and you are in the best hands I know of. I'll be back, I promise."

Shock waves rushed through her heart, and she almost hyperventilated. "Please stay with me the rest of the night. I don't mean make love to me, although the thought had crossed my mind. You can see your enemy better in daylight. I don't understand why you are helping me, but I'm eternally grateful," she said.

Chris looked at his watch. "I can only stay a few minutes." He led her to a small grass hut behind Gappy's, and stretched out across the straw bed with Anita cuddling up against his chest. She could hear his heart beating. She looked up at him with adornment, and he bent down and kissed her. She dreamily closed her peepers and was fast asleep. Careful not to disturb her, Chris slipped out to continue on his mission.

Like someone had turned on a light switch, Anita's eyes shot open and not seeing Chris, she pulled the covers over her and heeded his warning; to stay in her hut. Daylight broke and Gappy brought Anita an unbelievable hot cooked meal made from scratch. The mere thought of eating made her stomach wheezy, but the lessons she had learned from Chris dictated otherwise; she would eat to conserve her energy.

Getting cabin fever, Anita talked to her host about needing to venture out and was told precaution was her only priority, to which she agreed. The sun was shining and, as Gappy escorted her to an excluded area, Anita witnessed the most spectacular view. The sun caressed the valley, showing off its luscious colors, taking her breath away and melting her fears. She instantly fell in love with the beauty. Gazing at the sky in the distance, clouds began to form growing heavier and the smell of rain filled the air. Gappy warned her that a storm was headed their way, but she was not to worry about her accommodations; the little hut would withstand the elements. Anita's face had doubt written all over it, and the two ran to their potential homes. The force of the high winds, the pounding rain and rolling thunder, forced Anita to seek shelter in her little adobe. Huddled in a corner with her blanket wrapped solidly around her for warmth, she contemplated where and what Chris was doing, visualizing he was with Maureen, and she scoffed at the thought.

With the howl of the winds, the patter of the rain on the roof, and total darkness, sleep was the last thing on her mind. She could feel the temperature change on the ground below her; it was getting cold and wet. Taking some straw off her bed, Anita put it in the corner where she had been sitting, and curled into a ball under her blanket; thinking she was safer on the ground, and anticipated what would happen next.

Hearing a strange noise prompted Anita to strain her ears, and all hopes diminished when the sound stopped. Hiding under her blanket, she saw a light flash in her room and instantly knew it was Chris; he had come back for her. Anita ran to him for comfort and was surprised at his reaction as he held her tight, and then pushed her away.

Chris's voice was low as he spoke, "We need to talk and we don't have much time." He threw her some military clothes, and said, "Put these on and I'll explain a few things."

Worried about him, Anita asked, "How much trouble are you in?"

Chris changed the subject. "Let me worry about that. Hurry and get dressed," he said.

Anita felt as though she could tease Chris. "I could say turn around, but you've seen everything already, and besides, it's dark so you'd have to rely on your memory to remember such details."

He chuckled as he turned around, and shone the light over his shoulder so she could get dressed. "Anita believe me when I say I care what happens to you. I've arranged to have a plane meet us. Inside this folder," holding it up for her to see, Chris continued, "is a credit card, money and documents needed to get you home. You will be boarding planes that have been specifically arranged for your safe passage home. When you pass your bar exam, your first case will be to annul our marriage and those papers are included inside the folder. Should you, for any reason, need to get in touch with me, I've left a phone number. That should take of it."

Anita dressed the whole time and listened. When he was done, she spun him around so they were face to face within inches of each other. "Suppose *I don't* want to leave. Suppose *I don't* want to annul our marriage," she said.

Chris placed both hands on her shoulders, shaking her slightly. "You are in great danger and it's non-negotiable. You are leaving. As for the marriage, I did it to protect you, and that didn't work out. Our lives are so different. Do you understand?" he said, trying to prove his point.

Shaking her head, Anita's words barely came out for Chris to hear. "No one can put themselves in so much danger without caring. I care for you also. I'll not give out any information, unless it's beaten out of me. As for our marriage, well that isn't important right now. I want to find Carolyn and I may be forced to leave right now, but come hell or high water, I will return." She paused for a moment, and then added, "Umm, the phone number, is it Maureen's?"

Chris couldn't believe his ears. "Young lady, be happy your own life was spared. Get out and stay out before something happens to you. Chances of finding Carolyn are slim," he said.

An impulse overtook Anita's emotions and she planted a kiss on Chris. Chris found it harder to pull away than he imagined. Anita, feeling his passion, coolly spoke, "Well does the phone number belong to Maureen?"

Chris was still in shock over the kiss, but also at her persistence about the number. "No. Why do you ask? And that stunt you just pulled, it doesn't mean a thing," he said.

Laughing, Anita headed to the door. "Yes it did, and you can't deny it."

Chris ignored her last statement, and recollected his own thoughts. "Listen, we must leave now because if you miss the plane, there's no telling what will happen to you. I thought as long as we were married, they'd back off. It appears that's not the case. I've been followed and we must leave to save Gappy from meeting with hardships. We'll be travelling on foot through the storm. It will be a lot harder to follow our trail. I believe I have it all covered."

Anita stopped in her tracks, and asked, "How did they know we were married?"

Chris went out the door, so Anita had to run to catch up to him. "I used one of their priests," he said, and left it at that.

Clad in her raingear, Anita sought out to find Gappy. She thanked him for his wonderful generosity and he wished her well. Chris tugged at her to get going, and she followed him closely. The rain felt damp through her gear and the nasty winds were cutting through her like sharp razors, but Anita was more terrified about the unthinkable: getting caught.

Chris held Anita's hand and broke trail. He pushed back a branch to clear the path and it sprung back causing her to lose her footing, and she tumbled down the ridge spraining her ankle. While waiting for Chris to rescue her, Anita was certain a bullet grazed passed her shoulders. In the darkened hurricane weather, Chris found Anita trying to get up and he ordered her to sit so he could examine her foot. Quickly working, Chris made a cane out of a branch, but her speed slowed them down, so he carried her as far as he could.

Anita was positive shots were being fired at them and felt Chris wince, like someone poked him in the back, but they carried on as the sound of engines roaring could be faintly heard through the traumatic storm. It was all she could do to keep from jumping down and running towards the plane, but her ankle had swollen to the size of a balloon, slowing down her walking ability. Being a backbreaking job carrying her for such a long distance, Chris sighed as he let her down in front of the plane. Anita turned and saw blood oozing from his side. "You've been shot. I knew we were dodging bullets."

Chris yelled, "Will you just get on the plane. I'll be fine. Here's the folder and happy travels."

Looking at him with sad, haunting eyes, Anita begged Chris, "Come with me."

Chris stood his ground and shook his head. "No, get going."

Seizing the opportunity, Anita draped her arms around his neck and kissed him. "You haven't seen the last of me and you know it." She turned and then looked at Chris. "Is this plane safe to fly in? I mean the weather and all," she asked.

This plane will fly below the radar to avoid being detected. It will be safe, as you will be flying at a low altitude. Now go," he commanded her.

Anita boarded the plane just in time, as they were taking off with or without her. Getting comfortable in her small seat, Anita's shoulder ached with pain, but the thought of going home melted away her blues. Realizing she was a free woman, her mind was now plagued with having left Carolyn and Chris behind, and she felt sick to her stomach.

CHAPTER TWELVE

Holding onto the folder tightly, Anita began to think that if she didn't read the papers, she wouldn't be lying if she told them she had no idea where she had been. Her train of thought led her to the question of whether she should phone her dad when she landed safely, or wait until she got home undetected.

Unexpectedly, one of the pilots ran back very excited and in very poor English, he told her to hide in the cargo container. They had been ordered to make an emergency landing for an inspection, due to a missing package. The pain in Anita's wounded shoulder proved to be more prominent that she first thought, but she was determined to do as ordered. A flashlight was handed to her by one of the pilots. Anita checked her seat for bloodstains that could pinpoint her existence and when satisfied it was clean, she went down into the cargo holding tank. She began to rearrange the boxes to conceal her body. Feeling the plane land, Anita controlled her breathing and prayed she would not be found.

Anita heard a commotion followed by yelling and then the cargo door was forced open. Several people entered talking loudly in Spanish. A thorough search was in progress, with boxes being moved and kicked around. The movement rearranged some of the packages that concealed her body, but she pressed even harder up against the wall, creating a flush illusion. Not finding what they were looking for, the intruders swore loudly, then shut the door behind them and the silence was golden to Anita's ears. The sound of engines starting disturbed the noiseless background, giving relief that represented music to her ears.

Kicking back the boxes and holding the flashlight, Anita waited patiently for the door to be opened. The young pilot entered and shook her hand, saying how brave she was in fooling her seekers, and that she had saved his ass as well. She laughed, for she was indeed on her way to freedom.

Feeling the plane's wheels touch down onto solid ground, Anita pulled the credit card out of the folder, and was surprised Chris had put her name on it as well. Thinking it was traceable, Anita decided cash was easier to make her unscheduled flights home. Unaware of where she was, Anita asked where the next stop was and she was told to sit tight, she would be in the air shortly. Watching them unload the plane, Anita wondered what was in the boxes, and then shuttered and decided the less she knew the better. It was the same plane that was taking her to the next stop, but before take off, she had to pay up front.

Fatigue had set in and Anita sat in her seat with her head resting on the window and before she knew it, she was landing. She was informed they had one more stop and then she was home free. Excitement ran through her veins like it was a race to the end, and Anita began to pace until they were set for take off. Again their hands were held out for the money, and again Anita paid cash. It was well worth it and she knew she had to repay Chris.

The little nap she had revitalized her and she was taking in the view from her window. Pictures of Chris, Carolyn, her dad, her brother and her mother raced through her mind and she felt torn apart; part of her was excited to be free, but part of her was left behind with her friends. Tears streamed down her face from the pain in her shoulder and the heartache she was enduring. Feeling the plane descend, Anita was preparing herself for the entrance into the lion's den: her father and the FBI.

Upon landing, she was told she would have to walk to the highway and perhaps there she could get a ride. This did not sit well with Anita, but she began the long trek. The heat made her sweat in the military uniform and she wanted to shed some clothes, but made a decision not to; it was best to leave no evidence behind that could incriminate oneself. Nursing her sore ankle, it took her a couple of long, hard hours to get to the freeway. After several attempts to flag a taxi down, she got frustrated and continued walking: hoping not to get run down. Walking backwards waving her hands in the air to oncoming traffic became tiring, and she resigned to the fact she was walking.

Checking out her surroundings, Anita discovered her home was only a couple of towns away. Her mind started spinning and stopped at the idea that, if she could find a bus station, she could just coast into town unannounced. She placed her hat on her head, pulled her hair tightly to the back, rolled up her rain jacket, and stuffed it against her waistline to camouflage her appearance. A taxi driver stopped and asked if she needed a ride, more out of kindness than a fare; he didn't want to see her killed on the busy freeway. She gladly accepted and he took her to the bus station.

Anita had never ridden on a bus and found it to be noisy, cramped, and a bumpy ride. She wondered how people could actually use this as a means of transportation, but then gave herself a lecture; you do what you have to do to survive. Seeing buildings she knew gave her peace of mind, but she knew once she got home, her life would be in turmoil.

Taxies were lined up at the bus depot and Anita quickly slid into one and sighed as she sat back. Her heart beat to a rhythm of its own and she swore it would soon escape its chest cavity. A block away from her home, Anita told the driver to stop, paid him and watched him leave, before attempting to sneak around obstacles until she reached her home.

Crossing her fingers her dear brother had left his window open, Anita ducked down, careful not to be noticed. She tested the window and laughed thinking that Jake was so predicable, slid the window open and crawled in. Once inside, Anita inched her way through the maze of the house, slipped into her bedroom, changed and headed boldly down the stairs in search of her parents.

Her parents were sitting in the living room with strange men when Anita strolled in; the entire room stopped all activity when they saw her. She ran over to her father and hugged him, and then lightly kissed her mother's cheek. The FBI threw questions at her, to which she was not prepared for, and she put her hands in the air. "Please, let me settle down and talk to my dad," she said. "He'll be representing me. I really need a nap, a shower, and a doctor. Tomorrow, after I confer with my lawyer, your questions will be answered, but for now I need a rest."

FBI agent, named Mike Bernard, spoke abruptly, "You will talk to us right now."

Anita's temper boiled over and spilled out uncontrollably. "I think not. You will wait. I have rights and I promise to go nowhere. It's been a long couple of weeks."

On behalf of his daughter, Douglas said, "I'll take full responsibility for Anita, and we will hold a press conference tomorrow, after we talk."

"You will NOT hold a 'PRESS' conference until the FBI say so." Agent Bernard was miffed at how she could just appear out of nowhere with no explanations and his voice was agitated, as he replied, "I'll be right here until you are ready to talk, even if I have to sleep in front of your doorstep."

Anita looked at her mother, and smiled. "Make sure he has plenty of blankets. I wouldn't want to see him catch a cold waiting on my behalf." Standing, Anita's father asked the agents to please excuse them for a few minutes. "Anita!" Douglas glared at his daughter. "Enough of this behavior! I will not tolerate your arrogance and hostility toward any law enforcement agency. You will talk to them or you will be arrested for obstruction, or even as an accomplice to the kidnapping. I have already been informed of your conduct with Lieutenant Giles."

Agent Bernard took his cue and left the family to talk. When Jake walked in, unaware of his sister's return, Anita ran over to him squeezing him tightly, and full of affection. She felt such relief to be home.

Anita's request not to be asked questions was honored; that meant she was to hold back any questions she had for her dad and found that hard to do. Anita hoped that turning in early would settle the uneasiness within her, but it didn't. Instead, she thrashed around, making her bed look like a good fight had taken place there. Her thoughts whirled around Chris and Carolyn, and wondered if she would ever see them again. The captors entered her head and she prayed to God, asking to never have to see them again.

CHAPTER THIRTEEN

As dawn approached, Anita managed to get a few winks to prepare her to face the day. As she showered, she felt a sharp sting on her right shoulder, indicating it needed medical attention immediately. Straining to get a good look at it in the mirror, Anita twisted her neck, causing a spasm, which made it difficult to get dressed. Rubbing the back of her neck, Anita met her parents at the breakfast table, and she said, "Dad, I'm in need of a doctor and, yes, it is warranted. I seem to have a bullet lodged in my shoulder that is probably becoming infected as we speak. And yes, it does hurt."

Her father reacted without hesitation; Douglas called for a doctor to come to the house, and then poured his daughter a cup of java. "We need to talk," he said, "so drink this fast. And before you ask, there has been no word regarding Carolyn."

Biting her lip after taking a sip of coffee, Anita's curiosity needed satisfying. She asked, "Was the ransom paid?"

Mike Bernard, the FBI agent from the previous night, had entered the room and now stood behind Anita. "Yes," he answered, and then moved to stand beside Douglas so he could see her square on.

Anita scanned the room with her eyes and then at each individual before asking, "Does anyone have any knowledge or evidence concerning the abductions?"

With annoyance in his voice, Agent Bernard replied, "You hold all the keys to unraveling the mystery. No more stalling."

Looking past her father Anita's eyes locked onto Mike's, like heat-seeking missiles, and through gritted teeth, she responded, "How dare you speak to me like that. Your friend didn't disappear. You didn't have to deal with incompetent police. You weren't hit over the head and stolen from a police car. You weren't in a hole in a ship half paralyzed and drugged out of your mind, and you weren't shot at." Douglas shut her down. "Anita!"

Anita stormed out of the room with Jake hot on her heels. Jake's common sense kicked in and he tried to reason with Anita to go back and tell her story. Anita became furious that he would even suggest such a preposterous thing and was about to leave, when Jake grabbed her arm slowing her down. He told her to take in some deep breaths, and while she was doing that, he convinced her to go back and tell all, because it was their only chance of finding Carolyn. She thanked her brother for his input, and reentered the room, where she knew she was going to be grilled.

Anita's mood mellowed. She choked back all her hostility and began to describe the whole episode, starting from her first meeting with Jeremy and Blake, right up to her escape. As he listened to her story, Agent Bernard had suspicion in his eyes, and when she had finished, he prodded her, saying, "You say this man nursed you back to health and planned your escape. Don't you find that odd?"

Now wishing she had kicked him out while she told her story, Anita squinted her eyes and through pursed lips, she inquired, "What are you driving at?"

Another agent, who had been standing in the doorway, cut in and redirected the question, "Can you tell me where you were taken?" he asked.

"I told you, I woke up bound and drugged in a dark room aboard a ship and when we docked, there was no sign to saying, *you are here.*" Anita snapped back.

Agent Bernard pursued his theory. "Surely you must've figured it out at the man's house – after all, you had full access to everywhere," he said, trying to bait her.

Anita stood before the FBI and shot a spitball of fire at them. "Let me see. Oh yah. I was weak and unable to walk so I had to trust him. He could've gotten rid of me at any time and yet, he didn't. I could've snooped, but I just couldn't see myself invading someone's privacy that way, and deep down I think he wanted me to find Carolyn. Furthermore, I am not bilingual and Spanish was the main language there. The escape on the plane was very real I assure you. When the plane landed, they loaded and unloaded their wares and then took me on to the next stop, until I was in familiar territory. Take it or leave it, but that's the truth. That's what happened."

Douglas remained silent and when he was ready, he asked, "Anita could you identify the captors, even one of them?"

Looking at her father and taking his cue to calm down, Anita let her temper cool before speaking. "Yes," she replied. "I'll look at mug shots, but keep in mind I was heavily drugged, and kept in the dark. Trying to see in the daylight was very hard on the eyes, and I kept them closed as much as possible, avoiding the glare."

Her father's hard look made her feel squeamish. "And the young man you stayed with?" he asked, demanding she be truthful.

"He's innocent," Anita said, with conviction.

Douglas's tone was even, but authoritative. "That may be so," he said, "but weren't you brought to him by the captors to regain your health, so you could be ready for your captors future plans? You're assuming the black market, but you also have to keep in mind they extorted money from me. Do you think he got his cut and turned you loose?"

Anita, who was sitting in a swivel chair, turned the chair around several time and toyed with the ring on her finger. "Dad, you can relax. I will cooperate. You know that."

The second agent walked by Anita several times before stopping right by her side. Peering down at her, he asked, "How'd you pay for the flights?"

Anita's mind was sharp. "Cash. He gave me cash."

Agent Bernard extended his open palm. "I want the receipts for the flights, right now," he said.

"There are no receipts. I told you, I had to pay cash each time the plane took off," she said, and clamed up before she decked him one.

Douglas threw his daughter a look that made a pit full of snakes look more inviting. He knew she was hiding something that could make the case easier to solve.

Agent Bernard swore as he looked at Anita. "You know where you were. Your friend is out there and we could find her, but no, you are holding back vital information preventing us from doing our job. Do you realize your father paid a great deal of money for both of you? And do you care? I highly doubt it. This guy, Chris that you're protecting, may be innocent in this particular case, but what about others? Think about it."

Anita slowly got of her chair, and stood toe to toe with Agent Bernard. "Don't you think I know that?" she replied. "Don't you think if I could tell you where I was, I would? A lot happened and it's still very fuzzy. Yes, I was nursed back to health, but I honestly do not know where I was. I flew home on what were probably unscheduled flights. I went from one small abandoned airstrip to another, in the same plane. I had no passport, but here I am. I'm sorry I don't have the itinerary, but unscheduled flights don't have regulated stops or logs. All I could think about was getting home."

Agent Bernard stepped back, but doubt came across in his voice, as he said, "I doubt that's all you thought about."

"You're right. I thought about the bullet in my shoulder. I thought about seeing my best friend's sunken baggy eyes and thin body. I also wondered if the captors were going to nab me again. Yah, you're right; getting home was *not* the only thing on my mind. Now, bring me a doctor and some mug shots. I have work to do."

"How did you get here, and from where?" Agent Bernard threw back at her.

"I walked for miles in the bush and eventually caught a cab, and had him drop me off a block away from the house. I didn't want a big scene," she said, hoping he wouldn't take it any farther, but was not shocked when he did.

"Can you tell me, or show me on a map where you walked from?" he asked, waiting anxiously for her response.

Swallowing hard, Anita looked directly at her father. "Get me a map. I'll do my best. Now, I need to see a doctor."

Douglas ended the conversation and led his daughter to the study. Entering the room, Anita found a doctor waiting for her. Baring her shoulder, the doctor took one look at the wound. "Sorry kiddo, but you have to have this surgically removed," he said. "It's badly infected."

The doctor's words had every ones attention, and a look of relief came over Anita's face, as she realized that recovery from surgery meant some quiet time to gather her thoughts. Her father announced that any further discussions would have to wait until she was up to par, and arrangements were made for her departure to the hospital.

When everyone left the room, Douglas pulled his daughter off to the side to avoid being overheard. Anita was worried about what her father had to say, and spoke first. "What's on your mind?" she asked.

He suggested she sit down, but Anita chose to stand and stay on even ground with her father, to avoid being intimidated. "Tell me about the ring on your finger, and right now," he demanded.

His tone forced her to look down at her ring. She quietly responded, "It's a friendship ring."

Her father's tone had a slight edge to it as he spoke. "And I was married yesterday. Speak up," he said.

Scared of her father's temper, Anita spoke quickly. "Dad, the man who protected me, married me. He did it to save my ass, but that didn't work out. He never hurt me, or touched me, and I'm in love with him. I don't want the FBI hounding him for doing a good deed. Can you understand?" Not getting the response she wanted, Anita added, "He knew of you." Still he gave no response, so Anita let him have all the ammunition as it unraveled from her wagging tongue. "You weren't there and have no idea what transpired. I thought I was sick, but Carolyn was worse, or she looked like she was. What I don't understand is why they wanted me in better shape. I know it's the black market and I'll bet you they were going for a double header: money from you, as well as the black market. And besides, it wouldn't be the first time a client of yours held back information and you helped them out anyway."

Knowing his daughter was right, Douglas tried to argue back with conviction. "This is different. Criminals lie all the time. Family members don't hold back secrets. This could prevent you from writing your bar exam," he said.

"So what you're trying to tell me is, I'll be an easy case for you. I don't lie," she said, with a huge grin that showed off her even white teeth.

Scratching his head, Douglas resigned himself to the fact that she had him under her thumb. He sighed, and said, "That you are. You have to be upfront and work with me honestly. Does he feel the same way?"

"Yup. He just doesn't know it yet, but he will when I go back. I'm determined to find Carolyn and reclaim my man. Dad, I truly love him," Anita declared.

Opening the door for his daughter, Douglas spoke earnestly. "*That's* what I wanted to know; the fact that you know where to return to. We'll discuss this later. One more thing, how does he know of me?"

"Who doesn't," she whipped back, and scurried to her room to get a few items for her stay in the hospital. She was looking forward to quiet time, but to her surprise, the FBI posted an agent to be with her. Finally, however, she relented to the fact one agent was better than a bunch.

Waiting to be prepped for surgery, Anita asked the agent to bring in some mug shot pictures. Going through the books, Anita was disappointed that not one recognizable face jumped out at her. Tired, she laid her head back and closed her eyes. A loud cough disturbed her peacefulness and Anita's eyes popped open and her head turned in the direction of the noise. There stood Mike Bernard, the FBI agent, "There was a woman resembling you on the flight from New York. Care to explain?" he asked.

"*Resembling* and *being* are two different things," Anita shot back.

The agent was not deterred. "The ring on your finger would represent a name change," he continued, "and that would make it possible for you to be aboard that plane. I'm giving you the opportunity to come clean."

Displeased with this turn of events, Anita responded. "I told you I had no passport. How would I get on the flight? My dad should be here any minute, but to ease your mind, I do not know where I was. I was on a small cargo plane, which landed and took off from abandoned airstrips. That's your job to find out where it all took place."

He placed a map in front of her. "Show me where you caught the cab," he said, and his voice held very little patience.

Douglas walked in and ended the conversation, stating that Anita knew nothing more, and should any further details arise, he insisted they be directed to him personally. He would then discuss the issues with his daughter. Anita thanked her dad for intervening.

Surgery took longer than expected; the bullet had chipped her shoulder blade and the fragments had to be removed. The infection was severe causing further complications. After the surgery and Anita's recovery, she was informed she would be there for a few days to be monitored. Trying to stay alert and awake, Anita picked up the map, which had been left on her table tray, and tried to pinpoint where she came out of the bush. Her motive was to steer them in the opposite direction, but it had to seem real.

Agent Bernard walked in as she was trying to focus. He studied her for a few minutes, and then spoke, "Trying to put us on a wild goose chase? There are no airstrips within a hundred miles. Care to fill me in?"

"Think what you will, but what I said was true," she said. "Now if you'll leave me alone, I really need to rest," and before he could say another word, she was asleep.

Her stay in hospital was for two days, and then sent home for rest and was given orders not to over use her shoulder. Taking advantage of having to rest, Anita took the time to study for her bar exam. Her only visitors were her family. This made it easier for her to concentrate and retain what she had learned. Recovery to most people would be enjoyable, but Anita had two things on her mind: passing the exam and finding Carolyn with Chris's help.

A month had passed and Anita became a recluse, rarely venturing out of her room. When she did, it was to do research for her exam in her father's office. She shut out her family and only had time for one thing: to become a lawyer with a degree. But during her quiet time, her thoughts swirled around her ordeal, and how she missed those cold blue eyes of Chris's. Her plans included working for her father to gain a little experience and, to be able to manipulate the law, in her favor. She had planned to head back to Chris's, and with his help, locate Carolyn. She was miserable and felt guilty inside, more so because she escaped and could lead a normal life, but all she could think about was Carolyn and the life she now had: nothing but abuse. And it was tearing her up inside.

Coming out dressed and ready to face the day took her family off guard; she was pleasant, smiling and chatting. She informed them she was going to write her one and only exam and when it was over, she would love to celebrate with them.

Taking a deep breath before entering the exam room, Anita could feel her heart race and sweat formed on the palms of her hands. Wiping them dry, she walked in and was given a chair to sit at the desk. Looking around, Anita was surprised there were no pictures on the wall, no books in the room, and a small window to let some natural light shine through. Her exam was placed before her, and time was starting now.

Her nerves kicked in and her mind went blank. Holding the paper in her hands, she remembered when that happens, it was suggested to read it over and soon the answers would come to you. She did this, and found once she began to read the exam, she was able to answer the questions. She took the entire allotted hours to write the remaining parts of her bar exam. When Anita handed it over, she felt good inside and was pretty confident that she had passed. Anita was told, before she left, that it would take a couple of weeks before she would receive the results. Not liking how long it would take, Anita was crushed because that meant she would dwell on her past, not her future.

Not wasting anytime, Anita hurried back and headed straight to her father's office. Walking in she felt at home. This seemed strange to her, but she thought that it was meant to be. She asked Wendy, her father's secretary, to let her father know she was there, and her father immediately came out and hugged his daughter. Without asking her, he had set up a small office for her to work in, and he had a case already for her to take on.

"Dad, are you sure you want to do this?" she asked.

"Do you know how proud of you, I am?" he asked. "Well, let me tell you it is an honor to have a child follow in one's footsteps," he continued. "Well, what do you say?"

A tear trickled down her cheek and she wiped it away, because her father had never shown any affection towards her, until now. "I hope I make you proud."

Douglas left his daughter in her office, and Anita picked up the file and read it over. "*Wow*," she thought. "*My first case.*" Placing the file on her desk, Anita walked out and closed the door behind her. Walking over to Wendy, Anita left a note for her dad to say she would see him at home, and that she needed the rest of the day to herself. Walking out she smiled and made a check mark in the air; she had completed her first course of action; she was a lawyer.

Her first case was to settle a business contract between two friends; one wanted to buy the other out. It was straight forward and an easy settlement, and Anita was happy with the outcome. Her father was pleased she did so well and thought she was ready to settle in to her new life.

The two weeks slipped by and when Anita received the news she had passed the bar exam, she was elated. Jumping for joy, she knew then, that she would be leaving to go back to Chris's; time was passing by quickly. Anita became quiet and Douglas knew she was not putting her best into her work.

Douglas called her into his office and suggested she sit down. They had some serious issues to work out. "What's going on? I thought this is what you wanted; to be a lawyer and work with me," he said.

"Dad, it is. But I can't shake these feelings that keep popping up all the time. I feel as though I have let Carolyn down. I want to know if Chris and I could make a go of it. Do you understand? I can't do my best, if I'm not at my best," she explained.

"What are you suggesting, dare I ask?" he said.

"Dad, I need professional help. I never thought I'd be asking this, but I feel like I'm going to explode inside," she said, hoping her father understood.

Douglas agreed to get her help in hopes she would get back to her old self. She gave her dad a nudge in the arm and said thank you. Anita agreed to continue working while getting therapy, and hoped they could sort out her rocky emotions. Douglas silently decided to monitor her progress and hoped things would really calm down.

After several sessions with her therapist, they both agreed she would never be at peace until she did something about her past. Rehearsing her speech all the way back to her father's office, she boldly walked in and announced she was going back.

Her father being a negotiator, looked at his daughter with intensity. "Your intentions are good," he said, "but you lack good judgment. I understand you will go with or without my blessing, and I knew this day was coming. I just wanted to be sure you had your head on straight." Anita's face reddened as he had read her so well. "There will be a few stipulations," he said. "The FBI is still trying to figure out where you were originally taken, so start talking."

"Please don't insult my intelligence. You've known from the start that I knew. Chris gave me an address, which I promptly destroyed, but kept it in my memory bank. So, do I have your blessing? And what about those stipulations?"

Sitting back and rubbing his hands for a few minutes, Douglas finally conceded. "I will accompany you on your journey, but I also want to take Jake. I think it's time he spread his wings. Should I be satisfied no harm will come to you, I will return with or without Jake. That'll be his decision. A small army of men will be hired, a helicopter will be at your disposal, and the FBI will be called if I deem it necessary. An old friend is ready to help, but at the first sign of trouble you are out of there. Those are my terms."

Anita couldn't contain her appreciation. She ran over and hugged her father. "We have a deal," she said.

Douglas sighed, and spoke musingly. "I must be getting soft. No one has ever trapped me into doing something I feel is wrong before."

Anita still had her arms around her father, and giggled. "The criminals you've defended or prosecuted have probably manipulated you more than you'd tell. Besides, I'm your daughter and daughters are supposed to be able to manipulate their fathers."

Letting out a belly laugh, Douglas replied, "Isn't that the truth."

Feeling despair, Douglas sat back and watched his daughter as she left the office. He wondered how she had the guts to go into a foreign country full of perils when she had been so sheltered – and how she would fare, once the reality of things settled in. Picking up the phone, Douglas discreetly made his plans and was careful the FBI were left out of the loop. In the back of his mind, he hoped that when things got tough, Anita would back away, and leave it to the experts.

Having the job of explaining the plans to his wife, Douglas soon found that she was dead-set against going on such an outrageous excursion. So rethinking, he concocted a plan that Millie should go abroad and visit with her sister. Jake was excited about the venture, and packed as though he were going on vacation, instead of into dense jungle areas in search of Carolyn.

Their sudden activities sparked the FBI's interest and a tail was put on the entire family. Douglas's sharp mind anticipated that they would come under scrutiny, so he devised a plan to elude them.

Travel arrangements were made for the family to stay in a villa in France, and tour the countryside. From there, Anita's mom went to see her sister and the rest of the group headed to Scotland to do more sightseeing. From there, they escaped the FBI's watchful eye. Anita's heart was doing flip-flops about returning. She broke out in a sweat as flashbacks occurred, making her feel edgy.

Resting peacefully in their first class recliners, Douglas turned his head slightly in the direction of his daughter, and asked, "Does Chris know we're on our way?"

"Not exactly," Anita said, as she peered out the plane window.

Douglas raised his seat to an upright position, and demanded, "What do you mean, *not exactly?*"

Intimidated by her father's irritability, Anita spoke meekly. "I wrote him a letter, because, if I had phoned him or sent something out by priority mail or the Internet, the FBI would've been all over it. This way was safer, and he should have received it by the time we arrive."

Her father covered his face with his large hands. "*Should have received it.* Do you have any idea how long it takes for mail to get there? Which brings a question to mind. Why didn't you write, call, or e-mail me from there? Wherever that is."

Anita replied, bluntly. "Couldn't find a phone in the house, couldn't send a letter because I was not near a post office, there was no computer to be found, and I was being constantly watched. And yes, I do know how long it takes a letter to get there and, as I stated, he should have received it by the time we arrive." Her father's face looked strained, prompting Anita to ask, "You know him, don't you? Chris, I mean."

Douglas flashed her a grave look, as he replied, "Why would you ask me such a stupid question?"

"You told us no question is stupid. But to answer yours, it's the way you speak about him that leads me to believe you know him. Also, it's how you seem to know where we're headed, even though I don't recall telling you."

"You were under sedation from the surgery when I acquired that pertinent information. It's amazing how much you can find out that way. If I've convinced you that I knew him, then I fooled the FBI as well," Douglas said.

Jake, who had remained quiet all this time, popped his head up and looked at the father-daughter team, and asked, "Are either of you going to fill me on what you're talking about, or is it learn-as-you-go?"

"Learn-as-you-go," Anita quipped back, with a smile. "The less you know the better."

"Will this Chris character be pissed when we arrive?" Jake asked.

Knowing full well Chris would be upset, Anita looked at her father and then at Jake. "I can safely say, yes."

Her dad shook his head, anticipating the worst, but said little. He was beginning to believe now that the trip would be short, and wished he hadn't gotten involved with this situation, and had left it strictly for the FBI to handle. He found it difficult to relax, but he realized this was one of the hardest tasks he had to conquer, and prayed for a speedy return home.

CHAPTER FOURTEEN

When the plane touched ground, Douglas thanked the pilots and the man who dropped off the car. He then turned and headed towards the vehicle. His large strides got him there ahead of the others, and he had to wait for the rest of the group to catch up. Before getting into the vehicle, Douglas barked, "Where the hell are we headed?"

It seemed as though every living creature stopped breathing, as nothing could be heard but the sound of the vehicle's motor running. Anita bored holes through her father, and spoke, "Why ask me? You seem to know the way."

Gently shoving her into the car, Douglas muttered, "We have no time to parley. My plan was good, but not fool proof."

Sitting in the back of the car, Anita folded her arms and had a stare that made it seem like Jack Frost had appeared. She fixated her eyes on her father, sending chilling electrodes to make his heart palpitate, and she remarked, "I haven't given you the coordinates, so either we're on a scavenger hunt, or you know where we're headed. I vote on the latter."

Not liking to be caught in a trap, Douglas blurted, "Don't look so smug. We've had this conversation before. It just so happens I have a very good map."

Smirking, because she thought she was one up on her dad, Anita simply stated, "Gee, I wonder what would make me think that – oh yah, you seem to be driving in the right direction, without looking at the map."

Jake opted to say nothing, and his quietness made him appear to be invisible; therefore, he was being excluded from the conversation.

With barely a word being spoken, Douglas drove right up to the driveway of Chris's house. Anita drew in a deep breath and slowly exhaled when she saw the door open. Chris walked out to greet them. He was horrible to Anita. "Why are you here? Wasn't it bad enough the first time?"

Trying to convince him that this was a good thing, Anita used her own logic. "I wrote you a letter explaining everything. Didn't you receive it?"

His face showed red, hot anger, and Anita swore steam escaped through his nose. "Letter or no letter, where is your common sense? Do you not remember what happened? Do you have any idea the danger you've put yourself in, not to mention your family's?"

Now standing firmly and squarely in front of the man she loved, Anita matched his temperament. "You have no idea what I've been through. I can't eat, sleep, or start a new life until I've tried every resource in finding Carolyn. Process that."

Chris stood with his arms folded. Anita was sure his eyes were like magnifying glasses, and they were beginning to burn her with their intensity. "In other words," he said, "you're a spoiled brat. Have to have it your own way."

Anita wanted to shake him, but instead she shook her fist at him, while hurling her words. "I've worked for everything I've ever received in my life, and if I must die trying to make a daring rescue, then so be it."

Not fazed by her little speech, Chris spat back, "Do you really expect me to help you commit suicide?"

Anita backed off and sucked in a deep breath to cool her emotions. "Well," she said, "I had hoped you would help prevent my death. So, the answer is yes."

Chris shook his head at the foolish woman who stood before him. He let his plans for her be known during her stay. "You can stay here at the house, and I will find other accommodations. Understand one thing, I want no part of anything you do. Do you read me? I mean, really understand what I'm saying?" he asked.

Her hurt feelings showed in her face. "If that's the way you want it, see you around. I wouldn't want you to do anything that goes against your principles. Heaven knows you are an angel. Just answer one question. Do you think Carolyn and others like her are still around?"

Chris glanced over at the lake, trying to change his facial expression before answering, and then turned back to the feisty woman who stood before him. "Hard to say," he said.

Lowering her voice, Anita wanted Chris to know a few details about her departure, in hopes of persuading him to change his mind. "The night you helped me to escape, I was shot and I have the bullet scar embedded in my shoulder. How about you? You heal from your wound?"

His senses became sharp and was amazed that she knew he had been shot, but he was totally unaware of hers. Still digesting her words, he replied slowly, "Yes."

"Before you go," Anita said, and handed him the folder with all the information in it. "All the money is accounted for, and I thank you for your assistance."

Accepting the folder, Chris held it in one hand and slapped it against the other hand. He paused, and then voiced his opinion. "I want to help you, but you are just going to get hurt. This is a jungle full of predators, and I'd hate to promote such a catastrophe."

Grateful for his generosity, Anita replied, "Living in the city has killers. It doesn't matter where I am, because if they want me, they'll get me. Now if you you'll excuse me, I had better converse with my father, whom, I'm assuming you already know, and my brother Jake. I need to let them know what's going on so they can get settled. Thanks for your hospitality, and when more suitable arrangements are made for us, you can have your home back. I see my training will take longer, but do not think for one moment I'm going away. I have a mission to complete and I will not rest until it's done: to the best of my capability. My life means nothing if I don't make an honest attempt."

Chris felt remorse for not staying, but he turned and picked up his packed belongings and left his house. Anita sought out her family, and disclosed the conversation she had with Chris. Douglas was not surprised at his daughter's description of what transpired between the two, but hoped now that she heard another point of view, she would come to her senses and put the whole charade behind her and leave.

The first morning, after settling in, Anita was up early with the birds doing exercises; something she was not accustomed to doing. After a vigorous workout, she went for a swim, followed by some weight lifting in the gym Chris had set up for himself. Words of caution, from her father and brother, about over doing it were a waste of their time; she was in total control of her own itinerary. Just before mealtime, which Chris was kind enough to loan them Delia, Anita could feel her muscles tighten up. Making a judgment call, Anita went in for a swim hoping the cool water would soothe the escalating pain, but by dinnertime she could barely move. Jake and Douglas showed her no mercy and wouldn't allow her to lie down. Instead, she was to join them on the porch for coffee and look at the view. Sitting was very painful, and Anita was getting antsy to leave.

With much pleading, they finally allowed her to leave, and watching her climb the stairs was good entertainment; she tackled the stairs one at a time by grabbing the railing and slowly pulled her body up to the next stair. When she finally reached the top stair, she walked bull-legged, like she had just lost her horse, and she could hear laughter coming from the bottom of the stairs.

The next morning there was no movement out of Anita. Jake kindly pulled her out of bed, escorted her to the shower, and waited for her to dress. It seemed to take a long time, but she finally emerged and he guided her down to breakfast, and a schedule for her morning routines awaited her. Not happy with the outcome of her previous days workout, Anita allowed Jake to punish her weary body by getting back at it. She found it very difficult to make her joints do as directed, but as the minutes turned into days, Anita felt better and could exercise easily. She was grateful that Jake hadn't given up on her.

At the end of the first week, Jake and Douglas were positive Anita would change her mind and decide to join her mother, rather than carry on this ridiculous notion of finding Carolyn. But they were disheartened to learn she was more enthusiastic than ever before. Douglas's perception, on the state of Anita's mind, was altered and he began to realize that she needed his help, not his cynicism, and offered his genuine assistance. Inquiring where Chris may be hiding out from Anita, Douglas received no response and decided to head into town to do some sleuthing. It was his belief that information was better than training the body; although they went hand in hand when the time was right. Anita, seizing the opportunity to escape her regimented routine, decided to tag along.

Looking for Jake and finding him on the porch, she beckoned him to tag along for the ride; she needed supplies to further along her skills and an extra pair of hands was needed. Piling into the car, Douglas was surprised he had company, but welcomed the idea of maybe finding out what Anita was truly up to. He was sadly disappointed when Anita chose not to speak, but to take in the wonderful view and plan her next move: to entice Chris back into her life.

Arriving in town, Douglas's stride was fast indicating he wanted to be alone, so Anita and Jake shopped around for a bow complete with arrows, and a gun. Jake listened as Anita did her best to barter the price down and smiled when she was satisfied she had done a good job. Anita looked at her brother, who had been giving her unwanted stares, and she remarked,

"They're for target practice. I need to learn to defend myself and besides, if you know the right retailer, money speaks in loud volumes. The best part is, no permit is required. I fully expect a war to break out, and I need to be prepared."

Once she had everything secured in the vehicle, Anita's heart began to pound as she surveyed the little town. She was heartbroken when Chris's vehicle was nowhere to be seen and drudgingly, she climbed into the vehicle bounded for home. Douglas quietly approached and slipped into the driver's seat. Knowing his daughter was upset because she hadn't seen Chris, Douglas chose to ignore her and let her stew a little longer. Jake described Anita's shopping tactics to his father, but he didn't seem interested and Jake sat back in his seat – feeling like he was out in left field and hoped one of them would clue him in so he could join the team. He was miffed at all the secrets his dad and sister held.

The sky dimmed, as though someone had turned the switch down. Being in a grizzly mood, Anita chose to let her items remain in the vehicle and she made way to her room, giving no explanation. Once inside her room, she ran hot water, poured in some bath salts, and submerged her body completely, letting dreamy thoughts of Chris swirl around her. Carolyn's face showed up, and she knew it was time to get out. She needed much rest to plan her next strategy – only she didn't know what that was exactly.

The next morning, with bags under her eyes big enough to pack a suitcase, Anita was running, and spotted Chris as he drove into the yard. She decided now was not the time to talk to him, and stripped off her pants and dove into the water for a swim, hoping Chris had seen her.

Douglas approached Chris, and held out his hand for a handshake. "I'm Douglas Jefferson."

Chris had a firm grip and shook the stretched hand. "I'm Chris Preston. It's a pleasure to meet you face to face. Thanks for the warning before your arrival, and for not telling Anita where you found me in town. Tell me, how long before Anita gives up this wild notion of finding Carolyn?"

Douglas watched his daughter swim, and then redirected his attention to Chris. "I was hoping it would've happened by now. But, it looks as though this is one of those times she will carry out her whim."

Chris, looking confused, opened up about his feelings. "If you're expecting me to help her, that won't happen. I am bowing out. She's going to get hurt and I don't want to live with that for the rest of my life. How could you let her think she'd be able to help out a useless situation?"

Douglas met Chris's gaze as he spoke fondly of his daughter. "You don't know my daughter. If she feels it's a worthy cause, she'll fight to the end, and there is nothing in this world that will stop her. If I don't stand behind her, I could lose her forever. If I do stand behind her, I will have much better control and she will listen to reason: when it's laid out carefully. Anita has the courage to find out the truth. I admire her for that, no matter the outcome."

Shocked by his praise for Anita, Chris was still doubtful. "Aren't you worried something will happen to her? I am."

Douglas more than understood how this young man felt, and clarified his own feelings. "If it were anyone else, I'd react differently. But with Anita, well she's not your every day typical young woman. She's determined, sensitive, and has willpower of her own. She'll do this charade, as you call it, with or without our help. If she feels strong enough about her cause, she will see it through to the finish line. I wish you'd reconsider and work with her."

Chris's feelings were jumping around like jackrabbits invading his body, and shared his views. "When she was ill, all she thought about was locating Carolyn. She made me aware she was not like anyone I'd ever met."

"So you'll help?" Douglas threw at him.

"I have to think about it. I was really wishing with no support, she had headed home by now. But I find that is not the case," he solemnly said.

"She'll prove it can be done, even if it means going off half cocked. With proper training, she'll succeed in her mission, and she can be counted on not to falter. Please reconsider," Douglas pleaded.

Angry he had been manipulated by a very intelligent man, Chris climbed into his vehicle and shouted over the sound of the engine, "I'll think about it. You're a very convincing man."

Douglas smiled and waved. Chris barely heard his words. "It's not me. It's Anita. Why do you think I'm here?"

Anita's timing was perfect; all she could see was dust scattering as Chris left the grounds. Douglas, smirking because he had won Chris over, explained to Anita that he and Chris had a good chat, and he would be returning later. This news lit up Anita's eyes and she thanked her father for the great news.

Jake, still not asking questions, vowed he would know the entirety of what was going on, because he needed to satisfy his hunger. Ignoring all those around her, Anita turned sharply and headed in the direction of the vehicle they had taken to town, and began to unload her prize possessions. Struggling to carry out her feat, Anita was unable to do the task and asked the men to loan her their muscles. Giving orders to put the items behind the house, she ran ahead and began to set up a target practice area – she couldn't wait to try it out.

With everything set in its place, Anita grasped the bow with one hand and picked up the arrow with the other. With no instructions of how to use it, she put her mind to work and recalled seeing how it was done on the television. She placed one foot slightly in front of the other, turned slightly so her body was facing away from the target, raised the bow and released the arrow. Her arm was too close to the whizzing weapon, and it singed her arm causing great amounts of pain. Throwing the bow to the ground, Anita stormed into the house to tend to her arm.

Jake, who had been in the background watching Anita's mishap, decided to try his hand at the weapon. Holding his arm away from the strings of the bow, he let the arrow whirl through the air and watched as it landed a few inches away from his target. Not being discouraged, Jake adjusted his stance, steadied his arm, lined up his target, and in one easy motion, he let the arrow sail right to the target – delighting him. Happy with his shooting, Jake sought out Anita, and when he found her nursing her arm with ice, he began to boast about his marksmanship. Instead of being happy for him, Anita was a little jealous, and told him to go away. This made Jake laugh, because he was now better than her: in a least one thing.

Sulking at her wounded ego, Anita sat on the porch with her ice pack wishing the stinging would go away. She looked at the marks on her arm; it was full of bright red bleeding lines. She was questioning herself if she was doing the right thing, when Jake sat beside her. He was doing his best to discourage her from finishing her wild fantasy about being a hero and finding Carolyn. Having heard enough negativity, Anita turned to her dear brother, and sharply spoke, "Enough. If you don't want to be here or help out, there is no anchor weighing you down. You have the right to abandon ship. If you decide to stay on board, then shut up and pool ideas. Be a crewmember, not a martyr."

Jake loved his sister, and admired her for her strengths that he lacked, and shook her hand. "I'm a member of your crew."

Thinking everything was going against her, Anita felt as though she had a boulder crushing her upper body and she couldn't breathe. Wanting a little time to herself, she took a walk along the beach keeping the house in sight as Chris's words haunted her, "*They can get you anywhere.*" Her body shuddered as the vision of seeing Carolyn before they were separated, taunting her, and she became more determined to investigate the extenuating circumstances of who made all this happen and why.

Grateful for her family support, Anita talked to herself out loud, and made a pact to master the bow and then the gun. Her gut was warning her that things were going to happen.

CHAPTER FIFTEEN

As she sat in her room planning her morning, a movement caught Anita's attention. Glancing out the window, she saw Chris diligently working amongst the trees and after several long minutes of watching him toil; Anita wondered what he was doing. Her heart began to flutter uncontrollably, and she hoped he was going to stay as her father predicted.

Hoping her father could shine a light upon the latest happenings so that her heart could settle down, she went to the kitchen, only to see her father disappear around the corner, as did she. Tracing his footsteps, Anita somehow lost his trail, and began to laugh at her feeble stalking skills.

Shrugging off the morning mishap, Anita was strolling over to the practice range when a car sped wildly up the driveway, creating dust swirls before coming to an abrupt halt. The car had barely stopped when Maureen swung open the car door, ran over to Anita and planted a right hook to her face, knocking her onto the ground. Looking up, Anita was sure her assailant had foam forming in the corners of her mouth. Maureen then let her words echo through the countryside. "Stay away from him. He's mine. Pack your bags, and leave or next time, I won't be so gentle."

Laying on the ground and rubbing her sore face, Anita was in total bewilderment, and simply stated, "He doesn't have anything to do with me."

"Right. I haven't seen him in weeks, so I come here and look who's back. How charming," Maureen said, as she held her hands up in a boxer's position.

Chris appeared, taking the ladies by surprise. He could see Anita's eye beginning to change color and, kneeling over her to ensure she hadn't sustained any further damage, he asked, "Can you get up? Can you see? Are you hurt anywhere else?" Anita's eyes were fixed on Maureen's, as she assured Chris she was going to survive.

Watching Chris's compassion for Anita angered Maureen even more. She ran to her car, catching Chris's attention with her untamable manner.

Releasing his hold on Anita, Chris sprinted after Maureen causing Anita to lose her balance. She fell back on the ground with a jolt. Maureen reached inside her car with her hand, but Chris pulled her away and a tussle developed between them. Then, with one rapid movement, Maureen had a gun in her hand. Chris brought his hand down hard on Maureen's arm, loosening her grip on the gun, and it fell to the ground. The commotion was more than Anita could handle. She walked up to the couple, and directed her words to Maureen. "Listen up," she said, "Chris has had nothing to do with me. The fact is, he wishes for me to leave. He was good enough to lend us his home and he sought lodgings elsewhere, so don't get yourself all worked up for nothing. I'm going to get an ice pack, and when I return, I had better not see a trace of you because, I too, have a temper."

Prickles from her swollen eye enticed her to cover it up with one hand, and Anita headed straight for the house to tend to her injury, and try to control the pain; both from the arm and her heart. But instead of tending to her eye, she retrieved a towel and headed for the beach. Her brother appeared, stopping her in her tracks. He threw her off as he asked, "What are you going to do about it?"

"Let it swell and then put ice on it," Anita replied, as she looked at her brother through her one good eye.

Jake, shocked at how evasive his sister's retort was, smiled. "That was a good answer," he said. "Too bad it didn't answer the question I asked. Aren't you annoyed by all this?"

"Of course I am. I'm developing a black eye and it hurts like hell," Anita quipped back. "Well, you coming to join me in a leisurely swim?" she asked.

Hesitation from her brother told her he was unsure, so she continued down to the inviting water without him. When he saw Chris heading towards the beach, Jake stopped him, preventing Chris from joining Anita. Jake's narrowed eyes controlled the situation as he confronted Chris. "Don't toy with my sister. Let her know how you really feel."

"I have no idea what you're talking about," Chris stated, and changed his plan to see if Douglas was near by.

Jake stood motionless for a few minutes, staring at Chris, and then ran after his sister. When he caught up to her, he asked breathlessly, "Who was that woman anyway?"

"One of his girlfriends, I assume," Anita answered, hoping to avoid a confrontation with her brother. Jake was hurt at how his sister was brushing him off; he sat on the beach staring into space and stewing. Anita's dander was raised a little and, instead of going for a swim, she hooked her arm around her brother's, and they slowly walked back to the house.

Chris found Douglas sitting on the porch, but before he could open his lips to speak, Douglas asked frankly, "Would you tell me why you rescued my daughter from a doomed fate?"

"I had to or Maureen would've shot her," Chris replied, wittily.

"You know what I'm referring to," Douglas said, chuckling when he noticed how much Chris reminded him of himself when he was younger; witty, but would protect those he loved, and yet, he had an armor-like exterior and hard to penetrated.

Sinking comfortably into his favorite chair, Chris leaned his head back, and looked up into the beautiful sky, sighing. "Maybe because she wasn't concerned with her own health and safety, and more worried about her friend. It was like I was appointed her guardian angel," he said.

"I had you checked out and I know your story," Douglas said. "Would you like to do the honors and tell Anita or should I?" He scratched his head, as he waited for Chris to reply.

Slowly raising his eyes to meet Douglas's, Chris's voice deepened. His defense mechanisms had engaged. "I've done nothing wrong to Anita," he said. "You know my gesture was genuine, so why does she need to know the rest?"

"What are you going to do to help her now? Do you still feel like her guardian angel?" Douglas responded, with conviction.

Feeling pressured, Chris got up and walked to the end of the porch. Turning on his heel, he again met Douglas's eyes, and said, "You won't give up, will you? I will be upfront in order to have a fresh beginning with her and yes, I will help her, but we both know where this could lead and it terrifies me that I could lose her."

Anita and Jake's slow walk turned into a canter as they raced back to the house. She was taken aback at seeing her father's rarely lit up face, and hearing his softly spoken words. "Jake and I are going to town," Douglas said. "Don't wait up for us."

Jake and Anita looked at each other in amazement before Jake vanished into the house to get dressed for his surprise outing. Anita beamed, knowing she would be alone with Chris. "Huh. That leaves Chris and me alone," she observed aloud. "So Chris, do you know of a secluded place we can go for a quiet getaway?"

Feeling a pinprick in his stomach and letting his held-breath out, Chris nodded. "I'll have Delia make a picnic basket," he said. "Bring your swimsuit. It'll be boring otherwise."

Life was just too good; Anita danced around feeling like her dreams were about to be fulfilled.

CHAPTER SIXTEEN

Preparing the basket was a delight for Delia, and she secretly hoped Anita and Chris would become allies instead of remaining enemies. As Anita hopped into the jeep with Chris, she had a sense that she was going to get a wish granted. She smiled broadly. When Chris veered onto an unfamiliar side road, Anita reflexively drew in a deep breath; but when she looked over at the driver, her momentary fear melted, and she put her faith and trust in him.

Before she was even out of the jeep, Anita was awestruck by the beauty of the place. The waterfall rushed down the mountain, creating a soft lullaby to the ears when the water hit the bottom, which formed a small tantalizing swimming pool that drew her to it like a magnet. Chris was left behind to carry the basket; he laughed as Anita's childlike joy made his emotions soar. He shook off his fears that bringing her here was not the best idea.

Guilt-stricken for having left Chris to carry their supplies, Anita sauntered back, but he had already had everything laid out nicely. Her heart seemed to jump into her throat, causing her voice to take on a high unrecognizable pitch. She sat as close to him as she dared, and felt both the uneasy tension and heated closeness.

As he broke the ice, Chris's voice seemed to echo in the dense forest. "You've got one butte of a shiner," he said. "Doesn't it hurt?"

"Yes, and I can honestly say she has a sure hit," Anita replied, as she touch her distended eye.

Chris handed her an ice pack, and said, "Here, keep it covered with this."

"Chris, I need to know why you helped me to safety," Anita said, as she looked at him with one eye.

Changing the subject, Chris turned the questions to Anita, asking, "Did you pass your bar exam?"

"Yes, and with all that had happened, I was surprised at how well I did. So why did you rescue me? Was it because you *knew* of my father or did you *know* my father?" The look Chris gave, told her that her father was indeed the reason, and she shifted positions. Once she was comfortable, Anita continued, "Let me fill you in on what happened to me. They forced the plane I was occupying to make an unscheduled landing, so they could do a thorough search, but I managed to hide, and here I am. I know we were both shot. I healed, but did you?" she asked, really wanting to know.

Taking his cue, Chris got comfortable. He knew her batting eyes were telling him to speak, so he began his story. "When I was carrying you to the plane, I felt a thud as something struck me on the back of the shoulders. That was the first one. The second one was when you had just taken off. I felt pain in my arm and I could faintly hear someone saying that I could have caused them to lose a bundle of money if you arrived home before the ransom was paid. They dragged me to a tiny shack, sat me down in the chair, tied me up, and bashed me around – but I can honestly say I didn't end up with an eye like yours," Chris said, laughing. Anita wasn't amused, and he continued, "The room was dimly lit, so I wasn't able to identify any of them, and they left me for several days with no food or water. When they returned, it was dark. They untied me and said I was free to go. I had to find my own way home. When I saw my jeep, I was ecstatic, climbed aboard and headed straight home for Delia to take care of me." Then testing Anita to see if her curiosity was satisfied, he asked, "Did I feed your hunger for knowledge?"

Smiling at Chris, Anita had to be sure she wasn't drooling, and dabbed her mouth before answering. "Do you know you have the most gorgeous eyes? They are most expressive, tender and caring one minute, and the coldest weapons a person could possess, the next."

"Can we get back on track here?" Chris asked, feeling his face grow crimson in color. "What else would you like to know?" he asked, hoping she would stay on the subject.

Pleased she had flustered him, Anita's next question was simple. "Tell a little about yourself."

Playing with a piece of fruit in his hand, Chris sighed as he began to speak. "Seems I'm doing all the talking. I was a stockbroker making a good living until I received a call from my father's attorney to come down, and help clean up the mess my father had created. I told my dad I wouldn't come, and he retaliated by threatening to say I was embezzling money.

The consequences of that accusation would have been astronomical. My father didn't play fair, and I knew he would carry out his threat, so I took a leave of absence and joined my loving father."

"It seemed my dear father had gotten in very deep with the wrong crowd, and he could see no way out. That's when his lawyer contacted your father and a deal was made for my dad to testify at a trial, in lieu of his freedom. I was to be his bodyguard, but I resented both what my father had gotten into, and the way he had manipulated me into joining his affairs. The last thing I wanted was a tarnished name, especially if I wanted to go back to my career; any career for that matter."

"Anyway, a contract had been put out on my father and it was just a matter of time before they got him. Fifty thousand dollars goes a long way around here. My job was to get him to the Embassy, but I was knocked out and they shot my father. As much as I resented his profession, he was still my dad. After the funeral, I stayed on and began to see what he saw here. The peace, landscape and tranquility beat the city lifestyle: no sirens, no crowds, and best of all, people leave you alone here – that is until now. Quite different from living on the edge, don't you think?"

"The people my father dealt with tried to get me involved in their business, but I was not for sale. In the end though, to keep the peace, I agreed to do them the odd favor – like in your case. You probably think I am a man with no means of income, but that's not the case. I do errands for the villagers, my father left me a sizeable inheritance, and I have my own nest egg."

"Now, to answer your question. The night you ran away desperately searching for your friend, made me realize you weren't just any girl, but at that point, I was already thinking of a plan to help you escape. When you told me who your father was, I knew I had to help you. He helped my father. And yes, your father had been here before to confer with my father, but I had never met him. Does that satisfy your curiosity?" he asked, hoping it was going to be the end.

Anita's face scrunched up as she looked at Chris. "Wouldn't it have been easier to tell me instead of being so secretive?" she asked.

"I had my reasons for not trusting anyone," Chris said, somberly.

Taking it all in, Anita had to push one last time. "Tell me about Maureen."

Chris shook his index finger at her. "That topic doesn't concern you," he replied.

Anita's words bolted from her lips. "It most certainly does – especially when I'm disfigured from her jab."

Defending his honor, Chris responded, "As she told you, I haven't seen her for a very long time. I'm done. Your turn."

Flippantly Anita asked, "Do you want the story in one or two sentences?" causing Chris to laugh heartily. Anita studied him for a few seconds and then looked towards the pond. Finally she said, "I don't have any friends, other than Carolyn and she nurtured me through life. Her parents were killed in a car crash, so she moved in with us until she could support herself. That was her choice. I have no idea why a man would ever marry me because I can't cook, sew or clean a house. I don't relax enough to have fun, and Carolyn always called me stuffy."

"My dad went abroad as often as he could with or without my mom. I decided to follow in my dad's footsteps, trying to win his affection, while Jake did what he was best at: throwing parties and living it up. This one particular party Jake threw, he insisted I attend and said I had to bring a date. Finding a date myself was a lost cause, so I called Carolyn and she arranged everything for me. The night was a disaster, but to make up for our first date, a Valentine's dance was proposed and I agreed to try again. Just before the ship was about to dock, both Carolyn and her date, Blake, vanished and a ransom note was handed to me. I thought everything was being sloppily handled, so when I noticed I was unattended, I jumped overboard, swam to shore, and hitched a ride to the police station. To make a long story short, I was assigned protection, but then I was snatched right out of the squad care, while my "protection" was following a lead. I might add, that he was torn between leaving and going and we chose for him to go. The rest you know," she said, and waited to see if he had anything else he might want to ask.

Chris, making light of the conversation, asked, "So, what about this date you had?"

Not sure where his question was heading, Anita put the ice pack down. "Touché. His name is Jeremy, and Carolyn arranged the date, as I said. That's all, but somehow I think he was involved in the disappearance of Carolyn and Blake."

There was a thousand questions going through her head, but she tuned them out. Seductively she took off her blouse and shorts, exposing her bathing suit. "Enough talking," she said. "Time for a breather."

"You go," Chris said, squirming around to a get a good view of the pond.

Wanting his undivided attention, Anita walked over to the pond and bent over to let the cooling liquid run through her hands as she splashed around in the water. From where he sat, Chris could vividly see the scar on Anita's shoulder. He got up and knelt down next to her, running his fingers over the scar, causing her to break out in a sweat. She made a quick decision to turn around, and she planted a firm kiss on his lips. Her impulse caught him off guard and he resisted at first, but soon found his arms wrapping around her, embracing her so closely, she could barely breath. Excited, Anita made her feelings clear by pressing hard against his body.

Coming to his senses, Chris held her at arm's length, and breathlessly asked, "Do you have any idea what you're doing?"

Wiggling to get closer to the man who was torturing her emotions, she responded, "Yes. When I'm close to your body, you make me feel secure, my body heats up, and for the first time in my life, I feel as though I belong."

Still holding her at a distance, Chris scoured her body for other unusual marks. He saw her singed wrist, and asked, "The scrape on your arm, what's it from?"

"You don't miss much do you?" asked Anita. "I bought a bow and arrow thinking I knew how to shoot one. Just use your imagination to fill in the blanks. That scar has been cleaned, so let's move on," she said, and stopped squirming.

Chris let go of her, but Anita's movement was so smooth, that she caught Chris unaware. She again had him in a lip lock, as though she had used crazy glue, and Chris's willpower weakened. The kiss bloomed into more passion than either of them had realized, and Chris gently lowered Anita onto the blanket. He kissed every inch of her body sending little electric shocks through her. Anita felt so alive inside, that her pent up emotions unleashed and she exploded with excitement. After sweet love making, Anita giggled. "I never annulled the marriage," she said, "and now that we've consummated it, there's no turning back."

As Chris laughed heartily, his whole body wiggled. "Somehow I knew that. You stole my heart the first time you eluded me."

She was content just to lay there in his arms, but he decided they should go for a swim and they planned the rest of their day; it was to be followed with a fabulous meal and perhaps dancing, if they could fit it in. Chris also indicated he would teach her all he could, but she needed to be the best pupil ever, to which she fully agreed.

The ride home, for Anita, was definitely better than the trip up. Adjusting her seat and body, Anita found a way to almost sit on Chris's lap, and began running her hand up and down his leg, creating friction he didn't necessarily want.

Out of the blue, Chris said something that made Anita's hair stand up. "When the men untied me," he said, "they were talking. Although my head was splitting with pain, I am sure I heard them say Carolyn was ill and had been taken to a camp to recover."

Anita squealed with delight, and said, "She could still be around here. Yes! That makes me happy." She hugged Chris's neck, something he was not prepared for and wondered briefly whether he could handle her sudden impulses. He concluded they were part of her charm, and that he would easily adjust. She whispered in his ear to pull over, and Chris did as he was asked. Anita passionately kissed him, making him yearn for more.

Out of the corner of her eye, Anita saw a car missing the curve in the road; it was heading straight for them. She screamed and Chris had just enough time to pull the vehicle ahead, before they saw the car sail past them, diving down the embankment. Climbing out of their vehicle, Chris and Anita peered over the edge and wondered if it was an accident, or was it someone out to get them. They had no phone that worked in these parts, and since Anita didn't know her way around the area, they had to decide whether to help the people in the car right away, or go for help. Chris went down to see how badly they were hurt and discovered they were conscious, but needed help to get out of the wreckage. He told them he would send for help and suggested they keep talking to one another to stay awake until the professionals arrived. He then pointed for Anita to get into the vehicle, and drove like a madman to the nearest town. He described to the authorities how the accident occurred, and before anyone could ask him further questions, he and Anita disappeared down the road towards their home.

Finding the first available mirror in the house, Anita laughed until tears rolled down her cheeks. "Chris, you still want to go out this evening?" she asked. "This is an awfully messed up face."

As he slipped his hands around Anita's waist, his comeback warmed her heart. "You look just fine. This way I won't have to fight off the other guys trying to steal you away. Come, Mrs. Preston, I want to show you your new room."

Having opened the doors to the master bedroom, Anita looked around in awe. There were windows all around the room, with French doors leading to a deck, and a spectacular view. Off to one side was a very cozy sitting area with a fireplace and the biggest bed she had ever seen.

Pleased that she was in awe, Chris's words were full of passion. "Glad you approve. I need to look at that wound. It looks like it may have become infected, but I'll be back in a sec," he said. He headed downstairs, and Anita hurriedly took off her blouse and sprawled out in the middle of the humungous bed. Chris reappeared, stating that Delia would be up shortly with a homemade poultice. Taking advantage of the few minutes before Delia arrive, Chris cuddled with Anita on the bed. He was feeling contentment and resentment at the same time; contentment because he deeply loved this woman, and resentment because he did love her so much that he may lose her.

Delia was up the stairs faster than anyone could've imagined and was shocked to see Chris and Anita embracing. She broke out in a broad smile worth a million dollars. Chris beamed at Delia's approval when he explained that he and Anita had made their marriage legal and he was home to stay. Anita and Chris laughed when Delia did a little dance bringing joy into the room. To add to the lighthearted mood in the house, Chris gave Delia the much-needed night off, and her smile was bright enough to light up a darkened room.

Having handed Chris the concoction, Delia left the room. Chris, looking at the wound, applied pressure on the tender spot, and Anita let out a yelp. As he worked his magic, a tiny piece of shrapnel popped out and he immediately applied the poultice, warning her strictly not to get it wet for a few days, and to keep the medicinal wrapping in place.

Wanting the evening to be perfect, Anita dressed as best she could and when the task was done, she looked stunning - despite the colorful eye. Amused by the effect her black eye had on her husband, Anita coyly hung her arms around Chris's neck, and whispered, "I tried to match my outfit to a color in my eye. What do you think?"

Trying hard not to laugh, Chris whipped back, "It'll do in a pinch," but in the back of his mind he was proud to have this woman as his wife, and wanted to show her off.

CHAPTER SEVENTEEN

As Chris and Anita entered the cantina music was playing, enticing Anita to dance, but Chris wanted to kick back and relax for a few minutes. After a couple of social drinks, Anita forced him up to the dance floor for a slow song so she could snuggle closely and listen to the beat of his racing heart. She felt her legs go rubbery from passion, and her pulsating heart pumped her blood through her veins, making her feel light-headed and dizzy in love.

Suddenly a cold sensation came over them as they saw Maureen headed their way. Maureen pushed her way over to the couple, separated them, and whisked Chris away to the other side of the dance floor. Anita was furious and wanted to take action, but instead, she went out for a breath of fresh air and surmised that being in love had its good and bad points. Jealously was not a good trait to show, Anita decided. Counting the minutes to her cool-down period, Anita had just decided it was safe to intervene, when she caught a glimpse of a man resembling Jeremy getting out of a vehicle. Tiptoeing over to get a closer look at the figure, Anita became more certain that it was Jeremy. She flew straight into the cantina and butted between Chris and Maureen. She was full of anxiety. Chris has hoping she'd explain her sudden mood change but, instead of getting an answer, he was asked to join her outside, sparking more inquisitiveness.

Chris obeyed Anita's request, upsetting Maureen, and the two slipped out the door; only one knew of the forthcoming adventure. Without saying a word, Anita lowered her hand to signify that they should squat, and she waddled like a duck to her hiding place behind their vehicle. Before Chris could ask what was going on, a door slammed shut and there stood Maureen as large as a boulder that inconveniently rolled down a mountainside, preventing any further activity. Chris was compelled to take the initiative and stop her in her tracks. Gently pushing Maureen off the side, Chris explained he was working on a case for Anita's father and asked that she not give them away. He promised he would give her a full, detailed report as to what was really going on, if she would only leave them alone. To this, Maureen agreed, but as she walked away, her gait was that of a very hurt woman. Chris sighed and refocused on what was happening in the other direction.

Crouching down beside Anita, his words barely reached her ears as he whispered, "What's going on?"

Anita raised her body slightly to peer through the car window, and whispered back, "Do you have binoculars in the jeep? I swear I saw Jeremy."

Chris was taken aback. He repeated, "Jeremy?"

"Yes, and I'm going to spy on him until I find out where he's staying," she said, "so, do you have a pair of binoculars or not?"

Chris retrieved the binoculars and handing them over to her, his tone was full of sarcasm. "Is this business or because you want a rendezvous?"

Anita slapped him on the arm to get his attention, and didn't look at him when she responded, "Was dancing with Maureen pleasure or business?"

"I'm sorry. I'll straighten things out with Maureen," Chris said, trying to shake off his feelings and recognizing he was jealous for the first time.

Anita watched the little hotel across the street as Jeremy entered it, and her hopes rose. "He may be the link we need to find Carolyn," she told Chris. Anita monitored Jeremy's movements and could see him carrying his suitcase into the building. Gambling that he was staying put for the night; she conjured up her next move. Turning to face Chris with a sheepish look, Anita whispered, "I've never been in love before and it makes me want to dance, but a jealous feeling came over me in there. I wanted to scratch Maureen's eyes out and tell the whole world I love you and that I'm your wife."

Chris touched her face with his hands, making her entire being light up. His eyes were soft. "That's how I feel," he said. "I'm worried someone from your past will sweep you away. We know so little about each other."

"The mystery is what makes it more exciting and attractive," Anita said, with a smile that stretched from ear to ear. She kissed him with fevered passion. He broke the wonderful sensation by putting his hand in the air indicating that she should wait one minute. Then he crept forward to his vehicle.

Digging in the back of his jeep, Chris pulled out some articles of clothing and handed them to Anita. She gave him a quizzical look and he explained that if the town people saw her dressed like that on the street, it would cause speculation that something wasn't right and their cover might be blown.

With his help, Anita managed to change her clothes on the street. When she was done, they both laughed at her attire: baggy pants, a sloppy sweatshirt, and dress shoes. Rummaging through his vehicle, Chris found an old pair of boots. Anita changed into them and the transformation was complete; her hobo style attire would draw less attention on the street and, therefore, she could follow Jeremy without drawing attention to herself.

After hanging around the streets for several hours, the couple agreed that Jeremy was in the hotel for the night, and being extremely tired, they headed home so they could stretch their weary bones and get a good night's rest. Once home, they decided a hot shower would help. Chris was ready to retire for the night, but Anita had other plans. She entered the bedroom wearing the slinkiest negligee Chris had ever seen and she headed towards the open arms of the man she loved, making the rest of the night spectacular – complete with fireworks.

CHAPTER EIGHTEEN

The morning was bright and sunny, inviting Anita and Chris to get up and do a rigorous workout. Having jogged five miles, they were both ready for a good hearty breakfast. After their meal, they had decided to begin Anita's self-defense lessons. Debating whether to start with the bow and arrow, or the gun, they decided that the gun would be a good starting point for her education, since it was more commonly used. Chris handed Anita a rifle to get the feel of it, and instructed her to start slowly by placing it up and down to her shoulder several times. Feeling cocky, and without waiting for further instructions, Anita aimed the rifle, pulled the trigger, and without warning, she received a kick from the butt of the gun, which knocked her on her ass. Chris was annoyed and scolded Anita, shaking his head as the beginning stages of bruises could be seen forming on her lower cheek and shoulder.

Chris argued that if she wasn't going to pay attention, she had best leave it alone. A very apologetic Anita swore to be attentive; Jeremy was in town and that meant business was going to start soon. Chris showed Anita how to place the rifle on her shoulder, but having him so close to her it made Anita's body temperature rise and her knees began knocking. She spontaneously turned around and kissed him.

Breaking off the tender moment, Chris scolded her again, promising that if she didn't behave and concentrate on the project at hand, he would call the whole thing off, and go inside to have a well-deserved cup of coffee. Turning off her emotions was very difficult, but Anita made up her mind to concentrate and found that, with perseverance, she was hitting her target, pleasing both of them.

Having achieved a degree of accomplishment on the firing range, Anita followed Chris to an area where she was shown how to dismantle the gun, clean it and reload it. Chris wouldn't let her stop practicing until the task was second nature for her. It was late afternoon when they laid the weapons to rest, and went inside for a bite to eat. Since Anita was proving to be an attentive student, Chris decided it was time to teach her some self-defense moves.

Making a mat out of leaves and blankets was hard work, but it built character – as had all lessons of the day. As Chris was demonstrating a stance to Anita, a silver streak headed their way, catching their full attention. Maureen was back. When she climbed out of the truck, Chris and Anita stood still. The visitor stormed over to them and hotly demanded an explanation for their closeness. Maureen began to speak in Spanish and Chris responded in the same language. This prompted Anita to loudly request that they speak in English so she could understand what was being said. Gently picking up Anita's hand, Chris showed Maureen the matching rings. The hurt look on her face was more than Anita could bear, and her heart went out to this woman. At the same time, however, she was certain that she'd made the right choice in this man. She had no intention of letting him go.

Maureen began to cry and Anita, against her own judgment, urged Chris to comfort her. Not knowing what else to do, Chris have Maureen a hug. His touch seemed to reawaken Maureen's earlier rage, and she aimed her haunted eyes at Anita. Like a fire-breathing dragon, Maureen said, "It won't last long. He'll return to me sooner than you think."

Anger ripped through Maureen's body as Anita hurled back at her reply. "I don't scare easily," she said, "and he'll only come back to you when hell freezes over."

Vengefully, Anita turned around, picked up the gun, pointed it at its target, and shot a can lying on the ground. She hoped she had proved her point. Maureen left dirt in their faces as she sped away.

Biting her lip and waiting for a lecture from Chris, Anita was surprised when Chris embraced her and said, laughingly, "You're becoming a tough little woman. I think I preferred you better when you were meek and mild."

Her eyebrows shot up, and her eyes clouded over with worry. "You mean that?" she asked.

Retracting his words, Chris brushed her hair away from her face with his hands. "No. I don't think I could stop loving you no matter what you did. Young lady, you are embedded so far under my skin. If I had the choice of letting you continue your mission or holding you back, I would hold you back and build a wall around you to keep you safe and I would have you all to myself."

Beaming, Anita could feel heat simmering inside her and wanted him to make love to her so he could cool her down. "You make me feel so special," she said.

"Oh come now. I'm sure you've felt that way before," Chris said, teasingly.

"Nope. My dad was good at making others feel good, but not me. It felt like he just pushed me off to the side. That may have been his way, but it was cold to me. He always wanted Jake to be like him and when that didn't happen, I took it upon myself to walk alongside of dad, thinking it was my duty. I passed the bar exam and he hinted that I had done well; and he took me out for dinner. It's like he bottles everything up inside. I tried to be the same way, but I found out that expressing your feelings opens many doors," she said, and changed the subject. "By the way, if I hadn't kissed you yesterday, would you have kissed me?"

Chris cupped his hands lightly around her face. He wanted to tell her why he thought she was so special. His blue eyes seemed to deepen, to Anita, when he spoke. "I love you with all my heart and I am the happiest I've ever been. The mere thought of anything happening to you scares the crap out of me. Your spontaneity gives me warmth that I cannot express, and I like the change I've seen in myself since you came along. Would I have kissed you? Yah, that was inevitable."

Anita's smile was intoxicating to Chris. She replied, "When Maureen turned up, I decided I had to win, once and for all. I had to prove to her that I'm not going anywhere and I did just that. Now, I feel bad for my actions, because I let my feelings trounce over someone else's. Does that mean I'm becoming cold like my dad?"

"No, sweetheart. But being aware how easily we can hurt others for our own gain, will play an important part in our future behavior," Chris said.

His words were barely spoken, when Chris leaned in and kissed his wife passionately, but before they could get another bite of the forbidden fruit, the whines of a fast approaching engine told them they were about to be interrupted. They walked in the direction of the noise, and saw Jake stepping out of the vehicle that he and Douglas just pulled up in. A bewildered look crossed Jake's face and his eyes flashed, as he asked, "What happened while we were away? I don't recall Anita ever having had a sparkle in her eyes like that – and I'm not referring to the shiner. No one leaves until my curiosity has been quenched."

Chris looked at Anita and then at Jake before asking. "Anita, you didn't tell Jake?" Anita shook her head and Chris turned his attention back to Jake. "We were married," he explained.

"Married? When?" Jake asked, and had disappointment written all over his face.

As she gently clasped her bother's hands, Anita felt ashamed that she hadn't informed Jake of all the events that had led to this moment. "Jake," she said, "I'm so sorry I didn't tell you, but I thought the less you knew, the less harm could come to you. To protect me from harm and from being sold on the black market, Chris gave me his name in hopes to discourage such a transaction. It didn't work, so we parted, but the attraction grew and we've decided to make a go of it, rather than end it. It just happened."

Indignantly, Jake replied, "You have no faith in me, isn't that right? You all think I'm a bozo because I like to have fun. How wrong you all are. I am educated, and smart, and I can think for myself. I am sadly disappointed in your narrow view of me."

As he yanked his hand away from hers, Anita took a second look at her brother and admitted that she should have told him about the marriage. "I'm sorry," she began. "You never showed any interest in what went on and it never occurred to me to clue you in. From now on, you'll be a part of everything. Forgive me?"

"You'll have to prove it," Jake said, as he walked away. Anita felt like a rabbit wanting to jump into a hole and hide.

Looking at her father, Anita could see the corners of his mouth had a slight upward tilt. "Dad, get it off your chest – whatever it is you're thinking about," she said.

"I've known for the longest time how you truly felt. You never took off your ring, and would toy with it for long periods of time when you were thinking. Congrats are in order I assure you. Now, what do you have on your mind?" Douglas asked, as he embraced his daughter.

"Dad, you don't miss much," Anita said, and suggested they all go for a cup of Delia's superb coffee and catch up on each others exper

As everyone sat around the table with a cup in their hand, Anita couldn't' wait to fill Jake and Douglas in on her news. "Last night, we were in town and I saw Jeremy."

"Are you sure?" asked a very enthusiastic Jake.

Trying to remain placid, Anita picked up her cup and took a sip, but every part of her body vibrated when she announced, "I'm positive. He stayed at the little hotel right in the middle of town. I'd like to spy on him, but it would spook him if he spotted me."

Bravely, Jake stood up, cleared his throat, and said, "Let's go to town this evening. While we're there, I'll do some sleuthing."

"Do you know what perils are out there?" Douglas asked his son.

Feeling that he was being treated like a child, Jake became very defensive. "*That's* what I'm talking about. You don't respect me as the mature, thinking adult that I am. Yes, I know danger looms out there and that I could get hurt, but this is my contribution. For the first time, I feel like I can make a difference and that I am part of the intelligent human race – not the partying self absorbed person you think I am."

Anita hugged her brother, and stated, "You are the best brother ever, even though you tease me relentlessly about being stuffy. Welcome aboard." Anita then looked at her father, and continued, "Dad, Chris believes there is a slight chance Carolyn is still in the area, and I believe she may be in poor health. What's our next step?"

Douglas fell silent and then swiftly walked out of the room, leaving a current of air in his wake. Anita, Chris and Jake wondered what he had on his mind. A few minutes later Douglas returned and ordered Chris and Anita to get prepared; things would begin happening in the next day or so. Coffee cups were dropped as the siblings and Chris headed outside for some much-needed shooting practice. Chris praised Jake for being a great sharp shooter, but what shocked Chris was the fact that Anita was *good.* Both sister and brother appeared to be ready for whatever confrontation came their way. The three stood and shook hands on a job well done. Douglas appeared from out of nowhere, and asked them to convene in the dining room for a briefing.

Anita took a little extra time to freshen up before joining the group in the dining room. She entered after the others, and her father's cold stares gave her chills. Trying not to let him intimidate her, Anita sat beside Chris, cupped her hands on her lap, and looked at her father to indicate she was ready to listen.

His words rang out like a siren going off. "Due to the fact there has been kidnapping, and extortion of money out of the country, the FBI will be involved. They will be here in a matter of days," he said. His words left an uneasy feeling amongst those present in the room. After they digested the news, Douglas announced they would all head to town, leaving them hanging as to the reason for the trip. They felt as thought they were hanging on a cliff and there was no way down, but to fall and hoped the landing would be safe.

Deciding it was for the best, Anita promptly left the room. She ransacked her belongings and dressed in dark clothes: resembling those of a cat burglar. She tied her hair back, exposing her colorful face, took a flashlight, and tucked a revolver into her tight pants. Chris entered the room and his eyes took in Anita's state of preparedness. He threw her a jacket, instructing her to better conceal the gun that jutted out of her pants by placing it in her jacket pocket instead. Doing as instructed, Anita remarked, "Revealed too much, huh?"

"You could say that," Chris said, as he smiled back.

The foursome reconvened outside and taking two separate vehicles, they headed for the little cantina in anticipation of a night that was sure to be explosive.

CHAPTER NINETEEN

Meeting outside the cantina Anita took Jake by the hand and the two, dressed in dark clothes, blended into the darkness of the night, scouting around the perimeter of the hotel for any signs of Jeremy. Coming up empty handed, Anita bravely entered the hotel she had seen Jeremy enter. She asked the clerk if he spoke English, but the shake of his head indicated he did not, and Anita had to resort to other means of communication. Finding something to write on, Anita began to draw a picture of the man she sought. The clerk looked at her and, with his fingers he made a motion, describing a man walking away. Trying to use her universal language, Anita made the same swinging motion to indicate the man coming back towards the hotel, and the man shook his head to let her know that he had not returned. Bowing to say thank you, Anita headed out and kicked the staircase, relieving some of the aggravation that was brewing inside her body.

Needing some support from their co-conspirators, the siblings walked arm-in-arm into the cantina. The others were waiting for the news, with drinks sitting in front of them. Anita took a second look; her father had never had a drink with the family before and this triggered something in her. She decided to put her suspicions aside for now and would address it later: at the right time.

Jake informed everyone he would stay in town and do some snooping on his own: an announcement that drew disapproval from the other members of the group. But he was determined, and demanded they leave him a vehicle so he would have transportation to go home when he was ready. Finally the others conceded, and Jake made a promise to phone home around one in the morning if he wasn't returning. Leaving him alone to fend for himself, Douglas and Chris felt edgy inside. But even though Anita feared for his safety, she was proud of Jake for standing up for what he believed in - himself. The night ended early for the other three, who were unnerved at leaving Jake behind.

Feeling as though his life was crashing in on him, Douglas retired early. He was not prepared for the strong will of his kids, and was at a loss as how to deal with them. He was ashamed of not knowing his children, and wished he had been home more often.

Anita was mystified how her father could just shut everything off and not worry about his son, out in the cruel world in a strange country. A gnawing pain in the pit of her stomach grew with each passing moment, causing Anita to panic and break out in hives. Chris talked gently to Anita, calming her down as they cuddled on the couch and fell asleep wrapped in each other's arms. Later, Chris woke suddenly as if a bell had gone off in his head. Peeking at the clock, he saw that is was four in the morning. Gently easing himself free of Anita, Chris was startled when she opened her mouth before her eyes. "What time is it?" she asked.

"Four in the morning," was Chris's response.

Anita's eyes shot open, and she jumped off the couch in alarm. "Where's Jake? Is he home?" she asked, with urgency in her voice.

Doing his best to remain calm, Chris placed his hands on her shoulder, and said, "I was about to check and see if he snuck in while we were sleeping. Wait here."

Heading towards Jake's room Chris found he had a dark shadow looming over him, but he accepted the fact that Anita would do what she wanted, and he continued on his mission. The room was empty, and the wrinkle-free bed indicated that Jake had not been home. Chris and Anita checked the grounds to see if his vehicle was around, but the bright moon revealed no stationary shadows – just an empty driveway.

Anita's blood curdling scream woke Douglas. He sprung out of bed. His feet barely touched the floor, and in an instant, he was down the stairs facing his daughter's haunted look. He rubbed his tired eyes, and yelled, "What the hell?"

Tears ran down Anita's cheek like a jet steam, and she cried. "Jake hasn't returned or called. I knew something awful would happen."

Annoyed that his sleep had been disturbed, Douglas replied, "You know very well he's irresponsible."

Anita's nostrils flared with every deep breath she took. Her words were those of a woman out of control. "He's changed since his arrival," she replied. "You were always happiest when we were out of sight because then we were out of mind. So, why are you really here?"

Intervening, Chris defended Douglas, and said, "His concern for you brought him here."

Anita felt defiance throughout her entire body and her voice quivered, as she said, "No. He had another motive and I want straight answers. He's never had a drink with us or even listened enough to know what we were about. He's good at keeping secrets, but secrets have a way of biting you in the ass in times of disaster. Am I right, Dad?"

Douglas, lost for words, slumped onto the couch and after several strained minutes, he replied, "Part of what you said is true. My reason for being here is my concern for you, to make sure you are safe and not going off half-cocked, before I leave. When you were growing up, I may not have been there physically for you both, but I cared. I just couldn't tolerate being around kids. After you and Carolyn disappeared, I watched how Jake agonized over you both and it was like watching someone taking over my role. I realized how selfish I'd been over the years. I am trying to make amends, but I seem to be doing a poor job."

"You're here because of guilt?" Anita said, rolling her eyes back.

Having heard enough, Chris grabbed Anita by the shoulders and guided her to a chair. "You listen up," he said to her. "Now is not the time to be drudging up the past because it's just that; the past. This is now. Take it for what it is. Becoming suspicious of everyone and everything is going to destroy you, and I need you with a clear mind and trust in your heart. Otherwise, I'll not help either of you. Do you understand?"

The stern cold look Chris had in his eyes, penetrated so deep it gave Anita a wake-up call, and she nodded. "I agree," she said. "I apologize to you both. Our main concern is Jake. Should we go searching for him?"

"It's too dark and we have no idea where he may have gone. Let's wait until morning, and then we can try to retrace his steps," Douglas said, as he scratched the itchy hairs that had begun to grow on his chin.

Taking a vote, it was agreed they would wait for daylight, and then headed to the kitchen where Chris put on coffee. Out of the blue the phone rang. Anita instinctively picked it up and handed it to Chris knowing in her heart it was not Jake. She watched the facial expressions on Chris's face as he talked into the phone. Placing the receiver down on the cradle, Chris did not look up. His eyes looked downward and stared at the floor as he explained that Jake was being held and if the three of them, Chris, Anita and Douglas, didn't back off, they would not guarantee the condition Jake would return in.

Tapping her foot, Anita couldn't believe Jake's misfortune. "What are you hiding?" she demanded of Chris. "What else did the person on the phone say?"

"He said we shouldn't have sent a kid to do a man's job," Chris said, reluctantly.

Anita regained her composure, and spoke in a tone no one had heard her use before. "I wonder how they'd feel if something precious were to be taken from them?" she mused. "Do we know who they are?"

No one dared reply, so Anita pushed her coffee aside, left the room, and retrieved the liquor bottle. Reentering the kitchen, she poured some liquor into her coffee cup, and said accusingly, "Dad, you know who *they* are, don't you?"

As she sipped her coffee, Anita's eyes were full of evil. Feeling uncomfortable, Douglas replied, "I swear I don't; but I will find out."

Not taking her eyes off Douglas, Anita took another drink and put him on the spot. "You've been here before, and that is a fact. But you know who is behind this. You can deny it, but the truth *will* surface and it's usually ugly when it does."

The shrill of the phone gave them goose bumps. Chris put the call on speakerphone for them all to hear. The voice was clear and demanded that they not interfere any further, just leave well enough alone. In exchange for their silence, the caller said they could have Jake. Anita couldn't let it go at that. She stated that she wanted Carolyn as well, and if this demand wasn't met, the caller should start looking over their own shoulder, since *their* precious possessions may very well start to disappear. The person calling was not in a mood to barter, and snapped back, saying that Jake would be home, but that Anita could only blame herself for the condition Jake would be in. The caller then hung up.

In the silence that followed, both men looked at Anita. Her eyes glazed over, and then she said, "Dad, what game are they playing?"

Douglas replied, "You may have gotten Jake killed. You will have to live with the consequences of that conversation. Had it been my mouth, though, it may have come to the same result. What's done is done. Let's see what happens. No, I don't blame you. I blame myself. I believe this is a scare tactic, and the next one will be for keeps."

Anger stirred inside of Anita, driving her to grab the liquor bottle. Instead of pouring it into her coffee cup, however, she put the bottle to her lips and chugged. When she put it down, Chris placed his hand over the bottle tightly and moved it out of her reach. He stood between Anita and the bottle. Icicles dripped from the tone of Anita's voice. "Just whose side are you on?" she asked him.

"Yours," Chris replied, resolutely. "You can't learn anything with a hangover, so I suggest you stay sober. We have a lot of ground to cover in the next few days."

The alcohol kicked in and she found her legs unstable and words slurred. "Would you escort me to the shower?" she asked.

Obliging his wife, Chris slipped one arm around her waist, the other under her knees, and carried her up to the bathroom. He turned the shower on and she gently pushed him in, following closely behind. She closed the door and began to seduce him with a soft, tantalizing kiss. About to surrender to her passion, Chris broke it off suddenly, thinking of Douglas and how much trouble awaited them. The two raced to see who could get dressed the fastest and be downstairs first; Chris won the contest.

Douglas's steamy temper told them where they stood as they joined him in the kitchen. "Do you two have any compassion for what is happening here?"

Before anyone could say another word, the phone startled the trio, and Chris again turned on the speaker. They all listened intently to the instructions on where to meet up with Jake, and then the phone went dead. No words were needed as they clamored into the vehicle and headed out, as fast as they dared, to the meeting place. As they neared the location, their headlights outlined a figure on the ground ahead of them, and they approached with caution. It was Jake, or at least they thought it was, as his face had been rearranged. His shredded clothes scantily covered his body and his breathing was shallow. Instincts told them he was running out of time, so with as much caution as possible, they positioned Jake into he back seat and drove like they had a pilot's license to the nearest hospital.

Waiting for news in the hospital, seemed to take an eternity for Anita. She paced the floor, mumbling to herself as the guilt overtook her. "*What have I done?*" she asked herself. "*This may be the last time I see my brother alive.*" Seeing Chris's loving, tender eyes, Anita fell into his waiting arms. But, somehow they didn't console her, and she choked back the tears since, according to her father, was a sign of weakness.

Finally, the news came; Jake never regained consciousness and had passed away quietly. The internal damage was too severe and he bled to death internally. Douglas was horrified. Anita went numb. Chris was speechless.

Doing his best to keep Anita calm, Chris took charge. "I'll make the arrangements," he said. Chris then turned to Douglas, and said with compassion, "Douglas, I think you should stay here for a bit. Is there anything you specifically want done?"

"Could you arrange to have his body sent back home? Millie will want to view the body and she's not going to take the news well," Douglas said, with sadness in his voice.

Chris kissed Anita on her clammy forehead. Receiving no response, he patted Douglas on the shoulder and left to make sure that everything would be handled properly. Douglas then turned towards his daughter and watched her still body sitting there, as though she were a zombie. Tracking down a nurse, Douglas arranged for Anita to have a relaxant, in hopes of keeping her subdued, rather than becoming a wild person.

After all the paper work was finalized, Chris rejoined his wife and father-in-law. To his surprise, he found Anita to be very docile. Looking up at Douglas with a confused look, Douglas explained what he'd ordered for Anita, and Chris conceded that the shot had been a good preventative measure.

Douglas offered to get the car, and Chris said he would slip Anita into a wheelchair and meet him at the front doors. When the car pulled up, Chris forced Anita to sit up and slid her into the backseat, strapping her in. It was as if she were in another world and the effects of the drug made her desolate inside.

CHAPTER TWENTY

Anita sighed, as the familiar surroundings of home made her feel comfortable. She was grateful when Chris put her to bed, and she fell asleep immediately. Douglas was furious that the paperwork had been botched, and because of bureaucracy, it would be another few days before he could take Jake's body home. Explaining to the authorities what had taken place, in Douglas's own version, it was decided that there would be no investigation regarding Jake's death; but silently Douglas made a deal with himself - to make sure his death wouldn't go without punishment when the time came. Chris held his own thoughts on this; he, too, knew that pursing those responsible was a waste of time, but he believed that someone would pay for their actions, sooner or later. Changing his thought pattern, Douglas made his intentions very clear. He informed Chris he was flying out to tell Millie about Jake's death in person, and he asked Chris if he and Anita would escort the body home once it was released. Not wanting to leave his humble domain, Chris reluctantly agreed. The two men shook hands, and then sat down and had a couple of stiff drinks.

In Anita's absence, Douglas spoke candidly about his plans regarding Carolyn. Chris listened intently, but was not sure he wanted to be involved. He soon recanted, after hearing Douglas's full explanation of why he wanted to do this, and Chris gave his full attention to the details being presented. Chris agreed not to reveal much of the plans to Anita, which he knew went against his promise to her about being honest. As Chris and Douglas said their goodnights, Chris could hear whimpering noises coming from the bedroom. He went in and calmed Anita by lying beside her, but the events of the evening spun around his head, forbidding him to sleep. Sitting by the window and looking out, Chris could feel a ghost-like movement in the room and, when he turned around, he was met with the most elegiac eyes he had ever seen.

Groggily, Anita sat up and, said, "I feel like I've been on a drinking binge. I had the wildest nightmare . . . Please tell me that Jake is alright and that he is waiting to do a workout."

Chris could barely get the words out of his mouth. "I'm sorry," he said. "It wasn't a bad dream. Jake will be ready for a workout, but only in spirit, not in body."

Anita's eyes reacted like a waterfall he had once seen on the mountain, and she raised her arms out to him, to which he reciprocated the gesture. She let out all of her emotions, and when she regained her self-control, she asked where her father was. Chris took time to walk her through her father's agenda, and finished with his promise to escort the body home.

"You'd go with me?" Anita exclaimed, as she hugged her husband tightly.

"Of course. If you think I'd let you go home alone, you're sadly mistaken. My next train of thought is that we stay there – never to come back here. What do you say?" Chris asked, solemnly.

Puckering up her lips, Anita gave him the evil eye, and replied, "No. That would be admitting to defeat. Jake died for what he thought was important: finding Carolyn. If we don't continue, his death would've been a waste."

"Damn it girl. I love you. It would rip me apart if anything happened to you," Chris declared, and his voice let her know that he was upset.

Anita's gaze burned a hole right thought him, but she remained resolute. "I love you more than you'll ever know, but it would be wrong to leave and we both know it."

These words rang though his head and he knew she was right. Chris leaned over to kiss Anita's head, and sighed, "I'm with you. I need you, love you, and want you around for a very long time, and I don't know if I could handle it if you weren't."

As Anita kissed her husband, she found him to be passionate. She knew she was safe as long as he was around, though neither of them knew what the future had in store for them.

CHAPTER TWENTY-ONE

In the days that followed before flying home, Anita grieved Jake's death. Chris tried to get her to do a workout to keep her mind occupied, but her enthusiasm was very low and she sat around staring at virtually nothing. She seemed to drag her listless body and shuffled her feet whenever she needed to change rooms, and her tear-stained faced with red, swollen eyes told her story that she was not accepting Jake's death well.

Brushing off Chris's attempts to get her back to her normal stubborn self, Anita finally stood before her mirror. She was shocked at what she saw; she had an old ladies appearance. Her eyes were saggy from crying, her skin was dry from no cream being applied, her hair was stringy from lack of being washed daily, and she was wearing clothes that not even a beggar would wear. Anita put one hand on her hip, pointed her extended finger towards the mirror and shook it at her reflection, saying, "Get it together girl". Jake would be angry if he saw you like this. Get your act together. There is much to do."

With that being said, she felt much better and headed for the shower. After cleaning herself up, she proudly went downstairs, and poured a cup of coffee. Chris entered the room and was happy to see his wife looking like she belonged among the living and gave her a kiss. "We leave tomorrow," he said. "Are you ready?"

Raising her coffee cup Anita saluted Chris, and replied, "Yes. I know mom will be angry, and I must be strong for her backlashes. And, I apologize to you for my recent rude behavior."

Embracing her with a warm hug, Chris replied, "You were grieving. I understand that. I must admit though, you look a lot more appealing now, than before," and he pulled away quickly before Anita could hit him on the arm for his comment.

Smiling they went out for a breath of fresh air and walked down to the lake. Sitting on the shore, they said little, but being there together was all they needed. It was like they were connected through the universe, and they felt peaceful inside. After they walked back to the house, they went up and packed for their trip; one that neither of them wanted to make. Chris made sure Delia was taken care of, and she went home to see her family, and she promised to be there upon their return, which meant everything to Anita.

They rose early the next morning and drove out to the airport. Sitting in the plane with Jake's body being placed in the cargo compartment made Anita feel guilty. She became edgy at how her mother would react, and pondered over her own reactions. Hearing the engines whine, they felt the plane take off in an upward motion and Anita knew it was too late to back out.

Chris, looking over at his saddened wife, commented, "You can change your mind. We could stay in Montana."

"You're so sweet, but my mind's made up. We have work to do upon our return home. My father knows more that he's letting on, and it's time to get the show on the road," Anita said, as she patted Chris's hand.

Arriving at her childhood home, Anita drew some deep breaths to calm her nerves, and walked into the house. Finding her mother sitting in the formal living room with a colorless face and absence of vitality ripped Anita's heart in half. Running to her mother to give her support, Anita felt Millie's cold reaction to her and Anita's heart sunk, knowing her mother blamed her for the tragedy of Jake's death.

Stepping back from the cold reception, Anita introduced Chris, but her mother's response to the introduction was odd and frigid. Millie got up from her chair and bypassed her daughter and mechanically extended her hand to shake Chris's. Her words were those of a stranger: short and cordial. She thanked him for chaperoning Jake's body home. Millie then turned to face her daughter, gave her a chilling stare, and walked away.

Outraged at how her mother had behaved, Anita ran after her mother and demanded to know why the frigid reception. Millie's facial expression did not change, but she merely told Anita that, as far as she was concerned, she was holding Anita responsible for Jake's death and Carolyn's disappearance, and anything she had to say was going to deaf ears. Absorbing all the guilt that had been laid upon her, Anita took a stunned step back. Then, without warning, Millie's unsympathetic voice blurted out that she was no longer welcome in the family home, and that she had to leave. The color left Anita's face and she felt like the aftermath of an erupting volcano; it totally buried all form of life inside her body.

Not sure what to do in response to this confrontation, Chris slipped out of the room in search of Douglas. Anita, not realizing Chris was nowhere to be seen, stormed off into the study, where she found a bottle of liquor, and pounded it back, letting the strong taste slip down her throat. By the time she was discovered by Chris and her father, Anita was incoherent and rambling on about how she was being mistreated by her mother.

Douglas stormed off to find his wife and, returning with her a few minutes later, he tried in vain to reconcile the two ladies. Millie was adamant she no longer had a daughter, and stated that Anita was not welcome to attend the funeral.

Chris was stunned at this turn of events, and tried to comfort Anita. But, the guilt she felt weighed her down and her flair for life seemed to no longer exist. Quietly Anita explained to Chris that she needed to be alone, and she walked for the last time out to the garden she so loved. Trying to resolve the issue with her mother would be a waste of time, and she resigned herself to the fact that she was just a pawn in a nasty game. But, she wasn't the pushover she had once been, and she decided to ignore her mother's wish and she would, in fact, attend the funeral. She said goodbye to her childhood home, and asked Chris to take her to a hotel; the home she so loved was now filled with nastiness.

Anita convinced Chris to attend the funeral with her, and they stood in the shadows during the ceremony. As soon as the coffin was lowered into the grave, however, Anita stepped out into full view. She went and stood beside the remains of her bother and placed a dozen roses on the coffin. Touching its wooden lid, she said aloud, "Jake, I promise you I will finish our mission. Please be there for me when the time comes." She looked daringly at her mother to stop her, took the shovel from the cemetery worker, and carefully placed some dirt over the roses. Then she blew a kiss.

Shortly after the funeral, Anita said her goodbyes to those who attended Jake's final resting place and left with Chris to return to their home: her only home.

CHAPTER TWENTY-TWO

As Chris coached Anita for the fireworks that were about to come, Chris found her momentum and accuracy to be that of a professionally trained soldier. As they sat on the couch going over maps of the country, Anita looked up at Chris, and asked, "Do you feel the same way my mother does? You know, that it's all my fault terrible things happen to my loved ones?"

Putting the papers down on the table, Chris directed his blue eyes directly at her green ones, and answered, "What do you think? Would I be here if I felt that way?"

"Suppose she's right," Anita continued. "Even my father hasn't been in contact with me. I feel like I'm at a crossroad in my life; only each road comes to a dead-end. It's like no one wants me around for fear that I'll jinx them." Her expression and thoughts matched those of an orphaned animal wanting to be loved.

Hugging his wife, Chris's kind words soothed Anita. "That's where you're so wrong," he said. "Your mother needs to blame someone, and so we are the targets for her unhappiness. She needs your father's support and I am going to assume he's a big part of this – as you keep pointing out. Your father will be returning very soon and I assure you, I wanted us to be together from the start, and I haven't regretted it for one moment." He stopped, and then added, "Oh yes I do. I didn't keep you here the first time." He watched Anita's expression soften up, and he continued, "As for Carolyn, we will find her, but it could take some time. Jake will smile when the time comes, and will know that his premature death wasn't for nothing. Your mother, I predict, will come around in time. Last of all, stop blaming yourself and turn the page. A new chapter of life is on the horizon."

"You are the best. I'm so lucky. I understand why Maureen fought so hard for you. I'd do the same," Anita said. She kissed her husband's cheek, and smiled as she thought, '*he really loves me.*'

Suddenly, Douglas walked in unannounced. After a round of greetings and explanations, Douglas took Chris aside, explaining to Anita that they would be consulting on a private matter. They needed some time alone, he said, and didn't want to be disturbed. Resentment grew in Anita, who didn't appreciate her father's secrecy. She decided to take matters into her own hands. She eavesdropped on their conversation, through the small slit in the door, all the while taking notes about what she overheard. Douglas would engage Chris on many such private conversations in the days ahead, and Anita would sneak up and try out her skills at being invisible and undetectable. That did not always work, and she was caught on more than one occasion, which did not deter her. Instead, it only made her inquisitiveness grow that much more. She tried to be more discreet, thinking that if they'd only share their knowledge with her, she wouldn't have to snoop.

On one such occasion, the men left the room without saying a word. Anita, in the vicinity, heard the sound of a vehicle leaving the grounds. She snuck into the den to look for evidence of what they had been planning. Her perseverance paid off when she discovered bits of paper on the floor and she tried to piece them together as though they were pieces of a jigsaw puzzle. Being so enthralled in her project, she hadn't felt the presence of both men standing in the doorway watching her work intently, with twinkles in their eyes. Glancing at her watch, Anita knew they'd be back soon and without looking up, she scurried to leave the room exactly as it had been. Suddenly, Anita caught sight of a shadow off to one side and, with a sharp intake of a breath, saw both men watching her. Clearly they had seen the whole procedure. Anita tried to hide the visual truth. "I was just tidying up. This place is a mess."

The men burst out laughing, and Chris said, "Honey, we all know you are not a housekeeper. Did you find what you were looking for?"

Douglas spoke from his spot in the doorway. "Anita my dear," he said, "when the details are set in place you'll be the first one notified. The less you know, the better. Patience is a virtue."

"Do you know a store where I can buy some patience, because I seem to be running short these days?" Anita whipped back.

Sympathy was not one of Douglas's greatest traits, but his words expressed his amusement. "Honey, if you want to play Sherlock Holmes, you have to learn to be a little more subtle."

Anita hung her head in embarrassment, but Chris's words were full of love when he said, "Anita, you are definitely one of a kind."

To appease Anita, the men included her for the rest of the evening, and she felt like she was accepted. Deep down, though, she knew they were doing what they thought was best for her, but she didn't want seclusion; she wanted to be in the know.

The next morning, Anita greeted the sun off the bedroom balcony with her arms held out to capture the ray's warmth. The moment was suddenly broken, however, when she noticed a strange vehicle sitting in the driveway. Hurriedly changing her clothes, Anita shot down the stairs towards the study like an arrow, arriving out of breath. She was introduced to the FBI agents, and Anita noticed that one of them looked familiar to her. While being briefed, Anita's eyes bored holes into the agent like a drill. Douglas announced that he and the agents would be leaving to gather materials needed for the up coming events, but did not disclose what they were, keeping the secret to himself. This trade secret Douglas had of keeping things to himself irked Anita, but she soon found another interest to occupy her mind; she had to figure out where she had seen the agent before. Douglas made a conscious decision to leave an agent with Anita, while Douglas took several men to help him set up a communication's Centre in a nearby location, out in the woods that he had once discovered, when he was counseling Chris's dad.

Much to Anita's surprise, they left the agent that held her interest. She watched him as he began his duties of checking out the house for hidden microphones. He then stopped midway in his tasks and got out his notebook and pen. As he asked Anita questions about the last time she saw Carolyn, his hand glided across the paper as he wrote the information down. This triggered a hot spot within Anita's heart making it race, and she wanted a reason to extinguish the burning hot spot down to ambers. Narrowing her eyes and watching his moves, Anita finally connected the dots. "Blake," she said, simply.

The agent faltered slightly, and then said, "I'm sorry, but the name is Brent."

"Drop your pants," Anita demanded, unconvinced by his denial. Both Chris and the agent looked at her in bewilderment.

At first the agent tried to divert Anita's attention by putting his notebook back into his pocket and continued on with the scanning for unwanted microphones, but Anita was insistent on getting the facts straight and wouldn't stay quiet. "That can wait. You started this," she said, with authority. "You forgot how close Carolyn and I were. She told me about the little ship tattoo on your butt. If, indeed you are really Brent and not Blake, this will clear you. Now drop your pants."

The agent became agitated, and said harshly, "You listen to me. I am not the person you think I am. My name is Brent. I have work to do, so let me get at it."

Anita stared him down and lowered her voice. "If you don't show me your butt now, you will show my father. This matter will not go away until it's verified one way or another. I know you're Blake, and that you have an accomplice in Carolyn's and my disappearance. All the disguises in the world cannot protect you, and I certainly hope you were paid well."

At that precise moment Brent got up and said, angrily, "Ask lover boy what he had to do with all this."

Anita started to turn her head towards Chris, but decided it was a ploy and directed her gaze back to Brent. "Nice try in trying to avert the attention away from you. You're trying to play me for a sucker," she said. "Besides, Chris was brought into it after our quick departure from our home in Montana. I'm not in the mood for games, just clarification."

"How can you be so sure?" Brent said, as he stepped away from Anita.

"I'm sure about you. I'm sure about Chris. I'm sure about my father. You are the one running away from something that could end this right now," Anita whipped back, as she stepped closer to the agent.

Anita was so close to Brent's face that she was invading his personal space, forcing him to draw his gun to get her to back off. Chris, still sitting in his chair, watched the showdown; he knew Anita could handle the situation. Anita, not liking the idea of having a gun pointed at her, toyed with the agent by pacing around in circles, then back and forth mumbling about Chris, her father, and trust. Through the tops of her eyes, Anita watched the agent's eyes follow her and, when she was sure she had him off guard, she was in his face, and using her arm for leverage, she swung it hard, knocking the gun out of his hand.

The agent went to make a move for the gun, but Anita's movements were quick and she had his arms yanked behind his back and forced him to sit down. She then picked up the gun, sat on the edge of the coffee table, and pointed it at him. "Now, let's discuss this like adults. This includes you Chris, so please sit in my eyes focus range," she said. Surprised, Chris slid over so she could see his face, intriguing him with her mannerism.

Now with both men sitting down like gentlemen, Anita's hand began to sweat, and as she continued to point the gun at Brent, it began to shake.

Trying to keep leverage on the agent, Anita stood up again, regaining control over the pointed gun. "Okay, let's hear what you have to say Brent. Tell me what part Chris plays in this, and it had better be the truth," she demanded of the agent.

Brent sat back and grinned, showing his uneven teeth, which reminded Anita of seeing Dracula before her, and she cringed. She wanted to wipe the smug look right of his face, but instead, she waited for his words to pave the crooked path. The agent's attitude was that of someone with nine lives; he seemed sure she couldn't hurt him, and taunted her, saying, "You shouldn't play with things you have no knowledge of."

His goading angered her, prompting her to speak fast. "I want you to drop your pants right now. I want this crap cleared up. It's obvious you can't connect Chris to any of this and it's very clear you can't clear your name. So, judging by your nasty personality, I know I'm right. You are Blake."

"You don't even know how to handle one of those," the agent replied, disdainfully, "so do us all a favor, and put it down before someone gets hurt."

"How would you know that unless Carolyn told you," Anita said, sharply.

Not sure how good Anita was with a gun, the agent put his hands up so his hands were on either side of his face, and confessed. "I'm Blake. Now what?"

Chris remained silent, but chuckled, putting his hand over his mouth to stifle the sound. Anita still had the gun pointed on the agent, but now her hand and voice were steady. "Now that we finally have that dealt with, tell me what Chris's part consists of."

"He's the master planner of all this," Blake said, deliberately trying to anger Anita.

Pointing the gun at the lamp near Blake, Anita cocked and shot it squarely at the base, shattering it. She then turned her attention – and her precise aim – back to Blake. "Your turn," she said steadily. "I have this pointed right at your heart, and if you've forgotten what the truth is, I'll make sure I miss just enough to make your life hell. So think about the question. Where does Chris fit into all of this?"

"Okay," Blake said, squirming in his chair. "He had nothing to do with any of this, that I'm aware of. It's obvious you aren't the weakling everyone made you out to be."

Annoyed to no end, Anita had Chris call her father back to the house, because she wasn't sure how long she could keep herself from shooting the horrid creature that sat before her. Taking a seat on the edge of the coffee table, Anita placed her legs slightly apart and kept her stance - in case Blake tried to jump her – and pointed the gun directly at his heart. Wanting to learn more, Anita said, "Tell me. Where is Carolyn and is she alright?"

"You're the smart one. You tell me," Blake shot back boldly, as he moved around uncomfortably in his chair.

Finding him irritating, Anita spoke in a high-pitched voice. "If you move again, I'll shoot you so you *won't* move again. Got it?" To her amazement, Blake put his hands on his lap and remained still. She was proud of how she handled this situation and couldn't wait for her father to arrive.

The door blew open like it had no hinges and in stomped Douglas. He saw Anita pointing a gun on his agent, and growled, "What the hell is going on?"

Not moving a muscle, Anita smiled, and coolly replied, "Father, I'd like you to meet the young man who escorted Carolyn to the dance. Seems he tried to disguise himself, but you can't fool a walk. It's like a DNA. His name is Blake. It appears this wretched soul is a double agent. According to Carolyn, he had a ship tattooed on his butt with the initials "T.T.S." He smugly denied it, but I know the truth. He's all yours – but dear Father, I'd think twice about letting him go. Just remember, your actions could imply you know something," she said, and handed the gun to her father.

Anita left the room. The men were speechless. Finally, Douglas turned to Chris, and said, "She's going to make a hell of a lawyer or investigator. Is there anything you would like to add to the ugly events that has just occurred?"

"You know better than to ask that. You'll just have to take my word for it." Chris's annoyance showed as he turned his back to Douglas and began to walk out.

"I hope so for your sake. My daughter is becoming a little terror and I feel sorry for anyone who crosses her. Between us, we have taught her well. Go talk to her. I'll handle this," Douglas said, as he projected his voice loud enough for Chris to hear. He then turned his hardened eyes back towards Blake and he studied him – wondering what kind of jerk would show up at a job site knowing full well he could be caught. Then again, Douglas thought, maybe that's what he wanted.

Not ready to interrogate this agent, Douglas sat down very close to Blake, and Blake could smell Douglas's old stinky breath, and he gagged. Douglas ignored the actions of Blake and shook his head, totally befuddled at this stupid man. Finally saying his peace, Douglas's words were quiet – as though he were in a church – and Blake had to strain to hear them. "I don't know what kind of idiot would take a job action knowing full well his cover could be blown. I am to assume you wanted to be one step ahead of the rest of us, but now you will always be behind the eight ball – you just played a bad game of snookers." With that, Douglas had Blake placed under heavy security until he could find a place to hold him - so that he could be dealt with at a later time. The interruption caused Douglas some despair, but he chalked it up to being adaptable and he continued on his set goal: to help Anita find Carolyn.

Chris searched the house for Anita, but unable to find her, he walked down to the beach where she loved to sit. He saw a small stooped figure sitting on the rocks and walked directly towards her. She could hear him coming and wanted to run, but a part of her wanted him to console her. As he approached, Anita lifted her head, and even though it was dark, Chris could tell she had been crying. He knew he would have to tread lightly, and spoke, with a soft voice, "Anita let it all out. You were excellent in there. I didn't step in because I knew you could handle it. You have grown into such a feisty woman, and with each passing day, I fall more in love with you." He then stood beside her, gently put his arm around her shoulders, and she leaned into his body.

"If that's true, how come I feel so awful?" Anita responded.

The soft sound of the water on the shore was a delight to hear, and Chris's positive, comforting response eased her heart. "Think of it this way," he said. "You've started to unravel the puzzle."

Throwing a rock into the water, Anita took in her last sob, and blurted, "You are genuine and I almost believed what that creep said about you. How can I forgive myself?"

Rubbing her arm with his warm hand, Chris had a positive outlook. "You're like your father. He says he feels sorry for anyone who double-crosses you. As for how you felt about what Blake said, well the man was taunting you, but you showed restraint. Considering you've never been in a situation like that before, I'd say you fared well. No, I'm not angry with you. You are a special person."

Anita lifted her teary eyes. "My dad said that about me?" she asked, beaming. Chris hugged her and he knew her spirits had been lifted. At that moment, she was sure she saw Jake smiling down at her, and it gave her a warm glow inside.

CHAPTER TWENTY-THREE

Because of the delicacy of the matter concerning Blake, Douglas had him taken to the Embassy and placed under heavy guard. Under Douglas's orders, Blake was interrogated several times a day by investigators, but his lips were well sealed. Blake was more upset by *how* he had been caught, than the fact that he *had* been caught. Anita had been a thorn in his side since day one, but he never dreamed she had the wits to out smart him. The only satisfaction Blake got from the situation was that he had planted a seed of mistrust between Anita and Chris. "And now," he thought, "the only thing the FBI had, was an agent out of commission, but no hard evidence to substantiate his involvement."

Douglas thought he was fully in-control of the situation and thought he had it all mapped out, but this latest incident made him realize he had tunnel vision – he only saw what he wanted to see – and knew he had to think outside of the box. He had been duped.

Being a man short, and time constraints, Douglas sent word to have another agent meet them at the designated location in the woods and coordinates were given. Adrenaline rushed through Anita's veins, building her excitement. She was now getting her wish: they were finally looking for her best friend.

Gathering all the papers and files, Chris, Anita, and Douglas headed out to the destination – to which Chris didn't know existed, and he thought he knew the area well.

"Dad, what other information are you holding back?" Anita asked. "Is there something I should know, before we meet up with the others? After all, you and Chris have been in a hush-hush consultation, and I have been left out in the cold."

The look Douglas gave his daughter was one that read – *don't push it.*

Anita knew better than to push it with her father and concentrated on where they were headed. She was surprised when they pulled up in front of a small, dimly lit shack with two tiny rooms adjoining the main area.

Coffee and donuts were waiting on a foldout table and lit lanterns were hung around the room, as their source of light. Anita imagined that this was how soldiers lived in the jungle, and was grateful for her own lifestyle.

Introductions were made and Anita looked over at a silhouetted agent, who was standing in the dimness. "Dad what's going on?" she asked, and then, pointing to the barely noticeable agent, she added, "that man is Jeremy – my date for the dance."

Seeing her father's facial expressions change, and hearing his authoritative voice, scared Anita. Clenching his jaw, Douglas said, "Jeremy, or whatever the hell your name is, sit down. It seems we have a lot to discuss. May as well get comfy."

Anita felt rage in every bone of her body. When she tensed her body and clenched her fists, Chris knew something was going to happen. Without further warning, Anita let her fist strike Jeremy across the jaw, and the force of the blow threw him back into his chair. She was about to repeat the move, when Chris intervened. Anita fought with all her strength to beak Chris's hold, but was unable to break free. Anita withdrew and walked a few yards away, hoping to get another round in when the opportunity arose.

Douglas was hard-pressed for words. He rallied for a few moments and then collected his thoughts, and said, "I have a very angry daughter. I won't be responsible if things don't go right, so it would be in your best interest to start talking. Do we understand each other?"

Jeremy nodded and sat straight in his chair as he rubbed his sore jaw, and his eyes scoured the room. Then he folded his arms, looked straight ahead and in an even voice he said, "First of all, I'm an FBI agent working undercover. My real name is Duane Wright. Jeremy is my cover name. For the last eight months I've been working on a case involving Blake. We were partnered up deliberately. My Commanding Officer had a hunch Blake was dealing in extortion, so we conspired a plan that I pose as a dancer putting myself through school, to gain his friendship. He frequented this particular nightclub, so it was an easy way to win his trust. Through the dancing club, I met Carolyn and we talked on several occasions, but one particular night, she asked if I could help a friend out, and having nothing to lose, I agreed. It was then I met Anita. I told Blake about the two ladies and he drew an interest, so I arranged to have him meet Carolyn. That was his choice, and as far as I know, they hit it off."

"Are you saying you put our lives in danger, when you suspected extortion?" Anita hurled at him.

"It wasn't like that. He told me he was looking for a special person in his life, and that he wanted to settle down. I thought Carolyn was the perfect girl for him, I swear," Jeremy said, quickly.

"You expect me to believe that hog-wash?" Anita asked. Douglas hushed his daughter as his interest in what the young man had to say grew, and let Jeremy continue his story.

Knowing what the results of his story could do to his career, he wanted to clam up, but instead he took a few minutes to make his decision. He then diverted his eyes straight ahead on the old wall, and continued. "For whatever reason, Blake was determined to go on this cruise ship dance for couples. It took a lot of persuasion, but Anita finally agreed to be my date and I was able to keep on eye on Blake, for the most part. Carolyn and Blake's disappearance took me my surprise, and Anita blew me away with her accusation that I was a part of it. My thinking was that Blake had pissed off one of his contacts, and they were both apprehended. He didn't make nice-nice with people; rather he bullied them. Anyway, after the abduction was reported and being taken care of, I split and started my own investigation. Just as I knew Anita would. And here I am, on the sweat it out seat, airing my story."

Throughout his speech, Anita had been tapping her toes. When he finished, she couldn't stop herself from getting in Jeremy's face again. Through clenched teeth, she said, "How do you explain coming down here, checking into a hotel, and then suddenly leaving? How do you explain my brother's death? Who do you know that brought you here? Blake perhaps?"

Douglas pulled his daughter away, cutting her off. "Explain," he said, to Jeremy. "I have a dead son, an angry daughter, and a missing person. I'm not in the mood for guessing games."

"I wish I had never met Anita. She has fouled up so many things," Jeremy hissed.

"Yah, like my getting away. Hadn't counted on that, did you?" Anita spat back.

Jeremy's hostility showed and venom poured out through his words. "What did you promise Chris in return for marriage?"

"We are talking about *you*," Chris snapped back at Jeremy. "Leave her out of this. Just to set the record straight, though, I initiated the marriage before she realized what I had done, and I might add, we are very happily married. Now concentrate on your own predicament. Doesn't seem like your life is a happy one right now."

Without having a second thought, Anita kicked the leg of the chair Jeremy was occupying, and it teetered over, setting him on his ass. She hurled her words, like a javelin hitting its target. "What have you done with Carolyn? We know where Blake is."

"Where is he?" was Jeremy's immediate response, as he struggled to get up off the floor.

"Don't bother getting back into the chair, you just sit there," Douglas ordered, his voice echoing in the little shack. "Answer my daughter's questions. How is it that when Jake was tailing you, he ended up being beaten to death?"

"You're not going to believe me, but here it is. After doing some research, I discovered Blake had headed this way. I picked up and followed his trail. The night your son tailed me, well, I'm not sure what happened."

Anita's fist hit the table hard, and the sound echoed in the room. "That's bull and you know it. We received a call saying we had sent a kid to do a man's job. You know what happened, you just don't want it known that you secretly met with Blake and Jake followed you." Jeremy's body tensed, his face flashing red. Anita was pleased with her direct aim; she had hit the bull's eye.

"I've told you all I know," Jeremy said, as he sat flexing his fists.

Douglas was mortified at having to deal with another misguided agent. This was another twist to the already complex saga. His manner was that of a courtroom lawyer bearing down on a witness. "I don't know if you are aware of this, but you've almost convinced me you are very much involved. What research did you do? You *must* have been in contact with Blake – other agents plus a police force couldn't track him down. Any agent withholding evidence in an ongoing investigation either wants to be a hero or is guilty. I suggest you get a lawyer or waive your rights. There are two lawyers here, but one is available – Anita. Your call."

Jeremy sneered at Douglas. "Like that's a fair deal. We were partnered up. He never told me what he'd done. He just let me know he was leaving town, and he wanted me to meet him at the bar; the one Anita was apprehended from. He didn't put a detailed map on the table to say where he was located. He divulged only what he thought I should know, and no, I don't know with whom he was conspiring Through the little hints here and there, like knowing Anita was here, I assumed this would be a good place to begin, and yes, Blake did eventually guide me here as well. I swear I didn't know Anita was your daughter. On the night Jake died, I drove to the remote meeting place and went inside. Two men guarding the outside perimeters got into a ruckus, but I never paid much attention, until they phoned you. By that time, it was too late and I can honestly say, I cannot identify the men. I can only assume they were part of the kidnappings." Jeremy then pursed his lips and said nothing more.

After waiting for Jeremy to finish his statement, Anita's tone was full of rage. "What do you mean you didn't know I was related to him? You've been in his house."

Jeremy opted not to answer, and Douglas sat down with folded arms, showing that he was unimpressed by his so-called statement. His ironclad face matched his voice, as he said, "Why didn't you come forward about this information before?"

"I didn't want my connections with Blake revealed," Jeremy shot back.

"Who is your C.O.?" Douglas asked.

"Look, my instructions were that if I got caught, I was on my own. What do you expect me to do with instructions like that?" Jeremy asked, sharply.

"An innocent person was killed. Now, give me the name of your C.O., or I'll have you arrested. Hell, I'm having you arrested anyway until this is over. From this point on, you will not be told a thing. You will not say anything unless an attorney is present, and you will remain under guard at the Embassy. What a mess," Douglas hurled in a menacing tone.

"Oh and one more question, to which I may regret asking," Douglas said to Jeremy. "What the hell were you thinking? You knew my daughter was here and you knew she would finger you."

"I honestly thought she wasn't going to be here and no one else knew me. She isn't the type to just jump into action. She's far too squeamish for that," Jeremy said, and was proud he could say it with honesty.

"As an agent, you have been taught to never assume. This is exactly why. My daughter is not squeamish, nor is she a bookworm. What she is, is a brave young lady who wants to find her friend, to which, I might add, and it connects to you. I can't wait to see how you fit into all this."

"May I talk with Anita privately?" Jeremy asked, suddenly. Douglas glanced at his daughter and she stood nodding her head: eager to know what he had to say.

Immediately a room was cleared and secured for Anita and Jeremy. Anita took refuge up against the wall with a stern look on her face, keeping Jeremy at a distance. Finally, he said, "I'm sorry for everything."

Anita was shocked at his vague apology. "You've caused this mess by pretending to be a vigilante, and innocent people paid the price for your actions. Chris saved me from being sold on the black market. What did you do as an agent to prevent it?"

"Little white knight out there isn't as innocent as he pretends," Jeremy said, narrowing his eyes so she knew he meant business.

Anita hunched over for a moment, to recover from the blow she had just received. Then, gaining strength and tightening every muscle in her body, she straightened up. Her veins popped out of her neck, as she said loudly, "You're just saying that to make me angry and you've succeeded."

Jeremy remained calm and replied, coly, "Cut me loose and I will prove everything."

Now locking her eyes on Jeremy's, Anita was defiant. "Not a chance in hell. I really thought you were innocent, but now…"

Jeremy cut her off, "I am what I say. If I don't walk free, there's no telling what will happen. You may never find Carolyn."

Taking in several deep breaths, and letting them out slowly, Anita knew she had the upper hand - she knew where Blake was and Jeremy was just chasing the wind. "Who's your C.O.?" Anita demanded.

His reply was like a knife cutting through the tension, deep and precise. "I can't."

Without hesitation, Anita walked over to the door, and barked, "This talk is over."

The haunting words of both agents about Chris's involvement made her see red, as if someone had flashed a bullfighting cape before her eyes. Anita charged over to Chris with her nostrils flaring. "Who are you?" She demanded to know. "What are you all about? You've been accused of being Mr. Deceiver twice in one day."

Chris did not flinch. Everyone around them listened as he simply stated. "I'm who I say I am. You'll have to trust me."

"That's what a snake wants you to believe before it strikes," Anita quipped back.

Douglas cleared his throat, gaining the full attention of those around them and put his arms around Anita. "Believe me when I say you can put your trust in Chris," he said.

Bewildered, Chris looked at Douglas, who gave him a wink that put a smile on his face. Anita didn't miss the exchange. "What's going on?"

Her father squeezed her shoulders tight, and said, "Nothing is going on. We have work to do and a few of the men will have to escort Jeremy – or rather Duane – to the Embassy. We will be a little short in numbers until they return, but in the meantime, we have to get ready; a plan has been put in place and every moment counts.

A whirling sound approached, getting stronger and louder, and everyone in the dingy little shack went out to greet the landing helicopter. A small brigade of twelve men entered the room, and Douglas apologized for not being ready, saying an important matter had come up that needed to be addressed.

The men, just arriving, were well equipped and with loaded backpacks, immediately trekked to the shack and sat down on the floor. Anita was feeling overwhelmed by everything that was happening. In her mind, she debated whether Chris was, in reality the trusted, innocent man she believed in, or was he a devious person who saved her for his own gain. Her thoughts then whirled around the fact that two agents placed him in the center of the master plan for abductions, and then one recanted and the other didn't. Did this mean they were toying with her emotions, or was it a real statement? Then there was her father. He said to trust him, and then he winked – what did that mean? Her father's booming voice caused Anita to startle, and she refocused on the search – which was long over due, according to her.

As information, notes, and diagrams were passed around it caught Anita's undivided attention. As she focused on the subject, Anita discovered the camp where they thought Carolyn was being held was in an open area, with very little brush surrounding the perimeter. There was a small tributary of water that flowed around the camp, but they weren't sure how deep it was or if there was any cover for them to hide in. What they were hoping to do was to study the area through observations. Once they had a full picture of the layout, they would then devise a plan of action. Their ultimate goal was to have as few casualties as possible. It was agreed this would be a start and the group cheered, because this was the first time an attempt had been made to invade a camp – and to rescue a specific person made it that much more personal.

The major decision made the conversation turn casual, so Chris scooped Anita up to settle her misconceptions regarding his involvement.

He planted a loving, tender kiss firmly on her lips, melting her like chocolate. Breathless, she said, "Chris I don't believe any of that garble. I know they were trying my patience. I couldn't bear the thought of losing you, and I will stand behind you no matter what happens."

Embracing her tightly, Chris rocked her back and forth. "Hold that thought until this is over. I have no involvement, in what happened to you and Carolyn, nor to anyone else for that matter, but my father's connections have me somewhat entangled with his misfortunes. Work with me and we can fight the demons of the past. You with me?"

Feeling the steady rhythm of his heartbeat, Anita could tell he was sincere and she grew weak in the knees. Still in his arms, she whispered into his ear, "I'm there for you through the rough patches and good times."

Rejoicing at her words, Chris snapped his fingers and, quickly spoke, "What do you say we get away from here for an hour or so? I promise to take you to a place that will take your breath away, and we can relax." He looked at her surprised look and said, "Damn it girl, I am so in love with you."

With a glint in her eye, Anita challenged him to a race to the vehicle. He nudged her, and she stumbled, trying hard not to fall. He had a head start and beat her to the vehicle. Not telling a soul where they were headed, they drove off – like kids sneaking out, but Douglas was one step ahead of them. He stood on the porch and watched them drive off, and smiled, knowing that when they returned they would be fresh and ready for action.

To Anita, it seemed like a short drive, but when Chris took a sharp turn, she felt a light panic attack creep through her body. When they came to a stop, Chris put his hand on her arm. "You look as though you had seen a ghost and harm was headed your way," he said. "I assure you, I'm here on a peaceful, but tantalizing mission of making you feel like you're in heaven."

"I trust you. It's just that. Never mind. Forgive me?" Anita said, with a red guilty face.

Pondering over the last few minutes, Chris turned slightly towards Anita. His eyes were soft as he said, "I understand. I'm not trying to sound mean, but if you don't start trusting, you won't win."

Feeling ashamed for her latest behavior, Anita looked at Chris wanting to take him and ravage his body. She smiled and gave him a kiss that made his head swim. Not wanting the moment to end, Chris pointed straight ahead and explained that were was the most beautiful outdoor hot tub in the world, and that's where they would unleash all the negativity and concentrate on the positive. Lights could be seen flickering as they approached the spot. Anita's movements were as swift as a cougars: light and straight to the target. She was taken aback at seeing hundreds of lit candles outlining the hot tub. She stopped in her tracks and stood staring as the flames flickered, projecting color upon the mighty tall trees. A small waterfall could be seen flowing flawlessly down the mountain into the warm pond. Anita peered into the small hot tub. Tiny bubbles formed in the water as though it were a spa. "What is this place?" Anita asked.

Chris, who had just caught up to her, was pleased with Anita's reaction, and responded, "It's a natural hot spring. The locals maintain it with lit candles, but who pays for it I'm not sure. Anyone who comes here, brings a candle for future use." He placed a candle in the designated spot, smiled coyly, and said, "The only way to enjoy the luxury of this pool is to go naked."

Swallowing hard, Anita said, "Skinny dipping?"

"What are you afraid of? You have a wonderful body," Chris retorted, with amusement in his voice.

"Thanks for the compliment, but I was hoping only you would ever see it," Anita responded, and laughed nervously.

Putting his finger in the air, Chris indicated "one minute", and he ran back to the vehicle to retrieve a couple of towels. Feeling naughty and scared at the same time, Anita wasn't sure what to do. But, when Chris took off his clothes seductively and sauntered into the pool, Anita had her clothes off in an instant and entered the pool like a bolt of lightening, making the water dance with waves. Never had Chris seen a performance such as this. He laughed so hard he had tears in his eyes. Feeling like a fool, Anita stared at Chris and forced him to make an apology. "I'm sorry," he said, "but you should have seen it from my point of view. I was hoping to get a sensuous vision when all I got was speed like lightening." Hearing his version of her approach, she began to laugh at how she clamored into the refreshing water.

The warmth of the pool, the passion for each other, and the beauty surrounding them made Anita's eyes water. Through quivering lips, she asked, "Do you think I'll ever become friends with my mom again?"

Chris placed his hand under her chin and tilted her face upwards so her eyes connected with his. "Yes, I do," he replied. "And when it happens, all this will be behind you. Now close your eyes and let your body unwind in the tranquility of the healing waters."

Anita's playful mind was working overtime. She leaped into Chris's arms and initiated a playful wrestling match. Suddenly, they were interrupted by voices. Looking around, Anita's eyes adjusted to the dim light. She groaned as she recognized Maureen, who was there with a date. Feeling awkward, Anita wanted to get out of the water, but her eyes wandered over Maureen's body; she sunk deeper into the pool with embarrassment. Chris, unsure of what to do, gestured for the couple to join them, but the tension was so overpowering, that Anita slowly crawled towards the towels. Exposing only what was necessary, Anita latched onto a towel and covered herself and walked away. Chris, close behind her, was stark naked. With his towel in his hand, he did his best to cover himself.

Being covered as much as possible with the towels, Chris and Anita climbed into their vehicle and drove off laughing, planning their next adventure before going back to the shack. As they were getting out of the jeep, their towels slid off them like dropping ropes. They scooped them up, laid them on the ground and in an instant they were in each other's arms – like bees to a honeycomb, enjoying intimate and stress-free moments.

After an exhilarating, but exhausting workout, Anita looked around. At first she felt closed-in by the tall trees, but then they seemed to express their peacefulness. The prettiest flowers covered the ground; their colors danced as they popped back up where their towels had been laying. Chris walked back to the jeep and grabbed their clothes so they could get dressed. After they had changed their attire, Anita looked around again and wanted to remain in this wonderful secluded hideaway. Looking up at the sky, she knew time was ticking and they had to get back. As the jeep's lights flashed down the wooded road to the shack, Anita chuckled. There were pup tents everywhere, and the scene reminded her of a Boy Scout camp. "Let the games begin," she said, aloud.

CHAPTER TWENTY-FOUR

Hearing hustling, bustling, and feet shuffling, Anita opened her eyes and was shocked to see that the hut had been cleaned. Someone handed her a plate of food and gave her strict orders to get ready, and put her things away immediately. Not wanting her father's disapproval, Anita dressed in record time and watched, enthralled as tents were dismantled, packed, and stowed away. Everyone was ready to go, so, with her cold breakfast in hand, Anita climbed into the waiting vehicle and it sped off like every second counted.

As they drove along the bumpy road, Anita had a hard time eating the morsels that were left on her plate. "Why didn't you wake me?" she asked Chris.

"I tried, but you kept rolling over and saying, 'a few minutes more,' so I let you rest. I was tempted to leave you there, but I knew you'd send out a posse to track me down. Forgive me?" Chris asked, teasingly.

Blaming herself, Anita said, "No. I had a lousy, cold breakfast and coffee." She looked over at Chris's puzzled expression, and added, "I'm kidding."

His smile told her he was toying with her, and she sat back to see where this journey was taking them. The hot sun beat down on them. Anita found that army gear was not pleasing apparel- she was hot and sweaty. Diverting her mind from her discomfort, Anita focused on how well her father adapted to any situation and came to the same conclusion about Chris. He, too, could adapt in any situation. At that precise moment, Jake popped into her mind and she smiled, because he would have been a misfit, just like her. A tear escaped and she tried hiding it with a quick wipe under her eyes so she wouldn't appear emotionally fragile.

Being so deep in her own thoughts, Anita had not been paying attention to their whereabouts. They had come to a stop in a well-hidden, wooded area. Here they would set up temporary lodgings. Each of them was handed a piece of paper designating the area they were to monitor.

They were given explicit orders not to utter a word and a brief course on sign language was given, so they could minimize the chance of being overheard. At sixteen hundred hours, they were to convene and assess the next steps.

Going solo on a stakeout was not what Anita preferred, but she took it in stride and found a spot near a little stream to settle in. Through her binoculars, Anita spotted movement over by several clumps of trees, and she noted there were smaller bushes at the mouth of the little stream. The stream ran into a small pond, which was about a half a mile wide. She observed two guards standing over a team of white women, and wrote down everything she saw. As she was observing the activity at the far end of the stream, something else caught her attention, and she turned her spyglasses towards the new action. Two additional young white women were joining the first group of six women. The two newcomers picked up a basket and marched to a point beyond the others, where they proceeded to hang clothes on a line. Making sure to take accurate notes, Anita wrote down the times, the coming and goings, and what the guards did as she watched. Anita also noted that the women themselves were clean, but that their clothes were tattered with stains and rips. The most appalling thing, however, was the fact that they were undernourished. Like a light bulb illuminating a dark place, Anita's mind began to form a plan.

Chris was staked out at the back of the prisoner camp, where tiny shacks were erected and his findings were not pleasant ones. He could hear a door open and several crying women emerged. As they walked away from the building, Chris could see fresh, oozing welts, like whip marks across their backs. They halted suddenly, and he could hear orders being barked at them. The women held each other's hands and tensed their muscles. Quick as a blink, huge buckets of water were thrown on them, leaving them to scream at the impact of the water on their fresh wounds. The guards laughed heartedly, their bellies heaving. Still laughing, a guard stood in front of the mistreated ladies and ordered them to march in single file towards another shack – one without windows, or ventilation. Chris was astounded as the door was locked behind them. Revolted, he was literally sick and heaved his morning breakfast onto the ground, and he quickly covered it up and headed back to the base camp.

At the designated time, the troops congregated to pool their observations. They expressed their fear that it would take several days to formulate a workable plan. In the meantime, they were fearful of being caught before they could execute their plan. Anita sat quietly, stewing about plans of her own. Suddenly, she got up and went to the jeep in hopes of finding a dress. Not able to find one, she rummaged through the vehicle until she found some old towels and blankets. Rethinking her situation, she began to imagine how to make a temporary dress out of the towels and blankets. Chris and Douglas watched as she took a sharp knife and began to shred the items. Several times she placed a blanket over her head and put marks on it so she would know where to cut. Twenty minutes went by and finally Douglas had to speak. "What in the hell are you doing?"

Anita replied, without looking up, "I'm making a dress."

"For what purpose?" Douglas asked, and Anita could sense irritation building in her father's voice.

"When I have what I want, I will sit down and explain it to you. And I assure you, neither of you will be happy," Anita said, as she continued on her project.

The men left her, both frustrated with her inability to follow orders. Anita heard them mumbling, but chose to ignore them and the rest of the world. She was on a mission and no one was going to stop her. Finally happy with her dress, she sprinkled some water on the ground to create mud, and dragged her dress through it. Happy with her new attire for the next day, she headed straight towards her father's tent. He was sitting there with a solemn look on his face when she entered. Anita was about to do an about face and leave, when she felt someone stand directly behind her. Without looking behind her, she knew it was Chris and reached behind her to grasp his hand, only Chris pulled it away and she knew she was on her own.

Very impatient, Douglas bellowed, "Sit down and start talking. I don't have time for people who cannot follow simple rules."

Taking her place on the chair that sat across from Douglas, Anita sat and folded her hands on her lap, as though she were in school and about to get a lecture for misbehaving. "We need to speed things up, so in my findings I noticed that they were doing laundry. There is a small stream that leads to the pond. Beside the stream is a clump of trees. Not a lot, but enough for me to hide in. When they are busy doing their chores, I could sneak in and talk to the ladies. I'm sure they would not reveal my presence. When I have what we need, in the way of information, I will sneak back and bring the much needed data to the base," Anita said, happy with her plan.

Douglas's eyes shot wide open and she was sure that when he opened his mouth, there was enough wind coming from his lungs to blow her hair back. "Are you insane? I thought I taught you better than that. That's like committing suicide."

Standing up to be at the same height at her father, Anita leaned into the small desk, and blasted back. "You taught me to resourceful and strategic. Well I was being resourceful when I made the dress, and I am being strategic in my plan. I know it will work. What other choice do we have? How long do you think we can camp here and not be ambushed. They aren't dummies. They have weapons, night goggles and who knows what else. They've been doing this a long time. We need action, and we need it now."

"Let me see what kind of information you have. How can you be so certain that they will be there tomorrow?" Douglas threw back at his daughter, and snatched the papers out of her hand.

"Okay, I can't say for sure they'll be there tomorrow. But look at the bigger picture. With all the soldiers and, from what I heard, there seems to be a few ladies. That spells a lot of laundry to me," Anita said, and was surprised at how quickly her thoughts came together.

Reading over her notes and checking them with those of the others, Douglas conceded that her plan was a good one, but was worried something was going to go wrong. His biggest fear was - could he handle the worst outcome possible – he might never see his daughter again. Chris, now beside Douglas and reviewing all the information, was appalled at her vague scheme, but he knew she was right. Torn between wanting to wring her neck for her sketchy master plan, and kissing her for being so focused on the mission, he just walked away; this way he didn't have to show his reaction to his wife.

Anita knew Chris was angry, but kept a lighthearted attitude in hopes of changing his mind. That night in bed, Chris kept to himself, and Anita had to reassure herself that this was a good plan – no mistakes were allowed.

The next morning a few of the brigade, including Chris and Douglas, followed Anita to the hidden area where they could monitor the comings and goings. Douglas swore lightly under his breath. "Damn. Anita was right. The ladies are being herded out in single file with baskets on their hips," he said.

Chris and Douglas stood watch, and when it was safe, Anita slithered on her belly until the stream was deep enough, so that she could swim noiselessly to the bank; closest to the where the ladies were washing the clothes. Slowly emerging her head from under the water, Anita was hoping to capture the eye of one of the captives. It took two tries at bobbing her head up out of the water, but when the rippling water caught the attention of one lady, Anita was ready to give the hush signal by placing her finger to her mouth. At first the woman ignored her, but she soon nudged another one of the captives, and both stared towards the vicinity where Anita was hiding. The staring caused one of the guards to look up and he tried to see what had caught their attention. When he asked them what was so fascinating, one replied, "A bird," quenching the guard's thirst for knowing what made them stare. He told them to keep their minds on their chores, as they had a lot to do.

One of the captives devised a plan to distract the guards so that the mysterious intruder could enter their domain. They were curious to find out what she was all about. They staged a fight. While a couple of the women pulled each other's hair and threw punches, the guards watched on, fully engrossed at such entertainment. As the women pretended to battle it out, Anita slipped out of the water with the help of another young lady, and joined the group. Anita bent down and began scrubbing clothes, hoping her wet hair and clothes wouldn't give her away. The guards stopped the fight by throwing the fighters into the stream to cool them off, and then reordered them back to work.

After the activity had died down, one of the guards counted heads. When his count came up one prisoner too many, the guard became alarmed. Maxine, the head girl of the little harem, tried to convince the guard he was mistaken, and argued that there had always been nine of them, and he must have been confused in his count. The guard called over the other guard and they conversed about the head count; they were certain there was an extra lady present. Spotting Anita, they wanted to know what was going on, and asked why she was wet when only two prisoners had been in the fight. One of the other women piped up that she was wet because she laughed so hard, she fell into the stream and they had to fish her out. The guards were reluctant to accept the explanation, but their main intent was to find out where the extra lady came from – they didn't recognize her from anywhere in the camp.

Maxine knew these guards had some smarts and that this made them a little dangerous. She took time to explain that they had simply miscounted and made a good argument that would deter them from investigating further. "Who in their right mind would volunteer to join a flock of soon-to-be slaves? Who would want to join this group waiting to be sold to the highest bidder? What would the boss think if he found out you screwed up the count?" Maxine said, with a great amount of conviction.

Still not convinced they were wrong, the guards decided to keep an eye on the unrecognized woman and watched her movements. The prisoners went back to their routines, but information flowed between them as they worked. Anita had to rely on her memory, as writing down what she heard would only draw more suspicion.

Every so often the guards would get in Anita's face. They were trying to determine who she was, but she kept her head down to avoid their eyes. Occasionally when she was asked to raise her head, she attempted to shield her identity by either putting soapsuds on her face or using her hands to camouflage it. In order to observe the group better, the guards demanded that everyone remain silent. They isolated each of their prisoners, which left Anita alone and vulnerable. Panic ripped through Anita like an ambulance on its way to a scene. Hours passed by and the hot sun made the women hungry, thirsty and sweaty. The task of washing the clothes was finally done. The women were then being collected and marched towards their shacks. Anita hadn't thought of a way out. One guard led the way, while the other followed in the rear with his gun cocked. A stir could be heard as the last woman in the line turned to the guard behind her, and began arousing his manhood, enticing him to grope her back. At the same time, Maxine attracted the leader's attention and kept him facing forward. Thankful for the diversion, Anita made her getaway back into the water. She submerged herself completely, and then hid amongst the small clump of weeds, as she watched the escorts make everyone come to a grinding halt.

The ladies stood straight in single file, facing forward while one of the guards did his count. When he came up one short, his yell echoed through the surrounding area. He demanded to know what was going on and where number nine was. The second guard took off to investigate their surroundings and headed for the water where the girls had been staring earlier. Everyone was tight-lipped. The guard looked squarely at Maxine, and said, with annoyance, "When I say speak, I mean speak."

Maxine knew the consequences, but chose to be flippant. "Woof, woof," she said.

He slapped her hard across the mouth, drawing blood. It was his way of showing his authority. "You know the rules," he said. "You speak when spoken to, and no funny business. Where is number nine?"

Maxine wiped the blood from her lips. She wasn't about to give them any satisfaction. "You've been in the sun too long, and have become delirious. Your brain is malfunctioning. Besides, the big honchos will be disappointed if you tell them there was a number nine and you lost her. They would see that your guarding techniques were sloppy, and we all know what that will mean for you. But hey, you can be obsessed about your miscount and face the music to the big boys, or you can forget about it and save your ass. Your choice," she said, knowing which route they were about to take.

He was about to hit her again, but Maxine blocked the blow and she muttered, "Do that again and I'll spill my guts that you've been fondling us for your own sexual purposes over the last few weeks."

The guard withdrew his hand; he knew the punishment would be harsh if that secret were revealed. These women were the prize captives, and should not be damaged in any way. He marched them on with no spoken words or gestures.

Anita couldn't see where the second guard went, but she heard a rustling noise. Taking a deep breath, she submerged herself completely. Through the water, she could see the end of the guard's gun probing the stream's edges for foreign objects. The guard was about to walk into the water for a more thorough search when a bird flew by, startling him. He then realized the ladies had told the truth about the bird, and now he could attest to it. As the guard retreated back to the group, Anita raised her head out of the water to take in some air. Stifling her cough the best she could, she buried her head into the dirt bank of the stream and covered her head. She found it difficult to breathe and all she wanted to do was cough, but mustered up the energy to stay invisible and tried to swim upstream. At this point all she wanted was for her to be rescued. Her energy level was petering out. She thought she was not going to make it, when she suddenly felt herself being hoisted up by her guardian angels and carried to safety in a swift noiseless motion.

The trio blended in with the landscape and disappeared into the dimness that was beginning to encase them. No sooner had they arrived at camp, Anita was then handed a blanket and a hot drink. Looking up she saw that the agents had circled her, as if she were a prisoner. Focusing on her imperfect memory for details, Anita talked and Chris wrote down all she could remember. Anita's recall was impressive and she noted that there were twenty women, fifteen guards that at precisely seven o'clock, a change of guards took place. According to her information, she told them there were eight guards before the shift change and seven afterwards. The two huts in the center were the sleeping quarters for the captives. Eight women stayed in one hut, which were classified as the better specimens, and the rest shared the hut with no windows, one door and one guard. At nine o'clock, the women were in bed with the lights out, and guards were stationed at the four corners surrounding the perimeter at each end of the camp. On these corners were huge generator-powered lights. At the end of each shift, the day guards would either go to their little rooms, or snatched a woman, took her to their quarters, and raped her in front of the others. Shuddering at what she had divulged, Anita said disgustedly, "It's a cruel sport which men thrive on." Looking around, the faces staring back at her made her feel uncomfortable and to mask her feelings she smiled, and said, "Not bad for a rookie, huh?"

"You should be punished and court marshaled for going against orders," said a member of the brigade.

Defending her triumph, Anita spat back, "Oh and you had a better plan? I got more information than we would've had we sat and waited. Besides, I'm not in the army or whatever you are a member of, and I can't be court marshaled."

Douglas intervened before the bickering got ugly. "We're on the same side here," he said. "But to be clear, Anita, you did act irrationally, and although you got great results, that stunt will never happen again. Do you hear me?" Anita nodded. Though Douglas dared not say another word, Anita knew he was proud of her; why else would he have helped her.

Everyone sat in a circle on the ground, with three lanterns set up in a triangle for lighting. The talk swayed heavily towards an evening ambush, because of the fewer guards on duty at that time, and lowers the chances of being seen in the dark.

Anita's motive for volunteering to help was that she wanted to give her best friend a hug upon her release. Deep down inside, however, Anita knew she was only kidding herself. She also wanted to escort the women to safety, once the doors to the huts were opened. It was then stated that when everyone was out of harms way, the entire compound would be blown up, so it could never be used again.

Anita was very upset that her best friend had not been amongst the ladies she met near the stream. In her anger, she began striking and lashing out at anything that stepped into her path. Chris saw her outburst and when he stepped in, Anita's mood was deadlier than a snake about to eat its prey. Her eyes were wild, like a fire out of control, and when Chris placed his hands on her shoulders, she looked at him somberly, and said, "Carolyn isn't here. I know it in my heart. Do you realize we'll have to go through this again? Well do you?"

His hands rested lightly on her shoulders and his voice was dead calm. "Yes," he replied. "We'll take it one step at a time. Now, settle down and concentrate. Keep your mind sharp, otherwise it could cost you your life and I would be very upset. Now, take a deep breath and release." Anita looked away, but Chris pressed the issue. She took several deep breaths and soon found she was much calmer and ready for action. Once again in control of her emotions, Anita threw her arms around Chris's strong, tense body, and thanked him for being a solid rock in her life.

Doing a little begging, Chris finally persuaded Anita to have a nap before the night's events. Taking his advice, Anita hibernated in the vehicle that was parked in the shade. Chris said a little prayer before joining the troops that were preparing for the siege.

When Anita awoke, she saw the men loading the helicopter with the last of the supplies. Butterflies filled her stomach and she knew that D-Day was upon them.

CHAPTER TWENTY-FIVE

The light dimmed as dusk overtook the main stage, and Anita's group waited for the deadly hour to begin. Even the sounds in the background grew quiet, and only a single bird was heard chirping; it was as though the entire universe knew something traumatic was about to happen.

The troops were camouflaged as they waited in the shadows for their first attempt to free the women in captivity. Papers with quickly sketched details about where to send the women were handed out to the soldiers, as they prepared to bolt through the doors of the huts. Once the prisoners were free they were to be directed to Anita; her job was to accompany the ladies to safer ground. While this action was taking place, Douglas and Chris's job was to scour the remaining huts for maps leading to, or information regarding other camps, such as the one they were taking over.

At precisely eleven o'clock, gunfire was heard echoing through the dark forest. Screams erupted like a volcano blowing its cap, and men scurried around like ants at a picnic. Much to Anita's gratefulness, a decoy had been set in place, making her job easier to help the women escape. Anita's heart raced so fast that it doubled her blood pressure and she almost passed out. Drawing in a few deep breaths, she prepared herself to guide the unfortunate victims to safety. She wasn't disappointed because, there in the distance, the ladies were heading in her direction. Anita made herself visible, and pointed to the area they were to take refuge. A young lady could be seen struggling to keep up. Anita ran towards her grabbing her by the hand, and pulled her along. Anita peered over her shoulder, as they ran, to ensure no one was following behind.

Through the gunfire, Chris and Douglas skillfully maneuvered over to the main hut. Chris stood off to one side and, using the butt of his gun, rammed the door open. A blast came from within, just missing Chris's head. Douglas reacted quickly; he stood in front of the door and fired on the shooter inside. His shot hit its mark, killing the man. Chris looked over at his partner with a stunned expression, and his mouth wide open.

Douglas shrugged his shoulders, and said, "Piece of cake. I may be old, but I still have a few tricks up my sleeve."

Searching the hut for evidence of other camps proved fruitless. As they left the hut, they looked in Anita's direction, and motioned for to her to get a move on it.

Not having to be told twice, Anita and her companion picked up the pace. Anita heard a faint cry for help and noticed the young girl she had been helping had become too weak to carry on, so Anita clasped her hands tightly around one of the girl's wrists, and began to run, almost dragging her.

Out of nowhere, a blast descended upon them. Anita looked over her shoulder and saw that the young girl's face had been blown away and her body slumped on the ground. Anita's horrific shock impaled her heart. As if she'd been stung, she immediately released her grip on the girl, and ran like never before. The vision of what she'd just witnessed was still imprinted on her memory. After ensuring all the ladies were accounted for, Anita paced, twisting her hands together to keep from crying. She listened intently, thinking something was wrong; no sounds came from the forest. She began to mumble under her breath.

Several pairs of eyes rested upon Anita, and she explained that when the bombing started, it meant the mission was over. The next step would be for them to be transported to the nearest hospital, checked over, and then sent home – compliments of the FBI. The freed group gleefully swarmed around Anita, and they couldn't thank her enough and the others for all they had done. Tears beaded on Anita's cheek; she was so disappointed Carolyn was not among the women.

An hour passed and still the bombing had not begun. Anita began to wonder whether both her husband and father were dead. As she took multiple breaths to hold back the tears, Anita's ears picked up the sweet sound of the helicopter. Then the sound of exploding bombs made her drop to her knees. She looked around and saw the trampled ground where she had had been pacing back and forth and smiled, thinking she had probably walked many a mile. Catching a glimpse of her husband, Anita scrambled to her feet and almost tripping, ran over into him. She threw her arms around him, cutting off his circulation, and he gently pulled her away so he could kiss her. Her father was in full view, and she spoke with panic in her voice, "You two had me scared that I would be orphaned and widowed at the same time."

Both men nodded with a slight upward curve at the edge of their lips, and then carried on as planned by ushering the ladies into the helicopter and taking the ladies towards freedom. Knowing their mission was accomplished, Chris, Anita, and Douglas headed for home, totally exhausted and in need of a good shower. They knew all to well that while they may have won this battle, there would be many more to come.

CHAPTER TWENTY-SIX

The army brigade packed up their belongings and headed off to destinations unknown. Feeling tired and exhausted, they were glad to see Delia as she greeted them at the door. Anita found it so peaceful, she couldn't fathom how she had just been through hell, and yet here she was in such tranquility; her insides were churning like rapids on a waterway. She felt sick inside because of the young girl who hadn't made it, yet the release of so many women moved her emotions and she couldn't find an even balance for how she felt. Her hands shaking like a leaf about to fall off a tree, Anita poured herself a drink and downed it in one gulp. She had another poured before setting the glass down on the table and gazed at Chris. He had been watching her, not daring to utter a word, or trying to stop her.

As Anita picked up her drink Chris said, in a concerned voice, "Honey, was it too much for you? I really want to know."

"I could handle the shots and the screams, but what I hadn't counted on was having to deal with a young girl's face being blown off," Anita said openly. As she nestled down into the sofa and propped up her feet, Anita wondered aloud, "Why is it no one ever found these women before, or helped them to escape?"

Observing his daughter, Douglas said with certainty, "To my knowledge, no one has ever escaped once the abduction had taken place, and no one took the time to find out where any of these ladies were being kept. The camps move often to avoid being ambushed, and therefore very little has been done about it. You could say you rattled a few cages because, not only did you escape, you knew a few of the players. I don't understand why these two so-called agents put themselves out there, but they will be dealt with in due time. Of that, I am sure. Now my dear daughter, your lives will never be without living in fear. In fact, your lives may not be worth spit in the future."

Chris was mellow, but his fleeting look at Douglas was as sharp as his tone, when he replied, "They know you were involved. Don't kid yourself."

Anita's calmness was disrupted by a sudden vision of the girl's faceless body. Trembling, she said, "I could have ended up like that poor girl tonight. If they had gotten rid of those of us in this room, there will always be someone to take our place. I believe they are trying to scare us off, not take us out. So, who are they, anyway?"

Chris poured two drinks: one for him and one for Douglas. As he handed the drink to his father-in-law, he spoke his thoughts precisely, "I don't know who they are, but they know we are here. They know people were rescued. They know someone betrayed them, but what they don't know is who. We will have to keep our wits about us. Do we agree?"

Raising their glasses, the trio clinked glasses and Douglas took charge, asking Chris, "Where's your phone?"

Embarrassed, Chris replied, "When it's not in use, I hide it. It's an old habit. I hid it to keep it out of sight because of my father. He had some strange friends and I didn't want to be involved in his dealings, so I thought if we couldn't hear or see the phone, no one would bother us – we simply weren't home. Worked most of the time." Chris then got up and produced the phone from the den. He reached out to hand it to Douglas, but Douglas refused it and indicated that Chris should give it to Anita. Douglas looked at his daughter with the softest eyes she had ever seen on his face, as she spoke to her, "Call your mother. I'm sure she'd love to hear from you."

Reluctantly, Anita agreed, and with shaking hands, she dialed the number. She was surprised when her aunt answered the phone. They had a great conversation, but when her mother got on the phone, she immediately asked to speak to Douglas. Hurt and disappointed, Anita handed the phone over to her father, and walked outside.

Empathetically, Chris followed her outside and wrapped his arms around her tightly. He kissed her forehead. In a monotone, she said, "I'm a bad person." Her tears spilled out uncontrollably then, and Chris stood patiently holding her until her mood subsided. He suggested she get ready for bed and she agreed. She made her lifeless body go into the house and headed directly to the bedroom.

Chris found Douglas stressed out as he re-entered the living room. He was surprised to see such a cold face staring at him, and his father-in-law's words were like ice. "I don't understand how my wife can be so cruel, especially at a time like this. I've never been so disgusted with a human being – and believe me, I've dealt with some hardened criminals."

Lost for words, Chris only nodded to let Douglas know he understood. Then, Chris found his words, and said, "Time heals all wounds." Douglas just grunted in reply, and when they finished their drinks, each of them went to his room, for some solace.

CHAPTER TWENTY-SEVEN

For the next few days, Anita stayed in her room. She analyzed the recent events until, finally she realized she had to put it all behind her and come out of her little cocoon. Without saying a word, Anita scrutinized Chris's every move. According to her observations, he was being secretive, and seemed preoccupied; she wanted to know what dirty little hidden treasure she would find upon her investigation. Talking to him, however, was getting her nowhere in this pursuit.

Sneaking up on Chris, while he was having a private conversation, was generally against her principles; in this case, though, she felt it was warranted. She stood just out of eyesight and, just close enough to catch the odd word or phrase. Frustrated, Anita sought out her father in hopes that he could satisfy her thirst for knowledge. He let her down, however, because he, too, seemed to be ignoring her. Throwing her hands up in the air, Anita decided that something would surface, and put an end to all this confidentiality.

Wandering around aimlessly, Anita noticed that the house was unusually quiet and that the den was empty. Her two consciences, devil and angel, played her like a fiddle as she debated whether to snoop or not. The devil won its case hands down, and she entered the room checking every bit of scrap paper with writing on it, in hopes of finding a clue revealing what Chris and her father were working on.

Anita's heart pounded when she saw crumpled papers in the wastebasket. She worked furiously to straighten them out and piece them together. Busy in her own little world, her heart stopped when the den door slammed shut. There stood Chris with the coldest look she had ever seen on his face. He accused her loudly of meddling in his affairs and invading his privacy, but the horrified look on her face made him recant and he rephrased his explosive words.

Not batting an eye, Anita bantered back that his secrecy was getting worse and so was his attitude. She demanded to know what he was hiding, and defensively he said that he was not withholding anything. Anita was feeling contented with herself for following her instincts and being inquisitive, when suddenly her expression changed as she remembered Jeremy's and Blake's statements regarding Chris. She took a step back and assessed her feelings, and her expression changed again from that of a defendant to that of someone who had seen a ghost.

Her changed expression prompted Chris to embrace her tightly. The affection he showed triggered an emotion in her that said, *I may never see you again,* rather than, *'I love you,'* scaring Anita out of her mind. "*This was it,*" she thought, "*our first real fight.*" She shook off the bad feelings that were rapidly travelling throughout her body, because this isn't how she imagined it; it felt like he was leaving her, not staying and loving her.

Anita pushed Chris away, and he fell back onto the desk. Without faltering, Anita said, "Something is going on. That display of affection tells me I may never see you again. Well?"

Getting back into an upright position, Chris rubbed his arm that had been banged against the edge of the desk. He sat down and then pulled Anita gently onto his lap. "I have to leave for a few days, but I will be back," he said.

Infuriated, Anita hurled back, "You knew this and kept it from me? What kind of a person do you think I am? I *can* be trusted – or do you not believe that? Right now I'm finding it a little difficult to believe in you." Anita slid off his lap and stood by the desk, staring at him. Chris remained tight-lipped, opting to say nothing in his defense. Anita's eyes were that of a wildcat and narrowed them, as she said, "I suppose my father is going with you?"

Trying to avoid a heated argument, Chris crossed his arms and kept a level tone. "I don't know what your father is up to," he said. "While I'm gone, will you please stay home and wait for me. That's all I ask."

As she stepped closer to the door, Anita's nostrils flared as if breathing out steam. Chris could almost see her digging her heels into the ground, as she replied, "Promise me you'll explain it all to me when you return."

Crossing his heart with his finger, Chris responded, "I swear."

Those were the couple's last spoken words that day; after that, they just lay in bed holding one another silently. Anita awoke early the next morning. She took her coffee out into the garden letting the sun's rays beam upon her. The sunlight gave her new energy. When she heard something drop behind her, she turned around; there stood her father with his luggage packed. With a somber expression, he explained that he was going home to see if he could persuade Millie to have a change of heart.

Anita scoffed at the idea, and said, "Fat chance of that happening."

"I can be very persuasive," Douglas replied. "And stranger things *have* happened."

As her father stood still, like he was indecisive as to what he was going to do, he picked up his luggage and carried them back towards the house. He knew Anita was going to question him, and he needed a cup of coffee. Anita followed him and asked, "Dad, what else are you planning? Mom isn't the only reason you're going back. Will there be more fireworks when you return?"

Reaching the kitchen, Douglas poured himself a coffee, and replied, "You're very intelligent. A series of things will happen that could be very ugly. I hope you're ready for tragedies."

Anita's temper flared. "Oh, like tragedy didn't happen already. I still think of that poor girl and shudder. I can handle whatever comes my way. I'm not the weakling everyone thought I was."

"Yes, you certainly have proven your obstinacy," Douglas said, smiling at his beautiful daughter.

The sound of tires rolling across the ground caught Anita And Douglas's attention. Chris appeared with his own packed suitcase, and the men nodded at each other rather than speaking. Douglas told Anita that he would return soon, and then he left the couple alone. Chris touched Anita's face and ran his caressing hands over her body, making her melt like heated chocolate. "Honey, I'll see you in a few days," he said. "I'm not telling you where I'm going, in order to protect you, but I swear good things are going to come of it."

Burying her face in his chest, Anita said, "You are going to see one of your father's contacts aren't you? You think this person can help. Am I right?"

Astonished at her astuteness, Chris replied, "Something like that." He then turned and left, without looking back. He knew that where he was headed to, was not just a business meeting: it was more like a witch-hunt.

Being alone and bored, Anita wondered around the back of the house to the gym and practiced shooting with the bow. Soon tiring of that, she picked up the rifle, aimed it, and got the results she wanted; a bulls-eye. She felt smug about her marksmanship.

Her stomach growling, Anita looked up at the sky and it dawned on her that night was fast approaching. Delia was in the house and Anita told her she could go home; she would make herself a bite to eat, soak in the tub, and get a good night's sleep. Delia argued that she should stay in case something happened at the house, but Anita was more persuasive and Delia was happy to leave, and promised to be back in the morning. Anita was happy to have the company and the two shook hands on the agreement, laughing. Anita went about her night's plans and then went to bed. To her amazement, sleep wouldn't come. Her thoughts sailed around her head, making her very restless.

The next morning, Anita talked to Delia and told her she was going shopping, since that always eased her tension. She went on to say she would grab a bite in town, so Delia could have the day off. It worried Delia that Anita was driving off alone, but after she cleaned up, she made her way back to her home. The drive for Anita was pleasant and she relaxed as the sun's warmth nourished her soul. Upon reaching the little town, Anita's senses took a turn. She began to feel uneasy. Shaking off the strange feelings, she went bargain hunting and scored some treasures that made her feel somewhat better. After putting her purchases into the jeep, she went over to the diner. She peered in and not seeing Maureen, she sat down.

A dark cloud soon loomed over Anita, however, as Maureen came out of the back and waltzed towards her. "Where's lover boy?" she asked, sarcastically.

Anita gritted her teeth and smiled, "Had a meeting and should be back soon."

Maureen taunted Anita with her knowledge about her husband. "I don't think so," she said. "Where he went, he'll never be back."

Anita's veins were making popping sounds as they grew and her voice was strained, as she replied, "Care to explain?"

Feeling power over her rival, Maureen goaded her. "Nope," she said, and left the diner. Anita tried to laugh it off, thinking it was a ploy to get back at her, but Maureen's confidence had indicated otherwise.

Intending to keep her promise to Chris, Anita drove home. She had a gnawing pain in her stomach, and a fear that something bad was going to happen to Chris. Trying to keep busy around the house took more energy than she had. Maureen's brown eyes mocked her in her mind, making her want to shake that woman's smug little world.

As she looked out the window, Anita saw that dusk was nearing, and that the heavenly light would soon be diminished. Anita's impetuousness soon got the better of her, and she quickly changed into dark clothes and packed a few items into her pocket – a gun included. She would go to see Maureen, even if it meant interrogating the unlucky woman.

Anita drove straight to the diner, but was disheartened when she found that Maureen was not there. She inquired where her rival lived, and getting directions, she drove over to the part of town, to which she'd been directed. She parked down the street and took a few moments in her car, debating on how best to approach the subject of Chris. Finally, the debate was settled. Anita decided that the element of surprise was the key to getting the right answer.

Anita turned her car lights off as she coasted up to the house. She quietly made her way around the back and found the door. Unsure at first, whether or not to knock, then Anita turned the door handle and found it unlocked. She entered, peering around with her flashlight. Her search of the ground floor proved fruitless and she skillfully, noiselessly prowled like a cat up the stairs, one at a time. Listening for any sound to indicate which room Maureen was occupying, she continued up the stairs. Reaching the top stair, Anita's hand started to quiver. She cocked the gun and began peering into each room. The bathroom door was closed, but she could smell a fruity aroma coming from that direction. She walked into the bathroom with the gun pointed straight at Maureen, who was soaking in the tub. Maureen smiled at Anita, showing how truly beautiful she was, and said, "What took you so long?"

"What do you mean, what took me so long?" Anita quipped back, puckering up her face trying to camouflage her surprised reaction.

Still smiling, Maureen played with the water and blew on the bubbles. "I knew you'd come," she said. "But, not like *this*, I must admit."

As Anita's eyes narrowed, she aimed the gun at Maureen's heart. Her voice had sadness in it, as she said, "Where's Chris? No games."

Closing her eyes and sliding further into the soapy water, Maureen replied, "What makes you think I'll help you? You took him from me, and besides, I could have you arrested for illegally entering my home with a loaded weapon."

"You could, but I could say you invited me over, prearranged to have the door left open because you had a score to settle. I can be very convincing when the need arises. It's my job. Besides, you can't lose what's not yours. So, are you going to help me? Where's Chris?" Anita said, and lowered the gun slightly while waiting for a reply.

"No," Maureen blurted out, "I will not."

At first Anita's words wouldn't come out and, when they did, they were a bit choppy. She sat on the floor beside the tub, with her knees up, her back against the toilet. "Listen," she began. "I feel that Chris is in grave danger. We both know you have a hunch as to where he is, and if you really cared for him, you'd do your part in helping him back to safety. Whether I like it or not, Chris *does* have a soft spot for you."

Maureen sat up, bubbles covering her body. She tilted her head to look at Anita, and said, "You're just saying that to give me a guilt complex."

"Think of me as you will, but it's true. He found it very difficult to tell you we were married and didn't want to hurt you. He only married me to save my bacon from becoming a slave on the black market, and that was because he knew of my father. He sent me away, but I came back to find my best friend, and I pushed to consummate the marriage. I couldn't let go. Going to help or not?"

Glancing over at the honest woman beside her, Maureen wanted to tell her to go home, but something snapped inside her and she succumbed to guilt. She agreed to help on one condition; Anita was never to tell anyone. As they shook hands, Maureen chuckled; Anita had no idea what she was getting into but revenge was oh so sweet.

Anita waited downstairs for Maureen to get dressed. When she came down, the women checked each other out, laughing at how they resembled thieves about to steal a precious gem. They traveled on foot for miles, or at least Anita thought so, until they came to a fortress. Maureen quietly explained that it belonged to the worst kind of criminal around, the kingpin of flesh-traders. He meant business and didn't play fair. Curiosity getting the better of Anita, she began to fire questions at Maureen about the man: what kind of business was he in, and what did he have to do with Chris. Maureen took advantage of Anita's vulnerability and explained that Chris had been to visit the tyrant before, but that she wasn't sure what business had transpired between them. Bowing to Anita, Maureen announced she was now on her own from this point on, and wished her good luck. Maureen then turned around and left the frightened young woman behind, and chuckled. Anita was stunned to be left to fend for herself, but soon overcame the shock and let her training take over.

Shimming up a nearby tree, Anita found a branch that could support her weight. There she sat and observed the surroundings. She saw at least four guards on duty, and wondered how she was ever going to get over that high wall, let alone into the house. Taking several deep breaths, everything she had been taught came back to her. She must use her common sense and her full concentration: she must be alert and observant.

Repositioning her body, Anita prayed that she would not be detected. Unable to get a clear view of the house, she looked for a new viewing spot. She wanted to inspect the eight-foot wall for the best possible way over, and swore when she saw that there were no decent climbing trees nearby. Looking in her pockets, Anita let out a word expressing her frustration. She realized she had only brought a small pocketknife. The branches of the tree she currently occupied gave her an idea. It was a type of a willow tree and, when tied together, its branches would be as strong as rope. Fidgeting with her small knife, she hacked off several branches and attempted to weave them together, but her temper flared when she couldn't make the branches stay united. In an angry anguished state, Anita felt her body jerking as she tried in vain to keep tears from forming. Not letting this moment stop her, Anita drew in a vital breath of air and picked up the branches once more. She pictured Chris's hands as he once demonstrated how to tie a slipknot. Succeeding this time, Anita was happy with her accomplishment, and beat her chest with her hand to celebrate her triumph.

When she was satisfied that she had enough rope to lower herself to the ground, she slid down using her feet to stabilize her, and to keep from spinning. Reaching the ground level, Anita proudly dragged the rope behind her as she surveyed the wall, wondering how she was going to get over it. She then pulled out the gun she had used on Maureen, and examined the length of the barrel deciding it would suffice. She then shimmied up the tree, and using what little light came from the house, she leaned forward to get a better view. Almost falling, Anita hung onto a branch to stop her. Once steady, she checked the corner of the wall and was positive it had ledges on it – a discovery that made her bubble with joy. Timing was of the essence. Getting back to ground level, she waited until no guard could be seen, tied the rope around the gun, and threw it over the wall. Then she slowly pulled it up to the corner, and to her amazement, it became wedged under the adjoining ledges as she had hoped. Squatting down on the ground, Anita checked her watch and waited another twenty minutes for a clear shot to scale the wall.

Hanging onto the rope for dear life, Anita walked her feet up the wall and when she reached the top, she stopped and looked around for any sign that she had been spotted. Finding no movement or hearing any sounds, Anita looked down at the ground on the other side of the wall and grimaced, anticipating a painful landing. Acting quickly, she hooked her fingers around the edge and pulled herself into a lying position. She held her breath, hoped for a safe landing, and jumped. Having made sure she was not hurt, Anita then picked up the rope she had woven, and hid it in the flower garden. She tucked the gun into her pants on the opposite side from the flashlight – all this extra gear made her feel bulky. Checking out the premises, Anita looked at the bare corners, free of guards, and then dashed towards the house, minimizing her body movements so as not to be noticed. Thankful it was a warm night, Anita prayed a window would be open, and was thankful to discover Lady Luck was on her side; she found one. Slithering in through the open window like a snake, Anita found herself in unfamiliar territory, but using her flashlight was out of the question – the flash might give away her presence in the house. She caused a slight noise when she bumped into something in the dark, so she waited for her eyes to adjust, and was relieved when she was finally able to navigate around the room. "*Being a burglar was a lot easier than I had once imagined,*" Anita thought, laughing silently to herself.

Ensuring nothing on her body could fall off or out of her pockets, she started to scan the hallway, treading lightly, and was amazed how quiet the house was. Her whole body surged with heat when she considered the possibility there were hidden cameras following her every move, but she pushed that thought aside, reasoning that if she got caught, then that was meant to be.

Hearing voices in a distant part of the house, Anita recognized Chris's voice and immediately made her way in that direction, knowing she had to rescue him. The muffled words spoken enticed her to lean up against the door. She listened, and distinctly heard a raspy voice say that it was relocating camps to avoid losing more valuable property. Anita couldn't believe her ears and didn't wait to hear Chris's response. Feeling betrayed, she cocked her gun, stuck her chest out, and was about to enter the room when two goons came up silently behind her, placing their arms under hers, and lifted her so that her feet dangled in mid-air. Completely caught off guard, Anita kicked and screamed foul language in desperation to free herself. They opened the door to the room she had been eavesdropping on, and threw her in; she landed sprawled out like a starfish with a gun pointed at her.

As though he had bagged a trophy, one of the goons said, "Found her about to charge in and shoot one of you."

Chris's tone was high and full of surprise. "Anita, what do you think you're doing?" he said, incredulously.

Sitting up, Anita hugged her knees, and responded, "Well, Mr. Goody-Goody. I came to rescue you, but as it turns out, you are knee deep in the shit that took away my best friend. Need I say more?"

The gentleman facing Chris then turned to get a better view of Anita, and said to her, "Shooting me won't help." Then he looked right at Chris, and barked, "Your explanation for this had better be good, or your fairy tale will end badly."

The gentleman, keeping Chris detained, nodded to one of his goons and the goon plunked a chair in the middle of the room. He then grabbed Anita and harshly pushed her onto the chair. Before she could wiggle her way free, she felt two strong arms pinning her shoulders down, disabling her movements. Letting the goon get comfortable in his stance, Anita lurched her body forward in desperation to get free, and she said, "I'll tell you what's going on. Chris led me to believe he was Mr. Nice Guy and I fell in love with him. Now I find out he's a traitor. My intentions were to rescue him, but I find I want to shoot him instead. You can relax."

Finding a little humor in this, the gentleman nodded for his guard to release his grip on Anita. She knew enough to stay put. Surprised at Anita's brazenness, and as she looked directly into Chris's eyes, she realized she had not seen that look in Chris's eyes before. They were cold, hard, and full of animosity. An arctic front moved through her body, as self-doubt crept in. *"Had I really made such a terrible misjudgment?"* she asked herself.

The man of the house walked around to his lavish red cherry desk, which was inlaid with gold edging. He sat in the luxurious, soft leather chair, and rocked back and forth, analyzing the situation. Without having to say a word, the man had the couple whisked off to a cold, damp cellar, and Anita's fears resurfaced. She kicked hard and braced her feet against bars to keep from entering the dungeon, but was unsuccessful. She and Chris were deposited with a thump, landing hard against a wall. The door was locked and now she had to face the one person who, at one time, had believed in her. A flood of emotions stirred inside her; she was angry with him for being a tycoon's friend and puppet, but on the other hand

155

she hadn't heard his response to the tycoon and she assumed. Her face grew hot. She felt on fire, and almost passed out. Sliding down against the wall for stability, she rested on her feet and waited a few moments to gain back her normal composure. Chris could hear her movements and reading between the noises, he knew she was struggling with her emotions. He left her there to stew and began to place his hands on the walls to see if there was any possible way out. Anita's senses kicked in. She produced a lighter from her pocket and struck the ignition cap, and its small light illuminated the room. Shining it around the small cramped quarters, it confirmed that the only way out was the way they came in.

The cold of the room caused goose bumps to form on her skin. Being confined in close quarters was not her idea of a good time. She took the initiative, and spoke, "Are you angry with me?"

His voice was sharp. "Yes. How did you find me?"

Keeping Maureen's name quiet was difficult and she had to choose her words carefully. "I searched your office for clues, found some scrap paper, and read between the lines. You were so secretive and shut me out. I felt I had to do something. I'm sorry, but I'm a lawyer, and I need to know what's going on."

He stepped away from her and with coolness in his voice, he said, "All I ever asked from you was to trust me. If you can't do that, we're through."

The words cut her heart in two, and Anita replied, "Seems we have a lot to discuss."

Shutting off the lighter was her way of making a bad situation disappear. She felt so alone, but within seconds, the door opened. They were ushered down the hallway, and there sat the man of the house with the meanest look in his eyes, tapping his pen on the desk. His voice matched his expression. "My, that was a good show," he said. "Tell me Anita, were you really going to shoot your husband?"

Keeping her eyes focused on the man behind the desk, Anita hissed, "Yes."

Still tapping his pen and finding amusement in the situation, the man said, "I would like to find a punishment for you two that would be suitable. Any suggestions?"

Like a fire-breathing dragon, Anita replied, "Send us home together."

Grinning, he looked from one to the other, and then said evenly, "I don't think so. That little act in there could have been set up for me."

Thinking she would have to do a better job at selling her story, Anita quipped back, "Are you nuts? I wanted to shoot him. He had my best friend kidnapped for his own gain, married me for who knows what reason, may have been involved in my brother's death, and now I fear he may trade me off. When we get home, he'll be sorry he ever met me. I assure you." She smugly sat back, proud of her soliloquy. She took a side-glance and saw Chris's uneasiness, then turned back to the man who was holding them against their will, daring him to refute her candidness.

The man got up from his chair, and looked at Chris squarely in the eye. His speech was purposely slow. "You had better be on the level. And if you're not, well, you know the rules. I'm sure this little lady will keep you on your toes, but you had better have more control over her. I wouldn't want the wrong person shot." The man then exchanged his tone for a more demanding. "What do you know about the raid on my camps?" he asked Anita.

Words flew out of her mouth faster than she anticipated. "Camps?" she asked. "You mean fishing camps? Quite frankly, I haven't seen any of those around here."

Deepening his gaze and intensifying his voice, the man slammed his fist down hard on his desk, making everyone in the room jump. "You had better not get tangled up with things you have no right to. Get the drift?"

Raising her hand to her forehead, Anita saluted the man and responded in military fashion. "Yes sir. Loud and clear sir! You are the boss, sir."

Feeling secure that nothing bad would happen to her, Anita swung around and landed a good right hook on Chris's jaw. "I may not be able to shoot you, but this was the next best thing, and honestly, it felt good," she sneered.

The man's gasping laughter filled the room. He found it difficult to form the words when he said, "Chris, we'll be in touch."

Chris's expression didn't change; he just instructed the guards to bind Anita and put her in the jeep. "If she makes so much as a whimper, you have my permission to gag her," he said. The men complied immediately, and when Anita tried to protest, a gag was placed in her mouth. A guard threw her over a shoulder, carried her out to the jeep, and dumped her into it like a bag of flour. Chris joined them, and his hateful words filled the air. "This is the way it's going to be from now on," he said loudly. He hoped the words were carried back to the tycoon and would satisfy that his releasing them had not been a mistake.

As he stepped on the accelerator, the jeep's tires spun dirt and rocks in every direction. Anita fought wildly to free herself. Chris drove like a crazed person for a distance before pulling over and removing the gag. All of Anita's anger was released through shouting and screaming, and Chris warned her that if she didn't shut up, the gag could easily be replaced. She sucked in some much-needed air, which sent her into a coughing fit, but finally settled down when Chris informed her that her acting had been so convincing, it had saved both their derrieres. He also made it clear that she was to remain tied up until they reached home, in case they were being followed. He also was very clear, that when they did return home, they indeed had much to discuss.

Pulling up to the house, Chris hotly untied Anita and let the ropes fall to the floor of the vehicle. He walked at a fast pace into the house, leaving Anita amongst the little web she had created. Leaving the door of the house open, Chris poured himself a stiff drink, and let it soothe his parched throat. Anita stormed in and spun him around. "Okay asshole," she said. "Start talking."

Taking her hand in his, Chris led her to the office. He revealed a hidden drawer, unlocked it, took out a small chest, handed it to Anita, and left the room. Her face went white as she sat down to examine the papers inside. The papers were hard to read since her hands shook so hard, but soon she became engrossed in what was written there. Chris was with the C.I.A. He was to establish a relationship with Joe Dante, whether within the bounds of the law or not. Reading further, Anita discovered a document from Chris's company that apologized for the loss of his father. According to the documents, his father had been one of the best agents they had, who had crossed over the line.

Scanning the other documents, Anita discovered Chris was her husband's real name, and that Quinn Harlem was his alias. Her mind went in several directions. She wondered how he must feel at this moment, and she wished the door would open between them. Putting everything back as it was, Anita opened the door and walked over to Chris with shame and guilt written all over her face. "I'm sorry I didn't have more faith in you," she said. "Will you forgive me?"

The two sat down on high wing-backed chairs facing the picture window. Chris expressed his annoyance with his own actions. "If I had been upfront with you in the first place," he said, "this would never have happened. I wanted to protect you and thought the less you knew the

Split Second Decision

better, but I hadn't counted on you being so persistent. The minute I laid eyes on you, I fell in love and was so scared of losing you. I couldn't hand you over to them, knowing who you were and how I felt, so I did what I thought was right. I married you. The meeting I had yesterday and today, well, it wasn't going well. They suspect I'm involved with the recent raid on the camp. Maybe your barging in helped, in a strange sort of way. We shall see. Speaking of which, how did you find me? Tell me the truth this time."

"Before I tell you, why aren't you using the name Quinn Harlem? Why use your real name. The background checks would reveal your real life style," Anita said.

"I chose not to use that name because of my father. He used his real name, so if I were to use an alias, they would know, and that would trigger a spark and set off alarm bells," Chris said, patiently waiting for Anita to answer his question.

Shuffling her feet and looking down, Anita cleared her throat. "You fascinated me from the start. You were so kind and every minute with you was like a silver lining to the darkest cloud – even though you *were* cold at times. I was so jealous of Maureen it made me crazy inside. As for the marriage, I was determined to make it work."

"Now to answer your question regarding today's fiasco. I held a gun on Maureen to find out where you were," she said, but the look she got from Chris surprised her. "Don't look so shocked. They do it in the movies all the time and get the results they want. Anyway, to get an answer from her, I had to confirm the fact that you did care for her, and that it was hard for you to tell her about our marriage. After our discussion, Maureen agreed to give me a small piece of information. She led me to Dante's – I'm assuming that's his name – and then she left me alone there. The rest I did on my own. She swore me to secrecy. I think she was hoping they would kill me off and you would be free. That's my guess," she said, half to herself and half to Chris. "So tell me, what does she have to do with all this, and why would she know where you were?" Anita said, with inquisitiveness in her voice.

Leaning back in his chair with his legs stretched out, Chris sighed. "You want the truth, you shall have it," he said. "Just remember that all this happened before I met you. Key word, *before*."

Wishing he were somewhere else, Chris began his story. "My father did get himself into trouble with the wrong people, and I did come down

159

to help him out. I had just finished a case in the stockbroker world, and I didn't want to come here, but circumstances forced the issue. I was introduced to Dante and his girlfriend, Maureen. She took a shine to me and, knowing no one, I went along for the ride. It was fun and dangerous at first, but seemed complicated, and soon I started to avoid her. She resented that and hunted me down. She threatened to tell Dante about us. I didn't need the repercussions of that in my life, and avoided her as much as possible."

"After my father died, I wanted to go home, but other plans were made for me. Dante called a meeting, trying to entice me with the promise of large sums of money. At first I resented the very idea, but again my orders were to befriend Dante, and so I accepted."

"That made Maureen happy because it meant I was around a lot more. Dante was good to her and I tried convincing her of that, but she had wedding plans for us. I, however, was not interested in her plans. When it finally sunk in for Maureen that it was over between us, she told me she was pregnant. I told her I cared for her, but that it was not going to go any farther. She went on a rampage. I was willing to support her and the child, but that wasn't good enough for her, so she told Dante that she was in the motherly way. He laughed at her, called her a cheap whore, and kicked her out. Apparently he was sterile and having kids was not an option for him."

"Maureen came after me and I felt I had to look after her. As it turned out, she had made the pregnancy up, and so I cooled the relationship. Every time I went out on a date, Maureen found out and made life miserable for me." Chris stopped talking suddenly and looked at his wife. "You want to ask me something? You have that look," he said.

Guilt was riding high on Anita's emotional scale and with a shaky voice, she replied, "I got more than I bargained for. Does she still have ties with Dante?"

Keeping his distance, Chris's voice was soft and full of tenderness. "No. As far as I know, that chapter is over," he said. "All I ask is that you believe me when I say I love you. Never have I ever felt like this before. I'm all torn up inside."

Anita stared out the window for a few moments before turning her head towards the gorgeous man she wanted to take pleasure with. "Does Dante know it was you?" she asked.

"I think so, although nothing was ever said about it. If he believes I betrayed him once, then that would make him suspicious and mistrustful of me," Chris answered, scratching his head.

Sitting still was no longer an option for Anita. She got up and circled the room, talking as she spoke. "I want you to know that I was angry with you for keeping me in the dark. But, I invaded your privacy and, for that, I ask forgiveness. At first, when I arrived at Dante's, I wanted to shoot him, but then I thought you had betrayed me. Confusion set in and I wanted to shoot you instead. When we were in Dante's office, the confusion about you and him was so powerful, that my emotions kicked in and I knew if I screwed up, we were done for. My heart was swaying towards you betraying me, but the surprised look in your eyes almost had me recanting, but I stuck to my guns and let you all have a taste of my anger. In the last twenty-four hours, I've learned more than I did going to school." Anita's circling stopped when she sat on Chris's lap, and continued, "I love you and that should've been enough. I went berserk and now I feel like a heel."

They embraced with heightened emotions and knew that no matter what they came across in life, they were there for each other. They agreed, for the moment, to no longer keep secrets from one another, and never again to act on assumptions.

Cradling his wife and kissing her forehead, Chris said earnestly, "You know, you were very persuasive when you pretended you were going to shoot me. I'm sure Dante was persuaded, too. I think he is up to something that involves you, so he can keep you quiet and on his side. By the way, you have a good right hook. My jaw still hurts. One more question. It's about Maureen. What made you ask her for help?"

"Well," Anita began, "I was in town and she popped out of nowhere and basically said she knew where you were and that you would never be coming home. At first I was mad that she knew more than I did, but then I went home on my promise to be there when you returned. Something gnawed at me and I had to find out where you were. Are you pissed?" Anita asked, as she looked lovingly at her husband. His smile told her he had forgiven her and then a thought flashed in her mind, and she jolted forward, "Dante will involve me how?" she asked.

"I don't know. I just know he will," Chris replied.

Chris didn't get a chance to say anything else. His lips were covered with Anita's warm, moist ones, and their explorations of each other's bodies began. The couple headed for the master bedroom, turned the lights out, and raced to see who would get into bed first. What followed next was the most relaxation either of them had felt and they knew what they had: love.

Waking up refreshed and looking at the beautiful sunrise, Anita beat Delia to the kitchen. She did her best to prepare breakfast and made a tray to take to Chris. Bursting through the door all bubbly, Anita was soon disappointed that Chris was too sleepy to participate in her lovemaking tactics. His resistance inspired her to get ice cubes to lay them across his body. She placed the delightful breakfast tray on the nightstand, and since Chris's eyes were still closed, Anita went to get a few ice-cold squares. Waltzing back into the bedroom, Anita curled up beside Chris and she let the tiny droplets of water drip upon his chest. He grumbled and groaned, and gently grasped her hand and tossed the cubes across the room, before sitting up to enjoy his morning feast. Anita sat patiently as he ate, sipping her coffee and chatting. Chris let her ramble on as he finished his gourmet meal, and then pushed the tray to the side. Anita slipped under the blankets, ready for an intimate reunion, but Chris got out of bed and headed towards the shower, laughing. Crossing her arms and pouting, Anita decided drastic measures were needed. She wrapped a robe around herself and headed downstairs for a bucket of water. Doing her very best not to spill it, she nonetheless tripped and splashed some over the stairs and down the banister. Anita decided the puddle could wait; this surprise was more important.

Checking to see that the coast was clear, Anita placed the water bucket out of sight, but in the perfect position in case it was needed. She climbed into bed. Chris came out of the shower, and seeing Anita still in bed, he laughed. He teasingly got dressed. This was not what Anita had intended to happen, but she narrowed her eyes to a squint and waited. Chris opened the balcony doors and stepped out to take in the warm rays. Noiselessly, Anita climbed out of bed and got into position. When Chris turned around, she let him have it: a full frontal deluge. This struck Anita as hilarious, and she burst out in uncontrollable laughter with tears streaming down her cheeks.

Chris's mouth fell agape and his shirt clung to his body making Anita's mouth water. Then he left the room without saying a word. Realizing he could be out for revenge, Anita dared not open the door, but instead headed for the bathroom in hopes of his giving up his rebuttal. After the shower, Anita sat down on the toilet seat to dry her hair just as Chris appeared in the window with a garden hose and unleashed a blast of icy cold water upon her. His laughter was full of gusto when he saw her hair dripping. She looked like a drowned cat and he almost fell off the roof from laughter. Anita laughed until she cried, and then they called a truce, agreeing to clean up before having a cup of coffee.

They came down the stairs still laughing, but their laughter stopped when they saw Douglas, who was in a hot, foul mood. "Just what the hell happened while I was away?" he demanded.

Anita responded lightly. "We had a water fight and just cleaned up. Speaking of which, there is still some water that needs to be wiped up on the stairs. Why do you ask?"

Anita noticed some of the veins on her father's neck were beginning to bulge, as he replied, "You know what I'm referring to, so cut the crap."

Douglas gestured for them to step outside onto the deck and while the three of them were deep in conversation, the phone rang. It was Dante calling to arrange a private meeting with Chris on neutral grounds. Chris accepted, but did not divulge any details to either his wife or his father-in-law. The hairs on the back of Anita's neck stood straight up when she heard it was Dante, but her questions would wait until she and Chris were alone.

Changing the subject Anita caught the men off guard, when she asked, "Dad, what about Jeremy and Blake? Have you checked out their stories? Did they both cross over the line?"

Douglas flashed her a menacing look, and snapped, "What's your interest? I want to know about Dante and the visit. Seems like you played cat woman and rescued Chris."

"How do you know about that?" Anita said, as she looked her father squarely in the eyes.

"I have my ways," he said, "and don't ever question me like that again."

"If you know all, then I don't need to tell all," Anita whipped back.

"Answer my question," Douglas said, with no patience in his voice.

Not happy with her father's tone, Anita responded by changing the subject. "I knew both agents. Suppose I say I believe one and not the other. What then?"

Avoiding his daughter's question, Douglas turned his attention to Chris, throwing a question at him. "What does Dante want?"

Doing his best not to reveal too much, Chris stated, "Wants a private meeting with me. So, what about the agents?"

Disgruntled at being put in the hot seat, Douglas fired back, "Their stories are being checked out, but their statements need some corroboration to clear them. That hasn't happened yet. Now, tell me what went on at Dante's," Douglas said, and was not going to leave them alone until they did.

Chris's eyes burned holes into Anita's flesh, letting her know he disapproved of her wanting to get involved by talking to the agents. He then turned his attention to Douglas and began his story, starting with being held for questioning regarding the raid on the camps, and he finished with how he was released. Douglas looked at his son-in-law and was displeased at his vulnerability for letting Dante take charge, and was particularly upset with how Anita ended up at Dante's and could have been shot.

Anita sat up and stared at her father in disbelief that he even thought Chris had anything to do with her decision. She got up, pushing her chair back with so much force that it tipped over. Her words were that of an upset woman as she locked eyes with her father. "I gave him no choice. I would've done the same for you. You are both so secretive, and shame on you for that. I have a good mind and you both can trust me. I hope I've made that clear. About the agents, neither of you are fond of the idea that I want to get to the real truth, because, damn it, it involved me and I want to know how I was set up and by whom. One or both of you are hiding details, and I want to know what they are. We are supposed to be open and honest with one another. "Trust" is the word you once used. Try it. It just might surprise you – or it might bite you in the ass. Either way, give it a chance to work – as a team."

Her father's voice was deep and his eyes were wide open. He looked like he had had a big scare. "Young lady," he said, "you have no recourse for speaking to me in such a manner. If I feel something concerns you, you'll be the first to know about it."

With pride in her voice, Anita took a stab at setting her father straight. "My teacher taught me to be direct, forceful, and to know when the wool is being pulled over my eyes. Well, my eyes are wide open, and I am exercising them all the time." She then picked up her chair, sat it down with a thrust, and plunked herself in a position so she could see both men at the same time.

Trying his best not to smile, Douglas recanted. "Guess I asked for that one. An investigation is still going on, at least as far as I am aware."

Pondering over the words spoken, Anita's mouth opened and her thoughts flew out surprising even her. "I would like to talk to each one individually myself, and see if I can fill in the blanks. Because I have met them on a personal level, I may be able to get them to tip the pot and spill a few beans. It's worth a try. Hopefully, things could start to unravel," she said.

"Absolutely not," Douglas shouted.

"Why?" Anita asked. "Is there something you don't want me to find out?"

She could see his face grow a little pale, and his voice lowered to almost a normal tone. "I'll set it up, but I must be present and it must be taped."

Standing her ground, Anita shot back, "No. I'll consent to taping the conversation, but you will not be allowed to be present. I want to do this my way, and if it doesn't succeed, you do as you please."

Chris, after listening to all the arguments, coughed to get their full attention. "I believe Anita should do this alone. They just might say something valuable to her. Douglas I don't mean any disrespect, but you are a very intimidating man and not always easy to talk to," Chris said. "I, however, am not happy with Anita going to do this alone, but if she feels she can do this, then I say let her try," he said, and he was happy to have her kept busy, because he too, had his hands full - with Dante.

Once all the bantering died down, Douglas announced a camp had been found hear the fjords. This news didn't appease Anita in the least, and she cringed at the mere idea of entering another death-zone. The last one still haunted her.

After dropping the deadly bomb, Douglas assured them he would return with full details in a matter of days and he left the room. Anita, now alone with Chris, wouldn't let up on him and she demanded to know where and when the meeting was to take place.

"I already told you," Chris said, standoffish.

Not liking the brush-off, Anita placed a firm hand on his arm, leaned in, and with clenched teeth, she said, "I know what you want me to believe. Now, I want you to tell me the truth. We agreed, no secrets."

Clasping his hand around hers like a vice grip, Chris squeezed hard until he could feel the pressure release on his arm. Then he said, "If I reveal the extent of the conversation with Dante, do you swear not to tell a soul, including your father? I have a few reservations and the less said the better. Do I have your solemn promise? Otherwise, I shall remain quiet."

The news rocked Anita like an earthquake, and she whistled. "Wow. Not even my father. If I've learned anything it's to trust you. Okay, you have my promise, because I want to keep tabs on you, just in case you run into trouble."

Shaking hands, they exchanged vows to adhere to confidentially.

CHAPTER TWENTY-EIGHT

Synchronizing their departures, Anita and Chris left at the same time. While keeping secrets from her father still didn't sit well with her, her promise made to Chris was a done deal, and she would have to live with it.

Arriving at the Embassy, Anita stumbled across red tape in getting to talk with Jeremy and Blake. She had to produce several pieces of ID to prove she was a lawyer and that she was Douglas Jefferson's daughter. She also had to state her reasons for the visit. Hours ticked by, and when the red tape was finally lifted, she was told she could only have one hour with each agent, and that the rooms would be heavily guarded in case of an attempted escape. Anita graciously agreed; she wanted to get on with her mission.

Entering Blake's room, Anita found it to be small with all the amenities. It had bars on the windows, but it reminded her of a bachelor suite, and she commented under her breath, "This guy gets all the comforts of home, and what did I get? A dark, dingy hole infested with rats and with no bathroom."

A snapping of fingers in one corner caught her attention and she turned towards the sound. Blake's smugness caused her to gag. "What brings you here?" he asked. "The tattoo on my ass or just to take in the view of my body?"

Feeling as though he were a spider about to crawl towards her, the impulse to smack him was scoring high with Anita. Instead, she remarked, "Neither. So wipe that superior look off your face. I have some questions for you, and I had better hear the truth ooze out of those lips."

Blake's grin got wider and more satanic-looking as he walked around his little room, and then he sat down. "Look," he said. "You determined my weak spot, made your play, went for the throat and won the game. I'll be in for a couple of rough years, but things will settle down and I'll be on my way again. I don't hold a grudge against you, but I must admit I am angry at how it went down. I never expected a bookworm to be so coy."

Anita couldn't hide her shock at hearing his words and her facial expression betrayed her as her mouth fell open. "That's what this is to you? A game?" she said, and forced her arms to stay by her side. "What about the innocent lives destroyed? Do you not have any morals? How did you find out about my father, Carolyn, and me? What was the motive behind your actions? I really need to know."

Blake's grin diminished and his appearance became that of a gangster wanting to shoot his enemy. He remained seated in his chair, as he replied, "I was paid big bucks for a job well done, and I have no regrets. If you think for one moment I'm going to tell all, you've lost some sense along the way. I have my pride. I will tell you this, though, that your father bragged about Carolyn's charisma, and described you as being a boring bookworm, of which, believe it or not, he was equally proud."

Stammering, Anita held her head up and the words came out incoherently. "How did. Where did. How'd you meet my dad?"

Leaning forward on the edge of his chair a complacent look appear on his face. "Get real. Think about it."

Stiffening up, she sat as though she were a mannequin not daring to move, and the words that next blew from her mouth had no emotion behind them. "You realize I'm his daughter, and not Carolyn, right?"

Anita could tell he was shocked by the way his eyebrows shot up. He changed his posture, and replied, "The way he talked, and we knew he would pay dearly for both of you."

Catching his wording, Anita dived in for the kill. "*We* – as in you and Jeremy?"

Rubbing his head with his hands, Blake realized his slip and his eyes darted away from Anita. She could barely hear his response. "You ask him, that is if you can find him."

Picking up her chair, Anita plunked it down before the scummy jerk of a man, and got within inches of his face. Her breath was hot. "*You* tell me. Now."

Blake's hand extended automatically towards Anita as he replied, "Give me the tape. Anything we say is between us and I will deny anything you repeat. If you don't hand over the tape willingly, I will get it from you one way or another."

Getting the upper hand, Anita pinched Blake's cheek, and coyly said; "Nice try, but you see that guard over there? Or did you forget where you were?"

Blake turned slowly and eyed the guard. Then he turned back and stated simply, "I guess we don't talk then."

Assessing her options, Anita went over and spoke to the guard. Reluctantly, he agreed to leave the room, giving them some space. Somberly, she let Blake know she was unhappy with him. "I don't like being threatened," she said.

When Blake spoke, his voice had a tinge of malice in it. "Place the recorder over there," he said, pointing to the table. "I will carry out my threat if you don't. Screaming for the guard will only make your life more miserable. Besides, knowing and proving are two different things."

Feeling like a puppet and her strings were being pulled, she placed the small machine on the table. Then, with her back to Blake, she began firing questions at him. "What part, if any, does Chris play in this?"

Blake got up and checked the recorder to ensure it was off, and then sat down in his chair. "He's associated with a head flesh-trader, of the worst kind" he answered finally.

Walking over to the window, Anita looked out hoping for more. Then she turned around, trying to squeeze out every drop of information she could, and demanded, "That's it? That's all you have?"

Wanting to get a reaction out of her, Blake coyly implied there was more to the story. "He's as much a part of this as I am," he said. "But, judging by the lack of shock on your face, you suspected that already."

Walking around the tiny quarters, Anita smiled back at him, knowing she had the power. "Let's just say don't play poker with me. I can see you are of little value to me, so I'll just mosey on and go talk with Jeremy." As Anita collected her belongings, she leaned over, and whispered in Blake's ear, "Yes, I really do know where Jeremy is."

Trying to shake off the unwanted vibrations she had absorbed while in Blake's room, Anita sauntered slowly over to the door, where she was to meet the guard. She bid Blake farewell and headed straight to Jeremy's quarters with her new accessory - the guard at her side. Standing before the door, Anita patiently waited for it to be opened and when she walked in, Jeremy reached out to her as though he were about to hug her, and asked, "You here for business or pleasure?"

Admitting to herself that it was a cute approach, Anita pulled up a chair and pointed for him to sit. "Business. Take a seat," she said.

He interlaced his fingers and leaned forward on the table indicating that he may be ready to talk. "What makes you think I'll cozy with you and hand over all my dirty laundry?"

Playing his game, Anita sat with her hands wide open on the table, leaned in, and replied, "I believe in you. Start talking."

Jeremy got up and walked to his kitchen to get some coffee before flatly refusing. "I can't," he said.

Noticing how identical the rooms were, Anita was appalled at the luxury they received. Taking on the role of the aggressor, she placed her hands firmly on Jeremy's shoulders and her voice took on a hoarse tone. "You have to tell someone. Let it be me and we will keep this confidential." Jeremy's head did a slight nod and pointed in the direction of the guard. Anita sighed and spoke to the man in the uniform, who agreed to stand outside the door. Anita then folded her arms, waiting for the news to drop like dead flies. "I did as you requested," Anita said, expectantly.

Digging around for the recorder, Anita placed it on the table and Jeremy examined it to assure it was turned off. Then he looked her straight in the eyes, and said, "You're too close to the players. I don't know."

Her heart skipped a beat, and she could feel her face heat up. "Chris. What has he got to do with this?"

Getting up out of his chair, Jeremy placed his hands on his hips and began to pace. Skeptically, he replied, "How do I know you can be trusted?"

Scrambling for encouraging words, Anita blurted out, "We've had our ups and downs, but I swear to you I can be trusted. I believe in you and you've got to clarify your involvement. Talking is the only way to do that. My friend is out there somewhere, and I need to find her. Help me."

Struggling with his inner feelings, Jeremy remained silent for a few moments, and then sat down at the table. "Chris is associated with Joe Dante, a very mean tycoon," he said. "Judging by you response, you are already aware of that. My understanding is that Chris·does small favors for him – but what those favors entail, I'm not sure. I'm certain he's more innocent than guilty, though. As for Blake, well, we are both CIA agents, and my assignment was to befriend him and report any underhanded dealings he was involved with. He was suspected by the Agency of being on the take. I was to report in regularly, but my eagerness to bring him down single-handedly got the better of me, and I never reported any activity. That was my biggest mistake."

"Blake and I became fast friends and he confided in me. Thinking I could handle it all, I kept everything to myself. When I was on the job, I overheard your father talk about the two of you like you were princesses and before I knew it things started happening fast. Blake wanted to meet you both and it became my job to fraternize with Carolyn. That was easy, because she was always at the club, and she and I cooked up a scheme to entice you to meet with me, using school as the primary subject, and of course the party your brother threw fit in perfectly."

"I introduced Blake to Carolyn and as I said, things happened fast. Blake called to say he was taking Carolyn on a cruise, and not wanting to be left behind, I made my case for taking you. You were the final piece in the work of art that was my plan. I had no knowledge of his plans, but soon after their disappearance, Blake called to inform me he had taken the wrong girl. It turned out that Carolyn was *not* related to your father, he had told me, and plans were being made to correct the mistake. It took a few minutes for me to figure out what he was referring to, but finally I connected the dots; he had been the one to abduct Carolyn."

"I didn't find out you were missing until it was broadcasted on the news. I felt helpless and decided to remain quiet, hoping he would contact me again and share his plans – at that point, I was still his trusted friend."

"Then strange things started happening. His calls to me were cold, because he thought I had betrayed him – or so I assumed. During the last call I received from him, before I ended up here, his voice was sharp as he let me know where to meet him. At this point, I started to wonder about ratting him out, but something held me back. I couldn't correspond with my CO, because I had never reported in and he would've reamed me out and I didn't have time for that."

"I can only speculate, but I believe Blake had arranged to have someone tail you. When you spotted me, your tail must've spotted you. The night your brother died, I tried dodging him, hoping to lose him. My gut was telling me something atrocious was bout to happen. I really thought I had shaken free of him, but I guess not. He was good, I'll give you that."

"As I entered the cabin, or shall I say the meeting place, I heard a commotion outside, but was prevented from checking it out. Within minutes of the ruckus, a man I had never seen before entered the cabin and a call was placed to your home. Any goods I had on Blake, dissolved right at that very minute, because I hadn't reported any of his activities – and now I was just as much to blame as the team Blake had put together.

Blake laughed, saying the kid wouldn't make it through the night, and that this development would put you in a tailspin – that you'd run away and never look back. But you didn't do that."

Jeremy got up to stretch his body. Anita's emotions were divergent; she wanted to strangle him for his role, but she also had pity for him because of his stupidity. Her mouth was dry as she tried to speak, "Why didn't you contact your CO the minute you were alone?" she asked.

Wishing he had never started telling his tale, Jeremy snapped, "I told you; I had a gut feeling, not substantial evidence. After they had given Jake a work over, there was no way out. That's what I thought at the time, because the damage had already been done. If I had I made any attempt to make a phone call, well that would have been like signing a death warrant. I carry the guilt around everyday, and I keep telling myself I should've have told Jake what was happening and spared him the brutal beating. I'm truly sorry, but there's no way to correct the damage that's been done."

Anita's voice reached a high pitch as adrenalin pounded through every vein. "Are you insane? You may not be able to bring Jake back, but justice could've been done. For the last time, who's your CO?"

Jeremy stood facing Anita shaking his finger. He slightly raised his voice, "I'm sorry," he said, "but I'm not able to tell you that. Let me finish what I've started. Now, back to the beginning of your disappearance. Greed was high on the list, but what they hadn't counted on was your illness and that's where Chris enters the picture. One of them called in a favor and got him to nurse you back to health. Let's just say you were their cash cow. They expected you to bring in a higher price because you were the closest thing to being a virgin. No one suspected Chris would marry you, let alone help you escape the country. Well, they caught up to him, and beat the crap out of him much the same way they did Jake, hoping he would die jolly on the spot. To their surprise, your ransom was paid, making them very happy people."

"Then you came back, putting everyone up in arms. The initial plan was to kill you right away but for some unknown reason, that plan was nixed. Blake and his cohorts hoped to complete their mission of eliminating you somewhere down the road. A local was paid to watch your every move, but you seem to be very crafty and did a disappearing act. I was told to wait to be contacted about a new meeting place, but that never happened."

Looking at her watch, Anita realized her time with Jeremy was almost up. Her heart felt very heavy with the added burden of time running out, and she said quickly, "What do you mean I eluded them? I live at Chris's. How hard can that be to find? Something doesn't add up. They were playing games with you. You realize that don't you? They thought you were a snitch. Oh, and about that last meeting, you don't have to worry, because my dad and I have taken care of that. We met up with him."

Anita grabbed a glass of water to moisten her throat because it had become very dry. "You should really tell your CO all this, or at least a lawyer. You may be able to get out of here."

Jeremy's curiosity got the better of him. He approached Anita and grasped her shoulders; digging his fingers in so pain would travel throughout her body His voice was deep, scaring Anita. "Who are you going to expose this conversation to?"

Wincing in pain, Anita took a deep breath and, between clenched teeth, retorted, "I'm bound by confidentiality, so who can I tell? My father perhaps?"

Jeremy's hand tightened even more, bringing tears to her eyes. "No," he boomed. "You must not tell him."

Anita spilled her glass of water as she struggled to get free. "Why not," she shouted.

Releasing his grip, Jeremy's voice had a pleading tone. "Say what is necessary. I want you to find Carolyn because I botched it up. I honestly thought that I had it under control, and we both know that was the farthest thing from the truth."

Anita's eyes became little slits and she lowered her voice. "I'll need some help," she said. "Whom can I confide in?"

Rubbing his face and neck with his hands, Jeremy asked, "How much do you trust Chris?"

"With all my heart. Believe me when I say that," Anita answered, without hesitation.

Walking in circles, Jeremy talked softly under his breath. When he finally stopped, Anita looked at him, and he reminded her of a man with no soul. "Okay," he said. "You may tell Chris, but only what you think is relevant."

As the guard rattled the door to let her know her time was up, Anita looked at Jeremy with a puzzled expression. "What are you holding back?" she asked.

Jeremy's words rushed out like a babbling brook; aware that their time was at its end, took a deep breath, and as he said, "Chris's name always came up, but when it came to actual dealings, from my understanding, he was nowhere to be seen. I think he may be a plant. I tried to investigate him, but no records of him exist."

Time had run out and Anita spoke like someone running a marathon: fast and out of breath. "What do you mean, *a plant?*"

"You know, an agent or something. His actions aren't those of a participator, but more of a person who sets things up," said Jeremy, who was little baffled that Anita hadn't caught on.

Anita's heart was beating so fast she thought she could hear her blood pulsating. She looked at the guard who had entered the room, and then turned back to Jeremy and said, "I promise not to tell my father, and I swear to reveal only what is pertinent. Reconsider talking to your CO."

As she was about to leave the room, Anita heard Jeremy's tormented voice in her ear. "Its your father," he said, quietly.

"*My father,*" Anita repeated. She felt as though someone had just cut out her windpipe. "Tell him then."

"I can't because I believe he is more involved than anyone realizes. He's Dante's lawyer. That's one reason you weren't disposed of. Now do you understand? If Chris is an agent, he may not have his life for very long. Watch your backs, and be very careful who you confide in."

The guard was very impatient and hurried Anita out the door. As he did, she lost her footing and hit her head on the wall. She had a dazed look on her face as she staggered out of the Embassy. Pondering Jeremy's story, Anita didn't know which fork in the road to follow. In this case, flipping a coin was not the answer.

She climbed into the jeep, and her thoughts swirled around as she drove. The closer she got to home, the deeper her thoughts became – blocking everything else out. Refocusing her eyes on the road, Anita saw a car veering towards her. The results would've been deadly, but her instincts kicked in and she turned sharply, flying over the embankment. All she could do was brace herself and pray, as she flipped several times before coming to an abrupt stop. The jeep landed on its four wheels, and she was knocked unconscious by the impact of the landing. A passerby surveyed the damage and had to make a snap decision between leaving her there to burn – the vehicle was leaking fuel – or pulling her to safety on the off chance that he wouldn't aggravate her injuries. The passerby chose to pull her from the wreckage, drove her to the hospital, left her there, and vanished into thin air.

CHAPTER TWENTY-NINE

With a pounding head that felt like it would split her in two, Anita blinked a few times as she opened her eyes to the blinding light. She wished that whoever was pounding on her head would go away. Stirring, she felt a warm hand rest gently upon her and knew Chris was by her side. Just moving her lips hurt, but she smiled faintly to let him know she was aware he was there.

Chris's voice was soothing as he explained the accident as it had been told to him, and asked if there was anything she needed to add. As she tilted her head gradually towards her darling husband, the conversations she recently had, flooded the valves of her brain, compounding the pain.

Without warning Anita reached up to Chris's shirt collar and pulled his head down to her face. Hoarsely, she asked him not to leave her side, especially when her father was present. Sputtering at her unusual behavior, Chris saw the terror in her eyes. It sent messages throughout his body that something terrible had gone array while she was doing her interviews with the agents. As he listened, Anita seemed cold and empty, and at times she was incoherent. '*Maybe she had confused the events,*' he thought. Chris reeled at the change in Anita. He touched her face, promising he would be there when she woke up. Feeling secure, Anita closed her eyes and drifted away.

Douglas entered the room and nodded to Chris, indicating that he could leave to take care of business. Fulfilling Anita's request, Chris remained in the room. Both men sat watching the sleeping beauty as she moved around violently on her bed, and both wondered what torment had happened while she was at the Embassy.

Upon waking up, Anita noticed Chris's hand was turning blue. Realizing she was squeezing it tightly, she opened her fingers slightly to let the circulation flow and to let him know she was going to be okay. Groggily, she asked, "How long have you been here?"

Chris bent down and brushed his lips with his. "Three days," he replied, quietly.

The doctor came in and explained that Anita's health was good – except for a few bruised ribs, and a minor head trauma that was causing headaches. "She'll mend and be ready for new adventures, but it will take time," he said. "But for now, rest is your best medicine"

Applying her courtroom tactics, Anita persuaded the doctor to let her go home to recuperate. She promised that should there be any complications, she would head right back to the hospital. He agreed and said he would make house calls, only because he knew Douglas and Chris, and he had admiration for both men.

It was agreed that Douglas would meet them at home. Chris brought Anita out to the vehicle in a wheelchair, and with only a little struggle, got her into the front seat. Anita watched helplessly as Chris buckled her in. He drove with extreme caution, trying not to jar Anita's body. But when he looked over at her, he could see tears trickling down her face and asked if he should drive slower. Anita took Chris's hand in her and said she was fine, and to continue because she wanted a hot cup of coffee on the deck at home. Chris smiled. As they drove, Anita replayed Jeremy's words in her head; she felt tormented and torn in two.

As they entered the familiar door into the home she had grown to love, Anita was surprised when Delia came over and said she had made up a bed in the living room. That way, she explained, Anita wouldn't be isolated from the activities of the house while she recovered. Anita gave Delia a big hug, and planted a kiss on her cheek. As she looked around, she noted Delia had ensured she would have everything a person could want. She felt remorse for being such a burden, but Delia assured her it was okay. Getting settled on the new bed, Anita sheepishly asked Delia for one of her famous cups of coffee and Delia went about the task. Turning her attention to Chris, Anita asked, "Could we go to the den before my dad arrives?"

Chris helped Anita to walk, and the two headed to the den. Chris got her sitting comfortably in the chair and knelt down in front of her. He wiped her tears with his gentle thumbs, and then tenderly kissed her. "What's on your mind?"

Taking a deep breath proved painful. As Anita's lungs expanded, her ribs shot out causing the tears to fall like a tropical rainstorm. "I have to tell you a few things about Jeremy and Blake. My dad is Jeremy's CO and

Jeremy doesn't trust him. He also knows you are associated with Dante – only how deep it goes he wasn't sure. His mission was to tail Blake and report his dealings, but Jeremy wanted to be a vigilante and did nothing to stop any of it. He saw my brother tracking him, and yet, he led him to his death. He claims he didn't know that was going to happen at the time. Blake is very dirty. My personal opinion of Blake is that he is upset at *how* he got caught, not *that* he was caught. My question to you is - do you think my dad is aware of how he is perceived? Jeremy also told me my dad was Dante's lawyer, and he suspects my dad is way more involved than the surface shows. Can you add to this?"

Chris put his arms around her and held her close to his body. "Until I know what is going on," he said, "I'll trust no one except you. This conversation must remain between us for now. Do you think you can do that? I know it's asking a lot."

Delia tapped on the door, disrupting the conversation and told them dinner was ready. To Anita's surprise, her meal was handed to her on a tray in the den. Anita was overwhelmed with Delia's kindness and grateful to have her as her nurse. Delia's admiration for Anita made her secretly wish she could conjure up a remedy to make Anita's pain go away.

After Delia had left them, Anita searched Chris's eyes as she asked, "You suspect my father is deeply tied up in this somehow, don't you?"

Moving his head back and forth, as though he was tossing something around inside, Chris finally replied, "Let's just say I'm assuming he is - and by the way, the only reason I'm telling you, is so you don't shoot me."

Half laughing herself, Anita retorted, "Cut the crap. You're trying to tell me something, so let's have it?"

Walking to the window, Chris stood facing the garden. He crossed his arms and found it impossible to hide his theories from his wife. "I don't want to burden you, nor do I want to keep things from you, and yet, it seems that is no longer the case. Your father has been very good about finding camps, mainly because of your insistence, but I suspect he is being blackmailed and destroying camps is his way of getting revenge. I also believe he does not know where Carolyn is being held. As for Jeremy, he's an idiot for trying to go solo and will now pay the price, whichever way it goes."

Anita felt that her head was a drum, but the pounding was out of tune, and replied, "I'm not sure either, so would you please run a full report on Jeremy, Blake, and my dad? I need to know."

Chris whirled around to face her, and his words cut like a knife. "You have a soft spot for Jeremy?"

Not liking how the question was asked, Anita replied with shock in her voice, "Why should an innocent man be charged for something he didn't do?" she asked. "He should be charged for withholding evidence. Besides, he's a much better match for Carolyn than for me. There are three points I'd like to make clear. First, when Jeremy asked if I trusted you, I didn't hesitate for one second to answer, "yes." Second, I love you with all my heart and if I found out you were on the other side, I would still be there for you. Third, I want revenge – everyone I've ever loved has been taken away for me. And I know revenge is a deadly game. So let me put it this way, I want punishment for all those involved in ripping my family apart."

Chris's voice was deep, as he replied, "Never say 'revenge.' It destroys people inside. What I want you to do is rest, and I promise to get those files, and I will include my own file. Let's get to the root of the evil, and this is a good way to begin."

Taken aback at his tone, Anita dropped her voice to a softer tone. "Are you angry with me? I'm sorry I totaled the vehicle. When I'm better, I'll replace it."

Kneeling down in front of his wife, Chris's gentle approach amazed Anita by his transformation in mannerism. "You don't understand. I don't care about material things in life. They can be replaced. *You,* however, cannot. Too many speculations about who's honest and who's the bad guy has caused us much stress and anxiety. The only person I'm sure of is you. It's time I did my job." He kissed her nose and then her lips.

Anita grabbed his shirt, forcing him to stay close, and said, "You're still withholding something. Give."

Gently pushing against the arm of the chair for leverage, Chris broke her hold and stood up. He sat down on a chair opposite Anita and spread his legs, letting his hands drop between them, and said, "Your memory is intact." He then told her of his meeting with Dante. He remembered getting goose bumps the size of golf balls as he sat next to Dante and the conversation was so cold and manipulative. He explained that while they talked, Dante did something unusual. He got out his computer and punched in his name to get the run down of my life. The only information he got, was what the CIA had put in there, nothing more. He knew everything about his father; and from what he could tell, he ran his father. He explained that at first Dante didn't trust what the computer had printed for him, but eventually had to accept it. He then probed into their marriage and Chris told him they now had a strained marriage, and for some reason it satisfied him – or at least that's how it looked to him.

Chris rubbed the back of his neck and stated, "The main purpose of the meeting was to talk about the destroyed camp. "Only a few people knew of the camp's existence," Chris said mocking Dante." Anita giggled. Chris continued, "He then wanted to know what part I had played in the raid. I told him that secrecy was a tricky thing and that when more than one person knows about something, it's no longer a secret. I also explained that someone could've sold the information, or let it slip through a conversation, but the raid was a good indication that *someone* was selling him short."

Chris went on to finish his story. "We were quiet for some time, then Dante volunteered information that a new camp was being built to replace the one that he had lost. Knowing I was being scrutinized, I volunteered to help, to re-convince him I was part of his team. Nothing more was said, and Dante's last words were that he'd call when it was all set up."

Chris saw that Anita was exhausted. He carried her to the newly made bed with strict orders to get some shut-eye. Grateful for being able to stretch out her legs, Anita was almost asleep when she heard Chris enter the den and make a call. She succumbed to the fact that the little sandman's magic powder was powerful, and drifted off to sleep.

Quickly attending to business, Chris cleared his agenda and sat beside Anita, marveled at how innocent she looked and how much pain lived inside her body. These thoughts prompted him to call her mother to see if he could set things straight. Anita stirred and partially heard some of the conversation, but when he hung up swearing, she knew the detachment between her and her mother was still very much apparent. Seeing that she was awake, Chris kneeled on the floor beside her and explained that he had to go out, but promised to be back soon.

This triggered a panic attack in Anita that forced her to gasp for air. She begged him to help her to bed upstairs, saying that she needed to be near him for support now more than ever. Chris carried her to the bedroom upstairs and the two snuggled, comforting each other, and fell asleep.

Before the sun had a chance to shine, Chris went down and took up a breakfast for Anita. He served it to her in bed and explained that he had to go away for several days, but that a very special friend of his would be there in case she needed anything. Anita pulled her lips downward and, with her droopy eyes, she reminded him of a puppy. He smiled as he leaned over to kiss the woman who had stolen his heart.

Sitting up in bed with the tray before her, Anita said, "So, tell me a little about your friend."

Jittery inside, because he knew what her reaction would be, spoke methodically. "His name is Peter, and we've been friends since we were kids. He's a shrink – but that's not why he's here," Chris added this last bit quickly, since he could see she was about to explode. "The reason I'm leaving you is to get the details you asked for. I'm trusting Peter with my most precious gem: you. He needs a bit of a holiday. If you feel like talking, he's a great listener. If you don't, well try to make the best of it. That's all. Should Dante call, tell him I'll be back in a few days, and I will return his call then."

Anita felt like life wasn't fair, but if it made Chris's trip easier, she could accept his small donation and use the opportunity to get the goods on Chris's childhood. She smiled, thinking that this could be a good thing.

CHAPTER THIRTY

Watching Chris pack was hard for Anita. She decided to erase it from her mind and pretend he was just house cleaning or tidying things up. Escorting Anita to her new bedroom downstairs, he kissed her on the cheek and said his goodbyes. She wanted to lasso him, hog-tie him, and not let go. But, she knew the trip was important and she watched as he flew away like a butterfly shedding its cocoon.

She heard a vehicle approaching and knew it must be her new roommate. She had already established an attitude; she was not going to talk. When Peter entered the house, Delia greeted him with a hug. Anita watched thinking that if Delia liked him, he couldn't be all that bad.

Peter put his luggage down and walked into the living room. Spotting a pathetic-looking lady staring at him, he reached out his hand to shake hers and introduced himself. "Hi," he said, "I'm Peter, and you must be Anita. You are more beautiful than Chris described."

Anita shook his hand and looked him up and down, before saying, "Thanks for the compliment, but don't think for one moment I'll spill my guts. Welcome."

Peter sat down smiling, and replied, "Fair enough. Do you play chess?"

Unsure of his motives, Anita replied, "It's a mind game. What does the loser have to do?"

Digging around in his luggage, Peter pulled out a chess game and laid it on the table between them. "You're right," he said. "It's a mind game and the loser doesn't have to do anything. I like challenges, that's all."

Peter picked up his packed bags and headed upstairs to his room. Within a half hour, he was back downstairs talking to Delia and then faced his chess partner. "Well, up for the challenge? I'm fairly good at this game," Pere said, teasingly.

Against her will Anita smiled back, and said, "So am I – and you'll never get me to talk."

The game was interrupted when Delia brought out a light lunch. Anita, with a questionable look on her face, prompted Delia to ask, "Anita, what's on your mind?"

Placing her hand on Delia's, Anita asked with compassion, "Delia, when was the last time you had a day off?"

The smile on Delia's face showed even white teeth. "Long time," she replied. "I like to help. I can pay bills and help family."

Anita looked directly at Peter, and asked, "How good are you in a kitchen? You're lousy at chess."

Peter, who was busy clearing the table for lunch, looked up at the two pairs of eyes watching him, and responded, "I can make soup and a sandwich. Delia, go spend the rest of the day with your family. We'll take care of the fort."

Anita nodded and Delia's smile brightened up the room. She gave a courtesy, which made everyone laugh, took her apron off, threw it onto the table, and waltzed out the door. Anita smiled, and said, "I'll hold you to soup and sandwich later."

After eating their delightful lunch, Peter suggested Anita take a nap, while he finished settling in. She agreed, and then said, "Oh, and by the way, you will be in the hot seat later. We need to exchange stories. Deal?"

"Deal," Peter said, laughing heartily, and he left Anita so she could rest up for the in-depth chat they were scheduled to have later.

A creaking sound startled Anita, waking her up from her nap. Her eyes popped open and she saw Peter sneaking through the house. She burst out laughing, and said, "You look like you've done something terrible and are trying to get away with it. Care to enlighten me?"

Taken off guard, Peter stopped in his tracks. In a faltering voice, he replied, "Didn't want to wake you. Do you want anything from the kitchen?"

Anita surveyed the new bedroom and saw that everything she could possible want was there at her beck and call. "No," she replied. "I'm good. Delia has put everything I need nearby. Whatever you were hurrying to do, feel free to continue, but hurry back. We have a game to finish."

Taking his cue, Peter left the room and returned shortly. He was wearing shorts and looked very much at home. He carefully replaced the game on the table, and sat down thinking about his next move. "How is that I've never heard Chris talk about you?" Anita suddenly asked.

Distracted from the game, Peter got up and walked around the room. "We go way back to our childhood days. I went to school to become a shrink, and Chris went into law, which he never completed because he had to bail his father out of many fiascos. We both knew it was a mistake, but fate had its way and Chris, more or less, followed in his dad's way of life. We've been in contact all these years and, recently, I needed a change of pace and he needed a bodyguard, so here I am. I'm just getting out of a bad relationship, but I care for her deeply. Coming here is what I needed."

Picking up her drink, Anita eyed Peter. She took a sip, and said, "You're very professional. You haven't tried prying me open for my thoughts. You knew I would let the little monsters escape eventually. I'm not sure how much Chris had divulged, but I will give you a brief rundown of what's happened and on how I arrived here. Better get comfortable."

As she had promised, Anita began her tale, omitting the part about the girl at the camp, and not mentioning Jeremy and Blake. That, she thought, could wait until she felt more at ease.

After Anita had finished her story, Peter whistled. "Now I see what Chris sees in you. You are not what you seem."

"How do I seem? Like a spoiled brat?" Anita asked.

"What do you do – read minds? Yes, I thought of that, but it was the way he told the story. He neglected to tell me how stubborn and gentle you are."

Her face changed colors and, as she blushed, she changed the subject. "Do you think my mom will ever stop blaming me?"

Peter sat back in his chair, and thought for a moment. Then he said, "What I don't understand is why she blames you and not your father. Didn't you say he was the one who insisted on Jake tagging along?"

It was as if a light bulb had turned on in her head. Anita sat shaking her finger and said, "You know, that's a good point. I need to do some homework on my family."

"Please don't do anything rash. Really think about your next moves," Peter said, in a pleading tone.

"Why do you say that?" Anita asked, scrunching up her face.

Sitting down beside her, Peter took her hand in his and, like a true friend, he said, "I've never seen Chris so happy. You may be living in turmoil now, but when all is said and done, your lives will be completely fulfilled. Chris was always shy and never let his emotions show – he lost many a girlfriend because of that. You blew him away with your impulsive, unselfish ways, your stubbornness and caring, all the while making him guess what would happen next."

Anita raised her drink to Peter, took a sip, and then asked, "Chris and I come from the same kind of background. When I was younger, I was always in my mother's shadow, and she was always in my dad's. I decided to break the chain. I wanted to be strong, bold and independent, and therefore, dating was non-existent. I rarely got the chance to experiment with life, so books became my best friend. So you see, I became my father and he became his father, and together we became one hell of a match. Chris is everything I dreamed of and more."

Peter got up and gestured to his patient to lie down. He covered her up, and said quietly, "Rest. We'll talk later. I'll make us a bite to eat." When he left the room, Anita's head hit the pillow and instantly she was asleep.

In the semi-dark room where Anita was sleeping, a shadow loomed over her, causing her to stir. Upon waking up she felt fearful, and cautiously opened her eyes just as the dark shadow disappeared from the dimly lit room. Suspecting it was Dante; she crept out of bed to follow. Disappointment soon followed, as the only thing she managed to see was a partial license plate and the model of the vehicle as it drove away. As she crawled back into bed, every part of her body shook in terror and every muscle tightened as though she were being tied up in a knot. Anita dared not to close her eyes for the fear of never waking up, but fatigue and pain overpowered her and eventually she couldn't resist resting her eyes.

Peter gently shook her to wake her up. Feeling as though she were on a boat, Anita woke up swinging her arms and hit Peter. He had come to see if she was ready for the soup and sandwich feast that he had prepared. Anita gasping for air apologized profusely for the blow. She explained what had transpired earlier in the day, making them both feel like they were on the edge, waiting for the final push over.

Peter, fearful for Anita's life, did not let her out of his sight for the rest of the day; it was as though a chain bound them to one another. Anita was not overly fond of this new level of attachment, and secretly wished it were Chris who was there to protect her.

The following day, a car approached the house and Anita took out her binoculars to see if she recognized it. She swore under her breath at the unfamiliar car, and wanted to hide out. Peter walked outside to greet the guest and was pleased to find it was the doctor. He showed him in.

The doctor examined Anita and was pleased at her progress. He suggested she get out and do a little walking for exercise. This news pleased her immensely and she couldn't wait for the good doctor to leave. When he did, she ventured outside for a walk, taking in deep breaths of fresh air. The pain shot right down through to her lungs and forced her to hold her side making her realize that she wasn't out of the woods just yet. The walk took more out of her than she anticipated and she was compelled to go back to bed and rest.

Resting on the sofa, her ears perked up to rustling sounds and she waited for the intruder to appear. Feeling the heat radiate as the violator drew closer to her body, Anita's eyes flashed open; she was ready to pounce, when she realized it was Chris. She grabbed him around the neck and pulled him towards her harder than she intended. He lost his balance, but juggling his weight so that he wouldn't fall on top of her, he did a quick maneuver and landed on the floor instead, which made them both laugh so hard, they had tears in their eyes.

Picking himself up off the floor, Chris handed Anita some squashed flowers and gave her a kiss. She responded passionately, and his jealously of leaving Peter to monitor Anita relaxed, because he knew she really did love him; just from her kiss alone. Chris sat and talked with Anita a bit, and then nodded to Peter to join him on the deck. Grabbing a couple of beers along the way, the two men headed outside where they got deep into a conversation. Anita, who felt left out, decided she should be a part of their friendship and walked out to join them. As she was about to walk out, Delia called after her to rest, and until that moment, Anita hadn't realized Delia was in the house.

Hearing the commotion, Chris guessed what was happening. When he opened the door, he found a sheepish-looking Anita standing in the doorway. Chris wrapped his arm around her and gently guided her to the porch swing. Then he took a seat beside her and they saw Peter sitting there shaking his head.

Chuckling, Anita said, "Peter, if you shake your head one more time, it's going to fall off. You know all about our relationship, so let's hear about yours – unless you'd prefer not to talk about it."

"Does she always get her way?" Peter asked, with a smile.

"With me she does. As for you, you're on your own," Chris replied, smiling lovingly at his wife.

Peter moved his chair so it sat directly in the warmth of the sun. Sitting back down, he leaned back, took a drink, and began his version of his story. "I was with a special person for about ten years," he said. "People warned me no to let her take control, but I did and signed over all my assets into her name – to avoid being sued and lose everything I owned, more or less. As it turned out, though, she was having an affair. She wanted a divorce, and of course, had all the assets in her name. The lawyers are having a hay day sorting it all out, as there were provisions I had implemented. She is fighting it and costing me a fortune. As you know, the more the money a lawyer makes, the less you have in the end, so I hope the lawyer gets it all. Seriously. Anyway, Chris, being a good friend, offered me a retreat and being here does the trick. So, tell me, when your crisis is over, will you feel the same about each other?"

Anita blurted out her answer before Chris could even open his mouth. "I have plans for this man. I'm never leaving his side, we are going to have children, grow old together, and be surrounded by grandchildren, right here in this house."

Chris could feel goose bumps forming as she spoke and hugged Anita tightly. "Guess I don't have to worry about my future," he jested, and kissed his wife.

Delia served them dinner on the patio. The three of them enjoyed the sound of the birds, and watched the sunset, reminiscing about the things that had made them who they were today. They shared much joy and laughter that evening.

Eventually, Anita's eyes began to feel like paperweights, and she couldn't hold them open any longer. Chris said goodnight to Peter and carried Anita to their bed upstairs. He gently stripped off her clothes and replaced them with a nightie, but every time he touched her, her skin boiled with blood rushing through her veins. She locked her arms around his neck and kissed him as though it was their first time together. Chris surrendered to her emotions and they united together as one person. Neither of them could explain the feelings that raced through every part of their bodies, but relished in the swirl of bliss.

Waiting until Anita's eyes closed for the night, Chris went back downstairs and found Peter still sitting on the deck. Grabbing a couple more beers, the two closed off the night with general, but fun conversation.

CHAPTER THIRTY-ONE

Before they headed down to their morning meal, Chris handed Anita file folders containing the detailed information that she had requested. Shuffling through the stack, Anita tossed Chris's folder off to the side, but Chris picked it up and placed it back on the pile. "You may not think it's necessary now," he said, "but I guarantee it will come in handy somewhere along the way." Anita's heart did a complete stop for a second, but soon resumed its rhythm and she slid the files into a case.

A deep sigh come from Anita's windpipe, and Chris turned to face her with concern. "What do you have on your mind?" he asked.

Avoiding Chris's eyes, Anita began searching for something to wear and talked as though she were talking to herself. "Dante, or one of his goons, was here a couple of days ago, while I was sleeping. Peter was somewhere in the vicinity. I know this because I kind of woke up to see a figure leaving the house and I followed, getting a partial plate number," she said, and handed the paper with numbers scribbled on it to Chris.

Chris was about to ask her a question when he noticed a black sedan approaching the house. He banged his hand on the door and then opened it, rushing to greet the intruder. A brief conversation took place outside, and Chris shouted to Anita, who was standing on the balcony eavesdropping, that he would be back soon, but not to wait for him. Then he slipped into the vehicle and it drove off.

With her briefcase in hand, Anita hung onto the banister for support, and descended the stairs at a turtle's pace. When Peter saw her, he came towards her to help, but she waved him off, so he stood back and watched. Reaching the bottom step on her own gave her a sense of accomplishment and merrily she headed for the kitchen to get some coffee and sit down to scan the papers. Peter, noticing she had plans, told her he was going for a drive. Anita wished him a safe journey and snuggled up in her favorite recliner. Restlessness set in as she wondered what adventure was in store for Chris. She got up and began walking around the room, peering out the window as if he would magically appear. Coming to the conclusion that stewing about it wouldn't make it better, she sat down with her feet up, took a sip of her coffee, and began to read the files; thinking an occupied mind is better than an idle mind.

Having dozed off in the chair, Anita awoke to the sound of a door slamming. Chris's conscience was playing havoc with him. On one hand, he was excited to be helping Dante move some camps so he could see if Carolyn was among the women, but on the flip side, he also felt it was a trap. Anita looked at his tormented face and wanted to know what was going on. He explained that he had four hours to get ready, then he was to join Dante in moving a couple of mystery camps and only a few people knew. As Chris explained his imminent departure to Anita, Douglas showed up beaming with great news that he had found another camp. They were to execute the plan in the next two days. Anita placed her hands over her face, as she thought things weren't computing properly. She looked at Chris, and then at her father and was about to speak, when Chris cut her words off.

Chris's emotions were riding fast, as he said, "Not a good idea. I'm obligated to help move a camp and if it's the same one you're thinking about, it could be a trap."

Douglas, so certain he was doing the right thing, snapped back, "That's absurd. What do you base this on?"

Chris, wanted to throttle the man before him to knock some sense into him, ground his teeth, and replied, "I've had a meeting with Dante and he is suspicious of the last destroyed camp. He's playing with us. You want to eliminate this camp, be my guest, but keep in mind I may be there and you may have casualties you won't be expecting." Reigning in his anger, Chris continued, "Do either of you have a picture of Carolyn?"

Douglas pulled a snapshot out of his wallet and handed it over to Chris. Then Douglas asked, sharply, "What kind of relationship do you have with Dante?"

Chris's hand tightened on the picture he'd been handed, and he replied coldly, "You know very well. How could you even ask?"

Anita stepped in between the two men and cut them both off. "You both work for Dante in different ways," she said. "I can vouch for what Chris says about Dante being suspicious. That suspicion puts a whole new light on things, doesn't it Dad? What are you going to do now that you know how we feel?" She saw the confused look on her dad's face as she spoke, and threw in at the last moment a few kind words. "Dad, I know you are doing this for me, and believe me I appreciate it, but Dante isn't a trustworthy man. He plays games and enjoys watching his players kill each other off. Saves him the trouble. In my heart, I believe what Chris says; Dante is setting a trap. He's only telling a few people of his plans so he can weed out his traitors. Be careful, that's all I ask."

Chris added his own view, saying, "For all I know it could be a different camp, but this is spelling trap to me. Do what you must, and I'll do what I have to do. Now, if you'll excuse me, I must pack."

Anita followed her husband upstairs and watched him pack his belongings into a suitcase. "She has a strawberry shaped mark behind her right ear; Carolyn that is," she said thinking of her best friend. "Other than that, she has no distinguishing marks that I recall. Chris you were right to question my father. I, too, believe it's a trap. Just please, please, be careful. I want you back in one piece. I have plans for you."

Chris bent down to kiss the lovely woman he so desired. "I'll be back before you know it," he promised.

"Chris," Anita began, "my father spent much of his time overseas. In your absence I think Ill fly home and do some snooping. His recent behavior is out of character and something is wrong. I can feel it."

Chris's thoughts were of devastation surrounding them both, but he also knew that saying 'no' would only heat things up between them and he didn't want that, so he agreed. "I'm not overly fond of you traipsing around in your shape, so before I agree, you must promise to take Peter for support."

Anita clung to him like a bee to honey. Gradually he pulled away from her vise grip and kissed her forehead, eyes, nose and then her soft sensual lips. "Honey," he whispered, "it's time for me to leave. I'll phone you when I get home. Just let me know where you are. Maybe I'll join you if you are still abroad. Circumstances will dictate the outcome."

Holding her hand over her heart, Anita pledged. "I swear to keep a level head, take Peter with me, to return in one piece, and you can bet your ass I'll let you know where I am."

Chris placed his hand over his heart, and reciprocated. "I swear to dodge bullets and be here to share a life with you as we grow old." They both laughed and Anita escorted Chris to the car, just as Peter was pulling in.

Chris shook Peter's hand, saying, "Take care of my gem will you. She's going to her hometown for a few days and I would appreciate it if you tagged along. Besides, what else do you have to do?" Peter grinned as he shook Chris's hand, but in the back of his mind he wondered what he was getting himself into.

Waving goodbye to her husband, Anita turned and saw Douglas's tight-faced staring at her. He hurled sharp words, "I thought this is what you wanted," he said. "To destroy camps, release captives, and locate Carolyn."

Matching her father's temper, Anita replied, "What I want is to find Carolyn. It's obvious you have a score to settle with Dante. If you think blowing up this camp will do the trick, then do so. I thought Dante was your client, not your enemy." A look of anguish came over Douglas's face, and Anita blurted out, "You know he's got Carolyn, don't you?"

Douglas refuted her accusation. "When Chris gets home," he said, "we'll have much to discuss. I'll be gone for a few days so you can rest up."

It seemed that every nerve and muscle in her body was tap dancing, but she was also filled with heartache. Peter knew something was about to happen, and then the words flew from her mouth, "Pack," she said. "We leave as soon as I can book a flight." Peter nodded. He knew a new adventure was out to find him and, strangely enough, he welcomed it with open arms.

CHAPTER THIRTY-TWO

Jitteriness set in and Anita couldn't stay still in her seat on the plane, for even a moment. Peter watched her silently at first and then taking the first step, he placed his hand on hers, and said, "Whoa. You are traveling faster than the plane. What gives?"

At first Anita resented his hand being anywhere near hers, but she began to find it comforting, and replied, "My father traveled abroad a lot leaving us behind. And, by 'us' I mean my brother, mother and me. He always seemed agitated before he left and calm when he returned. I know my father is up to something and the key to his Pandora Box is hidden safely in his office. I know because he throws nothing out, just stashes it in places no one would ever look. You know, you don't have to join me in my crusade."

Peter's smile widened and his eyes twinkled. "And miss the outcome? I think not. Besides, I've been a shrink for so long that the change of pace is refreshing – it makes my problems seem trivial compared to yours."

Anita's hand twitched as though she was about to embark some deep, dark riddle, and had to find the clues to unravel a hidden treasure. "Peter," she said, earnestly, "I need your thoughts on this. Should I make amends with my mother, or wait until she makes the first move?" They discussed it in great detail, and concluded it would be a humanitarian gesture if Anita were to take the first step towards mending the relationship.

Several flight connections later, Anita and Peter arrived in her hometown in Montana. A dark cloud loomed over it, making for a gloomy reception, but Anita did her best to shrug it off. Peter was amazed at how well the long trip had gone, and the two checked into a five star hotel downtown.

Putting off meeting with her mother, Anita signaled for Peter to join her, and they drove off in their rented vehicle. She showed him the sights, and Peter was awestruck; he had been expecting a city atmosphere here, but instead he was in a little town filled with beauty. He also recognized

Anita's strong connection to this place, and could see what Chris saw in her: beauty, brains and compassion.

Getting an early start the next day, the pair headed to Douglas's office. A creepy feeling rushed over Anita and it gave her a sudden heat wave. She fanned herself to cool down. Pushing through her discomfort, Anita led the way to her father's office door, but Wendy, Douglas's assistant, stepped out in front creating a barricade, and said in a cold tone, "You have no right to be here."

"Why do you say that?" Anita whipped back, not having to worry now about being too hot – Wendy's voice had cooled her right down.

"He isn't here and left strict instructions that no one was permitted to enter his office unless he authorized it first, and that includes you," Wendy replied, her demeanor growing colder still as she folded her arms in front of Anita.

Dangling a key before everyone's eyes, Anita pushed Wendy to the side and unlocked the door, exposing the contents of the office. She pulled Peter in and slammed the door shut behind them. Panic was beginning to come through her voice. "I wonder what well-kept secrets my father doesn't want exposed," she said. Placing her purse down on the desk, Anita began the task of searching every nook and cranny, but came up empty handed. She had to admit her father was good. Eyeing the locked drawers and cupboards, Anita knew she was unable to access the well-concealed contents behind them. At the same time, she felt that some kind of evidence was sure to be lurking about in other parts of the office, and she aimed to find it, even if it was only a small fragment of the puzzle.

Having a sudden thought, Anita snapped her fingers and pulled Peter behind her as she headed down to the storage area. She was certain to find something that would incriminate her father in some shady deal there. Peter stood in the background surveying the scene as she diligently continued her crusade. Hours passed, and hunger set in making Peter want to eat anything in sight. Anita's temper escalated, but her obstinacy kept her in check and then the unexpected happened. Anita found an old passport of her father's. Squealing with delight, she beamed at this sliver of evidence, but Peter didn't see its significance, and asked, "So? He went to Aspen. What does that mean?"

Excited at the possibility of piecing some of Douglas's strange behavior together, Anita declared, "Hey, it's the turning point. We're going to Aspen. This should be fun." She stuffed some insignificant papers into a file folder and headed out of the storage room with a bounce to her step. Wishing everyone in the office farewell, Anita and Peter returned to the car and drove to her family's home. As she parked outside, she could feel tremors throughout her body, and sighed. "It's D-day. Time to face the two-headed dragon lady directly. Care to join me and give support."

"When you put it that way, how can I resist? There is one thing though, as soon as we are done here, we get a bit to eat. I am famished," Peter said, reluctantly. Anita shook his hand to show it was a deal, fixed her clothes, and walked up to the door, and Peter whispered encouragement. "You can do this."

A frail, thin woman, resembling her mother, answered the door and almost succeeded in slamming it in Anita's face, but Anita's foot found its way into the corner of the doorway, preventing its total closure. As she pushed the door open, Anita saw the fashionable entranceway that she had once loved; this homecoming, however, was not one of warmth and welcome. Peter, not sure what to do, crept in behind Anita and stayed quiet. An ugly episode erupted between mother and daughter and, without any warning; Anita's mom stopped and focused her sad, haunted eyes onto Peter, as if noticing him for the first time. Sarcastically, she said to Anita, "Who is he? Is this your boyfriend? Didn't take you long to get rid of Chris."

Anita's head made a movement like someone had punched her in the face. "You're out of line," she snarled. "I'm about to make your life complete. You will be a very lonely, bitter, old lady because I'm going to take my belongings, and when I step out that door, I'll never return. You'll never have the pleasure of seeing your grandkids."

Millie stepped aside, granting her daughter permission to go ahead and pack her bags. Anita stormed up the stairs and hastily packed what she could. Peter followed, and when he entered Anita's sitting room, he couldn't help compare it to his own prized study at home. The sitting room was lavishly decked out with settees, lounge chairs, a fireplace, unique wooden furniture, and walk-in closets that could encase most of his study. He chuckled to himself.

The banging of luggage hitting the floor caught his attention. He couldn't help letting his laughter escape as he watched Anita throw her belongings into the suitcase and sit on them to lock them. "You find this funny?" she demanded. "You could help instead of mocking me."

"I'll carry them downstairs for you," Peter said, as he put his hand over his mouth to stifle his laughter.

Satisfied that she had gathered her prized possessions, Anita turned her attention towards Peter and eyed him up from head to foot, making him feel uneasy. "You're about the same size as Jake. Let's see what kind of ski wear he had."

The corridor was long and before entering Jake's room, Anita hesitated, and drew in a deep breath. When she opened the door, she shrieked. "She's made his room into a shrine. I don't get it."

Peter tried to console her, but Anita pulled away and surveyed the candle-lit room. Jake's picture was plastered all over the walls, and it made her feel as though she was invading a crypt. She quickly took a few items of clothing and a baseball – it was one they had found on a treasure hunt and used to play catch. She then bowed in prayer, and left the room feeling shaken up.

Feeling like an abandoned child, Anita drove back to the hotel and went to the bar for a few drinks and to make sure Peter got his belly full. Looking as though she was in a trance, Peter clapped his hands to grab her attention and suggested she call home and check to see if Chris was back. Liking the idea, Anita dialed the number and when Chris answered, she had a spiritual feeling. "Hey, do you miss me?" she asked, beaming.

Chris's voice was so alluring it made her melt inside. "Hi, honey. Yah, maybe a little, but I didn't think you'd miss me now that you have Peter."

"He's not as good as the old one. Can you join us in Aspen?" Anita asked, laughing. "Seems my dad spent much of his time there alone. Mom has set up Jake's room as a shrine and refuses to acknowledge me. I feel so alone. I know I'll find some answers in Aspen. So, what do you say?"

Chris could hear the pain in her voice and didn't hesitate with his response. "Where in Aspen do you want to meet?" he asked.

Biting her lip, Anita answered, "I'm not sure, but I know it shouldn't be hard to find a house in my father's name."

Chris rubbed his sore arm and thought out loud. "I'll track it down and e-mail you the details. I wish you both well and I'll join you at the first possible flight out. What time is your flight?'

Checking her flight schedule, she replied, "First thing in the morning."

"Check your e-mail in about half an hour. I love you and I'm looking forward to seeing your sweet face."

Feeling relieved that Chris was going to be there for her, her heart was racing and she felt like a princess. "I love you."

Exhausted and full of anticipation, Anita and Peter had dinner, checked their e-mail for directions, and turned in early. The night seemed to last forever. Anita's eyes didn't close as everything she had been through in the last year ran through her head. Checking the clock periodically she decided it was time to get dressed, and be ready to roll. Peter, who had been observing his companion, was surprised at how well Anita managed to get things done in spite of her recent injuries, and before he knew it, she had whisked him off on another adventure. He had to admit he was enjoying it, especially because it wasn't on his dime.

They tightened their belt buckle as they waited for the plane to take off. Peter leaned towards Anita, and said, "Tell me about Carolyn."

Resting her head on the headrest, Anita smiled, and sighed. "She is carefree and makes me laugh," she said. "She's got the most innocent way about her. We are — were - so close as friends that people mistook us for sisters. There isn't anything we can't do. She is and will always be my mentor." Not daring to look at Peter, her mind now questioned his motives. "*Is he a plant or a really good friend of Chris's?*" she asked herself.

A soft whisper flowed passed her ear. "I'm a friend," he said.

Anita's head turned so sharp, she thought she heard it snap. "I don't follow."

"Your answers are very evasive, like those of someone who can't trust others. I assure you I can be trusted, and if I couldn't be, do you seriously think I'd follow you all over the world? I must say, though, this intrigue has replaced my depression and I thank you for that."

Anita apologized for her behavior, and Peter waved it off with a smile. They were quiet for the rest of the flight. Fatigued from many layovers, they finally arrived in Aspen. This was one of the most talked-about ski resorts in the world, and the land of discovery — that's what Anita was hoping for, anyway.

CHAPTER THIRTY-THREE

Dusk was showing that it would soon be dark and the lit-up mountain showed the skiers as they zigzagged down the slopes with ease. Anita wanted to be among them, but instead, her quest necessitated that she remain cautious and observant as she and Peter arrived at the front entrance to the many rows of condos protected by security.

Nervously, Anita approached the desk to sign in. She was worried she'd be turned away and was ready for a confrontation, but the clerk only smiled and printed off some forms for her to sign. "Douglas's daughter is always welcomed here," the clerk said.

Anita's head jerked back in surprise. She placed her left foot behind her to steady herself, and managed to keep her cool. "Thank you," she said, simply.

The clerk glanced down at the signature and questioned it. "That doesn't look like your normal handwriting. I'm sure it reads 'Anita'."

Scrambling for a comeback, Anita smiled sweetly, and said, "I'm trying out a new name and writing skills."

The clerk's face scrunched up as he replied, "I like Shelan better," and handed over the keys. Anita thanked him and told him a young man named Chris Preston would be joining them and would he please allow him to enter. The clerk nodded and Anita smiled, walked towards the door, and turned slowly, catching the smile on his face, before walking out the door in total bewilderment.

Like an obedient puppy, Peter was waiting for Anita outside and tagged along to their new dwelling. The condo took Anita's breath away. The picture window overlooked the ski hill and had a spectacular view of the town. Noticing that there were no curtains on the window, Anita looked more closely and discovered a sliding door. She stepped out onto the balcony. Endorphins were released, and Anita excitedly interlocked arms with Peter and the two of them scoped out the rest of the condo. There was a fireplace in each room, and the master bedroom had an en-suite filled with toiletries for every purpose imaginable – making Anita wonder for who they were intended. Choosing a room for their stay, Anita and Peter then headed down to the kitchen to see what was there to eat. Anita whistled as she opened each cupboard and drawer. They were well stocked. The fridge, too, was filled with items that could easily feed a family of four for a couple of months. Helping herself to some goodies, Anita prepared coffee along with a light snack for both of them. Peter flicked a switch to light the fireplace and the two sat in chairs, cozying up to the fire and taking in the ambiance. After they ate, Peter decided to turn in, but Anita was keyed up; she picked up the files and her coffee cup, and settled into her chair for some reading. Relaxing for the first time in ages, Anita could feel her ribs aching and found she was short of breath. She concluded that, for the first time in days, her adrenalin had been more powerful than her injuries, and she hadn't paid attention to them until now.

Propping a pillow up against her side, Anita got comfortable and picked up the first file. It was her father's, and she began with it because he intrigued her the most. As she scanned his history, his emergency contact names stood out and she carefully read the information that stated should anything happen to him, Carolyn, Shelan, Anita, Jake, Millie, and Suzanne were to be contacted immediately.

She was confused as to why Carolyn's name appeared on the list – and who were Shelan and Suzanne? Then she remembered Shelan was the daughter the clerk had mentioned. She desperately checked for any further details connecting the contact names, only to draw a blank and frustration. She threw the file to the floor and its impact caused a plunking sound. Not sure if she wanted to close her eyes or continue, Anita picked up the next file and it had Chris's name on it, and she began to read it. It stated that Chris's father had been a great agent who had gone one step too far. Even though he had volunteered to testify for the FBI, his father received no compensation for the years of service. It was their belief that he had signed his own death contract.

Chris had been brought in to protect his father so he could give his testimony. But, when his father was prematurely taken out of the picture, Chris resigned from the case, and wanted no further contact with the CIA or the FBI. After the CIA went over the entire case, they decided that Chris was eligible for some compensation from his father's pension.

Because they were such a powerful organization, they persuaded Chris to resume his position as an agent.

Chris's mother died mysteriously; very few details were known about her death. It was as if the investigation came to a dead end, and over the years, only Chris attempted to discover the truth. Anita read the highlighted part of the text that stated his mother's body had been found near an abandoned slave camp.

Anita's lips started quivering, and water flooding her eyes found a passage through the sockets and run down her cheek. Wiping away the tears, Anita pondered over a couple of questions: is Chris seeking revenge for his mother's death? Or is he afraid something unexplainable will happen to Anita herself? Making a silent vow, Anita swore to consider Chris's feelings more often and not act so hastily. The rest of the contents in his file she already knew, and she laid it carefully on the table.

Getting up to stretch her legs, Anita was drawn to the spectacular view. She told herself, under her breath, that if she were in better shape, she'd be skiing down the slopes, letting the rush of adrenalin fill her body. This thought put a long overdue smile on her face, and she hoped it would last until Chris showed up.

Trying her best to catch a few winks, Anita's restlessness won the battle. She picked up her cold coffee, drew her knees up, and absorbed herself in Blake's file. As she read, she whistled incredulously at his lack of good conduct. His not-so-squeaky-clean report was full of accounts of misconducts. All this led to his eventual suspension, and the timing couldn't have been better. He had been suspended right around the time that Carolyn was abducted, thus, confirming much of what Jeremy had told her. A question popped into her mind and Anita wondered: '*Did Jeremy know about the suspension and decided he wanted in on the cut of the abduction money? Or had he simply not contacted his CO, and therefore, was unaware of Blake's current status.*' Either way, Anita surmised, they were both where they should be: locked up.

Anita's eyes became heavy, but she picked up Jeremy's file and scanned it. His record was squeaky-clean, filled with accounts of good conducts, and accurate documentation that indicated he was a versatile, dependable agent. Despite this account, however, Anita's instincts told her not to put her faith in Jeremy; he had changed personalities, and could be a cunning predator. Skimming his file a little further, she noticed that his CO was named "Bedo". She quickly rifled through the other files searching for the same particulars, and was furious at how she could've missed such vital information. There it was in black ink; the same name on both Jeremy's and Chris's files; "Bedo". Anita could feel her color changing from her head right down to her toes. The change was accompanied by a head rush, and followed by pain. Her heart ached at the mere though of how deep her father's involvement might go, and her shaking hands became less cooperative.

She barely remembered closing her eyes, when a noise from the kitchen disturbed her peacefulness and she heard Peter ask, "Want a bite to eat? You look as though you pulled an all-nighter."

Wiping the drool from around her chin, Anita stretched her arms, and answered back, "Yah. That sounds good. I'm pretty sure I just closed my eyes, yet I feel strangely refreshed."

The early morning sun made its way through the vast window, enticing Anita to look out. It looked like someone had painted a mural. The beams of the sun lightly caressed the snow-packed mountains and formed little paths onto the main street, guiding the early risers to their destinations. Anita could see skiers with their snowboards and skis held tight to their shoulders as they met up with friends. How she longed to be one of them.

Totally absorbed in this vision, Anita did not hear the door open. She was startled when a booming voice hit the air in the room, and she turned to see her father standing there. "What do you mean by just walking in here?" he demanded.

Caught off guard, Anita replied without thinking, "My, you're in a good mood," she said.

Anita could see that his veins were about to explode as he said, furiously, "I want an explanation right this very minute."

Anita strolled coolly over to the sofa, sat down, and patted the files on the table. "Seems we both have some issues that need to be ironed out," she said, with a controlled voice. Anita then got up, walked to the kitchen and poured two cups of coffee. She handed one to her father and left Peter to kitchen detail.

Douglas accepted the coffee, but he was full of anger that his daughter had invaded his privacy. He said in a strained voice, "Where'd you get the files?"

Anita felt both anxiety and pleasure at having gotten one up on her dad, and spoke calmly. "When my life and family are in jeopardy, it's my right to be able to attain documents and use the information as necessary."

Darting his eyes around the room Douglas asked, hastily, "Where's Chris? I know he gave them to you." He shook his head at Anita, and yelled, "Well?"

Not sure what the question pertained to, Anita quipped back, "Well what?"

Douglas's voice went opera-like and Anita looked at him sharply – she had never heard him use that tone before. "Where's Chris?" he demanded again. "And who the hell is in the kitchen?"

Raising her hand and pointing around the room, Anita said cockily, "Do you see Chris anywhere? The person in the kitchen is Peter, Chris's best friend. I suggest we eat and wait for Chris. He'll be here soon."

Never had Douglas been challenged by one of his children before. He scoffed at her gesture of hospitality in this – *his* – space. "I could have you arrested for breaking and entering," he said.

Shrugging her shoulders, Anita brushed off his threat. "Go ahead," she said. "But then I'd have to tell mom a few things."

"Blackmail?" Douglas shouted. "You're trying to blackmail me. Your mother knows all she needs to know."

Calmly, Anita rebutted. "In case you've forgotten, you gave me a key to your office, and here as well. They let me in, indicating that your daughter was welcome anytime. The way I see it, I've never been here before, so that leads me to conclude you have another family, and that I look like my *sister.*" She watched her father squirm, and said, "I'm batting a hundred, aren't I?"

"That's none of your business," Douglas snapped back.

Leaning closer to her father, her legs slightly parted, and her elbows resting on her knees, Anita said, "It is if I have other siblings." Resting her hand on the stack of papers, she continued, "As for these files, I am on the case, and therefore, my access to these documents is valid. It's going to be a long, hard day unless we get some matters clarified."

Succumbing to his daughter's invitation, they headed to the kitchen where Anita made introductions and they ate a scrumptious meal. Peter, not wanting to be a party to the tension between Anita and her father, volunteered to clean up afterwards, so the father and daughter team could finish airing out their differences. But neither of them made the effort to restart the discussion where they had left off, and silence fell between them.

CHAPTER THIRTY-FOUR

Peter cleaned up the kitchen and headed for his room to change, so he could browse around town. Anita and Douglas had a staring competition, with neither of them backing down. A sharp rap on the door broke the trance and Anita, welcoming the diversion, galloped to the door. Opening the door, Anita didn't give the guest any time to enter; she just flung her arms around his neck, knocking him off balance. Chris lost his footing and landed in the snow with Anita on top of him. Before getting off, Anita gave him a hot kiss that could melt the snow, making him lick his lips for more.

Chris gently pushed her off into the snow and stood up, but Anita was laughing so hard that she had difficulty getting into an upright position. She grasped Chris's extended hand for support, and stood up.

Wanting one more hug, Anta threw her arms tightly around him, but Chris's face expressed pain and she backed off, asking, "What's wrong?"

He put his hand up indicating he didn't want to discuss it at that moment, and the couple walked into the condo together. Chris and Douglas stood facing each other for a few moments, before Chris blurted out, "You did it, didn't you?"

Anita stepped in between the men and growled while looking at Chris. "I want to know what happened to your arm," she demanded. Then a clear picture formed in her mind, and her gaze turned towards her father. "You blew up the camp, didn't you?" she asked.

Douglas dropped his eyes in avoidance, and replied, "Don't be ridiculous."

Daring not to get too close to her father, Anita kept her arms at her side and knelt down, so she could see her father's lowered face. She watched his expression as she said, "Yes you did. What were you thinking?"

Chris took charge, his voice full of annoyance. "I'll take it from here. Anita I'm sorry to say I didn't find Carolyn." Chris then sat down and, said harshly, "Douglas, I don't know why you did this, but we lost three men and five women. Six men were wounded, including me. It was a trap. I told you this would happen. That's right – it was a set-up. Dante, I believe, suspects you. He holds all the cards now."

Douglas did not utter a word, but fixed his eyes on the files. Chris followed his gaze. "I gave her those files," he admitted. "If you have any animosity, direct it at me. A new pair of eyes is needed, and I thought Anita could supply that because she hasn't seen any of the files. We all need to get our lives back, and the sooner the better. That's how I feel, anyway."

The room was so still, that Anita thought she could hear her own heartbeat. Suddenly, Douglas got up and disappeared into the hall closet. He returned with some photo albums. Sitting down beside his daughter, Douglas never looked up, but his words were soft. "Chris, stay," he said. "This isn't going to be easy for Anita."

Little electrodes ran the circuit of Anita's body, informing her she was about to be hit with a shock. She got up and grabbed a bottle of rum and a cup of coffee. Sitting back down on the couch with her legs crossed, Anita took a large gulp of her drink and waited for the tidal wave to strike. Chris sat down next to her, anticipating the rocking of an unstable ship.

Douglas sat on the edge of his chair, his hands moving in every direction; no part of him could remain still. He began his story at the beginning stating he had always been more married to his work than to Millie, and that this lead to infidelity on her part. Her affair resulted in a baby girl: Carolyn.

Douglas admitted openly to Anita, "I had given Millie two choices: either give up the child and stay, or leave with the baby. Millie was heartbroken. She decided to give custody to Carolyn's biological father. I stipulated to Millie that Carolyn's name was never to be mentioned again, and we tried in vain to patch the marriage. Our efforts were in vain, and I had an affair with a woman named Suzanne. Anita, you were the result of our affair."

"I had money and money talks," Douglas explained. "I won the custody battle between Suzanne and me. I took you home, expecting Millie would raise you like her own child. But, I suppose Millie was heartbroken over the double standard – I could keep mine, but she couldn't keep hers. Anyway, she walked out and went to live with her own daughter and the father of her baby. Several years later, Carolyn's father was killed. Millie had nowhere to turn, and came to me for help. I still had a soft spot for her, so I took her and Carolyn in, and again we tried to reconcile our differences. Jake was born."

"Doing the best we could, I still felt like something was missing, and I went abroad to rebuild my business. There, I met the most wonderful woman, who fulfilled my itch; life was good. Not long after meeting this woman, she was killed in an accident and her death tore my world apart. Not sure where my life was headed, I somehow got reacquainted with Suzanne. After that life seemed to smooth out and we built a house together. This condo in Aspen is our get-away place for quiet retreats. I had told Suzanne about Millie, and she didn't like the idea of sharing, but tolerated the situation – probably hoping to become a part of your life. Shelan was born, and the two of us couldn't have been happier."

Anita's eyes were wide open while she listened, sipping on her drink. Chris was certain she never blinked. When the words Douglas had spoken began to take effect, her words came out slightly slurred. "Does Mother – I mean *Millie* – know about Suzanne after all these years? When you and Millie went abroad, how did you handle the situation? Did you meet with Suzanne on the side or did you ignore her while you were otherwise occupied?"

"No," Douglas said, running his hands over the albums. "Millie was never told and I kept the two lives very separate. When I was with one, I did not see the other. I wanted to keep it the way it was."

"Pretty hard to do when everybody's names are listed to be contacted upon your death," Anita replied, with a snort. "No wonder she hates me. Her kids are gone, and I'm still among the living. This would explain the shrine in Jake's room."

Douglas had a tear in his eye as he replied, "I'm not proud of the way I did things, but I am proud of all my kids, you especially. You are so much like your mother. Whenever you are ready, you have a family that's dying to meet you."

Sobbing uncontrollably now, Anita managed to say, "Why didn't Suzanne fight harder for me?"

Wiping the tears from his own cheek, Douglas answered, "Money and power talk. Neither of the ladies could stand up to me. That said, Suzanne made me fight for her and our love couldn't be stronger."

In a near-frozen state, Anita asked, "And Millie?" The way she said it, she reminded Chris of a lost soul.

"Our love had always been weak. I needed more. She was like a zombie. Couldn't you see that?" he said with conviction.

"And Carolyn? Why is she in the list of contact names?" Anita asked, inquisitively.

Douglas wanted to avoid any further hardship for his daughter and replied, simply, "I owe her that at least."

Without explanation, Anita struggled to get up. She grabbed Chris's jacket, kissed him on the cheek, and said, almost inaudibly, "I need air. Time to think." She headed out the door into the cold, crisp afternoon. A couple of hours passed by before Douglas and Chris decided to go searching for the wayward Anita.

Chris walked into a small pub in hopes of finding Anita there, but was disappointed. He sat down and ordered a drink. The waitress placed his drink down in front of him and struck up a conversation. When Anita entered the pub, by chance, she heard their laughter and gasped at the sight of them getting along so well. Chris caught sight of her just as she bolted out the door. Being the better runner of the pair, he easily caught up to her.

Anita had little success in keeping her mouth closed. Her teeth chattered as she said, "Chris, I can't blame you. You really should be spending your time with someone who has a simple life."

Taken aback, Chris thought over what she may have seen in the bar. When he realized what she thought she saw, he melted inside and full of love, said, "Anita, I love you. We were just talking. When you left in such a state, your father and I got worried after a couple of hours, split up, and began searching for you. I stepped into the pub to see if you were there or had been there, got thirsty, and ordered a drink. The waitress struck up a conversation because I was the only one around. I swear. Besides, I wouldn't know what to do with a normal life. I'm partial to chaos."

Falling into his arms and feeling his genuine warmth, Anita sobbed. "I thought you were turning against me and I was left to face life alone. I love you so much; I guess my jealous side surfaced. What an ugly sight."

"I kind of admire the ugly side," Chris said, laughing, and hugged his wife with pure passion.

Feeling Anita shivering, Chris pointed to the pub and Anita accepted. She raced him to the table where she sat down. He immediately took her jacket off and began rubbing her arms to bring back the circulation.

The waitress took their order, and when she returned, she leaned into Anita and whispered, "You're a lucky lady."

Raising her drink in the air, to the waitress, Anita replied, "That I am."

The walk back was invigorating. The lovers had a snowball fight and pushed each other into snow banks. There was also a serious side to the walk home, however, and Chris convinced Anita to meet her new family before she would regret not doing so. The excitement of this prospect, combined with their playfulness, set the pace for the walk; she couldn't wait to tell her dad.

When Douglas heard the news, sweat dripped down his forehead, but his heart danced wildly at the prospect of this family reunion. Life was going to be good. He picked up the phone to arrange for them all to sit down to a dinner and get acquainted.

CHAPTER THIRTY-FIVE

Just as Douglas, Anita and Chris were about to decamp to their dinner, Peter flew through the door and announced he had plans for the night and not to wait up for him. Peter then turned to look at the trio and smiling, he said, "Huh. You all seem uptight, like you're about to embark on some secret mission."

Anita's mouth fell open, and she replied, "What are you, psychic?"

Peter only laughed in reply, and then headed upstairs. The trio continued on their quest to the meeting of two worlds. They were the first to arrive, and as they waited, Anita felt conflicted. Part of her told her to relax and be herself, while the other side told her to have a drink to calm her nerves. Before she could make a decision, the other guests arrived and Anita couldn't help but admire her mother and sister; they were gorgeous. Not sure what the next move should be, Anita's face went bright red, when she realized she was staring. She waited for the others to be seated so she could plan her next move.

Introductions were awkward, but Anita took the initiative and went over to hug her mother and sister, hoping to shake off the eerie feeling that rippled inside her. The lump in Douglas's throat prevented him from speaking, and Chris smiled at the clumsy reunion.

Questions flew around the table as the group ate dinner. To Anita's surprise, she felt comfortable with these women, as though she had always known them, and couldn't wait to learn more about her family – her *real* family. When the questions subsided, everyone remained quiet. Keeping her silence no more, Anita directed her bold question to her father. "Why didn't you tell me I had a mother who would actually care when I was going through hell and needed support?"

The look on Suzanne's face denoted she was about to say something pertinent. "What do you mean *'going through hell?'*" she asked.

Trying to avoid her father's stunned look at the question, Anita suspected her father was once again holding back secrets. "It appears to me," she began, "that dad doesn't always divulge details that may or may not be important to others. I had a best friend, who was kidnapped, and then I was kidnapped. We were both reunited briefly. I got really sick and when we docked, we were separated. I was ill and nursed back to health and escaped, while she went to who knows where. I've been trying to find her. We, or I rather, believe the purpose was to be sold on the black market, but I think a client of my dad's has her being held hostage. A rescue was made, and things didn't go so well. My mother – or should I say Millie – is very angry with me and has kicked me out of her life. That about sums it up," Anita finished, and picked up her drink.

Suzanne was speechless and Shelan looked at her father in disbelief that he could treat his daughter so shabbily. Suzanne managed to gain her self-control, and asked, "Douglas, how could you let this happen? How could you not tell me? How could you not tell Anita she had support? Where are your brains located? Are they out partying and forgot to come home? Is that it?"

Not liking the line of questioning, Douglas took a firm stand. "All that happened while I was away. I didn't tell Anita because she had been through so much and I felt she wasn't ready for such truths. Now that I see how responsive she has been, I do wish I had told her. But I assure you, everything is being rectified as we speak."

Suzanne's self-assurance shone through like a spotlight. "I will accompany my daughter to make sure she stays safe," she said. "I lost her once, I shall not lose her again." Suzanne then turned to Shelan, and said, "Shelan, close your mouth. You have your own home, your own life, and do as you please. This is something I want to do, and I expect your support."

"But. It's very dangerous," Anita stuttered. "I mean you could get seriously hurt."

Suzanne straightened up and placed her hands on her hips. With authority, she said, "Yes – but I could get hurt crossing the street. The only way I'll not go with you, is if you tell me not to."

Anita's face broke out in a smile. "Welcome to a world of mystery," she said, and got up to hug her mother. Sheepishly, Anita looked at her sibling, and asked, "Mind if I borrow her for awhile?"

"Just make sure she returns. I've kind of gotten used to her ways," Shelan replied. Anita beamed as she and Shelan first shook hands and then hugged each other. Anita solemnly promised to safely return her mother, but couldn't promise that the experiences she was about to face would not change her disposition. Shelan did not like what she heard and had some reservations about her mother's plans. Suzanne reassured her daughter that everything would be okay, because living with Douglas, had toughened her up. Shelan gave her blessing, but still was not happy about where her mother was going – across several boarders to the out-backs and jungles: the land of drugs, black markets, and kidnappings. The country is steeped in slave trading, back to the 1600's.

While the women chattered about girl topics, the men wandered off to the side for their own chat. Looking at Douglas, Chris demanded, "What's with you and Dante? Do you realize that was a nightmare you put me in?"

Douglas's face became distorted and his lips curled into a frown as he replied, "He has what I want: Carolyn. I believe she is kept captive in his house. I've dug him out of so many problems, he should have a plaque in the hall of fame for guilt, and he should be placed in an isolation cell. Mark my words, he'll involve Anita at some point." Observing Chris's reaction, Douglas commented, "You already suspect that, don't you?"

Nodding his head he took a drink, confirming that he suspected as much. "Yup, and there's no stopping it. Is that why you are risking your life? To prevent Anita, from falling into his clutches? If that's so, just remember you created this mess by your ties to Dante. He'll use every possible angle to get what he wants. Me, I'm associated, but I'm careful not to get too involved. But now, it seems I, too, am in his little web. I love Anita and I don't want to see her get into his clutches, and I will do whatever it takes to keep her out of harms way."

"Don't tell any of this to Anita," Douglas said, securing the secret between them.

Placing a cross over to his heart, Chris vowed he wouldn't. "But," he added, "you can be sure she will piece it all together. She has a very sharp mind."

The men rejoined the group and Douglas stood back, proud that the reunion of mother and siblings was going so well. The men joined in the conversation, and time had a way of passing. It was very late when everyone left the restaurant. They headed to the condo, and fell asleep wherever there was a spot available. Anita felt strange as she watched her father enter a room with a woman who was not Millie, knowing they would be together for the entire night. But a small glow ignited within her, and Anita beamed; for the first time in her life, she had a mother who truly believed in her.

Unable to sleep, Anita finally got up out of bed. Careful not to wake Chris, or any of their guests, she padded to the kitchen and brewed some coffee. Absorbed in her own thoughts, a rustling behind her made her freeze in her tracks. Her back arched like a cobra taken off guard, and she slowly turned around. When she saw Suzanne, she let out a huge sigh. "You scared me... I'm sorry but I'm not comfortable calling you 'Mom' yet. Give me a little time."

Getting a cup for coffee, Suzanne smiled genuinely. In a soft voice she said, "I'd be happy with 'hey you' right now. So, what are your plans?"

Sitting down at the kitchen island, with her cup in her hand, Anita waited for the coffee to finish brewing. "I've been here for less than two days," she said. "In that time, I've found out I have a new family, met my wonderful family members, and discovered that I have a mother who, despite never meeting me before, is willing to put her life in turmoil in order to support me. I've also found that, in spite of how crazy it sounds, it all makes perfect serene sense. And amongst it all, I know that I still need to go back and rescue Carolyn. Does that make sense to you?"

Placing her hand on her daughter's, Suzanne's frankness was supportive. "Yes," she said. "We'll go shopping tomorrow and I'll get Douglas to book us on the next flight back. I need to buy some proper clothing, if I want to fit into your world. Mine is dull and I need to bring a little life back into it myself. You okay with that?"

Anita's eyes couldn't focus through the film of tears that had formed in her eyes. She sniffed, and said, "I'd be a fool to say no, but there really is danger. I'd feel awful if anything happened to you."

Shushing her daughter, Suzanne replied, "It's my choice. Now tell me more about you. Your father has only told me enough to keep me satisfied, but I would like more details. Let me explain a few things. When you were conceived, Douglas was in a state of shock and instead of working it out, he just took you away. I was devastated and couldn't fight back. I was young and naïve; he was rich and powerful. All he had to do was snap his fingers, and he was granted everything he wanted. After he pulled the dominance card, I had no job, no money, no family, and no place to stay. He knew this and bought me off. I knew I couldn't provide for you, and I was grateful you would grow up with everything you needed. I went back to school, became a nurse, and took charge of my life. For whatever reason, Douglas reentered my life, rekindling the resentment and animosity between us, sending my defenses up. But, I had to admit, I was still in love with the lug and slowly, brick by brick, the wall came down. This time Shelan happened and things were good, but deep down I was still hoping for a reunion with you." Kissing her daughter, Suzanne continued, "Enough for tonight. I know I asked you to talk about you, but I think you needed to hear my side of the story, and I hope I haven't chased you away. We'll start again in the next few days, and I'm elated about that. My life is complete."

Chris entered the kitchen as Suzanne was walking out. They hugged in the doorway, and then each continued on. Finding Anita slumped over the table, Chris lovingly kissed her neck. She perked up when he said, "Can't sleep, huh?"

"I'm overwhelmed about the turn of events. I keep pinching myself. I have a mother who doesn't know me at all, and yet, will give me all her support. I can't help but wonder how someone could leave an already established life for one that is full of upheaval," Anita stated, dramatically.

Chris said tenderly, "Suzanne strikes me as the kind of woman, who, when her mind is make up, puts her all into it. Now my little lucky charm, let's get a little shut-eye and see what a new day brings." Happy to have such an understanding man, Anita didn't need a second invitation to share his bed; she was ready to snuggle up to his warmth.

Greeting the day with such a lighthearted spirit, Anita found it to be beautiful, peaceful, and with no burdens or worries. But that soon diminished when a feeling that something was amiss stirred in the back of her head, and she knew that only time would reveal the mystery. Giving herself a lecture to focus on now, and not on what could be, Anita joined her mother and sister in a day of shopping and gaiety. At one point during the day Carolyn's face appeared, and Anita felt almost guilty for enjoying her new life, and said a little prayer: "Your spirit is always with me and will share in my happiness and sorrows, but today we are going to rejoice for the start of a new beginnings."

After such a long day, Anita felt her ribs sending sharp stabs through her. She knew she had better rest, and dragging her weary body up the stairs, she fell deeply asleep. Chris quietly snuck into the room, and cuddled beside her. Instead of resting, though, his thoughts whirled around him. He was not aware that Anita had awoken, and her words hit him like a bomb. "Chris how do you feel about kids?" she asked.

Like someone had shot him in the stomach, Chris jumped up with a start and his voice held total surprise. "Excuse me?"

Dreamily, Anita reworded her statement. "How many do you want?"

Trying not to sound like he was against the idea of children, Chris stammered, "What are you implying, exactly?"

Anita sat up, and said apologetically, "I'm sorry. I didn't mean to imply I was pregnant. What I was trying to say was, that I want children. Do you?"

Chris's heart resumed its normal rate. His voice was less agitated when he replied, "Keep what I say in a rational mind. Can you do that?" He felt her nod, and continued, "I would like you to stay here for a couple of weeks with your mother and sister. Get to know them better. After the camp was blown to bits, Dante cannot be trusted, and I want to keep you out of his claws. Do you agree?"

Her first reaction was anger, but the thought of his mother's death slowed down her reaction, and she sighed. "Does it really have to be two weeks? I don't think I can handle being away from you that long?"

He had expected her to blow up and be defensive. He felt her forehead to see if she was running a fever, and found her temperature to be normal. "Okay," he said. "What gives? Where's my Anita?"

Avoiding his question, Anita answered him with a question of her own. "Chris do you know anything else surrounding your mother's death?"

Getting off the bed, Chris paced back and forth before stopping at the window and letting his memories take over. "The best I can figure, she found my father with another woman and they had an argument. Whether that's true, remains a riddle. The bits of data I accumulated told me that my father took her to the abandoned campsite, left her there, and came home alone. Her death certificate read: she self-inflicted the gun shot to the side of her head - so it was classified as a suicide and the case was closed. I can't see my father doing that, but he was a man with strange ways. I couldn't prove it, so I had to give him the benefit of the doubt. I don't know why you are asking me this now, unless this has something to do with the change of attitude."

Anita's body began to vibrate at such a tragedy, and she asked, "What a barbaric and inhumane way to die. Did you ever discuss it with your father?"

"Yes, but he just shrugged it off and told me she died of natural causes. It wasn't until after his death that I found out she had died at the camp and nothing else was verified. It wouldn't surprise me that Dante was a part of it. That, to me, makes more sense. My father would defend the man no matter what he did. My mother and I were not close, but a part of me feels like I let her down by not looking into her death." Then conveying his secret desire to Anita, Chris said, "Now to answer your question, yes I want a couple of kids."

Standing beside him, Anita's warmth and caring shone like a heat source. She draped her arms around him, and whispered, "Our kids will be close to us, and we'll always be there for them. Our parents missed out on so much, that I feel sorry for them. That won't happen with us."

Running his hands over her arms, Chris pieced it all together. "*That* is why you aren't going to argue about staying for a couple of weeks. So what's the real story behind it," Chris said, genuinely wanting to know where her mind was going.

Anita dropped her eyes and lowered her voice. "I love you and we have a lifetime together," she said. "I've been selfish and demanding and haven't taken the time to consider your feelings. So this time I'll abide by your wishes and, even though I'll miss you, I'll stay put."

Putting his hand under her chin and lifting her head up so her eyes met his, Chris said, "There will never be another woman for me. You are my world. I want to grow old with you and explore the future together. If you return with me right now, it's hard to know what Dante will do. I know he'll use you at his convenience. And, you can use this time to decide if you really want your mother with you."

As if a magnet were holding them together, Anita said breathlessly, "Chris, you're the greatest man on earth. When are you thinking of leaving?"

Chris thought about it, and replied, "I'll send Peter home, and take your dad with me… I'm thinking tomorrow."

Letting a tear escape down her cheek, Anita said, "Well, that means we have little homework to catch up on, so you will be all mine tonight. On the subject of files, is 'Bedo' the code name for my father?"

"Yes. Your father is the CO. How did you piece it together?" Chris asked, wanting to know more details of her logic.

"We haven't had a lot of time to talk. Jeremy told me when I went to see him. I thought my father was a lawyer, not an agent. What is he?" she asked.

Responding to Anita's question Chris said, gravely, "He's both, but I know something has gone wrong. Being in both professions, one always turn sour on you."

Sitting down, totally confused, Anita tried desperately to clear her thoughts. She wanted clarification from Chris. "Let me get this straight," she said. "He's a lawyer defending Dante, but also an agent who is working against his client, and could be disbarred if he leaks privileged client information. That would explain the raid on the camps, but how can he use the information without destroying himself? Why would he not step down and let someone else prosecute Dante – unless he plays a bigger part than that, and he can't turn away. What do you think?"

Chris didn't have to say a word; his facial expression said it all – Anita knew her father was suspected of treason. She also knew she should not ask any more questions, so she changed the subject. "So, what do you think of my new family addition?"

His eyes softened at the change in conversation, and he smiled, saying, "You are a very lucky young lady. Deep down, do you really want your mother to accompany you home? Think about it."

Playing with her rings seemed to create an energy that helped in clarifying her inner feelings. She stopped toying with them, looked up at Chris, and honestly replied, "Yes I do." She found an easement as she looked into his eyes and continued on a different track. "You realize I'll be home in two weeks no matter what happens. Oh, and one more thing, what if they choose you to set an example, what will you do then? I mean they seem to be dumping on you for my father's faults."

Amazed at how quickly Anita could change the subject, Chris said simply, "We'll cross that bridge if we have to."

"You realize I'll come for you should they take you, don't you?" Anita said, sternly.

"I'd rather you didn't," Chris replied, trying to convey how he felt.

Her words were like snapping dragons. "No one is going to hurt you or steal you, if I have anything to say about it. Call me selfish, but I'll not stand by and do nothing. You of all people should know that."

Chris stifled a giggle, and said, "Anita has returned. But, really, don't come looking for me again. Why should both of us be wiped out of the picture?"

Anita threw a pillow at him and got up to kiss him. "That'll never happen," she replied. "We're too good to let that happen to us. Now we must get down to real business," she said, and led him willing back to the bed, to begin the first lesson of their homework.

The next morning, sitting and relaxing in the living room, Chris and Douglas were working out their agendas, when Peter finally showed up. He was grateful for the wonderful hospitality and the freedom to explore on his own, but when he saw the devotion and love between Anita and Chris, he reflected on his own life and knew he had some changes to make. To his surprise, Peter was handed his airline ticket from Chris and his departure time was for early the next morning and he took it as a cue his services were no longer needed. He talked for a bit to his friends, and then headed up stairs to pack his belongings – happier than he had been in a long time.

Because of flight schedules, Chris and Douglas were leaving the same time as Peter, so in the wee hours of the morning, Anita watched them leave. She found it hard to accept Chris would not be there when she needed a hug, but she knew that two weeks were not a lifetime.

Excitedly, she turned to her new family and let the two weeks unfold new experiences. The shopping, dinners, meeting Suzanne and Shelan's friends filled in the gap, and before she knew it, the weeks went faster than anyone could imagine. Time had a way of fast forwarding and Anita and Suzanne were now boarding a plane and waving goodbye to Shelan.

CHAPTER THIRTY-SIX

On the plane Anita and Suzanne were, for the most part, quiet. Suzanne was feeling hyper because she was stepping into the unknown. She was scared half to death by the journey; but excitement was there in equal measure, making her heart pound wildly as she embarked on an adventure with her first child.

As the plane landed, Suzanne had to hold Anita down in her seat until it was safe to disembark. Anita's zealousness was apparent. As she stepped out onto the top step of the plane's ladder, Anita panicked; neither her father nor Chris was visible among those waiting at the small airport. Alarms sounded in her head as she frantically scanned the grounds, already anticipating the worst. Out of the corner of her eye, Anita saw a woman point to her as she handed a baggage worker something small. The man immediately headed towards Anita. Doing an about face, Anita grabbed her mother and they sat back down on the seat in the plane, to wait for the employee to reach them. Anita's hands shook as he handed her a note. The paper rattled and terror swept through her body as she read: *"Dante has Chris. They are after you and they are on the grounds. Be careful. Maureen."*

Wiping the tears from her face, Anita looked up and her voice held sadness. "Mom, we're in trouble," she said. "They have Chris and they want me too. They don't know you, so would you go rent a car and drive by the plane so I can jump in? They will frown upon such action, but we need to get out of here alive." Suzanne nodded that she would do just that, and Anita continued, "don't use your real name, and pay in cash. Oh yeah, welcome to my nightmare. You can always go back. I'd understand."

Her mother demonstrated her determination, and said, "I'm staying. I'll be right back."

Amazed at her mother's reaction, Anita's broad grin showed that she was happy she was staying; Anita knew her mother could be counted on in times of trouble. Suzanne didn't hurry to fulfill Anita's request, but rather walked at a normal pace, hoping not to give away their plan. Her heart was thumping hard; she thought for sure it could be heard across the airfield.

Minutes ticked by and Anita became antsy. She apologized profusely to the employees explaining she must remain on the plane until her ride arrived; her life was in danger. Once she showed them the note, they sat watch for her. Out of the corner of her eye through the window, Anita spotted a fast-moving vehicle headed her way. She hurriedly ran down the steps, tripping and tumbling to the ground. A few of the airline crewmembers were standing around and helped Anita back onto her feet. The speeding car's passenger door flew open and Anita jumped in yelling, "Thank you," as they sped away.

Peering behind them, Anita could see they were being followed; she racked her brain for a spot to hide. Suzanne yelled at her asking what direction to take. Anita finally located a place in her mind, and directed her mother towards it. Hiding in the bush, they shut off the car's engine, checking every angle to see if their predators were close by. About an hour went by and still no one came into view. Anita had it in her mind that they would be nabbed the minute they reappeared on the road, so the two took refuge on foot, praying they wouldn't get lost.

Walking as quietly as they could, they looked over their shoulders often to ensure they were still alone. Every so often they sat down, well hidden, to rest. Then they heard voices in the near distance, and crouching down to remain out of sight, Anita peered around. Surprised, she recognized one of the men as Gappy. Never so happy to see anyone, she ran out to greet him. When he saw her, his face went pale as a ghost, and Anita couldn't help but notice.

Taking a chance, Anita explained her dilemma as best she could, and he told her he would take care of it. Anita handed him the keys to the car, and called her mother out from her hiding spot. Gappy then sent his man to retrieve their car, and he personally drove the ladies to his village.

Suzanne was very paranoid and, when they stopped at the village, she had to be almost scrapped off the seat of the vehicle because of her reluctance to get out. Anita explained that Gappy was a friend and would help them do whatever was necessary to rescue Chris, and get them all home safely. The smell of food cooking made their mouths water, and they ate the meal presented to them as though they hadn't eaten in a week. While indulging in such a marvelous meal, Anita turned to Gappy, and asked, "Gappy, how is it you were there? I mean your timing couldn't have been more perfect?"

Not liking being asked about his whereabouts, Gappy stated, "Trying to catch a tiger. Brings in good money."

Anita was going to argue that she didn't see any guns for such an event, but she closed off her thoughts and went with the fact he was helping her, and left it at that. The villagers decided a night of festivities would help ease the tension; everyone sat back and enjoyed the night's events.

The early morning sun shone into their little huts, and when they poked their noses out, a feast and laughter greeted them. After the meal was consumed, Gappy took his guests to the side and in very explicit detail, mapped out his rescue plan. Upon hearing the plan, Anita interjected; it was dangerous, she said, and he should reconsider. But Gappy reaffirmed his intentions and stated that Chris was a friend who needed assistance. He added that Anita and Suzanne could stay in the village as long as they needed.

Taking advantage of their quiet time as the men assembled their equipment, Anita and Suzanne explored the mountains and all that Mother Nature had to offer, bringing tranquility deep into their souls. Approaching the village, Suzanne poked Anita in the shoulder and pointed towards the men talking to Gappy. They took refuge amongst the brush until the intruders left. Peering around like bandits hoping for a clear passage, mother and daughter quickly approached Gappy. Although he was happy to see them, he made them move quickly, all but shoving them into a little hut. He then gave them instructions to stay put and not to utter a word.

To Anita and Suzanne, it seemed the clock stood still. Finally someone entered their lodgings and they were stunned at the man's appearance. His face was painted and he looked like he was going on a manhunt. Plans of Dante's house were presented to them, and an X marked the specific spot in the house where Chris was being held hostage. Every detail of the plan was timed to the second, and Anita marveled at the sheer strength of the friendship that this plan sought to save. A loud voice startled both woman and, suddenly, they were face to face with Douglas. All three were stunned, momentarily speechless.

Douglas's loud voice was heard down the valley as he directed his exasperation towards Anita. "What the hell are you doing here?" he demanded.

217

Assuming a matching attitude, Anita responded, "We were warned that Dante had Chris and that I was his next target. Landing here was a fluke. Are you disappointed we're safe, or what?"

Anita swore she saw froth forming in the corner of her father's mouth as he snarled, "I didn't see you at the airport. How did you end up here?"

"We were there for some time, and never saw you anywhere on the grounds," Suzanne said, in an accusing tone.

Douglas's face went bright red, like someone who had been caught in a lie, and abruptly changed the subject. "This plan of yours must cease right now. Chris will know and understand when no one shows up."

Wide-eyed, Anita sprung to her feet and grabbed her father's shirt collar. "To you he's just an agent," she growled. "To me, he's my husband and will father my children. I already told him that should any harm come to him, I would come after him, and I will do just that – with or without your help. You do whatever it takes to help out, or you walk away. Your choice." She released her grip on his shirt collar, and added, "We are here because this area was a little familiar to me, and we parked our car, and walked on foot, met up with Gappy and the rest you know. You knew that anyway. There isn't much that gets by you."

"Douglas, how could you be so cold-hearted," Suzanne said, with a disappointed look on her face.

Shooting daggers from his eyes, Douglas replied, "You stay out of things you know nothing about. Do you hear me?"

"You brought me to my daughter and for that I thank you. But, I know a human being when I see one, but right now, I don't recognize you at all," Suzanne retorted.

Anita couldn't keep her mouth shut. "Why are you here?" she demanded. "At Gappy's I mean. How did you know we were here?"

Douglas stormed out of the hut and disappeared into thin air. Anita turned to Suzanne and burst out laughing. "In all my years, I've never seen anyone stand up to my dad like you just did. I'm impressed."

High-fiving each other, the ladies turned back to the men who were sitting on the floor waiting to go over the plans. Anita couldn't just let other people do all the work, and demanded that she be allowed into the house, as part of the rescue operation. She was shot down more than once, but when she told them she had been to the house before and could handle the mission, she was finally granted her wish. Suzanne volunteered to go as far as the gates, and now all they needed was nightfall.

As dusk settled in, the group boarded the jeeps and began their journey. By the time they arrived at Dante's, it was dark. Anita watched the men move swiftly and was amazed at their professionalism.

One of the men jumped the fence, avoiding setting off the laser light beams by wearing infrared glasses, and was able to reach the house with little difficultly. One minute he was with them, and the next it was as if the house had swallowed him up – he became invisible to the naked eye. Minutes ticked by and finally Anita got the go ahead to scale the fence. This time, she was provided proper equipment and she laughed, thinking this was way easier than when she had last done it.

The young man, who had entered the house, blew the breaker and hooked up a video to the surveillance cameras, before turning on the lights again in the house. Dante panicked and sent some men to scout out the premises. Hearing the extra footsteps pounding around the grounds, the invaders halted their movements. When all was quiet again, they resumed their posts. Anita was handed a little box with many buttons on it, should they get into trouble. She was told this would provide the diversion to enable their escape. Using sign language, two men along side Anita, snuck down the corridors noiselessly. One young man was surprised at how skillfully Anita maneuvered around, and was glad she didn't compromise their being in the house.

Hearing someone approach, they scurried to find shelter. Sweat trickled down their backs and face as they waited for the moment to pass so they could continue on their way. Quietly, they resumed their journey and found the den door ajar. They held their breath as they peered in, but saw no one. They agreed that Chris was probably being held in Dante's private room, but neither of them had any idea where that room might be. Listening in for further instructions through their earpieces as to where to go, they got no reception and had to rely on their own intellect. They traveled the corridors discreetly and listened at each door until they found the right one.

The element of surprise was to their advantage. One of the young men accompanying Anita, bolted through the door, taking everyone in the room off guard, while Anita snuck in and stood beside Dante with a revolver in her hand, pointing it straight at his head. No one dared move.

Proud of herself for capturing everyone's attention, Anita cocked the hammer back and spoke in a low, soft, yet demanding voice. "Mr. Dante," she said. "Now that I have your undivided attention, what have you done with Chris?"

Considering that this was the second time she had successfully snuck into his house, Dante was naturally worried about the caliber of his protection. She smiled as he asked, "How'd you get in?"

Resisting the urge to gloat, Anita answered quickly, "I'm a woman of many talents."

Dante lowered his eyes. When he spoke again, his voice was intimidating. "I could've had you blown away before this, if I had wanted to."

"I'm sure you could've." Anita replied simply. "You brought me into this mess, so let's negotiate a way out and go our separate ways." Despite her calm exterior, every organ of her body felt like jelly.

Sweat was beginning to slide down Dante's face, and he relented. "If I ask my men to leave, would you put your gun down?"

Hesitating, Anita looked at the young man who had first entered the room. He nodded for her to agree, and she replied, "Okay, but my man will keep his gun pointed for my safety. If any harm comes to Chris, I swear I'll not be held responsible for what happens to you."

Giving his men the nod to leave, Anita sat directly in front of Dante with her gun resting by her side. This prompted him to speak. "Go home," he said. "This is between Chris and myself, and besides I thought you wanted to shoot him at one time."

"We live like two people working against each other, but in actual fact, he is my husband, and I'll not rest until he's home. He's done nothing to harm you, I assure you," Anita said, with conviction in her voice.

Dante made his point known by yelling, "He betrayed me."

"How?" Anita yelled back. "You asked him to do you a favor, he got shot in the process, and *he* betrayed *you*? Not likely – unless he was suicidal. I have no idea what business you two have, but I do know he is loyal and keeps people's confidences. Now hand him over or I'll take him by force. What's it going to be?" Anita said, with such certainty that Dante couldn't resist engaging.

Anita was sure there was a snake in the room as Dante hissed at her, "If I do, would you stay away?"

"You don't get off that easily," Anita stated. "You still have Carolyn, and I want her back. Then, I'll stay out of your way." Her eyes were steady, as she waited for his reply.

"You can sure tell you're Douglas's child," Dante remarked.

Anita's lip began to quiver, while trying to stifle a snort, and she said, "I'm a individual who was kidnapped, brought overseas, became very ill, fell in love, escaped, got my law degree, and came back to find my friend. I'm someone who wants to have a normal life. What my father does is his business. What Chris does is his and my business. What you do is my business until I get satisfaction. My brother was taken from me, and I'll not take kindly to that happening to anyone else I love. Whatever business you have legal or otherwise, is not my concern. I want what's left of my family, intact. That's all."

For the first time, Dante stopped and stared at her for a few long moments. Then he announced, "I'll let Chris go, but should I find out he double-crossed me, you'll never see him again. Are we clear?"

Anita nodded her head fervently, and waited for the transition to take place. She was shocked when Chris was brought in all bloodied, barely able to walk or talk. Irate, Anita blew out her words like a fire hose putting out a fire. "How could you treat someone who is loyal to you like that? Are you human?" She retracted her statement then, and said, "Never mind, tycoons have no heart. I'm saddened and angered that you would do this. I ought to blow up your house or something of value to see how you'd feel. You think you are so well protected, and that no one can harm you. Well, you are only on top until someone better out-climbs you."

With that bold statement, Anita hit the panic button and blew up his back fence and shed. Dante got up to watch them burn, and Anita sneered, "You're only as good as you think you are. I could've blown you away and if I could do it once, I can do it again. If you hurt me, Chris, or anyone I'm associated with, I'd be looking over my shoulder, that is if I were you."

Dante looked at Anita and then at Chris. "You are not what I expected," he said. "No one has ever taken action like this right in front of my eyes. You have proven that you could be an asset to me, because you are up-front, bold, brazen, and wouldn't do anything behind one's back that you wouldn't in front of their face. I like that. I may have a proposition for you in the future."

Spitting on the floor, Anita's anger lit her up like a fiery dragon. "I'll never work for evil," she said, and then added, "but I respect you, as I believe you are a man of your word."

Stoking his chin, Dante looked at Chris, and said, "I may have been wrong about you, but I will tell you this. Had she not come for you, you would never have seen her beautiful face again. As for Carolyn, we'll negotiate about that sometime in the future. Now, you have ten minutes to leave the grounds, after that..." Dante stopped talking and started watching the minutes on the clock ticking away.

Chris was untied and carried out by Dante's men. As they approached the gate, help was there to secure Chris into the vehicle and as they sped off, a spray of gravel hit up against the gate causing dents. Dante was amazed how Anita and her partners had rigged the video cameras, maneuvered through the laser beams, and found him in his own home without being detected. All this made him smile; he knew Anita was smart, and he knew he would recruit her and her skills in negotiations. In the end, they would both get what they wanted.

All the way home Chris remained silent, and this bothered Anita; she hoped he would, in time, forgive her for coming after him. When they arrived at the house, Chris headed straight for the shower and then crawled into bed, giving Anita the silent treatment. She knew better than to talk, and instead, let him get it out of his system.

Delia was gracious enough to make a meal for all those who participated in the rescue, and after everyone had filled their bellies, they vanished like gypsies of the night. Suzanne wanted to know what had taken place, and Anita told her every detail. Suddenly, feeling like a ghost was present, Anita looked up to see Chris standing there with anger written on his face. Suzanne knew the look and left the room, leaving the two to sort things out.

Anita had not seen this side of Chris before. Angrily he said, "What in the hell did you think you were doing?"

Trying to keep calm, Anita stammered, "When you and my father weren't there to greet us at the airport, someone passed me a note telling me that Dante was holding you hostage, and that I was next on the hit list. So, my mother rented a car, met up with me at the plane – with shots being fired at us, I must add – and we headed out. I remembered a road you had taken once and we veered off. Scared of getting caught by taking the car back on the road, we headed off on foot. By chance, we met up with Gappy. He offered to help out, and I volunteered my services for the rescue mission. So tell me, what does Gappy have to do with this? He's brilliant at what he does, so I'm guessing he's an agent. How close am I?"

Plopping himself down on the couch, Chris was awestruck at what had happened, and said, "I don't believe it. Anita, you must have horseshoes planted in your skin, because Gappy is not an agent. He organizes or smuggles people into forbidden territories. He's very hard to locate, and charges astronomical fees. What did he charge you?" While waiting for her reply, Chris's eyes focused for a couple of seconds on his father's picture, and then he directed them back to his wife.

"Nothing, I swear," Anita responded, and was surprised at what Chris had told her.

Shaking his head, Chris had a hard time fathoming Gappy's motivation, and asked again, "He did this on his own?"

Unhappy at his mistrust of her account of the situation, Anita said, "I told you, when he heard Dante had you, he arranged everything. He asked for nothing in return – but come to think of it, my father showed up while we were at Gappy's. He shouted at me to let the matter lie and left in a stew when I said I was going after you. Dante would've killed you, would he not have?"

Stretching his legs, Chris got up to get a drink and spoke with uncertainty. "I want a detailed report of everything that happened, starting from when you arrived on the plane. I'll get my tape recorder. Something is wrong."

Before he could leave the room, Anita went over to him, and asked, "Do I get a welcome home kiss?" She batted her eyes.

Chris turned away and as he left the room, he called over his shoulder, "I'm still upset with you. I told you not to come."

Running after him, Anita turned him around so they were face-to-face. "You can be hard and cold," she said, "but I love you and if I can, I'll do whatever it takes to have you near me. You've taught me about survival, love, honesty, and to be cunning. If it were me he had, you'd come for me. So what makes the difference? You're a male and I'm a female. Is that it?"

Longing to hold her, Chris kept his distance and maintained his coolness. "You don't understand," he replied. "Had he gotten his hands on you, he could've sold you, or used you for negotiation power, or even raped you. Who knows? I love you so much it scares me to think that someone might hurt you. Are you following me on this?" he asked.

His words hit home making her feel ashamed of her rash behavior. She lowered her head and nodded that she completely understood. He then grabbed her close and his cold exterior melted as he kissed her passionately; she became jellied and soft inside.

The two sat down and while the events were still fresh in her mind, Chris had her repeat the entire procedure from beginning to end. He dared not say anything as she spoke, but was mystified at everything that had unfolded. Once everything had been recorded, Chris was about to ask Anita some questions when Douglas walked in. The shocked expression on his face told them that he knew something, but he began firing questions at Anita. "Just what the hell is going on here? What did you promise Dante in exchange for Chris?"

Chris said, coolly, "Honey, would you go make us a drink and then we'll play the tape for your father? Douglas, do not say a word until you've heard the whole tape."

Suzanne was invited to sit and share in the conversation, much against Douglas's protest. Anita argued that if she had missed a step, her mother could correct it right then and there. All sitting comfortably with a drink in their hand, Chris was about to play the tape when Anita's drink sprung a leak and she got up to fix herself a new one, making Chris laugh. He knew he was the luckiest man alive. When Anita sat down, Chris could tell the drinks had hit her, but he made no comment and cuddled her as the tape played.

When it was finished, Douglas was stunned and stared at his daughter, and said, "Dante never makes deals or lets anyone go unless there's something in it for him. What did you neglect to tell us?"

Chris stepped in to protect Anita. "Dante has something in mind for Anita and traded my freedom for it. He'd trade his mother if he thought he could away with it. It's all a game. What I want to know is how did you know where to find Gappy and the ladies?"

Douglas knew he was going to be interrogated, and declared, "I don't need to answer your questions? What I do is my business."

Suzanne, who had chosen to keep out of the squabble, now found her voice. "You'll answer the question," she said. "We looked for you and you weren't there. Your daughter's life was at stake."

Gazing at Suzanne always mellowed him, and he then looked at his daughter and realized he was outnumbered. "I must admit that you are one smart young lady," he said. "I knew Dante had his men at the airport waiting for you, so I hid. When Suzanne showed up in the car, I couldn't see what was happening as people surrounded the area for whatever reason.

You then climbed into the car and I sent a man to follow you. He saw you talking to Gappy, so I knew where to find everyone. Gappy's whereabouts are not a total secret. Once I'd found you, I said my peace and left."

Though she was feeling dulled by the liquor, Anita's reply was sharp. "When you barged in here just now, you never expected to see Chris, did you Dad? What did you expect to find? I don't think I can count on you for support in the future. You were willing to leave Chris for dead."

Douglas knew his daughter well, and he knew that every word she spoke she would uphold. "You don't understand," he pleaded.

Chris intervened with kind, but strong words. "Douglas, you are in over your head. Maybe you should sit back, and let someone else take over. It's not too late."

Douglas's response was out of character for him. He mellowed with words that sounded like defeat. "It's not what it seems and it isn't that easy."

"Dad, what is it that Dante wants or expects from you? Better yet, what does he have over you? Blackmail?" Anita said, trying to make her father talk.

Douglas's quiet moment turned to rage. "I don't need this. Suzanne, you and I are on the next flight home," he yelled, and headed towards the door.

Stepping into Douglas's path, Suzanne stood with her arms crossed and said with determination, "Don't you ever tell me what to do. I know where my priorities lie. Can you say the same? Besides, the kids are trying to help you, so give them some kind of consideration."

Douglas picked up an ornament and threw it across the room, smashing it into a thousand little pieces. His temper was explosive. "Pack your bags," he ordered again. "We're leaving."

Anita couldn't take any more. She ran after her father and tackled him to the ground. He threw her off and their eyes met, equally fiery. "Don't you ever do that to me again," Douglas said, to his daughter.

Getting into an upright position, Anita's temper was like a volcano about to erupt. "You barge in like a wounded bear, throw accusations around, bark orders, throw a temper tantrum, and *how dare I tackle you?* Dad, I love you, but you're a miserable man, and we are the only ones who can help you. Why would you want to walk away? Either you're on Dante's payroll for reasons other than that you're his lawyer, or you've messed up so badly, you don't want anyone to trace your ineptness, and ethics. Which is it?"

Ignoring his daughter, Douglas pulled Suzanne towards the stairs. She yanked back, breaking his hold. No one dared move, and Suzanne's words were soft, "Calm down first, then we can go to bed. It's been a very trying day for everyone. Let's go for a walk to the beach. It might help to put things into perspective."

Anita watched her father cave, and walk like an old man down the path to the beach with her mother. She felt his pain, but until he told them everything, there was nothing anyone could do for him.

Anita went into the kitchen and made herself a cup of coffee, and sat on the deck. Chris said he needed a little time to think, and went out towards the back of the house to release some frustrations. His thoughts of what had happened in the past few days came fast and furious. He didn't know what he wanted. He was angry with Anita for coming to his aide, yet he was happy she did so. He was upset she had to negotiate for his freedom, and yet he was pleased to be home. He was disillusioned by Douglas's reaction, and yet he was blown away at how his mother-in-law handled Douglas.

Giving Chris a few extra minutes of quiet time, Anita then went around back and approached him by waving a surrender stick, making him laugh. He threw his arms around her tightly and kissed her with such fury, she didn't want to let go. The excitement between them was deep with passion. Not caring if anyone found them, they made love right there amongst the colorful arrangements of nature's beauty. They were so elated with life that nothing would deter their love.

Heading back to the house for a much-needed cup of coffee, Anita's head quit swimming in love thoughts, and began to notice her surroundings. Now studying Chris, she noticed the wounds on his body and shrieked. Her reaction caused him to quickly put his shirt back on. Before they'd even been back in the house for a minute, Anita was asking Delia to make one of her magic poultices. Delia didn't need prompting in conjuring up her special healing bag. While Anita was applying the cool, homemade cure to Chris's wounds, Douglas and Suzanne entered the room.

Suzanne couldn't help staring at the open sores and commented that they looked like whip marks. Chris confirmed her guess to be accurate. Anita bore holes into her father's soul, promoting him to speak in his defense. "I'm not ready to be interrogated and need time to sort things out," was all he said.

Anita looked at Chris as he put his shirt on, and then she glanced back at her father. Nonchalantly, Douglas said, "You two take your time, because Chris and I have some unfinished business to tend to."

Anita nodded to her mother and the two ladies left the room, went to the liquor station, poured themselves a drink, and headed to the porch to bask in the serenity that surrounded the house. Anita raised her glass in cheers, to the acknowledgment, that they both knew the truth; her father was knee-deep in muck and was not yet ready to be pulled out to safety. After their night cap, it was obvious the men weren't ready to leave their conversation, the mother and daughter walked up the stairs together, and then went in their separate directions; it had been a hard day and a good nights sleep was needed.

CHAPTER THIRTY-SEVEN

After breakfast, Chris convinced Anita to join him in a mystery ride. Eager not to be alone, Anita jumped into the car and looked over at Chris, pulling a long face. "You still haven't forgiven me for recuing you at Dante's, have you?"

"Yes and no. I'm grateful to have my freedom, and to be with you, but my concern is for you. He's got something in mind for you and I can guarantee you won't be able to back out. That's why you were free to go unharmed that night," Chris said, gravely.

"If it should ever happen again, I can't say what I'd do. That is something the both of us will have deal with; my impulsiveness. Besides, there is no one else in this world that can put up with me. So, dear sir, you are stuck with me. Deal with it," she said, laughing until she had tears in her eyes. Chris smiled involuntarily.

He patted her hand, and said, "I love you, too."

Because of the conversation they were having, Anita had been unaware of where they were and, without any warning, her thoughts tuned-in to their surroundings. The dense trees and shrubbery almost jumped out at her, and couldn't believe how quickly her mind had changed. She could now see the true charm that was before her: the prettiest flowers peeked their little heads through the underbrush, exposing their vibrant colors. The road was very windy, and if she hadn't been buckled in, she would've flown out, because Chris had to dodge huge potholes and boulders in the roadway. They came to a stop in the most peculiar place, and Chris pointed to a tiny shed that was well hidden amongst the trees. They began their walk through the overgrown brush that tangled around their feet. Anita could feel herself falling, and hung onto Chris for support. They both tumbled to the ground. A smile appeared on Chris's face and right then he confirmed to himself that no one could even come close to the woman he married. He pulled her to her feet and they pushed onward.

Inside the shed was an ATV bike, which Chris climbed on and started up, leaving Anita speechless. Chris explained that this was the only way to get to the top of the mountain and gestured for her to hop on the back. Still not knowing where they were headed, other than up the mountainside, Anita's trust in Chris told her to go along for the ride.

Seeing the doubt written on her face, Chris took the time to clarify his motives. "Gappy and I have been friends for some time. He lets me use this when I need to contact him, and this location is where he hangs out the most. He has other places as well, but this is his own private hideout, so let's go. Time is wasting."

Anita threw her leg over the seat and hung on, greeting the new adventure with ease. After a few minutes of riding, she could see why the bike was a necessary tool; they had to cross some rough terrain, and she was almost knocked off a few times. She took a look behind them, and saw that the view was astounding. The underbrush swallowed up their trail. It moved back into place after they passed, making it appear as though no one had traveled there.

They waited there, at the top, and Gappy soon appeared, joining them at the end of the trail. "Gappy, how do I repay you?" Chris asked. "Anita says you didn't ask her for any form of payment. I don't get it?"

Staring at the couple for some time, Gappy quietly replied, "The payment will keep for now. All I can say is that Anita has Dante wrapped around her finger, and I may take advantage of that. But for now, go and I will be in touch."

Before they departed Anita found her voice, and asked, "What do you know about my father?"

"Can you handle the truth?" Gappy asked, and when Anita nodded her head, he continued. "Let's say he's not one to be trusted, now. He's been known to cross sides, but you, Anita are honest, and I will trust you. That's all for now."

Gappy signaled them off by waving his hands and he turned his back to them. The couple trudged their way back to the bike. Anita, deep in thought, out of the blue asked Chris, "Chris, could I drive the bike back?"

Chris agreed because he was unable to refuse his wife anything she asked for, but his inner thoughts were that it would take much longer to get back home. Explaining the proper procedure of changing gears and backing up, Chris hung on as Anita began to steer the bike. She felt as though she was born to drive the bike, and began picking up speed. Flying over rocks and debris in the roadway, Anita had a premonition to slow down, when Chris's hand suddenly pointed straight ahead. Skidding to a halt, and standing in their path, stood the meanest looking man she had ever seen. Not sure what to do, she let her legs dangle over the side of the bike like she was the boss, and waited for the ugly monster to let his intentions be known.

He told Chris and Anita their presence was expected at Dante's, immediately, but Anita refused saying she was hungry and it would have to wait until she'd had lunch. The man leaned over her; his breath stunk and Anita wanted to vomit as he said, "Now! Got it?" She was sure some spittle had landed on her, and fiercely wiped her face with her hand to get it off as it repulsed her.

The two men watched, as neither of them knew what had transpired, and when Anita realized the guys were peering at her, she clicked her heels, bowed and retorted, "This had better be good. How'd you find us?"

The man sneered and leaned even closer, and Anita waved her hand in front of her face to fan off the rancid smell the man was discharging from his mouth. The man's goal was to deliberately offend Anita's senses, and sneered as he spoke, "Followed you. Let's go."

Chris knew it was D-day. The hair on Anita's arm stood straight up, and shivers ran up and down her arms, causing her some confusion as to whether she was hot or cold. Arriving at Dante's house, they didn't have to knock; the doors opened and a butler was standing in the entranceway. He beckoned them to follow him to an enclosed room where lunch was being served. At first declining the invite, Anita received a harsh look from the butler; that and the pain in her stomach told her to indulge. Chris had a snack and afterwards, they were guided to the study and were told to wait.

Dante walked in, and the door hadn't closed yet when he began his sermon. "I don't know what games you two are playing, but I'm making a new one."

"Checkers or chess?" Anita piped up.

"Chess and you are going to be my pawns. I want to be king. Let's say I've just checked mated," Dante said, and his smile was more of a sneer, with a little gloating thrown in.

Silence filled the room, and Dante knew he had total control. "I see, lost for words. How interesting. I trust lunch was satisfactory?"

"Lunch was fine. Let's get on with it. I hate it when people aren't direct," Anita said, out of frustration.

Dante wanted to make sure his words had the right impact on Anita. "I really like your spunk," he said. "You are, shall we say, an unique person. So here's my proposition. You will work for me."

"Work for you? And what do I get in exchange?" Anita said, as her heart sunk at the mere thought of being in the same room as this repulsive man, let alone work for him.

Dante poured himself a drink and had it down before she could blink. He then turned to face his company, and stated, "In exchange, you get Carolyn and your father. Oh and I forgot to mention, you'll need to get me Blake."

"Blake? He isn't a part of this," Anita said, with defiance.

Putting his glass down with force Dante looked right at Anita. His cold tone made her shiver, as he said, "You will get me Blake or you can kiss your father goodbye, and Carolyn as well."

Clenching her fists and then releasing them, before clenching them again, Anita responded, "Suppose I don't."

"Ah, but you will. After all, hasn't your purpose here been to free Carolyn? You are a smart person, and I know the two of you can pull it off. You've already invaded my house twice," Dante said, clearly stating his position.

Interjecting, Chris asked, "Dante, what do you hold against Douglas?"

Shaking his finger at his guests, Dante opted not to tell. "What and reveal all?" he said. "Besides, Chris how do I know you are on the level? After all, weren't you and Maureen, shall we say, an item? If you screwed me once, you'll do it again. This is my insurance that you won't screw me over, especially when your wife is involved." He glanced at Anita's white face and smiled, adding, "I'm sorry. I didn't mean to tell tales out of school. Oops."

"That's old news. I want to see Carolyn, and I mean face-to-face. No gimmicks, no tapes or videos. As far as my father goes, what are your plans for him?" Anita asked.

"He'll be asked to be your aide. He's not working in my favor anymore. He's gone stale, but *you* are fresh." Dante was growing tired of the conversation and wanted to leave, but knowing he held the trump card, he waited for Anita to get her questions off her chest.

"And Blake? What does he have to do with all this?" Anita hurled the question at her host.

"Seems you got him arrested. He plays a small part. May I take this opportunity to welcome you to your first job," Dante said, with vindictiveness in his voice.

Not wanting Dante to have total control, Anita whipped back, "Set up the meeting with Carolyn and then we'll talk. Only then. If I should renege on your generous offer, what happens? Chris and my father will disappear?"

"I'll be in contact – and you won't renege," Dante said, with confidence, and strolled out the door.

As they reached their vehicle, Anita's legs buckled and she fell to the ground. She made an effort to get up, but instead she just sat there and cried. Chris came to her side and helped her into her seat and they drove off, neither of them saying a word.

Her parents were sitting on the couch when Anita entered. The look on her face disturbed them deeply but, ignoring their questions, Anita fixed herself a drink. With trembling hands, Anita spilled some of her drink down her blouse, but made no attempt to clean it off. She spoke without looking up. "Seems Gappy is truly a friend, however, Dante has made his move. He's holding Carolyn and you ransom so that I will act as his lawyer, and Dad, he wants you to be second chair. He has also made it clear he wants Blake sprung, and will keep his paws off Chris as long as I obey. What the hell have you done?"

Her father's lips parted and the words just spieled out. "I'm so sorry for the mess you're in. I'll talk to Dante."

"You weren't listening," Chris bellowed. "He doesn't want you. He's securing his empire. Seems Gappy, too, has been taken with my wife's spunk. Douglas, you had better work with us here and tell us what's going on. We need your help in springing Blake, or Dante will hold Carolyn over Anita's head for the rest of her life."

"I can't. Everyone will assume I'm guilty. You're on your own," was Douglas's reply.

"You asshole," Anita yelled at her father. "You're turning your back on us to save you own sorry ass? You are of no use to me, so maybe you should go home and play innocent."

Suzanne was astounded at Douglas's lack of integrity, and said, "You can't just leave the kids to fend for themselves. I now see the side of you I saw when we were younger. In your world, you are the only thing that matters. Well, here's a news flash; I'll help the kids out any way I can so that one day we can be a normal family, sharing in normal activities."

Chris's emotions were conflicted, as he thought about what Douglas had done to him and what it had done to Anita. He spoke kindly towards Suzanne, saying, "I appreciate the offer, but I couldn't ask you to do that."

Douglas's voice was loud, as he said, "Suzanne, this is too dangerous for you. You are leaving with me on the next plane out of here."

"I will not be intimidated by your actions or what is going on here. You created this mess, and one of us has to see our daughter and son-in-law through it," Suzanne responded, with clear resistance to Douglas's childish demands.

Everything closed in around Anita, and she felt sick to her stomach. She headed up to her room with Chris behind her. They sat talking, and all fired-up, Anita blurted out, "Chris, I am so sorry. I never dreamed any of this could happen. Even when Carolyn is free, Blake sprung, and my dad at my side, Dante will never let me go."

"Not to mention that he has a trial coming up. Are you ready for that?" Chris asked, wanting to know how she felt about the court case.

Running to the bathroom, Anita spilled her guts into the toilet and sighed. "I can't defend him," she said. "He makes my skin crawl and I'm still in it."

"Here's what we do," Chris began. "Let's play along with him, until we get a foolproof plan in order."

"Oh, like that's going to happen. We're doomed. You can still back out. Really, I'd understand," Anita said, and she meant every word of it.

"Where's the person with all the spunk that everyone likes so much?" Chris asked, teasingly.

"She's wallowing in self pity, and feels guilty for the mess she's made of your life," was Anita's feeble answer.

"Don't worry about it, I wasn't doing anything special with it anyway," Chris remarked, smiling at his pathetic sounding wife.

Feeling a little better, Anita went back downstairs to join her parents. She looked at them with intense eyes, and said, "I'll agree to Dante's terms. Just don't ask questions about my performance or behavior. All I ask is that you is there for the court case."

"Scrap your ideas. Dante will have you on the ropes for the rest of your life," Douglas said, without any life in his words.

"That's you," Anita snarled back. "This is me. I'll free Blake, Carolyn and you. Dante will get his, be assured of that. He's taken away people I love, but through it all, I've gained back a whole lot more, and it's worth fighting for. Life does work in mysterious ways."

Holding out her palm, Anita demanded that Douglas give her all the files he had on Dante. Suzanne left the three of them to sort out the paper work. After a couple of hours, Anita came out of the room with her head swimming. She sat beside her mother with her gaunt face and expressionless eyes. "Dad's in trouble. Chris and I will do everything we can to make sure he is cleared, but he's a stubborn man and does not want our help."

Her mother's intuition kicked in. She took Anita's hand, and said, "You want to talk don't you?" Nodding her head in agreement, Anita followed Suzanne outside for a walk. "Look, I'm here because I want to be, and I thank the heavens you know about me. If you have any reservations about my reason for being here – don't. As for your father, he has to justify to himself that *you* can help him. He has never had to rely on anyone before. It scares him," Suzanne explained.

Squeezing her mother's hand, Anita accepted the explanation of how Suzanne felt. Then Anita explained her feelings. "Mom, I'm scared to death. I feel like I'm caught in a spider web. Dante's the host spider, I'm the victim insect that's been lured into a trap, and the bug, being dad who did the luring, is now sneaking off leaving me to fend for myself. I feel as though I'm being devoured and I can't see my way clear. All I wanted was to find my best friend. I didn't get my best friend, but I got something just as good: a kind, gentle man, a great mother, and a sister I barely know. But on the other side, I've lost my brother, my best friend, Millie, and now my dad. Now lives rely on my *spunkiness,* as it's been put to me. I've put so many lives in jeopardy, yours included. How can I ask you to stay?" Anita said, but her heart was barely beating; it was as if all the life in her was fading.

Suzanne's smile was genuine, and she lightly placed her arms around her daughter in a gesture that said; *she was there,* and Anita let her tears flow freely. After a few minutes of reassurance that they would be okay, the subject was changed and the talk was enjoyable and refreshing. Walking back to the front of the house, they saw Douglas standing there like an old man, with his head bent down, and all his weight shifted to his stooping shoulders. "Dad," Anita said, "I'm not the brightest person, but I know you could be disbarred because of your arrangement with Dante. What could you have possibly been thinking? I'm going to assume that you had already crossed the line once and having done so, it was easy to do again. Am I close?"

Douglas perked up as he defended himself. "I'm not on trial. No one will find out, so, I'm safe."

Suzanne hushed Anita and then spoke up herself, saying, "Maybe not, but your daughter looked up to you, and now she is forced to look down. No one accomplishes anything if they are always looking down or over their shoulders."

Very calmly, Douglas began shuffling his feet towards the house. He had an emotionless face, and his voice reflected the same empty tone, when he replied, "Suzanne, we have to go. Our flight leaves tonight."

"Running away won't ease the pain," Suzanne countered, "nor will it stop the manifestation of what you've done. Face it like a man."

Douglas continued his task of preparing to leave, and Anita felt anger piercing her heart, as though she'd been shot. "Mom, do you think he'll leave? I mean, he's at an all-time low, and whatever he's done is eating him alive."

Watching the man she loved trek through the house, Suzanne replied, "Yes, he'll leave."

Now her heart stopped as the pain intensified. Gasping for air, Anita said, "He can't. He's part of the package. He's leaving me holding the bag."

Anita was about to bolt when she felt herself being held back by her mother's hand that had been placed on her arm, but somehow her mother's words were of no comfort to her. "Anita, leave him. When he's in this mood, the best thing to do is to let him go. I promise, he'll return when he calms down.

Stopping in her tracks, Anita gazed at her mother wondering why her father ill-treated her. She was the kind of person you would want to be with, through thick and thin. She felt remorse for her father's actions towards this woman. Hearing a thud, they looked up to see Douglas standing with two suitcases in his hands. "Coming?" he asked Suzanne, with a sharp edge to his voice.

Suzanne drew in a deep breath, and then exhaled slowly. "No," she pronounced the word carefully. "We'll be here when you get your priorities straight."

Chris rounded the corner in time to see the standoff wind down, and waited for something to happen. Douglas dropped one suitcase, and then headed for the vehicle with the other. He did not utter a word of goodbye. The others stood silently in his wake, baffled. It was late in the day, and Chris took mother and daughter by the hand and guided them to the porch swing. Sitting between them, he placed a warm arm around each of them and he could feel them begin to release their stress. After a few minutes of silence, they headed in for a late snack, and then to their rooms to lick their wounds, and recover from the torture of the day.

Keyed up and unable to sleep, Anita opened Dante's files and, after carefully reviewing them, mumbled that she couldn't figure out what her father's defense was for Dante. She began rubbing her neck. Chris awoke and spotted her sitting by the window curled up in the chair, and walked over. The warmth of his hands, as he placed them on her shoulders, penetrated the knots that had formed and relaxed her into a semi-conscious state. Without warning, Anita turned giving him a kiss so deep that it drove them to heated passion, and, then, explosive fireworks.

Cuddled in each other's arms, Anita ran her fingers up and down Chris's arm sending a trail of little bumps up to his neck, and making him laugh. Her thoughts were no longer full of passion, but of strategy. "I'm going to need Gappy's help with breaking Blake out of the Embassy," she said, finally.

"I don't know where that came from, but it's going to cost you big bucks," Chris remarked, chuckling at how fast her mind worked. "He doesn't work cheaply."

"I expected that. My mother told me about funds I didn't know I had. Can't spend it all anyway, so may as well spend it on a rescue mission," Anita said. The night fairy had just sprinkled her sleeping dust, and the two had fallen asleep when Suzanne bolted through the bedroom door. Her words echoed through the room like someone had taken a shot. "Your dad's plane went down, and no bodies have been found."

Instantaneously, the ladies sought comfort in a warm embrace. Chris, being the strong one, put his arms around both of them and they let loose a small flood of tears. Suzanne wiped away the water that had accumulated on her face, and announced she was going to the crash site and Chris and Anita were right behind her.

Quickly getting dressed, the trio then headed as fast as they dared to the crash site. They were detained while the site was being investigated for any remnants of Douglas's or the pilot's bodies. Impatiently, Anita hounded the officials until they were finally allowed onto the site. Wearing gloves, they were allowed to sift through the debris in hopes of finding anything pertinent. Nudging a piece of the wreckage that stuck out to one side, Anita discovered a briefcase with her father's initials on it. Excitedly, she asked one of the authorities to open it. It had a numbered lock on it, and it seemed to take forever for them to pry it open. Intoxicated with the contents inside the case, Anita was shocked when they opened it. It was empty, and she was equally surprised when she learned he had hired a private plane and pilot for the journey, not a commercial one.

Overhearing a conversation between some officials, Anita strained her ears and, with the skill of an animal moving noiselessly in the bush, she crept closer to better hear what was said. She was blown away when one official mentioned the crash looked like sabotage. Charging like a bull at a stampede, Anita herded Suzanne and Chris and marched them to the car. She took control of the driving, and drove straight to Dante's - as far as she was concerned, he was the only one who'd benefit from her father's death.

Leaving everyone else behind in the car, Anita ran past the guard at the entranceway and straight to Dante's door, banging on it like she had enough power to push it in. In the wee hours of the morning, Anita was expecting to see the butler answer the door, but there stood Dante – as though he was waiting for her.

Dante was pleased to see Anita, and smiled as he gestured for her to enter his domain. He was taken off guard, however, when Anita stormed in and paced around like she was about to lock horns with her opponent, and she retorted, "Why did you have my father killed? He's not the one that can hurt you, it's me."

"Whoa, little lady," he said. "I know nothing about this. Do tell me what happened," Dante responded, with sincerity.

"Oh please," she quipped back, sarcastically. "Nothing happens without you knowing about it, so don't play innocent with me." Anita stood back and watched the man's face fall, and said, "You didn't know, did you?"

"Your father had many enemies, and I was not one of them. Believe what you like, but your father was a good man, but *I* swear to you, I had nothing to with his death," Dante said. He paused for a few moments, and then began, "Since you are here, I may as well tell you that I'll be calling you later, say anywhere from today onward, with detailed instructions of time and place you will meet Carolyn. In the meantime, you do your part. I expect nothing less than perfection from you," he said. Dante hesitated for a moment and then turned to Anita, and asked, "What do you mean when you said *you're* the one that can hurt me? You know the rules: follow them or be destroyed."

"Precisely, and at this time, until I see my friend, we have no deal. *I'm* not on your payroll, nor am I a friend. *I am* someone who is trapped, so therefore, *I* am considered dangerous. My father, God rest his soul, was on your payroll," Anita stated.

Dante's grin was menacing. "So will you young lady – be on my payroll, standing in court defending me, and getting me a not guilty verdict. You'll become my friend," he said, still smiling with the same awful grin.

"You realize once court is over, I will no longer serve your purpose. I shall expect the same results as my father: to be eliminated. That's your way," Anita shot back.

"Oh, not true little lady. Chris is still around and he screwed me over with my woman," Dante threw back at her.

"You haven't finished with him yet. He's connected to me and you will make damn sure all your demands are met before he becomes exterminated like a rat that you see him as," Anita bantered back.

Tired of the truthful bantering, Dante showed Anita the door, opened it, and with a wave of his hand, his indicated she should leave. His words were cold. "You just do your part."

Judging the time she had spent with the obnoxious little man, Anita hurried back to the car and apologized to the occupants. They both greeted her with a look that told her she needed to explain the outcome of her chat. Anita threw her hands up in the air, and said, "I thought it could wait until we got home, but it seems dear old Dante knew nothing about Dad's death. I, for some stupid reason, believe him. Can you believe that, because I'm having a hard time myself?"

Pulling up in front of the house, Anita looked at her mother's tear stained face and threw her arms around her. Choking back her own feelings for her father's death, Anita said, "Mom, I must be cold inside right now. I know I grieve Dad's leaving this earth so suddenly, and yet my feelings won't come through. It seems I must pursue what happened, rather than sit and do nothing. Are you okay with that?"

Suzanne kissed Anita on the cheek, and said through her tears, "Yes. I understand. Be careful will you please."

Anita hopped back into the car, and Chris was in a preoccupied mood. "How did you know I was going to see Gappy?" he asked.

"Oh please. You are just as angry as I am, and we both know that if Dante doesn't know the answer, Gappy will," she said. Then she added, "Yes, I'll be fine. I'm numb inside and I know we're in for a rocky ride. But I also know this ride will come to a sudden stop, and then all will smooth out. I've had enough."

Taking advantage of the still somewhat darkened skies, they drove off and Chris said teasingly to his wife, "Got a plan in mind?"

"I've decided to play it safe. You know, wait to see what unfolds and then play the game," she said, and she let the tears fall down her cheeks. Instantly, she knew she was still human inside.

Time passed by quickly, mainly because Chris drove at record speed, and they arrived at the secret hideout of the ATV. Mounting the bike, Chris hadn't yet started the engine, when he felt a prickly pin stabbed into his arm, and his immediate reaction spooked Anita. Standing high on the bike, Chris surveyed the area, but was unable to see any movement or hear any unusual rustling in the tall grasses, and he debated whether to carry on or abort the mission. A gun fired from the direction in which they were to recede back towards home, and it whizzed by their ears. Chris, at that moment, chose to move onward. Starting the ATV, Chris barely let the engine start when he sped as fast as it would go, hitting a dip in the path, and both tumbled to the ground. The bike rested on its side with both of them pinned under it. Chris was about to push the bike back on it's wheels, when it toppled on top of them, and the steering handle bar crashed down onto his upper jaw bone, knocking him out. Anita, yelling at Chris to wake up, struggled to free herself, but when he didn't respond, she panicked. Her adrenalin kicked in and she managed to push the bike off her and wiggled free. Tapping his face gently, Chris finally came to; he was dazed and complained about having a headache and a sore jaw. Anita noticed he had a gash on the side of his head, but it wasn't bleeding profusely, and she thought it could wait a few more minutes.

Struggling as best they could, they managed to get the bike back on all four wheels. Once the bike was resting on it's wheels, he started the engine by reaching his hand up to turn the key. He then popped his head up out of the undergrowth to see if he could see or hear anything. All was quiet, so they flipped a coin: heads to continue, tails to go home. It was heads and they headed up to the mountain. A second shot was fired, just missing the tops of their head. Hurting and shaken up by the turn of events, they were hoping they were traveling faster than those firing upon them, and drove in a zigzag motion to dodge the shots, should there be any. Soon, the noise of the birds and crickets filled the airwaves, and both relaxed a little as they kept climbing up the mountain.

Feeling outraged and relieved at the same time for making it to the top, the couple sought out Gappy. Learning that Gappy had gone to one of his other hideouts, the couple just plopped to the ground in disappointment. The villager they had been talking to noticed the blood oozing from Chris's wound, and asked them if he would like to see a doctor. Chris knew it wasn't a conventional doctor that practiced in these parts, but welcomed the examination. Being led to a small little grass hut, Chris took his seat and the doctor did a quick review of his injuries. The strange little man, according to Anita's summation of his appearance, went to work and put a little magic powder together and applied it to Chris's wound. Much to Chris's surprise, the burning on the side of his head went away and he could no longer feel blood trickling down the side of his head. He was handed some tiny pills, and was told to swallow it and in a few minutes, his headache would dissipate, but his jaw would still be tender. True to the doctor's words, the headache was beginning to subside to a dull roar, but his jaw still let him know that it was sore and not going away any time soon.

Hoping enough time had lapsed, they said their thanks, and they jumped onto the bike. The skies were beginning to lighten up as dawn was settling in. Scouring the trail ahead of them, the two nervous people crouched down as low as they could get, and began the descent, into what they hoped would be smooth riding.

CHAPTER THIRTY-EIGHT

Hunger had set in and the couple went to a diner to calm the beast roaring within them. Chris's jaw was so sore, that he had to order soup and scrambled eggs as it was easier to "gum" the food than chew it. Chris made a decision to phone home and let them know they were safe and weren't sure what time they would be home. During the meal, the two discussed where Gappy could be hiding out, and both concluded to go to where he had once taken her for safekeeping – there was no name for it.

Feeling as though they had struck it rich in finding their intended resource, Gappy, Anita placed a proposal before him. He listened intently as Anita presented her request, and when she was done, he thought about it for a moment and then refused. At first she was stunned that he dared to refuse her, then she collected her thoughts and asked him what was his reason for rejecting her proposal – she was offering to pay his fee. Gappy tried to appease her by explaining his reasons why he wouldn't do it, but she was not hearing his words. Finally, Gappy relented and agreed to help with the expedition.

Thinking his price would deter her, he was surprised when she didn't blink and she shook his hand to confirm the deal. Gappy, for the second time, gave her his condolences for her father's death, prompting Anita to ask, "What do you know that I don't?"

"All will be disclosed sooner than you think; but for now, I will need some money up front to secure our agreement. You will be notified when we require your services," stated Gappy.

"Give me forty-eight hours and I will have the money for you," Anita promised. Then she bit her lip and looked up at Gappy. "Are you saying that I am to participate in Blake's release?"

"That I am," he said, and chose not to say another word.

A small cloud formed over Anita's head; she could tell Gappy's mind was a mile away. "What's on your mind?" she asked him.

He smiled, and said earnestly, "I've dealt with your father in the past. Now I shall see how you compare and that will determine if I shall deal with you in the future."

Anita's attractive face lit up, and she replied, "Let's say you'll be glad you dealt with me, not only in this case, but any others that may arise in the future; and let's hope that doesn't happen."

Gappy had a slight twinge around his mouth, and Anita took it for a smile of approval, but his words didn't indicate as much. "You are overzealous, and often it goes against you."

Recalling he had once mentioned he may use her in a battle with Dante, Anita just blurted out her words. "Dante will get his. Are you in?" asked Anita.

"One deal at a time," Gappy quipped back and, like a whisper in the wind, he was gone.

On the way back from the location, Anita was silent. She was drowning in her thoughts and to save herself from being totally consumed by them, she unleashed what she had been thinking. "I think my father is alive."

Chris's reaction was that of someone who had been hit on the head. Asking her how she had arrived at such a conclusion, Anita admitted that after putting some of the pieces of the puzzle together from the reactions of the main players and the crash site, she believed it was his way of getting out of the picture and saving his skin. Chris held her hand giving her comfort, and he, too, thought about her statement and surmised that she could be right; no bodies were found, only an empty briefcase.

Arriving at the place they now called home, they found Suzanne sitting at the table with a note in her hand. She was speechless. Chris gently tugged the piece of paper out of her hand and read it: '*Go home to where you belong before the same thing happens to you*'. There was nothing specifying for whom it was intended, but everyone in the room knew.

Her heart pounding, Anita could feel sweat running down her back as though she had just run a marathon. She raced to the den, closed the door, and picked up the phone, making several calls. Before returning to the group, Anita picked up the bottle of booze, tucked it under arm like a football, and dragged her body back to the kitchen. She poured herself a stiff drink hoping it would lift her spirits and not let her have a heavy heart, but still the heavy heart emerged.

With all eyes on Anita, she quietly said, "Seems my father has left two wills, and Millie is steamed up because she read them both and wants to choose the one that fits her needs the best. I know this because I just made some calls and one was to her. This is the one time she spoke to me. What she doesn't want to hear is that no matter what will is the right one, it cannot be executed until my father's body has been recovered. Without that, we may have to wait seven years. We are invited to go and hear the reading of the wills, and I think we should go. My intuition has kicked in, and I think I may find humor in it after all, as well as a few answers." She turned to Suzanne and continued her speech, "Mom, I would very much like to have you come with me, but I feel things may become volatile and someone could get burned. I do, however, know you will be in the will."

"Sweetie, thank you for your concern, but I knew this day would come – although, I hadn't counted on it happening like this. Deep down I believe your father is alive and this is a mockery for him. Should I get to see him again, I will personally make him feel the pain and torture he's put us through," Suzanne said, weakly.

Anita now directed her focus on her adoring husband. "I would very much like it if you were to join us, but I do understand if you don't wish to accompany me – us."

Chris knew Anita was vulnerable and that now would not be a good time to leave her alone: especially if the two mothers got together. He considered her concerns. "I'll be there for you. You must be aware, though, that Millie will be unbearable because all her loved ones have left her, and now she's alone."

With haunting, glazed eyes, Anita turned to face her loving husband. "I'm anticipating the worst. Neither of you have any idea how thankful I am that I'll have you both there by my side. My father was or is a man of many deceits, and is leaving us to sort out the details. What was he thinking?"

Suzanne's lips quivered as she held her tears back, and tried to speak. "Losing him once was hard, but losing him twice is devastating. We must cherish what we have because life if full of uncertainties."

Feeling the alcohol numb her senses, Anita spoke with sadness. "I've lost Jake, Carolyn, Millie and now my father. All this happened because of a maladroit kidnapping. Now there's a book that could be written," she said, and laughed falsely.

Chris stood by silently as the two ladies expressed their frustrations. Suzanne took the stand and threw her glass against the wall. "Anita," she said. "I've lost you once also, and now I'm afraid of losing you again. I can't let his happen. I'll do whatever it takes to keep what's left of my family."

Anita picked up the shattered glass and then poured her mother and Chris each a drink. Handing them their glasses, Anita raised her own, and said, "You know, with all the chaos, going home will be much deadlier than staying here. Millie will wish me dead, and may even try her hand at it; while Dante will do everything he can to keep me alive – until his court case is over. Thanks to my father, he left a hell of a tidal wave, and so my guess is that we'll be riding some rapid waves. It'll be anyone's guess who will survive." Everyone raised their glass and made a toast to the ride of the rocky waters they were about to embark upon – knowing they were going to win.

CHAPTER THIRTY-NINE

Money had been transferred into Anita's account so she and Chris made a quick trip to Gappy's, and before the money changed hands, Anita quickly explained the circumstances of her short absence. Gappy said his plans for Blake's breakout could wait a few days and complimented her for handling business in a timely fashion. Anita smiled sweetly and announced the best of her business dealing was yet to come.

All packed, Chris, Suzanne, and Anita headed to the airport. Because Anita was dreading the fact of seeing Millie, the time just snuck up on her and, suddenly, they were headed to the lawyer's office. They arrived a few days before the reading of the will so Anita could read both wills and determine which one was correct. Proudly walking into the lawyer's office, as a lawyer to a lawyer, Anita introduced herself. She was unimpressed with the lawyer, who claimed to be a good friend of her father's, because he knew nothing of Douglas's family situation or family. To further her less impressive overview of the lawyer, he was uncertain which of the wills was the latest written. Using professional mannerism, Anita asked to see both wills and began to read each of them. The dates seemed to be smudged and Anita shook her head. "How on earth did you manage to bumble the wills? The dates are illegible, and the contents are totally different. How are we supposed to know which one is right? You'd better have an answer, like right now," Anita stated.

The lawyer's eyes bounced from one person in the room to another, and his hands began to shake as he examined the papers. "This is all I have," he said. His sheepish eyes did a side-glance at Anita. He held up the documents to the light and there was a faint legible date on the one document. Anita examined the contents of the will and threw them down on the desk.

"That will never hold up in court, and you know it. Now, where's the real one, you know the one where the date and signature is readable?" She asked, again.

The lawyer spoke, cautiously. "If there is another one, he didn't draw it up with me. Perhaps he has another somewhere else. Should you not find one, this one will hold up in court. I will swear to it."

"Hogwash," Anita spit back. "And who is Ivan? You should know that if you were a friend of my dad's?"

"I can't answer that question," the lawyer said, angrily because she was poking her nose into his business.

Wanting to throw something, Anita stood in the middle of the office and threw a temper tantrum by stomping her feet and making several growling noises, taking everyone in the room by surprise. Seeing their shocked eyes focused on her, Anita looked around, and said coolly, "It was a dance of prayer that Ivan, and my dad's true will, will show up. Hmm, I guess it didn't quite work." She then opened the door and left, leaving everyone laughing behind her.

Looking at her watch, Anita knew her dad's office wasn't closed yet. She was worried that her father was coyly playing with all of them. She gathered her troops and headed straight for her father's office. Entering the main office, the staff were dabbing their eyes as though they had been crying. Anita's somewhat compassion came out when she said that she had no intentions of closing the office at this time, but should they wish to seek other employment, they would receive a glowing letter of reference. Nodding her head, she indicated to those traveling with her to enter her father's office with her.

Opening the door to the luxurious office, Anita could feel tears trickling down her cheeks as memories flooded her head of her father. Being entrusted with the combination to his safe, she did so in front of witnesses and when the door opened, she rifled through the papers it contained. There it was, nicely tucked away: the will. Carefully reading it over, Anita saw that it had a date on it and matched the one with the strange name of Ivan. Checking to see if the other papers held any significant information, Anita was not surprised they held nothing but useless information. Wendy interrupted them when she knocked on the door and entered the room. She asked Anita to join the partners in a meeting.

Rubbing her temples in an attempt to make her headache go away, Anita suggested that Chris and Suzanne get comfortable while she attended the meeting. She then followed Wendy out. When Anita took her place at the boardroom table, she was presented with a buy out; they wanted to run the firm their way. Agreeing that would be the best move, Anita told the board members she would hire a lawyer to look after her interest. She also said she would have her father's belongings sorted out, and that any case files he had been working on, she would hand over to the firm. They all shook hands in agreement. After the meeting Anita collected her entourage and they headed onward to new experiences.

Arriving at the much-dreaded place she once called home, Anita knocked on the door, half-expecting to be greeted with a knife aimed at her heart. But no one answered the door, so she let herself in, calling, "Mom, Millie are you home?"

"Get out of here before I kill you. You don't belong here," a weak voice replied.

Clenching her fists and holding them by her side and taking in a few breaths, Anita remained calm. "How can you turn your back on me? You raised me," she said, hoping to be able to have a decent conversation.

A ghostly figure of a woman stood before her. "You killed my son, my daughter, and now my husband. I've nothing left. You are his daughter, not mine," Millie said, making her point of view very well known

Anita's feelings were hurt, and she felt a combination of guilt, animosity, and pity for the woman before her. "Oh please," Anita said hotly, "you've been wallowing in self-pity for so long, you've missed the boat. Your husband, my father as you put it, is the one responsible. Carolyn and I were pawns he played at his convenience and the game went terribly wrong. You know more than you ever let on. So, cut the crap and let's get on with it." Anita's clenched fists rested on her hips and she hoped they would stay there, rather than lash out at the first thing in her path.

Suzanne and Chris stood slightly in the shadows, still as statues, daring not to draw Millie's attention, but it was too late. Millie captured their presence, and remarked, "It's you isn't it? The woman who stole my life, my husband." Without receiving a response from Suzanne, Millie turned sharply to Anita, "How dare you bring that woman here. What is it you want? To torment me more?"

"They are here to support me, because you, who was once my mother, turned your back on me. Yes, this is Suzanne. Don't pretend you're surprised; you've always known, just never admitted it. What I want to know is, who is Ivan? And before you tell me to get lost again, you'd better think – because that will with Ivan's name on it, is his latest will. Unless we locate him, when it comes time to executing Dad's will, we'll need to find everybody mentioned or it all goes to charity. I don't have energy to fight, so I'm asking again, who is Ivan?"

Millie and Suzanne passed some dangerous looks between them making everyone feel ill at ease. Meanwhile, Anita's patience was running thin as she waited for Millie to respond. Tapping her toes to show her agitation, Anita couldn't take another minute in the house, and yelled, "*Now* Millie."

Startled by Anita's tone, Millie yelled back, "I don't know, really."

"Okay, ladies put your own conflicts aside and think. Did dad have a brother he never talked about? Or a cousin?" Anita was hoping that this was the answer to the riddle.

Millie had had enough of the whole thing; she told them she knew nothing and ordered them to leave her house. Infuriated, Anita let uncensored words fly. "I hope you have some savings because I'll not cover your ass." Still Millie didn't offer any clue, and the trio headed back to the office, totally mystified about Douglas's hidden secrets. The three of them searched every inch of the office, and the only item they found was an old check stub with Ivan's name on it. Their stomachs were growling, and they knew they needed nourishment. They noticed a diner nearby. The walked in, sat down, ordered, and discussed their next move. Not letting the issue die, Anita remembered she had put some information into storage. After they ate, Anita dragged everyone to the storage unit to search for anything pointing to Ivan, or his whereabouts. Again they came up empty handed. Frustrated and excited about the manhunt and discovering Douglas's dark side, they turned in for the night, and their tired bodies collapsed onto their beds.

Rising early the next morning, Anita anxiously waited for the bank to open. She presented the stub to the teller and inquired about the person who cashed it, and any information regarding the location of this individual. At first the bank refused to help, which irked Anita, but in talking to the manager, she found out two small bits of information; the stamp on the back of the check was old and there was a glimmer of chance that it could be from the next town's branch. Annoyance and exasperation seemed to run a circuit between the three of them, and as they drove to the next town, they speculated about the mystery; what was it they were going to find?

Suzanne pondered over the situation. "I wonder if it's an alias for Douglas to keep money separate in case of disaster."

Chris tried not to make her feel silly for her suggestion. "Maybe, but then why would he name him in the will?"

"Because Dad's an idiot, and I know he's not dead. He wanted to cop out so he could save face for his involvement. Ivan is just another well-kept hidden treasure of his that we must sort out. Then there's Dante. What does he have on my father; another hidden treasure kept inside his vault – the one in his head," Anita said, pointing out her views.

Upon arrival into the small town, they agreed they would each go to a bank with a copy of the check stub to see if anyone had an idea about the individual it named. It was Suzanne who struck oil. Bouncing out of the bank, she waved the paper, calling to the others and getting the attention of everyone around her. Feeling a little embarrassed about her happy reaction, she sheepishly went about her business of gathering up her comrades and they entered the bank. Crossing their fingers in hopes of getting good news, they followed the teller to the manager's desk.

The manager sat them down and he studied the stub. The name rang a bell to him and he methodically thought about the person until a vision came to his mind. He described him as being a short, balding man, who had someone come in and do his banking because he lived in a nursing home. The bank manager's face frowned because he was unable to recall the name of the nursing home. Almost jumping off her chair with excitement, Anita asked the manager if he could possibly check his computer and see if he was still in the system; while he was checking the computer, Anita pulled out a picture of her father. When the man looked up at her, she asked if he had ever seen that man. The manager nodded and confirmed that he had accompanied Ivan on a few occasions, but was unable to give him a current address, only an old one. At this point, however, Anita was hungry for any tidbits thrown her way.

Anita's heart pounded so hard she could feel her veins pulsate with each beat. She scurried out the door of the bank, eager to gain more data, and knew they were closing in on the mysterious little man. They checked each nursing home in the vicinity, but there was no Ivan registered at any of them. Buying a map, they checked nearby towns and began the task of eliminating homes, one by one. They had two left on their list, and were ecstatic to hear there was an Ivan registered at one of them. They were disappointed when they were told they could only see him at seven o'clock in the evening to visit, however, they were told no to get too excited because his memory was poor. Indulging in a bite to eat seemed fitting at this point in their day, and they waited eagerly until it was time to end the wild goose chase.

Entering Ivan's room, they found the little man hooked up to an oxygen tank with a companion sitting by his side. Ivan opened his eyes, taking the mask off. "Douglas, is that you?" he asked.

Anita's heart did some flips and she shivered at the mere thought that she looked like her father. Responding to the man's question, she said, "I'm Anita, Douglas asked me to check up on you for him."

The man's face was pale and his body nearly lifeless. "He left me here to die and I'm not too happy about that," he wheezed.

Tears welled up in Anita's eyes as she saw the resemblance of her father in his face. "Ivan, Douglas died in a plane crash. I promise you'll get the best care and you can live wherever you want to."

His weak little smile changed his gaunt face to that of a little boy. "You mean that?" he asked, and reached for her hand.

"Yes, I do. Where do you want to live?" Anita asked her uncle.

"The place where we grew up," Ivan said, beaming.

"Ivan, is Douglas your brother?" Anita asked, wanting to know the truth.

"Yes. He always took care of me, but I wasn't very happy when he just left me here." Ivan managed to say. Then he added, "Nobody wanted me after I fell out of the tree. They said I was too much trouble, but Douglas always cared for me."

Wiping away her tears, Anita asked, "Ivan, can you tell me where you grew up so I can arrange for you to move back there?"

His voice began to trail off. "I just want to look at the lake and the stars. That's all."

"Ivan," Anita spoke with a gentle voice, "could you please tell me your last name."

Ivan got a blank look on his face and he blurted out, "Who are you?"

Stroking his arm gently with her hand, Anita responded, "Douglas's daughter. Please what is your last name?"

Ivan turned away and closed his eyes, and Anita was about to walk out the door when very faintly she heard him say, "Ivan Jefferson. My name is Ivan Jefferson."

She hugged the little man and said she would be back soon, and Suzanne, Chris and Anita collapsed on the waiting room chairs. How had no one known about Ivan, they wondered. When they arrived back at the hotel, Chris got on the computer and after relentless hours, he found the birth records of Douglas's mother and – yes, there it was – confirmation that Ivan was the brother to Douglas, along with their place of birth. Checking through all the newspaper clippings, they discovered that Ivan had been climbing a tree, trying to rescue a cat when he slipped and fell to the ground. The fall caused a severe head trauma, and possible permanent damage. Suzanne, not able to sit any longer, drove out to the nursing home to talk with a nurse, and had learned it was only a matter of time before Ivan closed his eyes, never to open them again.

Suzanne took her time in getting back to the hotel, and was horrified that Douglas never talked about his brother. She was thinking how cold he was on the exterior, but so kind on the interior of his body. She couldn't make sense of how his mind operated at keeping such secrets, that most people would've shared. When she arrived back at the hotel, Anita was busy searching for a place to rent for Ivan. Upon hearing the news of Ivan's fate, Anita quickly made a decision on a cottage by the lake, even though it wasn't anywhere close to their home town. She then found several retail stores that had every type of medical equipment, and couldn't wait to get it set up.

Chris was quiet, and just watched his wife become alive as she made notations of what may be needed, which store was the best, and most of all, she fell in love with the cottage. He suggested that they go to bed, and get an early start on putting her plan of action into gear. She was so excited she barely slept. Rising early the next morning, she was on the phone and had an appointment to rent the cottage. Her next step was to visit the nursing home and get a list of equipment Ivan would need, and when she had the entire list, she was on her way to the cottage.

The view of the lake was awe-inspiring. She was sure it would satisfy Ivan. Taking a tour inside, she found that it needed a lot of work to make it livable for the intended tenant. The owner shot down her asking permission to renovate some of the walls, and Anita decided that she would just buy it and then she could do as she pleased. The owner wasn't ready to sell, but Anita made an offer so tempting, that he agreed to the price. She told him to get the papers ready, and in the mean time, she would have some carpenters come in and make it accessible and functional for Ivan.

Now looking at Chris and Suzanne, they were both staring at her and she grinned. "We are staying here until the work is done. The view is so invigorating. It's what we need right now. Peace and tranquility. It will give us time to regroup and rethink our strategy when we return. What do you say?"

Suzanne, at first, thought her daughter had lost it, but looking at the view and hearing the sounds of nature in the distance, had to agree. "I think it's a wonderful idea."

Chris was anxious to get back home, but knew there was no way they were headed in that direction until Anita had her uncle settled in, so he threw his hands up in the air and said, "Let's do it. I figure a couple of days."

Chris and Suzanne left Anita behind and they went back to the hotel to collect their belongings and did some grocery shopping along the way. They knew they would have to eat at some point. Suzanne decided that they should have a glass of wine and threw in a few bottles. This was some adventure they were on. Knowing time was precious for Ivan, Anita hired a renovation team to do the work until it was done – and that meant day and night. She had barely gotten off the phone when they arrived; ready to start the project. Still not having the papers signed, Anita went over the plans for the house and made decisions as to where to make the changes. The little man showed up with all the papers, and Anita read them over quickly, signed the papers, wrote the check and handed them back to him. He was astonished that this lady meant business, and he danced all the way to his lawyer's.

Sitting by the lake and hearing the workers diligently working on the house project, Anita dug a little whole in the ground, threw some rocks around and from the old bits of boards that were being torn down, she lit a fire. In her own little world, she hadn't heard anyone approaching and when the person stood directly behind her casting a shadow over her, she was startled. Trying to catch her breath, she turned sharply to see who was standing behind her, but was wacked over the head. She tried to focus on keeping herself awake and held her eyes as wide open as she could. What she really wanted to do was to pass out from the pain.

A worker came out to ask Anita a question, and the brute of the man who wacked Anita did a fast disappearing act. Dazed at what he saw, the worker rushed over and checked to see if she was all right. Everything from her neck up was like someone had dropped a boulder on her and the inside of her head was scattered into a million pieces, leaving the nerve endings exposed and throbbing. With his help Anita got up and staggered into the cottage, and she searched her purse for meds that could cure her unwelcomed pain –but none were to be found.

In a state of panic to heal the pounding in her head, the worker asked if she wanted him to see if he could track down the assailant, but Anita suggested he go back to work and she would take care of it. Reluctantly, he obeyed his boss and put before her two different ways to reconstruct the wall, and she gave him her version of what she wanted. Noticing how much pain she was in, he searched his tool kit and then he handed her something for the pain. When she asked what it was, he smiled and told her to take it, and she'd be good in about an hour. Not liking the idea of doing such a daring thing, she weighed the pros and cons: the constant pounding pain or easy feeling – she chose easy feeling and popped the magic pill.

Taking her place, once again by the fire, she sat still and meditated. The pain had begun to mellow and she could feel her whole body relax and was enjoying the moment. The worker was now keeping a close eye on her until the others returned.

When Suzanne and Chris arrived, Suzanne hurriedly went over to her daughter with a bottle of wine in her hand. The fire was an addition that made things a lot better. The worker pulled Chris over to the side and explained what happened and what he had given Anita for pain. Chris was devastated with what happened to Anita, but was grateful with how the worker helped out in her hour of need.

Walking down to the fire, Chris took one look at Anita and started laughing. "How's the pain?" he asked.

Anita's glassy eyes looked up at Chris and she had a smile on her face. "Don't have any," she remarked, still smiling.

"Can you focus and tell me what happened?" Chris asked.

Suzanne now looked at the couple, and asked, "What do you mean?"

Anita's words had a slight impairment to them. "Mom, I was hit on the back of the head, while I was just sitting here. Didn't see who, but I can guess – dad's lawyer. I think he's got a little thing for Millie. Why else would there be so much confusion on the wills? I mean really, think about it," Anita said, and her words held a lot of truth.

Chris chuckled, and asked his wife, "How are you feeling right now?"

"I know that pill the worker gave me was probably illegal, but I tell you it worked miracles. I don't feel a thing, literally I don't feel a thing." Looking over the lake, Anita sighed. "I told the workers to work day and night, but now I'm beginning to think we should stop for at least six hours so we can catch a few winks.

Suzanne taking in the view of the whole area they were occupying said in response. "Yeah, that would be nice. I could use a little R and R because my head will hurt after I drink these bottles of wine. I think we are overdue for such activities and we need to vent over your father's untimely disappearance. Did you catch that, his *disappearance?* I know he's still alive, but a apart of me is wishing otherwise right at this very moment."

Chris took the initiative and went into the cottage. He was glad he had purchased paper cups, but more important, he made a snack; the ladies were going to need it if they were contemplating having wine for their main choice of beverage.

Bringing out the goodies Chris had prepared, the ladies thanked him and the three sat by the fire looking at the lake and taking in the sounds in the distant valley. Before Anita had consumed enough alcohol to make her oblivious to things, she tried to stand up but her wobbly legs wouldn't cooperate and she staggered around the little area until she steadied herself. Raising her cup, she made a toast. "Dad, thanks for the wild goose chase, it was pretty intense and frustrating, but I gained an uncle I didn't know I had. Thanks for the most wonderful family one could hope to get. And Jake, I know you're here with us right now because I feel your presence as you brush up against my arm. My promise to you is to find Carolyn and get those involved in your death. I miss you little brother." The tears fell in huge drops and she let her body sink into the ground – she was hurting inside.

Chris gave her and her mother a big hug. Suzanne took the stand and raised her glass. "Douglas, if I didn't know better, I would swear you were a tycoon yourself. You are not one to divulge any information all in one package. No, you need everyone guessing and playing games – your hidden treasure games. Unraveling them has been difficult, but I may be starting to think like you – to look in the most peculiar places to find small puzzle pieces and that's not good. It's a terrible way – not to trust. You are devious yet can be kind, ruthless yet can be compassionate, cunning yet straightforward. Of course, you use these traits when the purpose serves you. I love you with all my heart and, we will find you – that is my promise."

Chris asked the crew to come back in the morning around six o'clock and happily they went home. But at six in the morning, the pounding started and Anita covered her head because it felt like - for every nail pounded into a board, it was pounding in her head. Chris gave Anita some aspirins for her headache and a motion pill to help ease the rocking emotions from within her body, to which she was grateful for.

Seeing how well things were shaping up, Anita, Chris and Suzanne headed out to the nursing home. In talking to the gentleman in charge of the home, he was reluctant to release Ivan, but he also knew Ivan was near the end of his life. Anita asked for the man to put Ivan's companion on leave of absence so she could stay with Ivan. He declined her request. When she offered to pay for lost wages during that time, the man shook hands and offered anything she needed. Pleased with his mannerism, Anita asked the man if he would oversea that Ivan had everything he needed before he left. Transportation was arranged and that it was explained they would go ahead and await his arrival.

The workers were busily retouching the walls when the trio arrived. But something didn't seem right. There was a smell of smoke in the air. The three asked any of the workers if they had noticed anyone lurking around or saw anything unusual. When they all shook their heads indicating they hadn't, the three spread out and began their hunt for the cause of the smell.

Chris found the source. It was where some tools had been left laying around and his first thought was that it was set off accidentally, but upon further investigating, it was pretty evident that it was started deliberately; there was a match found just off to the side of the small blaze. Running to get something to put the fire out with, he found a small container and made many trips to the lake and doused the fire. Now it was a fact; no one wanted Ivan to live there. Whistling loudly, Chris caught everyone's attention and explained what he had found. Each and every person said they would be more aware of what's around them. Anita had a small rage of fire burning within her own body. But when the man from whom she bought the house appeared, her simmering insides cooled down when he handed her the papers. He told her he had never had a deal go through so quickly, and that he was pleased to have done business with her. She smiled knowing full well she had overpaid him, but it was worth it to her.

The last of the touches were done when Ivan showed up. The work crew aided in getting his equipment set up, and before long, Ivan's bed was situated so it faced the lake. His weary eyes were heavy from the travelling, and yet when he looked out the window, it was as if he had a sudden burst of energy. His face lit up when he smiled and his eyes shone. His dream had been fulfilled and he was able to see the sky and the lake, and he knew come nighttime, he would see the stars. The cottage was cozy, yet spacious with a wide-open kitchen and a fireplace. The bathroom wasn't needed as Ivan had a portable one, but all the necessities were at close hand.

Anita sat beside him, held his hand in hers, and kissed him on the cheek. "Ivan, I hope you'll be happy here."

His soft whisper reached her ears. "Thank you," he said.

Anita's eyes filled with tears that soon found their way down her cheeks. Giving him a hug, Anita explained about Douglas's departure from earth. At first, Ivan didn't grasp her meaning, but a few words clicked within his memory, and he turned to Anita with sad eyes, asking, "Are you going to look after me?"

Brushing his forehead with a kiss, Anita answered, "Yes. You are family. This house will be your home, and your companion will live here with you for as long as you want. I will come to visit from time to time. Would that be okay?"

"I'd like that," Ivan said, as he turned his head to look out the window. Anita could see him smile: she knew he was content and that he was going to be okay. The companion was pleased to see him happy, but Anita left with a heavy heart, because no one else knew of this cute little man.

Now that her mission was accomplished, a meeting was scheduled at the lawyer's office. Everyone was to attend, and Anita couldn't wait to shock Millie and the lawyer with her news – because according to Anita, they may think Ivan is no longer in the picture. Arriving at the office, Anita was in a hurry to use the facilities before the meeting, so Suzanne entered the lawyer's office alone. As she did, she witnessed a kiss between Millie – the weakling she saw at the house – and the lawyer. Suzanne smiled and mumbled under her breath, "Anita was right."

Chris walked in behind Suzanne and saw the lawyer and Millie in a lip lock, and cleared his throat. The guilty parties pulled apart like someone had sliced them in two. Even though they had red faces, they pretended as though it was a friendly gesture of greeting. Anita walked in and could sense that something was amiss, but knew it would wait until the reading of the will was over.

Sitting smugly in her chair, Anita's smile revealed that she was about to ambush them all with something she was dying to tell. Waiting for the others to settle down, Anita glanced around the room and noticed that the office was plain, with only his credentials on the wall, some law books, and a moderately sized desk with leather chairs – which were comfortable, she had to admit. She was surprised her father had hired this lawyer to handle his affairs. The lawyer cleared his throat and was about to speak when Anita stood up, and announced, "I hold the latest will in my hands. It actually has a date on it and that, my fellow companions, makes it legit. I have also located the whereabouts of Ivan and at this very moment, he is being well cared for." Looking at the lawyer, Anita continued, "Other than those who came here with me today, I am getting the notion that you are not totally shocked that I know of him, but are shocked I know where he is. This will, that I am holding is similar, yet different from the ones you've read. Now the truth will come out where my dad's heart really lived."

Millie's sharp eyes turned to Suzanne, then to Chris, then to Anita, and lastly back to the lawyer. Clearly she had a heart of stone. "What are you talking about?"

Waving the papers in her raised hand, Anita once again took the stand. "Dad had this will in his safe in his office. I had the combination, so I retrieved it. From there, we searched his office for clues regarding Ivan, and after a wild goose chase, we located him. Chris searched the Internet for all the proper documentation, and as it turns out, I have an uncle: a very frail and weak uncle. Someone, I presume, wanted to keep him tucked away so they could take his fair share. By this I mean I was attacked with a board slammed across my head and a fire was deliberately set on the grounds that Ivan now resides on. Dad kept his life very private, but it was obvious Ivan was important enough for him to be put in his will; just not important enough to disclose his actual existence. There will be no need to contest the will. I assure you it is legitimate and all those mentioned are presently accounted for, with the exception of Carolyn. I am Ivan's advocate. So, let's move on," she said, feeling as though she had won a battle of the minds.

Millie grabbed the papers out of Anita's hands, and laughed. "He's a mental case."

Snatching the papers back, Anita replied, "I thought you had never heard of him." She relished in the way Millie blushed in that moment.

Not letting Millie distract her, Anita stared her down. "How can you shun a human being like that? He was family."

Stuttering, Millie's mind went blank for a few seconds, then regained her thoughts. "I knew of him, but Douglas never spoke about him. I thought he was dead."

Picking up on the last phrase, Anita threw in. "Speaking of dead. Seems they can't confirm Dad was on the plane as no bodies were found, so that means all of this is for nothing. Unless his body miraculously turns up, the will cannot be executed for seven years. I really hope you have enough funds to get you through the years," Anita said, and sat down knowing she had made a huge impact on Millie.

Crying like a baby, Millie looked at the lawyer, and asked, "Is that true?"

The lawyer nodded. "I'm afraid so. They have to tie Douglas to the plane, and so far it doesn't look very promising."

Millie hurled her anger towards Suzanne. "It's all your fault," she said. "You were his mistress. This should've all been mine." Millie then looked at the lawyer and begged him to read the will anyway, so they could get on with their lives.

Suzanne put her hand up to hush the lawyer, and directed her comment directly to Millie. "If you weren't so cold and bitter, he wouldn't have had to turn to me. I have a beautiful daughter, and I thank you for raising her to be a proper lady."

Millie shot back, "You can have her. I never wanted her, but she came with stipulations. She was nothing but trouble. Look what she has done to this family."

Suzanne got out of her chair and slapped Millie across the face. "Don't you blame Anita for our mistakes," she said loudly. "Douglas created this mess."

Millie got up and returned the slap before anyone could blink. Chris pulled Suzanne away by the waist, while the lawyer grabbed Millie, and the two were separated.

Calming down, Suzanne shook her head, and laughed, "Damn, that felt good," she said. "I've wanted to do that since the beginning." Millie was now sporting a black eye.

When everyone in the room was contained, the lawyer read the will. Ivan was the first on the list and was awarded a million dollars to be used for his wants and needs until he passed away; anything left over after he died was to go to Anita. Millie's face went a deep red as rage surged through her body. She glared at Suzanne. Anita was entitled to his share in the firm on the buy out, because she was the only one to show motivation and an interest in following his career.

The conditions of the will further stipulated that Millie was to be given the house and one million dollars. After that, she would receive no more income. Suzanne and Shelan were given the chalet, the house they lived in and two million dollars. Anita was mentioned again, that she was entitled to receive two million dollars to start her career, and Carolyn was given five hundred thousand dollars. The will, being dated a couple of weeks ago, omitted Jake and it seemed that his inheritance was distributed amongst the living. Millie was so fired up by the will, that she got up and punch Suzanne in the face, knocking her out, and then stormed out the door. Chris called 911, while Anita bolted out of her chair and, catching up to Millie, sneered, "This is *after* probate. Remember, it could take seven years."

Millie slapped Anita across the face, and said, "That felt good. I should've done that years ago." She was out the door so fast, that all Anita could do was feel the draft from her departure and the sting on her face.

The lawyer came out and shook Anita's hand. "Thanks for finding Ivan," he said. "I will check it out for myself. You know, to make sure it's all legal."

Anita slipped her hand quickly out of the lawyer's grip. "I noticed the way you were looking at Millie. I hope you are genuinely fond of her, and not her money," she said, and turned to check on Suzanne who had come to and was dazed. The paramedics came, but Suzanne refused to go to the hospital, waving off their offer of assistance. Anita had Chris drive Suzanne to the hospital, even though she protested. Anita smiled at her mother. "No need to argue. We are driving and you'll go where the car goes. You can thank me later," she said, laughing.

As they waited in the waiting room, Chris teased Anita. "I hope you are as good to me as you are to others, should the time ever come."

"Are you kidding?" she said, jokingly. "I'd give you the boot, take your money, and run."

"Pretty hard to do with a dozen kids around you," Chris said, ribbing his wife.

Suzanne, emerging from the emergency room, chided, "Speaking of which, will I ever see any?"

Other than apologizing for not staying in the emergency room with her mother, Anita was lost for words. Suzanne stated she had a minor concussion, but other than that, she was good. Changing the topic, Suzanne looked at the couple that stood before her. "Well?" she asked.

Batting her eyes at her adorable man, Anita replied, "Of course, but first we must get the opportunity to practice." The laughter gave them the much needed stress relief.

As they walked towards the exit door of the hospital, Suzanne said, "Just don't wait until I'm in a rocking chair, okay?"

Anita promised that wouldn't happen. Taking Suzanne to a hotel, Anita and Chris told her to stay put and relax, and they would be back shortly. Suzanne, grateful for the rest, knew Anita was going to visit with Ivan before departing for home. As Suzanne laid her head down to rest, she was surmising about how their worlds had been turned around. No one knew which was worse: the evil they left behind or the danger they were veering into. Suzanne admitted to herself that she loved every minute of it.

CHAPTER FORTY

As they approached the door to their home, Delia greeted them with a grim look on her face. In her broken English, she told them that a fire had burned their garage. Concerned for Delia's well being, Chris asked, "Are you okay?"

She nodded her head to show she was fine, and Chris went to survey the damaged area, while the others took their belongings inside. Chris detected a cheap model of an explosive bomb and scouted for any evidence of who may have set it off. Taking the remains of the bomb back to the house, he placed it in a bag, and went to join the group who were busy talking over coffee in the kitchen.

"How bad is it?" Anita asked, as he came in.

"Amateur bomb. It can't have been anyone with power. I think it says 'back off' more than anything else," Chris said, as he grabbed a cup of coffee himself. His face drawn, and he eyed each person at the table before saying, "I'd like you all to go somewhere safe."

Suzanne was the first to say she'd like to stay at the house, that she would become a scout so she could feel she was doing her part. Delia put up her hand to volunteer her services, and Anita agreed to do her part, remarking, "This reminds me of a western when everyone circles the wagon and protects each other. I like the way we knit together."

Chris was not happy at how the group had made this decision without to listening him, but he knew better than to argue and gave up. Out of the blue, Suzanne's eyes shot wide open, and she announced, "It was Douglas. He's alive and this is his way of getting me out of here. Well, that just backfired, didn't it?" She raised her cup of coffee and toasted her husband, saying, "I toast the man who lives in hell."

"Mom, you can't mean that?" Anita said, in a horrified voice.

"I do. It's obvious his own ass is more important than his family. It's just like him to avoid the important things, but these scare tactics aren't going to work. When I find him and settle the score, he'll wish I hadn't," Suzanne vowed.

Anita raised her cup, and toasted Suzanne. "You go Mom," she said. She then looked at Chris and asked, "You with us?"

"Do I have a choice?" Chris jibbed back.

"While we're on the subject of Dad, Mom, what do you think he did with all his money? I mean, he made millions each year and if you add up what's in his will, it comes up real short. I realize he lost a few million during the extortion and traveling back and forth, but this is minor compared to what he made," Anita said, half questioning and half reasoning her father's actions.

Suzanne went deep into thought, giving the appearance of being a million miles away. Suddenly, she said, "He tied up loose ends. He has an account under an assumed name and he is going to make a new life."

Chris agreed that Douglas definitely knew what he was doing, and finally accepted the fact that his father-in-law must still be alive, playing everyone for fools, and that one day very soon, he would be discovered.

The rest of the day was spent in quiet solitude as they gathered their thoughts, because they knew it was only a matter of time before little wakes of turmoil would disturb their peaceful bliss.

CHAPTER FORTY-ONE

Gearing up, Anita and Chris prepared to seek out Gappy and see what his plans were. Delia and Suzanne concocted a plan to explore the burnt garage to disperse their anxiety. Never having done anything around the house before, other than housework, Delia beamed with delight as the pair headed out on their sleuthing adventure with caution.

Looking for clues of any sort, Delia came across something of interest and Suzanne examined the treasure; it was a book of matches that Douglas always kept in his pocket in case of emergencies, and its presence at the scene confirmed that he had been the one to set off the warning signal. Their curiosity aroused, the two detectives placed the evidence into a secured pocket, careful not to touch the item, and carried on in hopes of finding more treasures. At one point, Suzanne stood up and glanced around, swearing she could feel eyes watching her. She shook off the notion, however, and continued checking every inch of the ground.

Suddenly, they stopped abruptly in their tracks. Suzanne bent down and had Delia confirm what she saw: a trail of blood leading away from the scene. The women held hands for support, and began to follow the trail of red droplets, giving each other courage to carry on.

An alarming feeling rushed between them like an electric shock, and they half expected to see a body on the ground or to be snagged by a trap. When a twig snapped behind them, they stopped dead in their tracks, and squeezed their hands tightly together. Turning their heads towards each other, the pair surveyed their surroundings. They saw nothing, but nonetheless, made a quick decision to head home. Doing an about-face, Delia noticed a piece of paper on the ground and scooped it up. They tried to read the faint writing by holding it up to the sun in hopes of deciphering the note's contents, but got very little results.

Delia looked at her companion. "Belong to your husband?" she asked.

Puzzled Suzanne studied the paper. "It looks like it could be and yet, it doesn't. I think someone planted it there either to spook us, or to make us believe Douglas is alive –or, it could really be Douglas. I just don't know."

Very earnestly, Delia asked, "You think they want us dead?"

"No, they could've done us in any time if that's what they wanted. It's a warning sign, like they are the hunters and we're the prey, and they will play with us until they tire. I say let's run," Suzanne said, feeling vulnerable.

"On three, we run," Delia said.

They began counting, but they only got as far as "two" and they sprang into action, running until they were panting for air. Catching their breath, Suzanne leaned over and noticed another blood trail. Petrified of becoming live bait, Suzanne beckoned to Delia to check out her latest findings. Debating, whether to run or follow the trail, Suzanne asked Delia to spot for her and she began to trek down the unfamiliar path, daring not to speak. Delia kept far enough away so that if either of them were caught, the other would have a chance to get away.

Suzanne was somewhat disorientated, but became more concerned when Delia, who had been behind her, now passed her on the path. She watched as Delia entered a hidden rundown shack. Suzanne followed her in, and watched the other woman kneel down by the baseboard, and tugged at it until it gave way. The gap housed a gun, which Delia placed in her pocket. Sharply, Suzanne said, "Explain."

Delia's usual pidgin dialect came out in perfect English. "I am very poor. The money I make goes towards my child's education so he can become a doctor. Please don't tell Chris. I love my job. This gun is how I survived all these years and we need it right now."

Terrified that Delia might be an assassin, Suzanne stuttered, "Chris likes you too, and puts his trust in you. Are you out to harm him or anyone involved?"

Defending her current status, Delia explained, "I may be a phony as far as my English, but it's your alleged dead husband who's the one not to fool with."

Licking her lips, Delia decided to spill the information she had been withholding. "Douglas knew every square inch of this place. I'd see him writing things down constantly. I'd like to know where those papers are. Find them, and you'll find answers to the riddles he left behind. I love your daughter as though she was my own. Chris too. I want no harm to come to either of them, and I plan to work for them as long as I can, and to be there when they have kids. We need to find those papers and stop danger before it strikes."

"I'm with you, but why didn't you tell me this before? I can keep a secret you know." Suzanne was indignant at this betrayal.

"Until now, I didn't know who to trust. I guess this way was kind of a shock to you and I apologize. Really, I wouldn't hurt the kids for anything," pleaded Delia, eager to be forgiven. Instantly, Suzanne threw her hands down by her side and a moment later, she hugged her companion tightly.

Suzanne needed time to adjust to this news and was pensive as she followed Delia home. She was grateful to see the familiar cottage. As dusk was setting in, Suzanne's imagination got the better of her and she thought that it was casting evil phantoms, and she felt like they were being surrounded. She outran Delia to the house and waited at the back door for her to catch up. No lights were on in the house, which indicated that the kids weren't home yet. Delia pushed Suzanne to the side, cocked her gun, and quietly entered the house, looking for signs of an unwanted presence. Sighing with relief that the house had not been invaded, the two new friends poured some wine, clinked glasses, and put the soothing liquid down the hatch in one swallow. They sat down, put their feet up, and laughed at their attempt of being detectives.

CHAPTER FORTY-TWO

As they ventured on another excursion to see Gappy, the young couple expressed their views on the latest event. Chris, thought it was a warning not to double-cross Dante; Anita swore it was her dad trying to sway her into thinking like him – in fact, the more she talked about it, the more it made sense to her; she would start thinking like him and perhaps unravel a thing or two.

Having not paid attention to their whereabouts, Anita became suddenly aware that Chris had taken a new route. "Is Gappy in a new location?" she inquired. "And if so, how do you know?"

"Don't miss much do you? Yes, it's a new route to you, but he keeps his equipment here and only a few know of it. I figured it was safe not to blindfold you. You can be trusted, right?" Chris said, as he tweaked her nose and laughed.

Gawking at her strange surroundings, Anita had no idea where they were. Even if she were tortured for information, she wouldn't be able to give the coordinates of this place, thus preserving the well-kept secret. Chris parked the vehicle under a thatched garage hidden from the elements, and they walked through a wooded area, coming to a halt at the base of a mountain. Dipping down and running his hand under what looked like a rock, a door automatically opened just enough for them to duck under and, within seconds, it was closed again. A spotlight shone on them and they stood still. Heavily armed guards, who met them at the door, searched the couple for weapons. Anita, upset at how they searched her, brought her knee up and let the guard have it between the legs, vowing that Gappy would hear about it.

The guard was about to backhand Anita, when Chris intervened, and they were closely escorted further into the cave, giving Anita the willies. Chris warned Anita to be very careful about what she said or did, because this was strictly business proposition. She let him know that she fully understood the situation.

The cave was cold and damp. Anita rubbed her arms to keep her circulation flowing and to warm up her slightly lowered body temperature. Coming to a dead end, a narrow steel door was opened, letting them pass through in single file. There, before her eyes, was artillery complete with rifles, handguns, grenades, missiles, rocket launchers, bombs, dynamite, explosives, gas, detonators, fuses and ammo enough to start a war. Men buzzed around them as they packed up what they needed for the forth-coming mission, supported by Anita.

Gappy was there, and when he snapped his fingers, a jacket was thrown over Anita's shoulders, warming her and making her feel much more comfortable. She was very grateful for the kind gesture. Gappy suggested they sit and he wanted to know what was on their minds.

Anita looked at Chris, who nodded for her to go ahead and state her requests. Anita then turned her focus back to her business partner, and said, "When Blake's free, he'll need to be kept under lock and key until I negotiate with Dante."

"What does Dante have to do with this?" Gappy asked, narrowing his eyes with suspicion.

Squaring herself in the chair that was warming beneath her, Anita gave a brief explanation. "As you know, Dante has my best friend and, in return, he wants Blake and my services as his lawyer." She noticed the look he gave her, and retaliated, "Don't look at me like that. I'm not my father, and believe me when I say Dante will get his when the time is right. When that happens, you can be sure I'll call on you for support, and I'll not take no for an answer. I know you want him eliminated as well, for whatever your purpose may be. I'll not defend such a man."

Sitting back in his chair, and stroking his chin, Gappy said, "I don't know why you are here. I've agreed to spring Blake, but what does Dante want with him? And suppose I tell you I know where your friend is being held hostage. What then?"

Leaning over his desk, Anita could feel his breath on her face. "I don't know what dealings Dante has with Blake, but I'm here to let you know I'm ready for the dastardly deed to be done. I'm sure all our questions will be answered soon enough. I say, let's get Carolyn out," she said, making everyone question her integrity.

Tapping his fingers on the desk, Gappy wanted to know what Anita's intentions were, and asked, "Before or after Blake?"

Leaning back in her chair, Anita mused, "You decide."

Chris held up his hand, and said, "Gappy, we've been friends for a long time, so I'm going to ask you, what do you know about Douglas's death? And before you answer, remember there is little you don't know."

"My source tells me it was a hoax. Though I can't prove it one way or the other," Gappy said, simply.

Interrupting, Anita brought the conversation back to the task at hand. "We'll spring Blake first so Dante will relax, then we'll hit the secret compound where Carolyn's being held, and lastly, we'll settle the score with Dante."

"It'll cost you," Gappy announced, flatly.

"I wouldn't have it any other way," Anita replied proudly. Then she asked, "So where is she? Carolyn – where is she?"

"It was a question to see what was more important and it's obvious. You are right, Dante will keep." Gappy shook her hand in a business-like fashion and then gave her his instructions. "I'll be in touch with you in a couple of days. Expect to partake in the action."

"Does my participation decrease the fee? Say by ten percent?" Anita asked Gappy.

He dropped her hand and opened the door. "I've already included that discount," he said. "You will also be included in the rescue of your friend. Have a great day."

Knowing the conversation was over, the couple was led out and found dusk fast approaching as they began their journey home. Breaking the silence, Anita shared her thoughts with Chris. "You know, my dad's empty briefcase was the clincher for me. Who would take an empty locked case on a plane? And Gappy, it seems, had his own beliefs on the matter. Dad thought Dante was holding Carolyn at the house, but that will remain a mystery until we force the issue. I seem to get the feeling Gappy is not on the up-and-up, but no matter, I'd rather have him on my side than against me."

Chris burst her little bubble. "Sorry to say this, but Gappy is on his own side, loyal to whom ever is paying him. He'll see to it the job gets done, because that's what he's good at. As for me and Gappy, yes, we are friends, but again, we know the boundaries of that friendship."

"There's more to it than that. You know all his hideouts and secrets," Anita said, factually.

Chris pulled off to the side of the road and turned to Anita. "I once saved his ass and now we're even," he explained. "Yes, he confides in me because I've never caused him grief, and I've used his services many times. We have a business trust, not a friend trust."

Her thoughts collected all the data and shot out her results. "I get it. You're like the middleman. Your mission is to make friends with the enemy, and because of your connections, you play both sides. Your discretion and confidentiality keeps that trust."

"Something like that," Chris confirmed, as he safely pulled back into the lane of traffic and headed for home.

Rushing into the house for a cup of Delia's famous coffee, the couple found Suzanne and Delia sitting with their feet up, and drinks in their hands. Chris turned around to stifle his laughter at the sight of this pair. Fearful of being reprimanded, Delia jumped up and spilled her drink down her shirt. When Chris turned around and saw the stain, he burst out laughing and told her to sit and relax, and that he and Anita would join them. Chris fixed them all a drink and everyone was quiet, but the ladies were bursting with news they wanted to share.

Suzanne beamed as she began their story. "I coaxed Delia to go with me and try our hand at becoming junior detectives at the burn site. We found a book of matches that, I believe, belongs to your father, and a fresh trail of blood. We started to follow the blood trail, got scared off, and high-tailed it home. We scoured the house to see if had been invaded while we were out, but the coast was clear." Suzanne carefully handed the matches to Chris.

"And you did this because?" Anita asked.

"Boredom. I didn't want to go alone, so I persuaded Delia to go with me. Are you angry?" Suzanne asked, though she knew it was okay.

Anita's eyes bounced back and forth between Suzanne and Delia. "Not really. You could've been hurt or kidnapped. Did you leave a note to indicate where you were headed?" Anita spoke, like she was scolding a couple of teenagers.

"Huh. That never crossed my mind. Thanks for the tip," Suzanne said, and took a sip of her drink.

Chris found his voice, and said, "Ladies, in future, I think it's best to keep your inquisitiveness on the home front." He watched their faces fall, and added, "Unless you have a back-up plan."

Not sure what she should say, Delia enlisted Suzanne's help in making a bite to eat. Anita and Chris soon joined them and the talk evolved around the day's activities. After hearing what had happened to the others, the junior detectives vowed to ensure their safety, complete with contingency plans. The waiting game had a way of making them all feel antsy, as if they were sitting on the edge of a mountain, fearful of falling off, and yet intrigued to see what would happen next.

CHAPTER FORTY-THREE

With plans of snooping around the burn site and following the blood trails, Chris and Anita discussed their ideas with her mother, who was bouncing like she had a hornet buzzing around her, prompting Anita to ask what she was up to. Suzanne simply stated that she was still spooked from the day before and Anita, more or less, settled for the vague explanation. The couple had a nourishing meal and headed out the door. Suzanne and Delia, who remained in the house, cleaned up and then set forth on their own agenda to do some treasure hunting within the boundaries of the house.

Heading to Suzanne's room, the two amateur detectives began rifling through every inch of the space for a sign of what Douglas had been up to. Frustrated, the pair sat down. They were disappointed because they had been sure they would find even the tiniest clue to affirm his continued existence, but instead, they came up with a handful of nothing.

Pondering over the lack of clues, Delia looked at Suzanne. "Think like Douglas. Where would he hide such papers?"

Shocked at Delia's statement, Suzanne shot back, "What do you mean, think like Douglas?"

Thinking she had been misunderstood, Delia rephrased her statement. "You lived with the man for a long time. Where would he hide such important papers?"

She had certainly been with Douglas a long time, so Suzanne sat on the bed with her hands firmly clasped and looked straight ahead, thinking. In this trance-like state, a mirage appeared as she slowly described Douglas's hiding spot; it was behind the mirror.

They pulled out the dresser, but the back looked untouched. They pulled out the drawers, turning them over and checking them both inside and outside, and for a false bottom. Still nothing was found. Delia then ran her hand over the back of the dresser and – there it was, a little concealed door. They needed a sharp object to pry it open. Their hearts were beating so fast, that Delia had to fan herself to cool down. Suzanne wiped the sweat off her face as their excitement climaxed. Searching frantically for something small, they found a nail file, and slid the small edge of the file along the seams, the door popped and out came some papers, making them laugh hysterically at their new-found talent. But, as they looked the papers over, they were unable to derive any meaning from them, and decided to leave them on Chris's desk. He'd know what to make of the documents. Now, looking at the mess they had made in the room, they knew it was time to clean up. When they were done, they shook hands on having one spring-cleaned room and went downstairs, satisfied and full of pride.

Sipping on their coffee, the ladies tossed a coin in the air to see whether they should tear the den apart to see if they could add to their discovery. The outcome of the coin-toss didn't really matter, as they were going to do it anyway. The coin, to them, was just a formality.

Now that they had a feel for Douglas's thoughts, Delia and Suzanne were very careful to look for hidden compartments, as they began their task. Every square inch of the room was examined more than once and coming up empty handed was not on their agenda. They knew Douglas had spent time in the room and, therefore, something had to be hidden there. The only thing they didn't examine was the chair behind the desk. When they turned it over, they found that inside the shaft was a carefully folded piece of paper with items listed on it that neither of them could decipher. They laid it on the table, proud of another job well done. They hadn't realized how much work investigating was – especially the clean up part. Still, they were pleased they found something and went off to celebrate.

Anita and Chris began their search for the trail of blood and had almost given up, when Chris noticed the little droplets leading to the heavily brushed area. With a weapon in his hand, Chris led the way and Anita stayed very close behind him. Along the new pathway, Chris noticed some white papers and stopped to pick them up. Anita trembled as she recognized the handwriting to be her father's, and asked Chris if perhaps her father had hidden some vital papers in the garage. Chris's response was that Douglas was a man with many secrets and that one could only guess.

Their trail went cold, and Chris ran his hand over the area, surmising whoever set the fire had used a quad to make their escape. There were definitely more than one set of footprints, excluding those of Suzanne and Delia, who had followed the tracks earlier.

"Dante," Anita said, softly. "He's out for revenge. He wants me to defend him, so I'm thinking he's planting a take-heed message here." A shiver traveled the circuit of her body, causing small, piercing shocks to give her a jolt.

"That's one theory, but it could also be Gappy," Chris said, as he studied the area closely.

"Gappy?" Anita repeated, surprised. "I'm paying him for a job."

Touching her face lightly with his hand, Chris affirmed his earlier comment. "Remember, Gappy is loyal to whoever pays him. He takes no sides. What I'm trying to say is - if someone out pays you, that job is done first. Of course, he wouldn't *kill* you until your job is done; he wants full payment. At that point, you become just another paid contract."

Shaking her head as she tried to rationalize his theory, Anita said, "I don't believe that for a second. I know Gappy wants my help to do something to Dante. No, I think my father is tangled up with another source, creating a perfect time to disappear. That makes the most sense."

A twig snapped, causing them both to freeze in their tracks, forcing them to crouch down. Chris got on his belly and glided along the ground noiselessly. Anita raised her head until she could see over the brush and looked around. The scene was a vast area covered with trees and shrubbery. She could not see any movement; even the air was still. Anita's insides turned a frigid temperature as she waited for Chris to give some sort of signal that the coast was clear. Anita waited a few more minutes and then couldn't wait any longer. She stood straight up, and yelled, "Come on out, you chicken."

Her voice carried well into the valley, but no reply was heard. She spoke again. "I'm going home now," she said, loudly. "What are you going to do, jump us from behind? Face us like a person, not a coward."

Still there was no sound, and Chris, who was now a ways from Anita, surveyed the area detecting nothing. He stayed quiet, but motioned for Anita to start walking, and he'd be close behind. Anita didn't like the idea, but agreed. Before he could see it coming, a large branch collided with Chris's head, knocking him briefly unconscious. Anita tried to follow the fresh tracks, but lost them. When she got back to Chris, she helped him up. He wanted to track the person, but at Anita's insistence, they headed home. Chris staggered from time to time, with blood dripping from the back of his head. As they reached their safe haven, Anita yelled and Delia was on the doorstep in a flash, knowing just what to do. Once they got Chris inside and put him on the sofa, Delia made up one of her concoctions and applied it to his head. He fell asleep, and they kept waking him up to ensure he was all right. Finally, certain he was going to come out of it okay, they let him sleep without interruption.

Pouring a drink to calm her nerves, Anita turned to look at her mother and, then at Delia. "Okay you two, what did you discover?"

Suzanne chuckled at her daughter's sixth sense. "You seem to be good at interpreting my facial expressions. You are going to make a very good lawyer."

Delia's head hung, as she spoke. "You angry at me being lazy?"

Anita's eyes peered over her glass and looked at the pair of ladies standing before her. "No. We've been neglecting you, leaving you on your own. So, if you are able to do a little relaxation, you are welcome to do so. You *are* just relaxing, right?"

A mischievous look was exchanged between Delia and Suzanne, but they agreed at the same time that they were just relaxing. Anita strolled into the den and saw some papers she knew were not there before. Quickly skimming over them, she laughed as she reentered the living room. "Seems our little detectives are up to more than rest and relaxation. Okay you two. Confess to your crime. It should be good." She held her finger up in the air to indicate they should wait a minute, and said, "Hang on. I think Chris should hear this." Anita gently awoke Chris and asked if he wanted to hear what the ladies had discovered. He groggily said yes and slowly got up.

Suzanne was pacing and wringing her hands together as the couple sat comfortably. Suzanne then sat down rubbing her hands together. "We were bored," she said. "After checking out the garage, we felt compelled to check out my bedroom for a secret stash of papers. He always carried papers with him and when his briefcase was empty, well the papers have to be somewhere. He was always one for putting things in places where people wouldn't look, so we vandalized the room in search of his missing papers. We came up with only a few. We also concluded he spent a lot of time in the den and again we tore it apart and came up with a few pieces of paper. So, technically we *were* relaxing and, I might add, we did some spring cleaning while we were at it."

Anita had to contain her laughter as Chris did his best to scold the unusual team. "You two be very careful," he told them. "This isn't a game. We were being followed out there and it could happen to you as well. I suggest you stay together and cover each other's back." He could feel their eyes upon him, but he knew they understood. "When do we eat?" he asked, changing the subject. "Oh, and by the way, Delia, you may go home whenever you wish. I didn't mean to keep you here all this time, but it is nice having you here."

Delia mumbled something in Spanish, and Chris laughing, retorted, "I do *not* take all the fun out of life. I am merely telling you to take precautions and you can choose to stay or go home."

The sharp, penetrating shrill of the phone echoed through the house and neither Chris nor Anita moved to answer it. Suzanne's keen sense of their avoidance prompted her to pick it up. She put her hand over the mouthpiece, and said, "Anita. It's Dante."

Clearing her throat, Anita's voice had a flaw in it. "Hello," she said into the phone.

Dante's patronizing voice made her want to throw up as he spoke. "Anita. We have a meeting scheduled for ten o'clock tomorrow morning. My men will pick you up."

"You know Chris will accompany me," she replied. Her tone was cold as she choked back the urge to be sick.

"Wouldn't have it any other way," Dante taunted back.

Something snapped inside Anita, and she became edgy and shook as she made her demand known to Dante. "This had better be about Carolyn." But she didn't hear a response, only the dial tone. She hung up the phone. Using her hands to wipe the excessive moisture off her face, Anita stared anxiously at Chris. "He wants to meet at ten in the morning," she said.

"Let's go to the den while dinner is being prepared. We'll go over your dad's papers and see if there is anything we can use," Chris suggested. Anita nodded, as they retreated to the den. The ladies were relieved they were off the hook for their activities and were happy at the diversion of making a meal. Anita sunk down into the sofa; her emotions were drag racing to see which was faster: anxiety or hatred. It was almost a tie.

Chris sat beside her and the two carefully read the papers, but between them, they were not able to decipher what it was Douglas was trying to pinpoint. What was clear, however, was that it was a map, and they knew by the terrain that it indicated a place somewhere within a hundred-mile radius.

Putting down the papers, Chris's thoughts diverted to his housekeeper, and marveled at how she had become a part of the family. Even with perils lurking on the outside, she was enjoying herself. Knowing that Anita was unable to spend a lot of time with her mother, he was glad that Suzanne and Delia became friends. And, yes, he had to admit; they were having innocent fun, which in the long run was feeding them leads as to what Douglas may have been planning. He only hoped their amusements stayed that way – innocent. After dinner, they all congregated in the living room, sat down, and had a drink. Delia was feeling right at home and thanked Chris for being the best employer in the world, making him blush.

CHAPTER FORTY-FOUR

Unable to sleep, Anita thought she might have the house to herself and, getting up, she headed to the kitchen. There she found Suzanne and Delia sitting with a cup of coffee, talking, Wanting to eavesdrop, Anita stood at the door, but was soon called in by Suzanne, which surprised her because she thought she was getting better at being sneaky. Guilt ridden, Anita turned to her mother, and said, "I'm so sorry I'm not spending more time with you, but if things go as planned, it won't be long until we can enjoy our reunion. These trials and tribulations I've put you through will tell you what kind of daughter I am. Maybe they'll make you reconsider whether to support me in the future."

Hugging her daughter, Suzanne spoke with pride. "Honey, I understand your dilemma and nothing could surprise or alter my feelings. I lived with your father for a number of years and the only difference is, *you* have compassion – something your father lacked."

Checking her watch, Anita knew Chris was an early riser and yet he hadn't come down. As she quickly fixed two cups of coffee to go, Chris appeared in the kitchen doorway. "I think Gappy is right," he said. "Dante is holding Carolyn in a camp and not at his house. There is a spot on the map your dad left and, I think that is where she is being held. Having her at the house would be far too risky."

Anita's impulse to run and check out the map was squashed, as the rendezvous with the repulsive man would soon be upon them. The couple went to the front porch and could hear a vehicle approaching. As it pulled up, a door automatically opened. They climbed in and were whisked away to unknown territory.

Watching until they departed, Delia suggest that they go to the village because she had something important she wanted to do. Suzanne was all for a venture and followed behind, both checking over their shoulders for unwanted company. Not feeling overly fearful for their lives, Suzanne took in the sight of the village and was finding it fascinating at how the little village homes were built with bamboo and thatched roofs. When Delia took her to a very small, smelly shack, the strangely labeled bottles filled with unfamiliar ingredients mesmerized Suzanne. Delia looked around and told Suzanne to stand guard while she pulled out a well-hidden book. She began to search through it causing Suzanne to question her motives. As Delia looked up from the book, it was as though her eyes were rolling back in her head. "I want to put a spell on Dante," she announced. "You know, play with his mind a bit. Make him nicer."

Totally intrigued by Delia's capabilities and naughtiness, Suzanne knelt beside Delia. "You can do that?" she said incredulously.

Getting back to her book and reading the titles, Delia replied with enthusiasm, "Don't know for sure, but I'm willing to try. This book belonged to my mother and she used it all the time. I never believed in playing around with minds, but I want the kids to be safe. Besides, it'll be fun."

Suzanne shook Delia's hand, and said, "You are amazing. I have much to learn. Let's do it. Coming here was the best thing I could've done. By the way, could you contact Douglas?"

"Only if he's truly dead. We will try that later, right now we have bigger fish to reel in," Delia said, in a tone that would cause anything that moved to come to a complete stop.

Suzanne smiled, and softly said, "Yes, we have much bigger game to manipulate," and burst out laughing at the prospect of being able to change minds.

Chris and Anita were blindfolded and found the journey rough, fast, and frustrating because they were unable to see where they were being taken. Her cup of coffee was the only solace Anita had to cling to, since Chris was seated behind her to prevent them from talking or conspiring.

Without warning, the vehicle stopped abruptly, tossing Anita around and spilling her coffee. She unleashed some colorful language. Their seat belts were released and both were forcefully taken out of their sitting position, but Anita twisted her foot, and fell to the ground. There was no gentleness when she was picked up. Both Anita and Chris could feel a forceful hand tighten around their shirt collars, as they were towed by brute strength to their next point of interest. Anita's foot throbbed and her limp became worse, but she dared not utter a word for fear of being struck in the head. The man who held Chris threw him to the ground, and his head struck a rock. He soon felt a warm, moist liquid trickle down the side of his face. Anita was more fortunate; she just ate some dirt as she was tossed to the ground.

The blindfolds were removed and Chris and Anita struggled to adjust their eyes to the bright sun. Chris looked around trying to get his bearings, but was unable to find any familiar landmarks. He made some mental notes in hopes of pinpointing their location on a map later, but his sense of direction seemed a little off for the moment. The long barrel of the gun that one of the men carried reached out and collided with Chris's head, making him wince in pain. Anita could only show empathy, and knew better than to get involved. In an instant, the butt of the gun connected to her head as well, generating excruciating pain. A whacking noise could be heard in the distance and, as time went on, the sound got closer and closer. When Dante finally emerged, he had a whip in his hand.

Dante had a smile of victory written on his face, and said, smugly, "I see you are both sharing again. You each have similar wounds to nurture. Sorry Chris, but the clobber on her head was to reduce your thoughts. Can't have you finding this place again. Who knows, this could be where Carolyn is being held hostage."

Anita raised her head; all she could see were mountains, shrub, and the menacing man who stood before her. "It's all part of your game," she said. "You never do anything without thinking it through."

Dante patter her on the top of her head. "Good observation," he said, patronizingly. "And that my dear, is why I chose you. You have spunk. Your dad had pep, but lost it over time."

Daring to defy the monster, Anita took a chance and slowly stood up, saying, "Enough about my father. Let's get on with the meeting. Where's Carolyn?"

Dante's neck stretched and he stuck out his square jaw. He sucked in his over-extended waistline, and cracked the whip he was holding, causing it to pop within inches of Anita. "Don't rush me," he said

Anita's eyes danced, as she replied, "Deal with it. I don't toy with people. Just get to the heart of the matter. I jump for no one."

Dante leaned in towards Anita, invading her personal space, and she could feel the hot stench, from his mouth, surround her. It made her cough. Dante knew he was the owner of the moment. "Okay. We'll see how it goes," he said, and stepped back motioning for Chris and Anita to follow him. The trail was shallow and the trees were dense, not allowing a clear vision of their whereabouts. Chris was unusually quiet and Anita hoped it was because of the lumps he had accumulated in the last few minutes, and not her attitude.

Glancing behind them, Anita noticed the small trail looked closed off and she knew it would be difficult to find it again. Turning back to face straight ahead, she saw that the trail led right to the mouth of a cave and, when they reached it, it magically opened. The damp musty smell opened her nostrils, like a whiff of ammonia, and Anita had to plug her nose to keep from gagging. Walking in, there were little alcoves with bars across them and the lighting was very dim.

Once her eyes became accustomed to the dimly lit cave, she noticed curtains on the walls, a small propane stove, a bar fridge, and a table with four chairs. She could see a corridor leading to the back and assumed it also had niches with bars on them to keep prisoners tucked away so no one could see them. Chris, too, was taking the details in as best he could. He knew it would be very difficult to make a rescue of any sort from this place, but looking up he saw a tiny beam of light peeking through some jagged rock formations, and thought, *that is the only way in.*

While Chris kept his thoughts to himself, Anita vocalized hers. "You sure did make this camp impossible to attack," she said, as she ran her hand along the cold walls.

The two men accompanying Dante each placed a hand on Chris and Anita's shoulders and forced them to sit at the table. Dante disappeared into the back, and reappeared with Carolyn, who sat directly across from Anita.

"I don't suppose we're allowed to hug, are we?" Anita asked, testing Dante's icy limits. Anita then held Carolyn's hand, squeezed it and, getting no response, drew back like it had given her frostbite. "Carolyn, it's me Anita. Just think your days of entrapment are soon to be over."

"That would be nice," Carolyn answered, mechanically.

Anita delved into her best friend's new attitude. "This isn't like you. Where's your vitality, your positive outlook on life, your sense of humor?"

Sharp glances shot between Dante and Carolyn. Then she turned to look at Anita, and said, "Being drugged, held hostage, and put in this hell hole with no sunlight tends to take away anything good in life."

Not accepting her answer, Anita shot back, "That's bull and you know it. The last time I saw you, you were willing to do anything to stay alive. Granted, this place is not great and, yes, it would take away some of your enthusiasm, but I know the Carolyn I grew up with would never have succumbed to this. And I know for a fact that, you have not been here all that along. I think you were planted here to make me believe it, but I'm not that gullible."

Dante stood up, and snapped, "That's enough. I held up my end of the bargain."

Still unsure of the person who sat across from her, Anita spoke loudly, attracting everyone's attention. "I want to see the birthmark on her neck, right now," she barked.

A nod came from Dante and Carolyn bared her neck, exposing her birthmark. It looked odd to Anita, but she conceded that the darkness could be distorting what she saw. Now taking a much closer look at her friend, Anita saw she was thin, her cheeks were sunken, her eyes bulged out, her hair was long and stringy, but the little twitches that forced her hands to move involuntarily, put doubt in her mind. The person before her, as Anita saw it, was always a gaunt, thin looking person; not a person who had become this way from being locked up. As far as Anita was concerned, she was a plant and Dante was hoping she had fallen for it.

After taking a photo with her memory, Anita got up to leave. Pretending to believe this was her best friend, Anita shook the young lady's hand. "We'll be the best of friends again, I assure you," she said.

Carolyn's voice was weak-sounding and the words barely came out of her mouth. "I hope so," she replied.

Unable to stand this place another moment, Anita spontaneously ran to the mouth of the cave to suck in some fresh air, and to let the sun warm her body, ridding her of the moldy smell. She was glad she hadn't eaten because what little there was in her stomach, now covered the grass beside the trail. The guards, who had taken the couple into the cave, now surrounded them, preventing them from leaving.

Dante stood like the lion of the jungle, proud of his haven that was safely tucked away. "You know my plan was to keep you here?"

"What changed your mind?" Chris asked, as he too breathed in the fresh air.

Playing with his gun, Dante stated, "I'm not sure. We now have a deal. I want Blake and you can have Carolyn."

Using force to break through the human barrier, Anita stood within inches of Dante, "And how would keeping me here have benefited you? I need to get Blake out. I don't need you to monitor every move I make. You know enough already. How soon do you want Blake?"

Dante's eyes became intense and Anita was sure his pupils changed shape to that of a cat. "I'll give you one week. Let's say one week from today at noon. I'll call you for a place and time for the exchange," he said, proudly establishing that he still ruled.

Anita, thinking to herself, "*What's with his eyes? Must be my imagination. No eyes can do that.*" She shook her head and refocused on what they were negotiating, and knew she could take control of the situation. She stood confidently shaking her finger in front of Dante's face. "No. You won't. I'll call you. And one more thing, if that woman is indeed Carolyn, she had better be in better shape the next time we meet. Are you getting my message?" Anita asked.

As Dante looked up at the sky, every muscle in his body tightened. Insulted that a woman was trying to call the shots, he lowered his eyes to meet with Anita's, and said, "That's not how I do business."

Anita's eyes become nothing more than a glint. She folded her arms and stood with one foot slightly ahead of the other. "It is now," she replied. "Should I succeed before the week is done, I'll give you a call. That's how I do business."

Dante's expression held bewilderment that she could just indicate the business dealings in this manner. "What about Carolyn?" he asked.

"Do we have a deal?" Anita asked, knowing she had won this round.

"I'll be expecting your call," he answered.

Unfolding her arms, Anita again looked at Dante strangely, wondering why he didn't retaliate against her defiance. Taking advantage of a good thing, Anita hooked her arm around Chris's and they began to limp away. "That woman in there may or may not be Carolyn. I will fulfill my end of the deal, and *I will* rescue my friend Carolyn," Anita said, letting her voice trail off as the two continued hobbling away.

Not being able to get far, they were apprehended, blindfolded, and led roughly to the vehicle. "I'll be expecting a call very soon," Dante said. He then turned to the driver and instructed the driver to drop them off a good distance from the cave, and let them fend for themselves in making their way back home.

Anita, not liking how they were being treated, called out. "And you want me to defend you after you treat us like this? Just take us to our home. Fair is fair," she yelled.

Dante smiled at her feistiness. Instead of taking the bite for another confrontation, he let his opinion be heard. "*You* will defend me, and *you* will get a not guilty verdict, and *this* is my way of telling you I'm still in control. Have a nice day."

The ride along the trail was about half way to their home and the two were dumped off at the side of the road. Chris did everything he could to get Anita to look at him. He had so much to ask her, but she just kept walking, saying nothing. Her head ached with every step she took; the pain pounded in her brain, but at least it camouflaged the pain in her foot. Chris's head felt as though it had been split in two, and when he had to take a rest, he found Anita right by his side.

"When are you going to tell me what you're thinking?" Chris wanted to know.

Holding her head to keep the shooting pain from lifting it off her shoulders, Anita made a quick assessment. "That *looked* like Carolyn, but in my heart I know it wasn't. There was no happy response to seeing me; it was as though she didn't recognize me. I believe it was a ploy. Why he's doing that is because I think he will use it against me at a later time. As for Dante, himself, I can't let him beat me, but I found it strange that he relented. It was like I was talking to someone else. I swear his pupils changed shape. It was just plain weird."

Chris held his wife's hand and guided them back onto the road in hopes of catching a ride should someone drive by. "You're right," he said, "it was weird. I have sharp jabs of pain rushing through my head, how about you?"

"With every step I hear echoes in my head and it feels like it could blow off at any time. My foot feels detached… I don't feel it. Dante is such a jerk and he will get his. That I vow. As for Carolyn, or whoever that woman in the cave is, I now feel as though I have lost her. If it is Carolyn, then it may take years for her to regain her true self and if it isn't, well she'll be gone forever because once I'm through with Dante, he'll never reveal where she really is. The woman is a decoy and as along as he has the real Carolyn, he can keep me dancing. Only I won't dance for long," Anita said, and the tone of her voice made her statement believable.

The walk was long and very tiring, and the couple had to rest from to time to catch their breath. Then, in what looked like a mirage to Chris, an old bus was heading their way. They waved their hands in desperation, and the bus stopped. The pair clamored on, taking refuge amongst the chickens and people spitting on the floor; but to them it was heaven not to have walk the rest of the distance. Getting off at a stop close to their home, the two began their final journey to the house smelling of chickens and cigarettes, and when they entered the house, Suzanne immediately sent them to their room to clean up. Trying their best not to laugh too heartily, the couple carefully headed up the stairs, took some pain meds, showered, and threw their clothes into the garbage. With careful placement of their feet to save extra pounding in their weary heads, they headed downstairs for a good cup of coffee and a bite to eat. Anita was parched and guzzled a couple glasses of water before eating. Then the conversation began.

Suzanne and Delia were held in suspense, at whether their magic had worked, and every so often they glanced at each other, each silently prompting the other to ask the question. *"Did Dante have a change of heart?"* Chris had his eyes fixed on the pair. "What kind of mischief have you two been up to? I know you have, just by watching your facial expressions," he asked.

Suzanne spoke up first. "We – I, were wondering if you got to see Carolyn. Also, why did you smell so awful when you got home?"

"Weird. It was weird," Anita began. "Dante, to me, acted a little out of character. At first he clobbered us across the head to show he was the one running the show, but sort of mellowed out. As for Carolyn, I felt it was an imposter. Oh, I will say she looked like her and had a birthmark like Carolyn's but she had no life, no spark in her eyes, and gave no real acknowledgement of even knowing me. It was like it was rehearsed for my benefit. I could be wrong; it could be that she has been through hell and that it stripped her of all personality, but deep down, I know I'm right. Dante let me win a business settlement, and then blindfolded us and had us dumped off the side of the road. We were forced to walk home – a very long walk home. Luckily, we caught a ride on an old, smelly bus and here we are. I still find the whole thing strange."

When she finished talking, she noticed both ladies grinning from ear to ear, their faces a little flushed. When asked about their sudden joy, they both denied any mischievousness, and said they were grinning because they were happy she got to see her friend. Still unconvinced, but needing to act on her new thoughts, Anita nudged Chris and gestured for him to follow her to the den for some consulting. As they headed out the door, Anita turned and saw Delia and Suzanne give each other the high-five. She could have sworn they were doing the happy dance in their seats. Puzzled, Anita turned her focus to her next project.

In the den, Anita almost pushed Chris into the computer chair. Full of enthusiasm, she wanted to know if he could find a program to show what people would look like as they aged. She wanted to see if that person in the cave was really Carolyn. Chris's nimble fingers danced across the keyboard and retrieved the program Anita was looking for; he gave her the chair to begin her request. He showed her how it worked and then left her dutifully pouring over the program. While she was doing that, Chris picked up the papers that Deli and Suzanne had found, and began to study them in detail. Getting out his magnifying glass, Chris began to analyze every square inch of the map. Some of its features jogged his memory, and he let out an excitable cheer. Anita's fingers froze in mid-air as she looked at Chris's ecstatic expression and waited for his explanation.

Chris's fingers hit the map. "Your dad already knew of the place where we were today. He had it mapped out and must've thought that was where Carolyn was being held. How are you doing with comparisons?"

"Well," Anita began, "there seems to be a woman missing that fits the description of the person in the cave, but the person in the cave has a striking resemblance to Carolyn. No matter how gaunt and tired I make Carolyn's face, though, it does not match exactly to the woman I saw today. I've taken into consideration the lack of lighting, and my memory, but it just doesn't seem right. So what plan did my dad have mapped out? Are we able to break in?" she asked.

Carefully looking over the vague map, Chris answered, "We would need help and I wouldn't want to involve Gappy. He concerns me a little. Can't put my finger on it, but he just does."

Now excited at the prospect of blowing up another camp, Anita got up and began to ramble, as she paced. "Who then? Maybe the same team my father used. That would make sense."

"There's no paper trail leading to who that team was, but I know a few men who could use a little spending cash," Chris said, disturbed by the whole thing.

Excitement poured out of Anita's body as the idea of getting even with Dante grew. "I want to rescue as many women as humanly possible and see Dante's world crash with him behind bars."

Chris stretched his arms behind his head locking his fingers for support. "Hmm. Your first obligation is to Dante though. Remember Blake?"

A sunken feeling put a frown on Anita's face, and she sat back down at the desk. "Oh yah, but that doesn't mean *you* can't do it," she said, hoping he would agree.

Unlocking his fingers, Chris shook his head at Anita. "Oh no you don't. One task at a time."

Throwing a pillow at him Anita said, teasingly, "Party pooper."

Shadows danced amongst the trees, and the darkness dimmed the lighting in the den telling the couple it was time for bed. They both knew that when the sun rose, it would be a new day with new revelations.

CHAPTER FORTY-FIVE

A frightful noise disturbed the silence in the house, waking Anita up suddenly. In her semi-awake state, she answered the phone. The voice on the other end spoke in a broken English accent. "Be ready in one hour," it said, "and dress in a professional manner. Meet us at the end of your driveway." The phone then went dead.

Placing the phone down, Anita shook Chris, and mumbled, "I think that was Gappy's call regarding Blake. They want me to dress professionally. What do you think?" she asked.

"My guess would be the same. I'll go with you, just in case. I haven't traveled this much since I got here." He looked at his wife and kissed her. "Can't say its been boring though," and got up to get dressed.

Not sure whether they were both invited to the party, Chris and Anita waited in the driveway. They saw puffs of exhaust form as a vehicle approached. It was traveling at such a speed, Chris was sure it had no brakes; he half expected to see a parachute pop out the back to slow it down.

The car came to a semi-stop in front of them and the door flew open. The couple had to run to get into the moving vehicle and, when they were in, the door closed from the force of movement, and the car continued on. Getting herself settled Anita said, smartly, "Not in a hurry are you?"

No one looked at her. She was handed a briefcase and a pair of clear eyeglasses. One of the car's occupants explained that the glasses contained a hidden camera so a visual layout of the Embassy could be seen. To keep the briefcase looking legit, they had placed papers inside, just in case anyone became suspicious. Anita was then shown a hidden camera in the bottom of briefcase, and its purpose was to monitor the lower part of the Embassy. This would give them much greater detail as to the entire layout of the Embassy and those who worked there. Anita was instructed to do whatever it took to get inside the building, and into Blake's locked quarters. From there she would be given instructions through an earpiece, which they now placed roughly in her ear. Chris was given strict orders to be there as support only – nothing more.

Anita was shocked at their mannerism, but knew to keep her cool and let them do whatever it was they had to do. The glasses were fitted to her face, and adjusted to make it look like she always wore them. There was no mirror in the backseat, so she relied on Chris's opinion of how they looked on her face. He told her she looked more like a professor than an attorney, which made her laugh. Her next task was to test out the earpiece. She found it uncomfortable and readjusted it. Sweat poured out of every pore in her body, and she knew she had to control her anxiety or she would give away her disguise.

Arriving at the Embassy, Chris was informed he would remain behind. Anita, taking one last stab at making herself look professional, straightened her clothes, took a deep breath and walked confidently in, and waited to be cleared by security. Watching the second hand on the clock move slowly around, Anita took advantage of this time by surveying every inch of the office. The man who manages the Embassy came out and shook her hand, offering his condolences for the passing of her father, which she genuinely accepted. Just as she thought all was clear, another official joined her in the office. He asked Anita if she was Blake's lawyer. "Yes," she replied, and waited for the next set of stalled events before meeting with Blake. It felt awkward as she patiently waited for one of the gentlemen to speak. One of the gentlemen, in the office, was not sure if Anita was truly Blake's attorney but, told her that Blake would be transported to a new, secret lodging. Once he was settled in his new quarters, she could then set up a meeting to talk to him.

Anita looked at the men in the office, who seemed to dare her to contest the offer put before her, said in a professional tone, "Thanks for the update. But, seeing as to how I'm here, would you escort me so that I can at least talk to him before he leaves?"

The two men conferred and one graciously opened the door and held his arm out indicating for her to lead the way out of the room. Taking the initiative, Anita was the first out of the room and soon found herself being escorted down the corridors. Anita's head bobbed a couple of times, and she swung the briefcase around trying to record the space with the hidden camera. The man escorting her stopped, looked at her, and noticed she was a little sweaty. "You have a nervous twitch?"

Her eyes focused on a painting on the wall and she calmed right down. "I'm sorry," she said, "but these paintings are of the same taste as my father's, and I found it very eerie for a moment."

The man sighed, releasing his held breath, and replied, "For a minute there I thought you were surveying the place."

Terror blanketed her body and seemed to crush her windpipe. She gasped for air, and said, "What would make you say a thing like that?"

He turned right at that precise moment in front of a spiritual painting laden with angel imagery, and Anita's guilt rose to the surface, as he spoke, "You work for Dante, right?'

She could see his eyes shifting as though he were interrogating her, and she spoke without hesitation. "Let me clarify that," she said. "I have been coerced into representing him. And just to be clear, I have to finish what my father started. I owe my father that." Anita was about to walk away, but then hesitated and slowly turned to her companion, and asked, "What do you know, I don't?"

He raised his hand pointing to the route they were to take, and replied honestly, "I was hoping you'd tell me."

Reaching the door of Blake's room, Anita waited for the man to open it. "This is an awfully extravagant room for a double agent," she said. "All I got when he kidnapped me were drugs to immobilize me on a ship infested with rats, and a bathroom about as far away as I could move. I hope that wherever he's headed, he gets the same treatment."

The man leaned against the door and made eye contact with Anita. "You mean to say he treated you like a criminal and you are defending him? What kind of justice will he get?"

Pushing the man to the side, Anita barked, "Open the door. From here on in it's client confidentiality. As for justice, he'll get the best. It's my duty."

Inserting the key, the man opened the door. "I'll be right outside the door standing guard. Wouldn't want him to get away now, would we?" the man said, condescendingly.

Her eyes glazed over as though she did not hear or see him, and he let her in. Closing the door behind her, Anita set the glasses and briefcase on the table, and strutted over to stand right in front of Blake. "What does Dante want with you?" she asked. "Are you on his payroll?

Blake's eyes hardened, like stone, and he crossed his arms. "You're prying. That's not like you."

A surge of strength found its way through the circuits of her veins, bringing her new energy. She grabbed Blake by the shirt collar and shoved him against the wall. "Call it what you like. I want straight answers."

In her earpiece, she could hear a voice speaking softly. "Don't do anything rash," it said. "We have another plan in motion." This caught her completely off guard and she swore as she released him.

Blake smiled at her temper, and adjusted his clothes. "What, your conscious got the better of you?"

Feeling a little rattled, and with sweat dripping from her armpits, she retorted, "Yah, something like that."

Blake took a chair straddling it backwards, leaning on the chair forward with his arms hanging over in case she decided to lash out again. "I've decided to get a new lawyer," he said. "You know, one that will protect my rights, not use them against me. I hope you aren't offended. You know too much about me, and may be too emotionally involved."

The pressure lifted from her heavy heart. "So granted. I guess this means that any questions I have for you, I'll need to research it for myself."

He nodded and his smile brightened his face. "You're a smart girl. You'll make a good ally for whichever side you choose. Just for the record, I believe your dad is alive, and doing well. That's where my concern would take me, that is, if I were you."

Shaking his hand, Anita replied coolly, "I'll keep that in mind. They say you are getting new quarters. All the best to you."

Blake's teeth were now showing and his voice was hot, as he said, "Could be a decoy. It's for my best interests. After all, they don't know what side of the coin I'm liable to take."

Anita smiled back, as she replied, "You are so pompous. If I were you, I'd be looking over my shoulders. You may not be as safe as you think. Just an observation, that's all. Remember, I'm on the outside and hear things. Best of luck to you." Anita smugly picked up her glasses and briefcase and banged on the door. She waved goodbye to Blake as she stepped across the threshold.

Stepping out of the room, Anita caught a glimpse of two armed men trying to camouflage themselves behind the peaked corner where the walls met. She quickened her pace to leave, but was escorted to the office and was left there alone. Taking advantage of the silence, she sat down before her legs gave way. The door swung open and a man veered straight for Anita, pulled her glasses off, and thoroughly examined them. Terrified he would spot the camera; Anita began to fumble around and yelled that she couldn't see without her glasses, which compelled the man to look at her in a different light.

Handing back her glasses he said, sharply, "Seems the last time you were here, you weren't wearing any glasses, and could see quite well."

Putting her glasses on and then taking them off to clean them, Anita replaced them again, and calmly replied, "Ever hear of contacts?" Anita then handed the man her briefcase and suggested he check that out as well, and he did just that. He handed it back to Anita and she sat squarely in her seat, and asked casually, "What's next?"

"So what happened in there?" the man asked. He knew the answer, but wanted to see if she would tell him.

"You know very well. You had the place bugged. He fired me," Anita stated, simply.

"You here to see Jeremy?" the man asked, wondering what her next move was.

Anita rolled her head back and forth and rubbed her neck. "Sorry, I must be tensed up. Never thought about Jeremy, although I am researching his activities to see which side of the fence he's leaning on." As Anita spoke, she carefully watched the man change his stance.

"Well," the man began, "we need to move Jeremy, and he has stipulated he wants you to be his lawyer and contact. Don't know what that's all about." He unnerved Anita a little with his intensity.

Shocked at this news, Anita stood up with composure, and stated, "Let's make an appointment for, say, two weeks from now." She shivered as his look became inhospitable, and she added, "You mean *now*, don't you?"

With his arms folded and a look of intimidation on his face, the man appeared to have an unscheduled task for her to do. She fought off the urge to run, but followed the man down a dark corridor and her thoughts turned to the room Jeremy was in when she last saw him. This was not the same area of the building, and she could feel panic attacks set in. "Did you already move Jeremy, because this looks more like a dungeon," Anita said, frankly.

The man didn't skip a beat in his stride, but turned sharply to face Anita, walking backwards. His mannerism took Anita by surprise and she almost ran into an ugly gargoyle statue. It gave her the creeps. In a tone so sharp it could've sliced her throat, the man asked, "You have something to hide?"

In her earpiece she could hear giggling from the man on the other end, and Anita knew any slight wrong wording would give her away, so she tapped the earpiece hoping to create a sore ear at the other end. However, she just couldn't resist spitting back, "You have no idea what I've been through, so don't think you're so smug. Jeremy had a room like Blake's – who by the way is dirty – and now Jeremy is in the cellar of the Embassy. What did he do wrong? This is unacceptable."

"We ran out of room upstairs, shall we say," the man replied in a complacent manner. The dim lighting played games with Anita's eyes. When the man opened the door, she was sure he turned into a vampire and she couldn't wait to get inside Jeremy's cell.

Once inside, Anita's eyes had to adjust to the dim lighting. She could hear heavy breathing and when Jeremy spoke, his tone was like that of a madman. "What's with these accommodations?"

Trying to cope with her own fears of being in a confined area, and with the untrusting man still standing at the doorway, Anita responded, "I agree. What's with the dungeon?"

Anita wanted to wipe the sneer off the man's face. She found him nauseating along with every word that came out of his mouth. "We needed room for the diplomats." He then turned to Jeremy, and said, "It's up to your lawyer friend to find you new lodgings," and left the room, laughing.

Jeremy stood, in what could be described as a broom closet. It had a small bathroom; one would have to back up into it to be sure of hitting the right target. Jeremy looked like he could devour Anita. Her immediate instincts were to leave, but instead she said calmly, "This is the first I've heard of any of this. If I'm your lawyer, why didn't you call me?"

His temper was beginning to show. He appeared agitated, and every time he spoke, his voice raised and lowered. "Didn't have your number."

Letting her briefcase fall noisily to the ground, Anita leaned up against the wall. "You're an agent. Surely you could've figured it out. You could've got the Embassy to call me. They have all the information. My father was a regular here. So, let's try again. Who cooked up this scheme and why?"

Jeremy could feel the heat in his body build up from his toes to his face, and was glad she couldn't see the change of color taking place. "What makes you say that?"

"Cut the crap," she said. "I really don't have time for this. What is it I'm suppose to do?"

292

Jeremy yelled back at her. "Get out if you don't believe me. You know I'm a good agent, just a little stupid."

Standing firmly to reassure him she was going nowhere, Anita had questions she needed answered. "Did you persuade the officials to bring you down here to lay a guilt trip on me? Who are you in cahoots with on the inside? Why didn't they just let you go?"

Wiping his brow with his shirtsleeve, Jeremy's temperature went from hot to cold. "Don't miss much do you?"

Anita took off he glasses and twirled them around. She could hear swearing in her earpiece and realized that the motion was making her helpers sick. She laughed and gently tucked one arm of the glasses into her shirt. Acting like she was in a courtroom with a hostile witness, Anita began her assessment of what was going on. "What is your plan? Let me guess. You want to be released into my custody so you can, what, go after Dante? Blake? Me? Who?"

Jeremy's stance was erect and statuesque when he responded to her accusations. "Something like that?"

In one step, Anita was in his face. She verbally tore him to shreds. "Something like that doesn't cut it. Tell you what. I'll be back in two days. If by then you have a better attitude, and if you're willing to be honest and will cooperate with me, I'll help you. Until then, consider these your permanent quarters. If you think I'm gullible, and you dare to play games with me, which I don't have time for, then you will have to wait until I'm ready. Have a nice day."

Anita tapped the door, and put her hand to hush anything Jeremy wanted to say. When the door opened, she stepped out and spoke loudly to the man, who had walked her down to Jeremy's room. "We have some negotiating to do. He will remain here until my next visit. Is that clear?" The man nodded and Jeremy hung his head knowing all to well it was his turn to become a minion.

Rushing down the dark eerie corridor, Anita passed the man and headed straight for the office. She bolted in like she owned the place and turned the swivel chair around so its occupant was facing her. "Your neck is on the line. I don't know what you and Jeremy have cooked up, or who bribed you to pull this little scheme, but I assure you that if you don't leave Jeremy here until I return, your ass is mine. I will get to the bottom of things and heads will roll. Do I make myself clear?"

The man barreled out of his chair and placed his arms on Anita's, pinning them down. "Who do you think you are coming in here with insinuations and threats? Who do you think they'd believe – a cocky lady lawyer or someone who has held a position for many years?"

Not backing down, Anita broke his grip, and replied, "Me. You have been in the business long enough to attain seedy friends, which wouldn't be hard to prove. *Now,* do I make myself clear?"

He sat back in his chair and smiled like syrup was running out of his mouth as he licked his lips. "You're on Dante's payroll," he said. "Now who do you think they'll believe?"

Leaning over the desk, she quickly spotted the man's name on a plaque sitting on his desk and pushed it off to the side. Getting close to his face, Anita could smell moisture pouring out of every pore of his body. "Me. I may be Dante's lawyer, but I'm clean, and never has any money exchanged hands between us. Oh, and don't think of trying to hide your assets, because paper always leaves ugly trails, and that includes under-the-table payments. You see, my father taught me well. I *will* find what I'm looking for." She stood up, winked at him, and danced out of the office, hurrying out of the Embassy. When she was far enough away, she told her back-up crew to start a background check on a Mr. Roger Thornton."

The fresh air felt good. As she hopped into the vehicle, everyone was astonished at her beaming face. She looked around at every pair of eyes and, said, "Oh, like I planned meeting with Jeremy? Besides, I'm paying for it no matter how you look at it. So now what? Blake is being escorted to a new destination. How are we going to know if it's a decoy?"

The shifty looking man behind the wheel spoke up. "Leave that to us. We've wasted enough time. You will change your clothes and await our call, both of you." Anita knew she was being dismissed and kept her other thoughts to herself.

The trip home was like being on a jet. Anita was sure the vehicle did not touch ground until it came to a stop at the end of the driveway. Two very angry people stood waiting for them on the stairs, and Suzanne wagged her finger at them both saying, "No note. Where have you two been? You had us worried."

Stopping dead in her tracks, Anita tried to speak, but her thoughts worked faster than her mouth and the words came out garbled. Covering her mouth, Anita focused on her mom and calmed down. "Mom. In the next few days, we will be coming and going, so please don't get uptight.

We're not at liberty to explain our peculiar behavior, but you will be told everything at the right time. What we need right now is a bite to eat, and maybe a light lunch packed – if that's not asking too much. Really, I'm sorry."

Suzanne and Delia didn't argue, they just turned and vanished into the house. Anita and Chris plodded up the stairs to shower and freshen up. Once they were able to keep momentum going, the couple met with Suzanne and Delia in the kitchen for a much-needed meal. Anita took the opportunity to inform the rest of the group that they may be having a temporary houseguest. Chris dropped his utensils, and sputtered, "Let me guess, Jeremy? And, your arterial motive is what?"

His tone caught Anita off guard, and she responded with a rush of uncensored words. "We'll need him when the time comes. Like maybe to keep an eye on Blake."

Chris was very unhappy Anita hadn't taken the time to discuss what she was thinking and although he loved her for her spontaneity, this was one time it bothered him. As he was about to speak, Anita changed the subject, and smiled at her mother. "Mom, I'm very happy you and Delia have become friends. I feel much better knowing you are in good hands."

Suzanne bowed her head for a moment, and then raised her glass. "I don't know how it can be arranged, but I would like to stay here. I feel very close to Douglas and Delia. This place has, shall we say, cast a spell on me." She took a sip and winked at Delia, who blushed.

Chris and Anita looked at one another, puzzled. Chris looked back at Suzanne and Delia, and said, "You two are up to something, aren't you?" Even though Delia's complexion was dark, it was obvious she was blushing. He continued, "You think by holding a séance, you'll prove whether or not Douglas is dead, don't you?"

Suzanne choked on her drink. Coughing, she said, "How'd you know?"

Placing his elbows on the table, and locking his hands over his plate, Chris grinned showing off his charming features, and replied, "I know more than you think. All I can say to you both is be careful. Things don't always turn out the way they should." He then looked at Anita. She could see his lips moving, but the words were barely audible. "That goes for you as well," was all she heard. She was embarrassed that she hadn't discussed her plans for Jeremy with him, and he knew what was going through her mind.

Suzanne's hand began to shake and she placed her drink on the table. "Now that you've opened the conversation, I may as well stir the pot and add the rest of the ingredients. Your presence is required – both of you. Please."

Sheepishly, Anita looked at Chris and he shrugged his shoulders. She knew this man was a saint, and there was nothing she wouldn't do to keep him around for a long time. Rubbing her neck, Anita finally asked, "Do you two know what you're dabbling in?" She felt two pairs of eyes looking back at her in the answer to her question. "Okay. When – and only when – things calm down, we will attend your séance: but not another word about it until then. Now that baking lessons are done, Chris and I need to get ready for phase two. For the next few days, you ladies have fun, do whatever you like. We don't know when we will be around, but we can fend for ourselves."

Delia laughed, and said, "We fix meals to warm up. We know about your cooking skills."

The smile on Chris's face broadened and he couldn't contain his laughter. "Much appreciated. I wasn't prepared to go on a diet just yet." Anita threw her napkin at him to show her discontent, but laughed with them just the same.

While Anita packed, Chris watched her in the mirror. Seeing which items she threw into her bag, he commented. "Seems I've taught you well."

Proud he had noticed, Anita whipped back, "You mean the lighter, thermal blanket, rain gear, and things like that?"

Chris placed his bag beside the bed and stretched out on it. "Yup. So tell me, what are your plans for Jeremy?"

Putting her hands over her face, Anita turned away from Chris. "I'm sorry I didn't confer with you, but in all honesty, I don't know what I'm going to do with him. I've suddenly acquired an extra burden, one that I didn't ask for, I might add. What do you think should happen to him?"

Mulling over the thoughts in his mind, Chris spoke with kindness. "Honey, turn around. I would like to see you face to face, not behind a mask." Waiting for Anita to turn around and face him, he patted the spot beside him on the bed. She gently climbed up beside him and he put his arm around her. "I know you didn't ask for this, and I know you don't always think things through, and I know you work on spontaneity, so I'm going to assume that was just being tossed out there. I'd prefer he didn't stay here, but if that's what you want, I'll be okay with it. Should you change your mind, please let me know, in advance. Some surprises I like, some I don't."

Squeezing him tightly, the two just cuddled because they knew they could be called upon at any moment to start the mission. No plans had been outlined for them, which made Chris believe that Gappy wanted to keep them guessing, and that he didn't want anyone to know the whole plan. It was his way of preventing leakage.

CHAPTER FORTY-SIX

Barely awake, Anita heard a horn sounding: D-day had arrived. Getting up, they grabbed their packed bags, ran through the kitchen grabbing the little basket of goodies and bolted out the door as though they were in a relay race. A van was parked at the front door, and before anyone could say a word, Anita was sitting in the comfiest seat. Chris took a seat in the back and studied the contents of the vehicle. Anita, too, surveyed the equipment in the van and whistled at the technology, which included much of what she had seen in Gappy's hideout. Now looking at the people in the van, Anita asked with surprise, "Just the four of us? Where's Gappy?"

A man closed the door and signaled to the driver to go. "My name is Jack," he said to Chris and Anita. "I'm the liaison between Gappy and yourselves. You will be notified of what your part is, nothing more. Do you understand?" Anita and Chris nodded in agreement and let the mystery of their future fall into strange hands.

Biting her lip and fidgeting in her seat, Anita finally broke the silence. "Just us, huh?" she asked, again.

Jack was busy getting the equipment set up, as he replied, "There will be others."

Prying Anita asked, bravely, "Are we getting Blake before he's released or after?"

Jack, still working on the equipment replied, with annoyance in his voice. "Timing couldn't have been better."

As a lawyer it was her business to ask questions, so she persevered. "How can you be certain it isn't a ploy to ambush us?"

Jack stopped what he was doing, raised his head, and with penetrating eyes, wordlessly ordered her to keep quiet. Anita's intuition told her to hold her tongue, and yet she said, "I get it. You have someone on the inside." The menacing look she got from Chris told her that silence was golden, at least for now.

Chris was confident in the countryside surrounding his home, but when he observed the areas they were now entering, he felt lost and tried to recover his bearings. As they drove over unbroken trails, many items bounced around the van. Anita held on so tightly, her knuckles went white and she was sure she had left imprints in the chair she was occupying. The driver skillfully dodged the trees and shrubbery in the path, and Anita reluctantly let one hand go and covered her eyes, because she didn't want to witness her final moments.

When they came to a stop, Anita uncovered her eyes and smiled; they were still alive and unharmed. Anita and Chris were ushered out of the van, and escorted to a plank straddling a vast ravine. Terrified, Anita turned back towards the van, but was pushed with force to meet her fear, twisting her already damaged ankle. Giving herself a good pep talk, Anita took a deep breath and was able to defeat her fears by walking to the other end of the plank; she congratulated herself on a job well done.

Chris joined her on the other side of the ravine, and the two turned to watch as Jack pulled the plank away and headed back to the van. Feeling vulnerable, the couple were suddenly grabbed from behind, and pulled into the bush. Anita's first instinct was to let out a scream, but her assailant had placed his hand over her mouth, stifling the noise. Chris was angry at how they were being treated, and wasn't sure whether the men were friends or foes. Soon he pieced it together, however, and told Anita to settle down; they were Gappy's men. He told Anita that the reason for this rough treatment, was so no one could follow them, and they must remain discreet. But deep down, Chris knew he would have a few words with Gappy, after it was over. No longer allowed to stand in one spot, they were pushed deeper into the dense forest of trees; time was being wasted.

The brush was thick, and they couldn't see past the next tree. Taking a sharp left, the foursome met up with Gappy. Anita took a few minutes down time to nurse her sore ankle. "You're all business, aren't you?" she blurted.

Gappy's expression hardened. "Have a job to do. The rest of my men should be here anytime. I want you two to wear these earpieces. You will walk two miles in a straight line from here, and stagger yourselves a half-mile apart. You'll be part of the lookout team, and will tell us how many vehicles, men, and weapons they have. We'll do the rest. I have other armed men planted at various points in case of trouble."

As she placed the earpiece in her ear, Anita replied, "Trouble? How can there be trouble if we're spotters?"

Gappy gave Chris a stern look and, because he was already set up with his earpiece, he turned to Anita, and explained, "The enemies have spotters, too."

Her outrage overtook her emotions and found her hand grasping Gappy's shirt collar. Her voice dripped with ice, as she said, "And you aren't going to arm us? Are you going to leave us out there for target practice?"

Gappy was strong. He cupped her hand and brought it down, releasing his shirt from her grip. "You're a menace to this operation," he said. "But I assure you, you'll be okay. Do you think you can follow orders or do you want to abort?"

Raising both hands in the air to signify a truce, Anita saluted Gappy, turned and linked her arm though Chris's. She questioned their ability to survive this mission, but kept silent. Chris was very quiet and Anita felt his frustration with her heedlessness. She was sorry for getting involved and swore to herself when this was over, she would have a lot to make up for. The couple walked in total silence, and when a voice spoke over the earpiece, it startled them both. They were told that one of them should take cover and the other was to keep walking. Chris suggested that Anita be the first to take cover and said he would continue to the next post. Looking around for a place to hide but seeing none, Anita drew her wits about her and began gathering brush and leaves, piling it up. When the pile was high enough, she dug a little hole in the middle and squirmed inside with her binoculars and she was ready. Satisfied she was well hidden, she began her watch.

Chris searched for the right spot by climbing into a tree thick with branches and had a good position for monitoring the comings and goings for miles around. He laughed as he watched Anita work like a beaver setting up a dam. Gappy went to the van and waited for the fireworks to start – when the first oncoming vehicle appeared with the intended percussion of others following.

On the horizon, Chris could see the beginning of a convoy and, as it advanced, he let the others know to stand by. The hair on the back of Anita's neck stood straight up as she heard a branch snap behind her. Beads of sweat trickled down every side of her head and joined forces as they continued down her body. Her ears perked up and she held her breath, waiting for the next sound, and after a few moments, a foot rested softly on the pile of leaves covering her. By his quiet and light-footedness, Anita knew he was a pro.

The click of a gun hammer being pulled back echoed in her ears and she looked up to find a gun barrel pointed straight at her. The man reached down and yanked her out of her little alcove; he was stunned to find that she was an unarmed woman, and asked, "Where's your gun?"

Her body began to twitch and her eyes were wide-open with fright. Suddenly, she fainted, slumping to the ground. He shook her until her eyes fluttered open and she pointed over to her hiding place, and said, "All I have is my binoculars."

He badgered her, poking her with his gun, and picked her up by looping his arm under her armpit. "Whom do you work for?" he asked, loudly.

He let her go and she crumbled to the ground like a marionette's string being released, and as though someone tightened those strings, she slowly got back up on her feet.

Glancing at his watch, the man knew he was behind schedule; he held a gun on Anita, and swore," Damn. I've never shot a woman before, let alone an unarmed one."

Feeling a little cocky, Anita let her words fly out of her mouth. "Well then, just go about your business and leave me be."

"I would like to do that, but because it's impossible, I either have to shoot you or take you hostage, and seeing that you have no gun, I guess I have to take you hostage. Personally, I'd rather tell you to run so I could shoot you," the man said, and shoved the gun into her ribs to make her move.

Wincing from the pain in her side, Anita's feet moved double time and she prayed someone would notice and take care of business. He was in a hurry and pushed Anita to move faster, but she stumbled, sprawling out like a butterfly spreading its wings. He yanked her by the belt to an upright position, barking orders to move faster. Looking up towards the sky, Anita prayed that Chris would notice what was happening and come to her rescue.

Disgruntled that was not going to happen, Anita walked with confidence, relaxing the man, and they moved at a swift pace. Out of the corner of her eye, Anita saw a large branch lying loosely on the dense forest floor; she took a dive for her newly found weapon, startling her escort. With all her might, Anita grasped the branch, rolled over to a kneeling position, and swung the makeshift bat at his knees, barely making a connection. He cocked his gun, but before he pulled the trigger, a gunshot was heard, and the man fell to the ground face-first. Anita took advantage of the man lying still on the ground, and scrambled to get up and ran in the direction from which she had come.

A black shadow presented itself, making Anita stop in her tracks and gasp, thinking she was done for. The owner of the shadow appeared in full view and Anita's heart raced as she saw that it was Gappy. "Thanks for arming me," Anita said, sarcastically. "I wouldn't know what do without it."

"In case you're wondering how you were detected, the sniper watched you diligently dig a fox hole. You were easy picking. I must say, though, it was very well thought out," Gappy said, as he slung his gun over his shoulder.

Anita was pissed that he made fun of her attempt to hide, and defended her actions. "Then why didn't he just shoot me?"

"You were unarmed," Gappy stated, simply.

"What took you so long to shoot him?" Anita asked, letting him know she was unhappy about the recent events.

Smiling, Gappy responded, "You were moving too fast, and I couldn't get a clear shot. Seems you were able to arm yourself after all."

Anita couldn't fathom this man being a good back up for her, and shot back at him, "Then, why didn't you shoot him when he was attacking me?"

Avoiding her questions, Gappy pointed in the opposite direction from where she was heading, and barked, "Enough talk. I have other plans for you." Anita's feet began to move involuntarily and, almost tripping, she fumbled to keep up with his long strides. He resumed the conversation. "I wanted to see what kind of stigma you possessed and you actually surprised me. Chris has taught you well."

Running to keep up, Anita's words came out in spurts. "What do you mean you have other plans for me?"

Arriving at his vehicle, Gappy motioned to Anita to get in and, like a robot, she did as she was requested. Once she was in, Gappy threw her a dress and a pair of shoes, saying, "I retrieved these from your home. Get changed, and fix your hair. You are about to become the best actress of the year."

Anita looked down at the clothes and then back at him, "Now," he snapped.

The tone Gappy used told her there was no fooling around, that she was to do as instructed, so she changed carefully, trying not to reveal too much of her body in the process. She looked down at the dress's sagging breast area, and laughed, "What did you do, borrow this from Delia?"

A side-glance told him she was not properly dressed, and he stopped the vehicle in a sheltered area, got out, retrieved a bag from the trunk, and threw it at Anita. "Here, put the fake bra under your shirt, gauze in your cheeks to distort your face and voice, and put the wig and glasses on. Just do it, no questions," Gappy said, in an authoritative voice.

Peering into the bag, Anita did as she was told, every so often glaring at her business partner. Using the side mirror, Anita fixed herself up, and when the finished image looked back at her, she was astounded at the transformation; it did not resemble her at all. Now ready for the next step, Gappy jumped in and started the vehicle. Anita barely had enough time to climb on board before it shot off, and he drove furiously down the dry desert-like road.

Bravely, interrupting Gappy's train of thought, Anita commented. "I feel like my grandmother. Care to explain what it is I'm expected to do?"

They hadn't traveled very far when Gappy stopped the vehicle and motioned for Anita to get out and start walking. Doing as requested, she could feel the heat pounding down on her body, making her sweat, and when she turned around, she saw Gappy using a branch to erase their footprints. He pointed to a clump of trees and obliging him, Anita wandered over and waited there for Gappy to join her. When he did, he began tugging at a pile of branches, leaving Anita feeling vulnerable. She began to help him, in hopes of satisfying her curiosity.

As the last branches were pulled away, Anita saw a dilapidated old car. Gappy handed her a set of keys and shoved some papers to put in her purse. He briefly explained that the convoy would drive by without stopping. It was her job to get their attention and get them to help her back onto the road. Disbelieving her new assignment, Anita shook her head, leaned against the car, and looked up into the scorching sun as it reflected into the distant hazy mountains. "I take it you'll let me improvise as things unfold?" she asked, and then added, "And I'm going to assume that you will be doing your job of monitoring me. What if something goes wrong? Are you going to come to my rescue?"

Gappy's look told her that she was asking way too many questions, but her life was on the line, so she rephrased her words. "You will be there to rescue me if things go array." When Gappy nodded his head, it didn't give her much comfort, but sighed, and said, "Let the games begin."

Before she could blink her eyes, Gappy had abandoned her, and she sat down on the seat of the car laughing and talking to herself. "Wow, this is some outfit. I feel like I'm in a sauna. I wonder why Gappy didn't give me an earpiece. The action had better start soon or I'll be like a prune, all wrinkly with sharp edges and loose shape."

In the distance, Anita could see a heat wave as the warmth of the engines and the hot sun collided. The convoy of vehicles was headed her way. The rays from the heat source made her sweat even more, her throat was dry, and the gauze in her mouth was beginning to make her gag. Concentrating on the parade ahead, Anita forced herself to think about what was going to happen, rather than what was happening now. She choked back her gagging sensation.

Shielding her eyes from the sun with her hand, Anita's gaze was glued to the brigade moving steadily towards her spider's web. She counted the number of cars protecting one man, and the numbers struck her as odd. Her heart began to pound, her hands dripped with sweat, and her legs began to shake like branches in a strong wind. She noticed the convoy was veering slightly off course, and she tried in vain to wave her hands in hopes of grabbing their attention. Piqued at their lack of intelligence, Anita stormed off towards the band of vehicles. She let her body take on slow steps like an elderly person and stooped her shoulders like an old woman and shuffled across the treacherous undeveloped ground.

The first car decreased its speed. The driver rolled down the window and stuck his out, saying sharply, "We'll call for help."

Fear sprinted through her body, but Anita replied in a very tired, old voice. "I'm an old woman. You want me to wait in this tropical heat? I could die and I'm sure it would only take a few minutes of your time. Please."

"Look lady," the man said, "I'm unable to stop. I promise to send help."

"How would you feel if your mother or grandmother were left out here to die in the heat?" Anita said, with the intention of making him feel guilty.

Stopping the car completely, the man opened the door, and said, "Get in. I'll take you to the nearest town."

Surprised at his offer, Anita stuttered, "Couldn't you just fix it?"

"Either get in or stay," the man said, and she knew his equanimity was about to erupt. She clamored aboard, petrified at the outcome of this little operation.

CHAPTER FORTY-SEVEN

Gappy swore as he saw Anita climb into the vehicle. The parade carried on almost without skipping a beat. Inching his vehicle back, Gappy was careful not to give any signals that anyone was around. He didn't want to spook the convoy and risk Anita's life – she still had some unpaid bills he needed to collect on. Gathering his troops, a new plan was drawn up; each person involved had a new strategy to implement.

Chris could feel his heart beat out of rhythm, and he approached Gappy. "Where's Anita. I can't find her anywhere?"

Gappy's eyes darted away, as he replied, "I used her for a decoy, but it backfired and now we have to follow the new plan."

Chris locked his hand around Gappy's arm. "What do you mean you used her as a decoy?"

Gappy patted Chris's hand and replied, calmly, "Things will be okay. Just a slight misjudgment."

Every muscle in Chris's body seized up, so he was unable to carry out the task of strangling Gappy. Instead, he growled, "How on earth did that happen? I hope you had her wired."

The color in Gappy's face revealed the answer to the question. Gappy broke free of Chris's grip, and said, "Didn't think it was necessary at the time."

Chris's heart leaped up into his throat and he found it very hard to swallow. His words were faint when he said, "Gappy, she's all I've got."

Ignoring Chris, Gappy had radioed his men to find a well-hidden spot to hide out in the back of the mountain and park their vehicles. There they would wait for the convoy to reappear. The plan was to surround the convoy, force it to stop, and then attack. It was stipulated that they had two people to rescue, and both were to be taken alive. Once in position, they waited.

CHAPTER FORTY-EIGHT

Anita sat quietly in the car and wondered how she got into such a mess, when a voice broke her train of thought. "What were you doing out there in the middle of nowhere?"

Gazing around at the view, Anita looked at the empty land clad only in brush, straggly trees, and a few mountains completing the backdrop, Anita replied slowly, "I was lost. The car broke down."

Taking her hand in his, her questioner squeezed it hard, and hissed, "No tire marks. Try again."

A flame ignited in the pit of her stomach and the heat threatened to engulf her. "Didn't you notice the wind that blew over there?" Anita coughed and continued, "of course you didn't. You just arrived."

The man's eyes bored holes through Anita and he examined her hands while speaking, "We shall see. Something tells me we are bout to be attacked."

Anita's face expressed astonishment, and she asked, "What are you carrying? Gold?"

The man's eyes scoured the road and beyond, and seeing no indication of trouble on the horizon, he turned to Anita, and asked, "Where were you headed?"

Beads of sweat broke out on her skin. Putting on a false air to cover her nervousness, she replied, "I heard there was a hot spring in this area. Guess I goofed and took a wrong turn."

The man's hand stretched out with his palm facing up. His fingers wiggled as he said, "I suppose you had a map?"

Digging around in her purse, and thankful that Gappy had shoved some papers in it, she pulled out some crumpled notes. Looking over the papers, she found one with markings on it like a map of some sort and handed it to the man. "Pretty poor map, but that's my instructions. It was mostly verbal, I assure you."

Taking the paper and scanning it, he immediately extended his hand again, and yelled, "Passport."

Fury ripped through every inch of her, and her heart felt as though it would break through her chest wall. Her breathing became shallow, and she said, "Must've lost it."

Before he could make a decision as to what to do with the hitchhiker, a bullet pierced the vehicle behind them. An excited voice could be heard over the radio system. "Man down," it said. "What's the next move?"

Anita seized the moment, saying, "You want my passport? Care to explain the current events I seem to be involved in?"

Anita's companion scrunched down so his head was level with the window, and with the radio in his hand, his eyes raced back and forth across the landscape searching for the attackers. But nothing out of the ordinary had changed the view, and he was unsure of what their next step should be. His voice made it clear that he was taken off guard, as he asked Anita, "You scared?"

Sitting frozen in her seat, unable to move or twitch any important muscle, she looked at the man beside her, and responded, "Yes. I'm terrified. But you, you should've been expecting this."

The man shot a hostile look at Anita, and replied, "Expecting and being shot at are different. I only lost my plan of action for a moment."

The man commanded over the radio that his convoy were to move at a faster pace, and zigzag in an effort to dodge bullets. If they were shot at again, they were to strike back and their goal would be to capture a prisoner. With little emotion, Anita's hand slid off to the side, palm facing up. "Binoculars please."

His curiosity was piqued and he did as requested. He watched as Anita surveyed the perimeter of their convoy. She could see flashes of metal through the scantily placed trees and knew it wouldn't be long before a shower of bullets sprayed from their enemy's guns. Calmly, Anita said, "You have company. Whatever you're protecting, I hope it's worth it."

Snatching the eyeglasses from Anita, the man peered around, noticing a cloud of dust hovering above the tree line. "You are very observant," he said, agreeing.

"I may be old, but I'm not blind or stupid," Anita retorted.

His eyes focused straight ahead, leading the small army of vehicles to shelter amongst the trees, but his thoughts didn't miss a beat. "You seem a lot younger that you look," he said. "Your hands have that youthful, soft appearance."

Before she could answer in her defense, a voice could be heard radioing the other drivers to take refuge and stand their ground. Within a short time, the cars had pulled into their secluded positions. The man, Anita's rescuer, got out and found a concealed spot so they could ambush the enemy.

Squatting under hidden bushes against the mountains, everyone was secured and, as they anxiously waited for their enemy to make its next move, it was so quiet they could hear animals scurry to safety. Not even a whisper in the wind could detect what was about to happen, as a hand slipped around Anita's rescuer's mouth, and in one motion, his neck was twisted and he crumpled to the ground. The driver of the vehicle Anita had been occupying reached out, wrapped his arm around Anita's throat, and put a gun to her head. "One move and she gets it," the man yelled, pulling Anita backwards.

Anita heard the hammer click and knew if she didn't react, she was a dead person. With one swift movement, she stomped on his foot and elbowed him in the groin, causing him to lose his grip on her momentarily. Anita took advantage of the quick release, and she pushed his arm away, using both hands, before stepping off to the side, exposing him as an easy target. At that precise moment, a rifle shot, hitting her assailant and he dropped like a rock over a cliff: fast and straight to the ground. Not wanting Blake to get away, Anita took the gauze out of her mouth and stretched her mouth to give it time to bounce back to normal. Dropping to the ground, Anita slithered on her belly over to the vehicle where she thought Blake was being protected.

With a careful eye, Anita observed two men standing guard, near their precious cargo vehicle, and she looked around to see if she could spot a sniper's barrel. She hoped that if there were one, it would be one to shield her, not to shoot her. She heard a rustling of leaves, and felt something brush up against her. She held her breath, but she could feel a tight grip on her ankles. Then, her belly scratched along the earth's surface, drudging up dirt, and she found she had a mouthful of it. She tried spitting it out. Her mind raced and she wanted to give a big kick, but the hands wrapped firmly around her ankles made her powerless. A large warm hand with strong fingers clasped her by the collar and the other by her waist, and before she knew it, she was planted firmly on her two feet, face-to-face with the force behind the strength: Blake.

Blake's hand clenched Anita's shoulder tightly and it began to cut off her circulation. Tingling sensations traveled through every vein and artery in her body. His eyes were fixed on her, sending hateful vibrations to her brain, and forcing her to break the silence. "You can release your grip," she said. "I'm here to rescue you, not harm you." She then looked over at the men who were standing around the car, and then back to Blake. "How'd you get out without them seeing you?"

His long, strong fingers applied more pressure and his voice was serious, as he replied, "Like I believe that you are here to rescue me."

The pain was excruciating, and tears pooled in the corners of her eyes. "Ask yourself, why am I here?"

He studied Anita, and she could feel the heat coming from his fanatical eyes, and his voice cracked, as he said, "What's the catch?"

Feeling tears on her cheeks, Anita mustered her self-assurance, and replied, "You are surrounded, so no matter what you may be planning, it will fail. There really is no catch. You will be placed under my care. Now answer my question, how did you get away from the men guarding your vehicle?"

"Like you, you know when it's safe," he replied. He stood before Anita and let out a howl that set off other animal sounds in the distance. Still his grip was tight on her shoulders. "You don't do anything unless there's a plan. So again I ask you, what's the plan?"

The snapping of dry debris on the forest floor interrupted the two, and Blake's grip softened, as did his voice. "Friend's of yours?"

Not sure of which side this person was on, Anita's eyes danced frantically and relief took over her face and a half smile formed on her lips. "Friends. Told you," she replied.

Blake dropped both arms and let them relax by his sides. He shook his head in amazement; this woman was truly a thorn in his side. "Seems I'm at your mercy. How do you do that?"

"I don't do anything without a plan, remember?" she quipped back. Anita lifted her eyes from Blake and directed them towards the bush where she could see a gun appear. A full figure emerged behind it. Anita said, coyly, "It's my lucky charm here to help me out. It's time we made an exit. Seems all those on your side are no longer able to function – they are now incapacitate."

Blake made a show of surrendering as he waved his hands in the air and bowed to Anita. "I can't wait to see what's on the agenda for me – I'll assume you're not going to tell me."

Switching roles. Anita placed her hand on Blake's shoulder, playing his game. She felt powerful, as she replied, "All in due time. Let's vanish before we get bombarded." Blake turned on his heel and could feel eyes penetrating him like wild animals, as he slowly surrendered to his nemesis.

In the distance, Anita saw Chris and, instead of coming over to her, he winked, sending a gooey rush through her that ravished her body, making her feel warm inside. Like someone had changed the temperature, Anita then felt a cold object on her back and was instructed to move it, because they had quite a distance to hike to the hidden vehicle. Wanting to hamper any thoughts Blake may have of escaping, Anita asked for handcuffs, slapping one around his wrist and one around hers, and began to walk at a fast pace.

They reached an old army truck with canvas covering its top and sides. Anita protested riding in the back of this truck, but to her dismay, this was her ticket out of the bush. Blake beamed as he assessed the situation for a possible means of escape, but Anita noticed his keen expression, and chuckled as she said, "Don't let that thought give you hope. There will be other armed riders with us, I assure you."

Blake's head turned fast towards Anita and he wondered how she knew what he was thinking. "Why all this? You could've just signed me out."

Anita was the first to climb in to the back of the truck and when she felt stable, she yanked on the cuffs, forcing Blake to do a nosedive on the floor of the truck. She giggled and did not attempt to help him as he struggled to sit beside her. Anita leaned close and whispered into his ear, "You will be thanking me for this, I'm sure. However, I don't like it and, had Carolyn not been involved, I would have left you to rot in jail for treason."

Blake smiled and reminded Anita of the circumstances. "Just to be clear, I was being taken to new lodgings. I fired you, so how could you make me rot in jail?"

"You may have been transported to new living quarters, and you did fire me. But I could've put you away in a trial, and that my friend is a fact. Instead, all you have to do is help me out, and you will be free. That's it."

Chris and two other men joined them in the back of the truck, which took off before they were seated and they fell, like a couple of drunks.

Anita snickered. Chris looked at his wife fondly and took his place across from her. "Are you okay?" he asked.

She reached her hand out, and lovingly touched his. "Thought I was a goner a couple of times. I'm going to assume it was not you who rescued me."

Chris patted her hand, and responded, "You assume correctly. Now what do we do with the baggage we've acquired?"

Rubbing her chin, she sat quiet for a moment and then looked right through Blake as though he wasn't there. "He'll come home with us for a couple of days. Then he goes to his new home," she replied, loudly over the noise of the truck's engine.

Chris's expression showed remorse at her decision, but Anita's face expressed that he should trust her and, again, he surrendered to her silent proclamation. The ride was rough, but so slow that Anita could count the trees as they passed. This helped make the trip seem shorter – to her anyway. Her mind was fully engrossed in her thoughts, when suddenly the truck came to an abrupt halt and a man appeared around the back. He told Anita she was wanted up front. Obeying the command, Anita slid the key out of her pocket, released the clasp of her accessory, and had it secured around Chris's wrist before Blake could make a run for it. Chris was unimpressed by the turn of events and felt left out, but understood that it was she who had been summoned, not he.

Taking large steps to get to the cab of the truck, Anita saw Gappy giving orders to his men, who immediately began packing their belongings into a newer vehicle. Anita's lips parted only slightly, but her words had power behind them nonetheless. "You giving up?"

Gappy's response was cold. "My job is done," he said. "You are on your own."

Trying to grasp what was happening, Anita took in a few short breaths and stuttered when she spoke. "I'll pay you more. Where can I hide him out for a few days?"

Gappy turned to face Anita. A cold front grew between them. "That's your problem. You exposed yourself. I want nothing more to do with you."

Disappointed in the man who stood before her, Anita shot back, "You used me. You put me in that spot, and now you're just walking away?" Knowingly if she had been carrying a gun, she would've shot him right there on the spot. She turned away, and yelled over her shoulder, "Never mind. I'll figure something out. Your payment will be waiting for you upon my return. Thanks."

By the time she was at the end of the truck, Gappy and his men had vanished, leaving only the three of them. Anita released the handcuffs on Chris's side, and she explained they were on their own. Chris was now the designated driver and she would think about where Blake would stay. A bright flash went through her mind. She handcuffed Blake to the steering wheel, and guided Chris away from the truck to explain her idea. This was one time he was in complete agreement.

Anita found pleasure in keeping Blake in the dark, and a broad smile crossed her face, though she dared not say a word. Nightfall was upon them as they drove into the abandoned campsite that Dante had once occupied with his criminal activities. This was, according to Anita, a perfect place to house Blake, and she locked him in. She and Chris found a place to spend the night and checked to see, if by chance, there was any type of food around. Though they didn't find any, they did score a bottle of water, and had some of the refreshing, warm liquid, before taking some to Blake.

Blake's mouth was parched, and after the water had moistened his throat and lips, he licked them. "Okay, you've had your fun," he said. "Now let's eat and retire for the evening."

Anita's grin was like a beaming light. Her eyes danced wildly, as she said, "You are where you should be. This hut is where the likes of Carolyn and other girls lived until their fate was decided. Makes you want to puke, doesn't it. There's no escape. You'll remain here for a few days; provisions will be supplied when we get some. Right now, we have none. My goal is to keep you alive for a few more days anyway. Better say your prayers. Gets cold at night."

CHAPTER FORTY-NINE

Much to Anita's dislike, Chris decided to go home and recruit someone to watch over Blake until Anita decided to hand him over to Dante. After Chris left early in the morning, Anita sauntered over to Blake's hut and found him huddled in a corner, his eyes bloodshot from lack of sleep. Handing him a small glass of water, Anita removed the handcuffs so he could get up and stretch. The sun was warm and the two walked around, surveying the ghost camp hoping to find clues or documents indicating the existence of other sites like the one they were currently occupying. Climbing a rock in order to get a better scan the area, Blake's voice was filled with shame, as he said, "I always thought the girls were put in a posh camp. This is the doings of a cold man."

Anita dug in her purse and found a mirror, which she held up in front of Blake. Her words were like a knife and cut deep. "Take a good look at the man who orchestrated the kidnappings and helped the cold scoundrel," she said.

Pushing the mirror away, Blake became unglued, walked a few steps, and then turned to face his captor. "Who do you think you're passing judgment on? What would you do if I just walked off?"

Anita stretched her arms and placed them behind her head as if for support. She leaned her head back to emphasize her point. "You were paid good money to abduct rich girls. You didn't care what happened to them – or their families, I might add. What you didn't realize is that Carolyn adored you and would've done anything for you. You are merely a player in a checkers game – I intent to trounce over you and become queen. Carolyn's freedom is my prize. Should you leave, you'll be an easy target because the vultures will give away your spot once you grow weak and weary from lack of water, food, and protection from the elements. Now sit down. Food will be here soon; then we can nourish our bodies."

Kicking dirt around and creating a fog of dust, Blake retorted, "Why didn't we all go? You said I'd be a guest at your house."

Now fully in a sitting position, Anita rubbed her hand on her pants and slowly stood up. She shook her head, and smiled. "This is more fitting. Bare bones. Make the best of it."

Being defeated many times over by the same cocky woman made Blake's blood boil, but he reasoned that she was her father's daughter and must have been taught well. Taking advantage of their quiet moment, Blake said, "I though you were a bookworm, that you hibernated and didn't come out unless dragged. At least, that's what Carolyn told me."

Flipping her hair back, Anita laughed, and she replied, "Situations have a way of changing people. I will find her."

The sound of a car engine filled the air and Anita was elated; she was hungry and dying for a cup of coffee. Blake's pupils grew wider and darkened, giving Anita the sensation that evil was overpowering his good traits. He sat down and watched with domineering eyes, hoping to get to freedom should the opportunity present itself. The car crept closer, and Blake's skills waited to be put to use. With tense bodies, it was a waiting game between Blake and Anita: survival of the fittest.

Chris had just opened the door when Anita shouted at him to get his gun and be ready to shoot. At that exact moment, Blake leaped like a leopard towards Chris. Chris's reflexes were quick and he had the gun drawn, telling Blake to step back. But it was too late; Blake pounced with intentions of regaining his freedom. The gun flew out of Chris's hand and landed with inches of them. The men fought, their fists connecting with one another, each vying for the nearby trophy. Anita raced down the hill and, as she was about to pick up the gun, Blake's hand grabbed hers. She bit him hard, getting an immediate release. She held the gun up and shot it in the air, making the men break apart. Blake was miffed that the gun was now once again pointed at him.

Hunger was gnawing at Anita, and she tucked the gun into her pants and walked briskly to the car. She picked up the basket of prepared food, and stole a piece of chicken, sighing at how good it tasted, hoping the men would follow her lead. The men were still standing facing one another, disappointing Anita with their stubbornness. Continuing her quest for a ceasefire, she headed to the main hut, laid out the food, poured a cup of coffee, and walked back to the stand-off smacking her lips, "Food's on," she said, and went back inside for more; all the while keeping a watchful eye on the men.

Blake was about to make his move towards Chris when Anita calmly appeared with the cocked gun in her hand. "Don't go there," she said, with steady eyes and hands. "Give it up. You'll be free sooner than you think."

Chris then turned to look at his tantalizing – yet menacing – wife, and said to her, "I've arranged for someone to stay with Blake for the next two days, and yes, this person is trustworthy."

Blake didn't utter a word, he just moved like someone being pulled by a rope and headed towards the food. When he passed by Anita, he pushed his elbow into her gut, knocking the wind out of her, and she automatically stuck her foot out, tripping him so that he landed on the side of the table. Chris laughed, thinking, not only was she beautiful, but also unfazed by cheap tactics!

As she sat enjoying the home-cooked meal, Anita stared at Blake's cruel expression until he couldn't take the insult any longer. "Don't stare," he told her.

As though waking up from a trance, Anita gave her head a little shake before defending herself. "For someone who claims he's innocent, you are acting peculiar," she said.

Blake opted to say nothing in reply, and Chris took the opportunity to explain that the guard would arrive sometime during the day. "Is it a female?" Blake asked, smirking.

"Thought about it, then decided it was a bad idea. I want you alive, not dead," Chris whipped back.

Every muscle in his body tensed up as Blake studied Chris and then Anita. "What are your plans for me?" Blake's curiosity had gotten the best of him, forcing him to ask.

His manner was icy and water vapor escaped from his lips as he spoke, causing Anita to be cautious in making her reply. "You'll be notified only at the appropriate time. For now, your no-frill quarters are all you need. Now it's *your* turn to sit and wait, uncertain of your future – with one difference; you won't be raped, tortured, or drugged like those women were. You'll just be left alone with your own morbid thoughts. Sooner or later, you'll understand the afflictions you caused those you hijacked for money."

Anita and Chris made the best of things, and the day went by. Finally, as dusk was beginning to creep in, the replacement arrived, making no sound upon entering the main hut and freaking Anita out. Chris made the introductions, and the man seemed to be well briefed about his duties.

The stranger told Blake to do his business before lock-up. At every chance, Blake tried to overtake his new protector. The new guard was ready for action and became the reigning champion when he put Blake in his place. This impressed Anita and she felt comfortable leaving them behind, so she could seek out her soft bed, a relaxing shower, and a hug from her mother. Anita knew that this very trying time was just the beginning of the finale.

CHAPTER FIFTY

The morning sun woke Anita with its gentle, caressing rays. She rolled over to give Chris a kiss, only to find that his side of the bed was unoccupied. Getting dressed in haste, Anita careened down the stairs and breathlessly entered the kitchen where she found Chris smiling as he was drinking his coffee. Delia had laid out breakfast. Anita reminded Chris of a vacuum cleaner as she inhaled the food and sucked back her coffee. Amused by her oddity, Chris asked Anita to join him on the deck when she was finished breakfast. They had much to discuss, he said.

Grateful for the beautiful day, Anita poured a second cup of coffee and went to sit on the deck with the man who rocked her world. "What are your plans?" he asked. "From here on in, they had better be well thought out."

Moving her lips back and forth, Anita mulled over his question in her mind and, then replied, "I'll call Dante to tell him he can have his protégé in two days, and that he can pick him up at the camp. Of course, the guard will have been long gone by then, so I will say Blake will be locked up in his quarters until he's bailed out."

"Uh huh. What about Jeremy?" Chris wanted to know what her plans for him were.

Anita's head spun around like an owl's, and her voice was piercingly high. "Jeremy. I forgot about him," she said. "I guess we'll have to sign him out under my care."

Chris narrowed his blue eyes and Anita thought for sure a rogue was lurking behind them. "And?" he prompted.

"Well, I can't say for sure because I haven't thought it out," Anita jested back, and Chris knew that it was going to be another plan full of improvising, just as everything else she does, is. But he loved her for it and knew deep down he was there no matter what.

Chris gestured for her to drink up and Anita took the notion they were heading to the Embassy. She dressed professionally, while Chris drove the vehicle up to the house and honked the horn, getting everyone's attention. Suzanne questioned her daughter about her plans and Anita replied honestly that she wasn't sure, but that they may have a houseguest until she could match the puzzle pieces together.

The trip was extremely quiet. Anita was thinking of the many different scenarios that could take place, and none of them made her smile or proceed with enthusiasm. The quieter Anita became, the more Chris was convinced she had a half-cocked scheme planned, and he patiently waited to see what ramifications would come of it.

Arriving at the Embassy, Anita asked Chris if he wanted to join her. At first he said he'd rather go for a walk, but then, reluctantly, he did accompany her, because of her pouty face. They took their time entering the building. It seemed they were expected, and the paper work was all signed and set to go. Before putting her name on the bottom line, Anita wanted to ensure Jeremy would cooperate with her and not fight her. If he did fight her, she would let him become a permanent fixture in the Embassy, and wouldn't care where they placed him.

An escort led the way to Jeremy's accommodations, and Anita was shocked that Jeremy was still living in the dark, dreary basement, or dungeon as it was in Anita's summation. She found that the dim light inside the tiny room was on, and it felt like she was in a fog; it was misty and she could barely see. Chris was disturbed at the conditions, but did not mention it upon entering the room.

Boldly, Anita pulled up a chair and sat down. The men opted to stand. Chris, being very untrusting of Jeremy, stood blocking the door, just in case he decided to bolt. Anita watched with caution how each of the men worked and then cleared her throat, getting their attention. "Jeremy, sit down. I'm here to offer you a way out. You will report to me directly. If you do not, you will be hunted down and shot like an untamed animal. Do we have a deal?" she asked.

Jeremy stretched as tall as he could, and declined both the options to sit and her offer of freedom. Anita was irked, but remained somewhat calm, tweaking Jeremy's curiosity, which finally got the better of him. He then sat down with his arms crossed. "I'm listening," he said.

With her hands folded and resting on the table, Anita was very precise and demanding in her speech. "You will do as you are directed," she stipulated. "You will report only to me. You will not try to escape. Should you meet my demands to the last detail, you will be a free man – which

I promise. But should you cross me, you'll be better off dead. That I can promise."

Jeremy looked at Chris, then turned back towards Anita and contemplated the bargain. When he finally spoke, his voice was so soft that Anita and Chris had to lean in to hear his words. "If I agree to all your demands, I will be a free man, forever. If I fail, I will be hunted down like a terrorist and either disposed, or placed in a dark dungeon to rot. Does that sum it up?"

Anita leaned over the table getting into his personal space. She knew, without a doubt, that he was caving. Even her words smiled, as she replied, "That sums it up."

Jeremy reached out and shook Anita's hand, and Chris sighed, knowing this could blow up in her face. He, however, did not have a better plan. Now that they were in an agreement, Anita let the escort take her back to the office, but instead of being presented with a handshake and her ward, the door closed behind them, and Anita and Chris were told to sit. Apparently it was question-and-answer time at the Embassy.

The director Mr. Rogers rocked back and forth behind the desk, in his lavishly expensive chair. "What do you know about the ambush on Blake?" he asked, point-blank.

Anita's response was very convincing; she gasped, and said, "What are you talking about? He fired me, and the last I heard, he was being transported to a new holding-place."

Mr. Rogers, who was behind the desk, was not convinced she was being candid with him, and he tore into her, as if she were a criminal. "Don't play innocent with me," he said. "You were among the few I told."

Anita didn't falter for a second. "He was left in your care," she rebutted. "He was a double agent. He was working under my father at the time. What makes you think I'd liberate him?"

Laughing, Mr. Rogers leaned in, and sneered. "Revenge. You have motive. As you said, he was a double agent working under your father."

Getting specific, Anita shot back, "I had him arrested. I had Jeremy arrested. You're letting me have Jeremy, when he's also considered a traitor – and by the way, Jeremy worked under my father as well. You begged me to take Jeremy. Why would I plan an ambush on Blake, when all I had to do was ask for him?"

The man sat back in his chair and tapped his desktop with his pen. Summing it up, he said, "You're involved. I could revoke your visa."

Crossing her legs and showing a little thigh, Anita slid back into her chair and made herself clear. "I may be new here," she said, "but if I wanted to I could make your life miserable. How do you think your supervisor would feel if they knew you favored one bad agent over another? One agent you sold out to his enemies, and the other you kept under guard. As for my visa, I am legally and happily married – as you know, since you've had me followed for months – so my position in this country is secure. Speaking of which, where were your men at the time of the ambush?"

The man looked over at Chris, who was showing off his ring, smiling. The man sighed knowing that this time, he had been defeated. He chose to remain silent. Anita and Chris's salvation was the fact that there were no survivors who could tell about the role they'd played in the ambush – except Blake, and he was in no position to tell at all. The gentleman behind the desk denied them access to Jeremy, and said he would call when he had the appropriate paperwork completed. Anita was baffled because all the paperwork was handed to her when she walked in, but said she would await their call. She then turned and walked out of the stale and very corrupt

CHAPTER FIFTY-ONE

Suzanne, Anita and Chris sat quietly, while Delia served up the meal. A smile appeared in the corner of Anita's mouth, and she patted the empty chair beside her. "Please, Delia, join us," Anita suggested.

Delia looked at each person at the table, but focused mainly on Chris and saw his head bobbing up and down in agreement, welcoming her to join them. Delia finished her tasks, making sure everything was laid out perfectly, and then quietly slid into the vacant chair. Once Delia was firmly planted, Anita looked at her mother, and said, "So, mom what have you and Delia been up to? We haven't been around much and this would be a good time to catch up. I guess what I'm asking is, are you bored?"

Suzanne clasped her hand and placed her elbows on either side of her dinner plate forming an inverted V, and rested her chin on her firmly locked hands. "I've never had so much fun," she replied.

Chris looked at Delia, and smiled. "You two are up to something and I'm almost certain it is quite involved. All I ask is that you be very careful. Anita and I could have potential enemies lurking about, but is should end soon."

Anita added her extra two cents worth - to the pot. "We may have a guest for a day or two, but that is *maybe*. If it does happen, would you two be able to keep an eye out for trouble?" Just then, a dark cloud came over Anita's face and she looked down at the floor. "Mom, do you think Dad is alive?"

Suzanne's head was swimming with all her daughter had to say, but her answer came from the heart. "No. Too much time has lapsed. I know he would've contacted me by now. I'm grateful to have such a wonderful friend in Delia." She reached out to touch Delia's hand, and continued. "We will be very careful and, yes, it would give us great pleasure to watch over the houseguest. You might say it will add to my adventures. Perhaps, one day, I'll write my memoirs. I know both of you have your hands full, so let's eat."

Anita's admiration for her mother was more than she could ever have imagined, and Chris, too, was delighted to know this spunky lady. The meal was topped off with a superb dessert and afterwards, the four had coffee on the deck. Delia was having a hard time relaxing, but Chris's kind words make her feel valued. "Delia," he said, "you are a very important part of the family. You may join us all the time, or some of the time, or not at all, but the invitation will always be there." Chris smiled and walked away, and Anita followed, but lagged a few feet behind him. Chris walked a bit farther, then stopped in his tracks, and waited for Anita to catch up. He took her hand, and they walked silently to the beach.

Unable to control her emotions, Anita questioned her own actions. "What have I done?" she lamented. "I ordered an ambush just for Dante. I'm no better than he is."

Chris draped his arms around Anita and held her close. They walked further down the beach and he tried to console her, saying, "No, you didn't order the ambush. Gappy does as he pleases. He doesn't care. He's an assassin. He didn't tell you what his plans were; he kept you out of the loop. I must admit you handled each situation well. You'd make a good CIA agent."

Anita managed a little chuckle, "No chance of that happening. I just wish it hadn't gone down like that. We get Jeremy tomorrow and, before you blow you stack, I *am* thinking of reuniting him with Blake." Chris's reaction to this news was an unhappy one, and he told her it was an outrageous plan. But to Anita, it made perfect sense; one would occupy the other, but both would fulfill her wishes by freeing all of them – each in their own way. Dante would get his wish, she would get hers, Blake and Jeremy would take care of each other, and then there was the trial. That, to Anita would be the end result of everything.

CHAPTER FIFTY-TWO

The next morning, the usual sun didn't greet the couple, and Anita commented that the grayness of the day added to her miserable mood; Chris felt the same way. Anxiously waiting for the call from the Embassy, the couple did their best to relax in their home and tried to carry on a normal routine. But when the phone rang, all was lost like a hurricane rolling into shore – fast and forceful.

At the Embassy, they were greeted with a gloomy salutation, and they followed the man into Jeremy's dreary room. They then escorted Jeremy down the semi-lit corridor to a natural lit area, which came from the surrounding multiple windows. Jeremy was placed in a private room until he was officially the ward of Anita. Anita and Chris were taken into the main office and there the man sat like someone without a guilt complex. He sat staring at the couple and finally put his thoughts into motion. "I don't know if this is a good idea."

Chris took the upper hand and his reply was blade-sharp. "You'd better hand him over to us," he said. "You made this deal, we've put our life on hold, and you turned our world upside down. So you could yank our chains whenever you felt like it? I'm tired of games. You hand him over right this minute, or you can keep him, but we are walking out that door with or without him. Your choice."

The man reacted suddenly. He quickly got out of his chair, and it took Anita's breath away as he left the room. Within seconds, Jeremy was produced. All the papers were in order, ready for signatures. The door was opened, and they were ushered out, giving Anita and Chris the impression that there was more to it than met the eye.

Once outside, Jeremy thought he was a free man, but Chris caught him by the shirttail, and his feet were going nowhere in a hurry. In a very low voice, Anita explained to Jeremy that his purpose in life was just beginning, and that he had better abide by the rules. She left it at that. Once strapped in the vehicle, Anita asked Chris to make a slight detour into town because she needed a few provisions. Before driving off, Chris secured Jeremy into the vehicle so he couldn't escape. After arriving at the little town, Anita went over the list of equipment and staples required, and handed the men a list to start shopping. Once they were out of earshot, she made an untraceable call to set things in motion, and then merrily skipped down the street to catch up with the men. She was happy because, according to her plans, things were going her way. Anita asked Chris if brought the map. He nodded, and said he had anticipated her next move, which brought a smile to her face.

It was late in the afternoon when the three of them arrived at the camp and were greeted by the guard. They asked him to retrieve Blake and join them in the kitchen shack, where Anita laid out an edible meal to tide them over. Met with their stares, Anita began to unfold the details of a plan that would involve the guard, Jeremy, and Blake. Mouths dropped open when she explained each of their involvement. She was not taking no for an answer. Her plan was to go to the cave, rescue Carolyn, and anyone else that was being held captive. Anita was very clear. "It is in everyone's best interest to do their part, and should anyone negate their task, well, let's just say, they will wish they hadn't. I really hope I made myself clear because in the past, two stupid agents clearly did not understand these simple words; 'Do as you are told, and you will be set free'," she said.

Chris knew that now was the time to bring out the map and pinpoint the exact locations needed to rescue Carolyn. Jeremy and Blake expressed their lack of enthusiasm for taking part in such a risky mission, but Anita voiced her subconscious thoughts when she told them to suck it up as their freedom was on the line. Finishing their business plans, Anita discreetly slipped a small bug into the guard's hand, and instructed him to take Blake and Jeremy to the same shack, and then to return, as they had more to discuss. The captives were not happy about the recent turn of events, and balked at being put into the same den, but Anita held up her hand to halt their whining, and grudgingly, they headed off to their quarters.

The guard rejoined Anita and Chris, and sat down to enjoy a cup of coffee. He had the monitor turned on so that they could hear everything said between the two agents, but to their surprise, nothing was said. The guard, listening to the plan, reassured them that he would do his part of making sure there would be plenty of back up amongst the trees, thus preventing any chance that either of the charges would escape. This made Chris feel more comfortable. The guard was asked to monitor what the agents had to say, and Anita apologized for not being there the next morning due to a court date, but promised to be there pronto once court was out. Chris was unsure whether to return with Anita the next day or stay the night and let her go home alone. The voice in the back of his head was screaming at him that he'd be a fool to let her go home alone. With that thought in mind, Chris sought out the guard and the two went over Chris's expectations for the next day. The guard assured him that it would all be taken care of and they would be ready for action the minute they arrived. Anita joined the men and had the guard swear to her that there would be no special privileges or favors for the captives, and that they were to share everything, and play nice. The guard gave his promise, stating that the orders were explicit and would be followed to specs.

With the captive's hut quiet, Anita asked for the men to be brought back so she could reiterate her expectations. While they were being brought back to the kitchen hut, Blake made a run for it and a gunshot rang out, narrowly missing him. The guard then grasped a hold of Blake, and roughly escorted him to the kitchen hut. Arriving at the door, the guard tossed Blake in, and Blake's stature was that of a man full of hatred.

"Don't underestimate me," Anita said, tyrannically. "You created this hell-hole mess, now live in it until I say otherwise." Her words hung like icicles between them.

Blake tried to stare her down, but found no human life in her eyes. Finally, he conceded to the fact that she really was in control. Anita, with a sinful smile, made a motion with her hand that Blake was to be dismissed; anything that was needed to say could wait until the next day.

Jeremy watched on. When Anita spoke to him, he noticed she didn't move even one part of her body. "Your mission is to work side-by-side with Blake," she said. "You are to report even the slightest detail, leaving nothing out. You will not lie or hide details. Your freedom depends on these orders. Now, get some sleep because you have a couple of long days ahead of you and we only have a short timeframe to complete the mission." Anita turned towards the door and watched while Chris and the guard escorted Jeremy back to his little abode.

While Anita was cleaning up the food, a head popped around the door of the shack, jolting every nerve ending in her body. She almost collapsed from the fright. The man gave her a chair before she fell, and he explained he was Rocky, the man she'd sent for. Relieved, Anita began to calm down. When Chris and the guard showed up, the guard drew

326

his gun ready to shoot this stranger. Anita quickly explained that she had asked him to join them and made introductions. Anita finally found out the guard's name was Daryl.

Chris was unhappy about her hiring an unknown, but finally gave up trying to win a losing battle with her and let it go. It was her plan that the four of them – Daryl, Rocky, Blake and Jeremy – could accomplish the rescue mission if Anita and Chris were detained due to the court session. Happy with the arrangement, Daryl and Rocky agreed to set things up, and Anita and Chris left with clear consciences. The only thing that sill made Anita shiver unhappily, was the thought of facing the worst tycoon she had ever heard of – Dante.

CHAPTER FIFTY-THREE

Usually court was exciting for Anita; she thrived on the hope of winning. But on this day, Anita slowed her pace as though she were a zombie going to an evil gala. Chris remained quiet giving her support and breathing space, and Anita reached out to find his hand to show her appreciation of his love and understanding. Walking up to the courthouse's majestic doors, Anita stood still as if she were at the gates of hell. She was abruptly brought back to reality when her opponent stopped beside her, and said, "Nice day for a triumph, don't you agree?"

Anita turned slightly to greet her colleague. "It *is* a nice day for a triumph," she agreed, and entered through the doors.

Taking a deep breath, Anita asked directions on where to find her client and was shown to her private room. She felt as though she were headed towards her doom. She tried to shake off the persistent, distasteful vibes, and entered the room to meet with her client.

Dante sat comfortably at the head of the table as though he were a king, waiting for his servant. His voice was full of arrogance, as he spoke to Anita. "How's the deal going?"

Anita was busy sorting out her papers and glanced quickly at Dante through the tops of her eyes. "Better than expected. Now, I am remanding your case for two weeks. I should then have all the necessary particulars in place and will be ready for action." She said, waiting for his reaction.

Dante's expression turned fiendish and barbaric. He kicked the table hard, sending it flying across the tiny room, and said, "I want to start now."

Anita's eyes were fierce and she did not hold back her temper. "You do as I say," she ordered. "I'm not my father. Your antics won't work on me. Now, sit down and shut up." She straightened the table to release her anger, before going into the courtroom.

Dante's eyes glazed over and his stare was like a brewing storm, but he crossed his arms and sat down. His words were just above a whisper, when he said, "I'm listening."

Glancing around the tiny room that offered just enough space for the table and chairs, and a side table to hold coffee and water, Anita's manner was professional when she spoke again. "If you want your freedom," she said, "grant me this request."

Silence filled the room and their eyes were in a deadlock; then Dante smiled, casually uncrossed his arms, and said, laughingly, "We'll play it your way, for now. You really are like your father. I like that."

Repulsed at the sight of him, Anita gathered her sorted papers and motioned for Dante to lead the way to the courtroom. As they entered, all eyes were pinned on them, and they gracefully took their seats. The Judge brought down his gavel to begin the court proceedings.

Being the first on the docket, Anita stood up. Her skirt showed a little leg and she knew this would entice the Judge. She asked to speak. The Judge granted her wish, making her feel more confident in asking for her plea. "Your Honor," she began, "since my father's untimely death, I've only just begun to find his paper work. I'm asking for an extension of two weeks. I will be fully prepared by then, and will not ask for any further delay."

The Judge's face showed discontentment at the request, but he asked the opposition if he had any objections to this delay. The lawyer looked over at Anita, and announced that two weeks would be fine. The Judge granted her appeal, stipulating that she was to uphold her promise not to ask for any further extensions. Anita assured him she would be ready in two weeks. Anita looked over at her opponent and asked why he was being so generous. He replied that he wanted to see how she would fare, and she laughed.

Dante, being a free man for the next two weeks, laughed sarcastically at his little lawyer. "Guess you'll be visiting me a lot over the next two weeks. You'll need to gather a lot of information. Shall I prepare a bed for you? The nights could be long."

"Only when hell freezes over," Anita retorted. "I'll be seeing you shortly. You just see to it that you go home."

Anita then turned to Chris, who had just walked in, and her angry mood flared. She ran out of the courthouse and jumped into the car, with Chris close behind. "We have to rescue Carolyn or whoever she is," she said, sharply. "I do not want to defend Dante. I bought us two weeks. That's it. Gappy once said we'd discuss Dante, and now's the time. Don't ask, I need to calm my brain and then I'll let you know what the scoundrel said to make me so bitter."

Being the dutiful husband, Chris did as he was told and drove home, but by the time they reached the driveway, Anita's composure was back to normal. She then blurted out the hideous remarks Dante had so smugly made. Now understanding the latest turn of events, Chris laughed because he thought she was premenstrual and she should've known better than to let Dante get to her. Once inside, the phone rang, and the caller said that all was in order and did they wish to join the escapade. Anita barely got changed before they were out the door again. She wanted to settle the dilemma of whether this was truly Carolyn or not. She, also, wanted the plight of defending Dante in court over with. She thought to herself, "One step at a time."

CHAPTER FIFTY-FOUR

Heading out to their given coordinates on the mountain, Anita had hopes of finally ending the charade of games and was already thinking of getting Chris's friend Peter to work with Carolyn. But as soon as the vehicle stopped, Anita was out and over to where the men were standing waiting for them to arrive and she grabbed Blake's binoculars. Surveying the terrain, she was not happy at what she saw. "Only one guard?" she asked. "Don't you think you can take him down and go through the entrance way?"

With a tone that could cause a freeze-over, Jeremy retorted, "Don't you think we would've done that if that were the case? Let me explain it to you. There are at least four heavily armed men *inside.*"

Searching her memory for details about the entrance to the cave, Anita replied, "Didn't seem like that many when I was in there. But, then again, Dante is expecting me, or someone, to come to their aide. Huh. He's trying to manipulate my good sense. Good work guys."

Blake, wanting to get this over with, jumped in and in an impatient voice, said, "Let's just do it. Anita, we'll go to the top of the mountain and I'll lower you in and you can send the girls out, one-by-one."

"Oh, right, like that's going to happen. You'll leave me there and run," Anita replied, sharply.

Jeremy thrust his hands into the air, catching everyone off guard to silence Anita, and said, "I'll be there to ensure that doesn't happen. Can we get on with it?"

"And the guards? Who's going to watch over our arch enemies?" Anita demanded.

Daryl, interjected with a whistle, and everyone stopped talking as he forcefully took the stand. "Listen to me. Anita, I've hired a few men who will take care of the guards. They will tell you over the walkie-talkie when to go ahead and you will then be lowered into the cave. When you find the ladies, you will lead them to the rope and they will then be pulled up.

The front entrance will be blocked and we have no other choice. Rocky is there to protect you. It will work, but darkness is our enemy."

Anita looked at Daryl, and asked, "And Chris?"

Rocky replied before anyone else could. "He'll be with us. Okay?"

Nodding her head meant that it was a go, and they carefully fanned out to their designated targeted areas. Anxiety and adrenaline were racing through her heart making it pound so hard that it sent tingles to her limbs. Anita prayed that the woman they were about to rescue was really her best friend; her thoughts were popped like a balloon by Chris's sharp tone. When he thought that didn't work, he nudged her, forcing her to stay on track. Coming to her senses, Anita realized that they had arrived at the top of the mountain. Chris stayed with Anita while Daryl, Jeremy and Blake searched the premises to ensure Dante didn't have any surprises waiting for them.

Rocky, Anita, Chris, Blake, and Jeremy climbed to the crest of the mountain and could see Daryl and his men head towards the mouth of the cave, but the terrain was too steep to see everything. Anita lost her footing when she got too close to the edge, and was able to stop herself before heading down the side of the cliff in a tumbling mode. The air was getting chilly and Anita hoped they would not have to stay the night due to the late start.

Rocky guided them down the crest a ways and stopped. Anita looked at him and, her voice quivering, said, "Please don't tell me we have to spend the night here?"

She could feel a warm hand on her shoulder and heard Chris's voice say, "No. We need to do a little digging." He saw relief pass through Anita from her head down to her toes. A call on the walkie-talkie announced they were clear to go ahead with their plans. The men picked up their shovels and began digging vigorously to accomplish their task in record time. A small device was placed carefully in the freshly dug area, and a loud booming sound, from below, filled the air. The earth shook under them, making Anita think they would topple over. She clung to a clump of bushes for stability. Anita's heart pounded as they could see through the freshly dug shaft and the explanation was very simple; it was the only opening into the cave and all they did was expand The next thing Anita knew, they were measuring her and then the hole to make sure she, and the others, would fit through it.

Geared up, Anita was lowered into the hellhole, and the darkness that surrounded her made her skin want to crawl back up the through the shaft. Using her flashlight, she could see the ground and tugged on the rope signaling them that she had reached the bottom. Squeezing the talking instrument she held in her hand, she immediately asked for help.

Blake was lowered down next, much to Anita's dislike. She flashed the light in his face, and said, "Just my luck."

Ignoring her, Blake began the job of flashing his light around and was soon joined by Anita; together they found their bearings and steered right for the back rooms. Not understanding the structure of the back cave, they found many locked doors and tried to pry them open with no success. Blake got on the horn and asked for explosives to be sent down and, like magic, they were at their fingertips in seconds.

Holding the light for Blake, Anita watched with intrigue as he tied the explosives together and applied them to the locked doors. When he was ready, he yelled in a loud voice for everyone to stand back, and hit a switch. A loud popping sound reflected throughout the cave and Anita had to cover her ears. Letting the dust settle from the explosion, they searched each room and were astonished to find them all empty. Shocked at their lack of discovering anyone behind the now open doors, they hustled to see if they had missed any other compartments resembling a cell. Coming up empty handed was not on Anita's agenda, and she suggested they look for a hidden tunnel or holding cell, but neither was found. Heart broken, Anita radioed their lack of findings, and they were hoisted back to the top of the mountain feeling distressed.

Anita was angry. "Dante's playing with me," she said. "Well, he's met his match. He knew we would attempt to rescue Carolyn and let us do his dirty job. Getting rid of the men he no longer had any use for. That son of a bitch."

A light went on inside Anita's head, and she turned to study each of the men as her smile stretched from ear to ear. Chris, disbelieving the expression on her face, cocked his head and blinked quickly checking to see if the vision before him was real. When he opened his eyes again, the grin was still plastered across her face. Anita's tight lips divulged nothing as they packed up their gear. Waiting for the right opportunity, Anita dismissed everyone except Blake and Chris, and the trio stood at the top of the mountain eyeing each other, waiting for the news flash from Anita.

Letting her arms dangle, Anita cleared her throat and began to let her mystery unfold. "Blake, you are going to your destination at this very moment. What you do is your business, but I hope you and I will never cross paths again."

Blake could feel the tension mounting in his body, and his eyes locked with Anita's. He wondered what evil motive she was hiding behind her mask, and yet, he admired her tenacity. He spoke with curiosity in his voice. "If it comes to that fork in the road, I shall take the one that leads away."

Chris stood in silence, wondering what it was they were referring to, and watched the performance play out. His wife stood ever so still, and squeezed her eyes together. Then, she quickly opened them as a signal to Blake that she agreed. Making a gesture of his own, Chris indicated that he wanted to get down the mountain before nightfall to avoid getting stuck there overnight.

Anita stepped behind everyone, still with her smile and still not saying a word about her plans, and slowly moved her hand to indicate to the others to head down first. It wasn't a second later, and they began to descend the mountain to the base. Anita was feeling awful inside that not only had she been duped, but also she came away without her friend.

CHAPTER FIFTY-FIVE

Now gathered at the base of the mountain, everyone was a little disgruntled that the risks they had just gone through were for nothing. Licking their wounds from the disaster, Anita told Rocky she needed another vehicle, because Blake was headed on another route to a new location, and that Jeremy would be their houseguest. Rocky was a little miffed that she had sprung it on him at such short notice, but arranged it so she could have a vehicle.

Blake couldn't hold back his fear, and asked, "Just where am I headed?"

Anita could see Chris's eyes grow cold and hard looking. She quickly darted hers away before she felt the nippy air, and spoke directly to Blake. "You know."

Blake looked as though he was about to bail, and Chris snapped, "Don't even think about it."

Blake's hands tensed up and his sharp tone caught everyone's attention. "Dante. I'm going to Dante's," he said.

Anita's hand pointed to the vehicle ordering for Blake to get in. She then climbed in, sat still not moving, nor did she respond. She just sat there, but Chris could see the wheels turning and he knew she was up to something. Rocky told the rest of the group to climb on board into the other vehicles and they would meet at a rendezvous point down the trail. Little was said to help the ride go smoothly, and it seemed to take forever. The vehicle eventually came to a halt and Anita was happy to see another vehicle waiting for them.

Before their departure, Anita took Chris by the hand and led him away so they were out of earshot. She touched his shoulder, and pleaded. "Please don't be angry with me. I'll drop Blake off at Dante's, and Jeremy will accompany you home. He'll be there one day, max. I want Jeremy and Rocky to follow Blake, but I don't want Blake to know. Blake will be reunited with Carolyn, of that I'm sure. I want to end this quickly. We have future plans to be upheld."

335

Chris stood looking at his wife and as his piercing look sent volcanic shock waves throughout her body. "You're hiding something," he said. "Care to enlighten me?"

Feeling wetness form inside her eyes, Anita lowered her head, and replied, "Can you wait until I get home? I need a clear head when I go to Dante's."

Feeling as though he had been beaten up, Chris walked briskly away and Anita wiped the tears that were spilling out from her eyes. She ordered Blake into the waiting car along with a driver, and climbed into the back seat, cocking her gun. Her words were that of someone with a vengeance. "Move, and you're dead," she said.

CHAPTER FIFTY-SIX

The ride was long and Blake was restless. She raised the gun to his head and told him without hesitation that he had better settle down. Knowing all too well she'd make good her promise, Blake chose to sit still. Approaching the hill that led to Dante's, they saw that the house was lit-up as though he were expecting company.

They pulled up to the gate and the guard let them in, triggering Anita's senses that he *was* waiting for them, and that she had been played like a wind-up toy. Getting out of the car, they were greeted by Dante's villainous smile; he was gloating over having won the game. "Didn't find Carolyn, and yet you still delivered Blake. What? Are you giving up?"

Before any one could respond, Anita threw a punch at Dante. While he was rubbing his jaw, she clutched his shoulders with her bare hands and her long fingers dug into his muscles, and brought his head into her personal space. "Get over yourself," she spat. "I'm through playing games. The next time I see you will be in court. As for Carolyn, that woman you showed me wasn't her. As far as I'm concerned right at this minute, my best friend is gone. Enough innocent people have been killed. If she ever gets free, she can find me."

Dante broke her hold and straightened out his posture. He gave her a menacing look, and his reply was cold and calculating. "In court? I thought you had to prep me."

Her face went white, and she retorted, "You'll be notified when court will be held and you will appear two hours prior. That's when you'll be prepped. If I see you before that, I might throw up all over you."

Anita was sure Dante's eyes went completely black and that fangs appeared as he wiped the drool away from his lips. "You had better win the case," he said, boldly.

Taunting the man before her Anita asked, bluntly, "Are you threatening me? What are you proposing to do, go after Chris?"

The silence told her the answer, and Anita did an about-face and climbed into the vehicle. She told the driver where to go next. She thought that whatever needed to be done; it had to be done *now.* She feared facing Chris more than she did Dante; she knew she had better be prepared for a storm because Chris was going to be pissed, and she stewed about it all the way home.

CHAPTER FIFTY-SEVEN

Chris was waiting for her on the porch and he didn't look happy. Putting a false grin on her face, Anita went over to him, and his eyes penetrated so hard, she felt like she'd been shot. Deflecting his intensity, Anita explained her encounter with Dante, and her forth-coming plans. Still Chris's demeanor hadn't changed, and his eyes held hers, prompting her to turn her away.

Chris's voice startled Anita, when he asked, "What aren't you telling me?"

This stopped her in her tracks. She was undecided as to what to say next, but then the words flew out, almost of their own accord. "I'm pregnant," she said.

Chris's expression turned to shock. His eyes were lit-up like sparklers, and he said, "Pregnant? When were you going to tell me?"

Anita was taken aback, and shot back, "Isn't that what you were thinking?"

Still in shock, Chris stammered, "No. I was thinking about your plans for Jeremy."

Kicking dirt at him in frustration Anita said, harshly, "You're an idiot. Jeremy? Please don't insult my intelligence."

Chris was lost for words, but managed to reply, "How could you get pregnant at a time like this?"

Anita hit him hard in the shoulder to get his attention, and screamed, "As if I planned it. Now what are you going to do about it – love us or leave us?"

His arms wrapped warmly around Anita and he choked back his tears. "I love you both. I must say I'm overwhelmed – but happy. Really, I am."

Their embrace was full of love, and they hung onto each other with every ounce of energy they had. After a few minutes, her mother disturbed their precious moment when she announced dinner was ready, and Anita signaled to her that they would be there shortly. Walking in hand-in-hand, their smiles lit up the house, and when they entered the dining room, it was as if someone had turned on floodlights. Suzanne asked what they had on their minds, and Chris gave Anita the nod to explain. But, to his amazement, she declined, and sat down and began a conversation on a different topic. Jeremy was sitting on the edge of his seat, because his future was unknown to him, but kept his cool, knowing Anita would tell all when she was ready.

Once dinner was done, Anita and Chris walked Jeremy to his room. The driver, that had accompanied him home, was to be his guard, and he was instructed to maim Jeremy should he try to escape. Assuring the windows and doors were rigged with an alarm system, they placed a fairly comfortable chair outside the door for the guard, and they merrily made their way to the den. Anita made it cozy and she and Chris sat down for a heart-to-heart talk.

Being as honest as she knew how, Anita began to express her feelings and thought process. "I don't want anyone to know our good news until this is over, because too much fuss will evolve, and I'm not ready for that. I'm meeting with Gappy tomorrow. He has a plan and this time, it's on his bill. He has wanted this for a long time, and I'm his way in. And, before you ask me why, I did not ask nor did I want to know what his personal vendetta is all about."

Chris's body language combined with his voice, deepened. "No," he said, "it's too dangerous."

Placing her hands on either side of Chris's face, Anita was placid when she spoke. "Yes, It will happen. Jeremy will spy on Dante and Blake for us. Gappy will set the trap – or whatever he's devised – in motion, and I will do my part. I swear that in less than a week, it will be over. Then we can tell the world."

Chris shook his head so hard, Anita wondered whether it might be detached from his body. He told her she would not be involved, but Anita was much stronger in her beliefs, and held her ground. "I do not want to go to court and defend that monster," she continued. "Somehow I believe my father planned the abductions, was a partner with Dante, but Dante got greedy, and rather than lose his license to practice law, my father ducked out, and is very much alive."

Chris placed his hands on top of hers and slowly brought her hands down to his lap, not taking his eyes off hers even for a second. He lowered his voice, and said, "You weren't going to tell me until this was over, were you? Don't you think I have a right to decide my child's safety?"

Daring not to move, Anita's response was methodical. "I only found out yesterday," she said. "I was trying to figure out the appropriate time to tell you, but it just seems there was none. When you wondered what else I had to tell you, well, I had to practice it. I knew you'd be happy and I knew you'd be pissed about the timing, but I swear to you I'll be careful. I've come a long way from being a bookworm. I've trained to be an assassin, an investigator, to roll with the punches, defend myself, and manipulate, but I've never trained to be a mom, and I'm scared to death. So very scared."

Chris's arms extended outward and she cuddled up to him. When he closed them tightly around her, he built a protective wall around them in his mind's eye. They both had tears of joy, and sadness that they couldn't rejoice in their wonderful news. Chris's words were barely a whisper, but they were full of compliments as he directed them to Anita. "You'll be the best mom ever. You will teach her good values, self-defense, but mostly to be true to herself. We will finish this adventure, but when it's over, it will stop. If your father is alive, let him resurface at his convenience, and Carolyn, well, we can only hope the best for her. I know deep down you will never stop looking, but it cannot posses you and take over your life. Do we agree?" Drawing Chris closer so she could hear his heartbeat, she agreed. "Should we get any leads on Carolyn, we will hire a detective and let him take all the risks," Chris said, confirming his views.

Nudging his body with her elbow, Anita giggled. "So you think we're having a girl?"

"Yah, and as pretty as her mother," Chris responded, lovingly. "Now are we in agreement about the detective? You know, let him be the risk taker?"

"Yes, Daddy," Anita answered, and their lips met letting their passion for each other flow through them. The heat between them escalated and they headed to their room to take advantage of the romance before it could be interrupted.

Before the sun could rise, Anita wandered down the hallway with two cups of coffee and headed towards Jeremy's room. The guard graciously accepted the warm liquid, and he let her in the room. She stomped in startling Jeremy, and he sat up like he was going to harm her, and shouted, "What the hell?"

Showing no emotion, Anita sat on the edge of the bed and handed him a cup of coffee. She spoke authoritatively and Jeremy's instincts were to listen and take notes. "You will go to Dante's house unannounced, and act like the agent you were trained to be," she said. "You will let me know what their exact daily activities are, what they do, and who they see. Afterwards you *will* report to me. I'll decide the next step. You will have several men at your command, but do not screw me over. Once the plans have been executed, you will be a free man. Double-cross me, and you'll live in a cave for the rest of your life. You decide. I'll be back with orders, and an escort will be placed at your disposal. There will be equipment set up to make it easier. Are we clear?"

Sipping on his coffee as though he had won a lottery, Jeremy paraphrased her orders. "I'll have men with me and you want us to discreetly monitors everyone's activities, comings, and goings. For how long?" he asked.

"You have a day to gather the necessary information," Anita said, and noiselessly left the room like a ghost going to a haunting.

Entering her bedroom, Chris was up, dressed, and looked at Anita. "Are you ok?" he asked.

Smiling, Anita nodded and gave him a kiss on the cheek, and whispered, "Somehow things are going to be just right. We meet with Gappy in two hours. You know the place with all the huts."

Chris's eyes shot wide open, and he replied, "That's more than a two-hour drive."

Anita quickly changed and they headed downstairs and into the kitchen. They grabbed coffee and a snack to consume on the road, and so not to be scolded when they returned, they left a brief note explaining some men would be coming to take Jeremy away for the day. Upon their return, all would be explained.

Not even five minutes after they left, some strange-looking men came for Jeremy. Suzanne, luckily had read the note, asked the men to wait while she fetched Jeremy. She then watched as they headed out the door. Delia walked silently up to Suzanne, and asked, "Are you okay, madam?"

Laughing, Suzanne turned around and repeated, "*Madam?*"

Delia laughed and beckoned Suzanne to follow her. "Come on. I have a feeling we will be having a house full tonight, and it will help take things off your mind. I'm sure when the two sleuths finally tell us what's going on, it'll be over very soon."

While those two ladies began their task of baking and preparing food, Suzanne dropped her hands onto the countertop, and asked, "How long do you think that spell on Dante's mind will last?"

Delia stood still for a moment, and then answered. "I don't know. Let's hope for a very long time. It was fun though and the results were not quite what I was expecting. I was expecting a little more tenderness."

"I hear you. I was thinking the same. He is such a brutal man. I would like to see him swim in his own flood of tears when things start going wrong, and I do believe his life will start deteriorating, now that he's met my daughter," Suzanne said, earnestly. Like someone who had poked her in the ribs, Suzanne asked, "Delia, do you think we could cast a spell for Anita's safety?"

Not sure of how much she wanted to dabble with the book, Delia responded, "Better not. We've casted one recently, and we don't want to upset the Gods by being greedy. They'll protect her."

Suzanne's heart said she wanted to get revenge on the tycoon, but reality told her Delia was right. Although, deep down she knew that something was wrong, and she couldn't turn off the gnawing feeling that grew inside her with each passing minute.

CHAPTER FIFTY-EIGHT

Chris drove like a maniac to the meeting point, and Anita held on for dear life to keep from being tossed around like a salad in a bowl. Anita said, in a loud voice, "Do you have to travel so fast?"

Chris shot her an ugly look, and retorted, "If you had told me sooner about this meet, this wouldn't have had to happen. You are like your father. Keeping everything a secret until the very last minute."

Horrified she had been compared to her father, Anita said in a harsh tone, "Don't compare me to my father. I don't mean to hold things back; it's just that I've had a lot on my mind. One of them being, I don't to go to court as Dante's lawyer. In the future, I'll try to keep you in the loop. You are, after all, my only real friend, lover, husband and soon-to-be daddy, to our little girl."

Still not impressed with her apology, Chris continued to drive wildly, and came to a sudden stop; there before them was a small barricade. Anita coughed when the dust engulfed them like a fog as they exited the vehicle. Waving her hands to clear the air, Anita sauntered backwards to escape the dust and bumped into a solid mass, scaring her enough to yelp. A hand reached out and tapped her arm. Every gland in her body secreted juices making Anita's body spasmodic, and she turned around slowly, hoping to see Gappy standing there. There, instead of Gappy, stood a stranger, and Anita yelled for Chris. Her piercing tone shook Chris up, and he ran as fast as he could. Upon arriving, he heard her say, "Chris, please tell me he's from Gappy's party."

Chris was annoyed at himself for not keeping an eye on Anita, and spoke in Spanish to the man. The man's hand dropped like he had touched something hot, and spoke back in Spanish to Chris. Chris then translated what the man had to say. "He says," Chris rephrased, "that we are to follow him to Gappy. But first I must hide my vehicle." Feeling relieved, and taking a few deep breaths to calm her entire body down, Anita patiently waited for Chris to find a spot to park the vehicle. He walked back to

Anita, held her hand and they followed the man, but looked over their shoulder, just in case.

Walking through the dense trail, Chris was surprised that he had never been this way before, but said nothing. Using his keen sense of direction, he made mental notes just in case not all went well; Gappy always had a second plan when things went awry. Up in the distance, they could see Gappy sitting at a table totally engrossed in a paper before him. They were told to wait until Gappy invited them to sit, and so the pair stood, and waited, and after several minutes, Gappy gestured for them to join him.

Chris, without hesitation, just blurted his words. "How come here? What's with the change of location?"

"Don't want to be disturbed. Too many people know that location. Here it's private and no one will interrupt us. Now let's get down to business," he said.

Anita was trying to keep her enthusiasm down to a dull roar. "What is your plan for Dante?" she asked.

Gappy's manner and words were those of a businessman as he looked over at Anita, and asked, "Are you going to do as I say and listen, rather than acting like a loose cannon?"

Anita's face took a slightly different color, and she nodded her head in agreement. Gappy then began explaining his plans for invading Dante's domain. His fingers walked over the paper that lay before them and described each section in detail. Then he looked up and told her what he wanted her to do. "Once you are in, you will plant explosive devices in these marked areas in the house, and while you are doing that, the rest of my team will plant them around the outside of the house."

Spitting out her unformed words, Anita let it be known how she felt. "Me? You want *me* to plant bombs? If that's the case, I want the detonator, too."

Gappy's words were sharp. "No. It will be my choice to blow it when the time is right."

Chris was livid at how the negotiations were going, and voiced his concern, saying, "Gappy. How could you ask that of her? She's putting herself at risk – alone, from what I can tell. No way that's going to happen."

Gappy's expression indicated he should not be fooled with. "This is what I want," he said.

Anita's temper displayed the traits of a maniac, and she said, "I'm risking my life. You got paid because that's what *you* do for a living."

Gappy's eyes darted from Anita's frightened face to Chris's concerned face and he relented. "Fine," he said. "I will send in two men. You will guide them through the house. Chris, you will accompany me."

Boldly, Anita stood up towering over Gappy. Her irritability was written all over her body, and her voice was strong and clear. "*That's* your plan? Chris and I are to ensure your men get in, help in the planting of devices, and then what? You'll set them off when you feel it's right? I think not. You could blow Chris and I up as well. Nope, that's not going to happen. You need me to carry this out. Rethink. This is your forte. Not mine."

Chris stood up and walked around the open area, and moved closer to his wife. "This is one time I'll agree with her."

Gappy's quick movement to stand up demonstrated that he was dismissing them, and his words coincided. "I don't need you."

Anita spread her feet slightly apart, and folded her arms. Her words were clear-cut, as she said, "Yes you do. As we speak, I have surveillance on Dante, and by dinnertime I will know some of their routines. After dark he will be monitored as well, so I'll know the appropriate time to enter his home. I can get invited in, therefore, it should be easy to get you in, and the task of getting the little hiding devices will be done that much easier."

Mulling it over in his mind, Gappy relented to the help she offered. He realized this young lady was not the fool her father made her out to be, and they shook hands. It was agreed that they'd meet at the same time the next day, and the strategy would be implemented. Anita's heart thumped at a much faster rate, and she could feel the rush of being home free.

CHAPTER FIFTY-NINE

Back at home, Anita and Chris sat somewhat calmly on the porch, and were soon joined by her mother. Suzanne looked ill, setting off an alarm in Anita's heart. "Are you alright?" she asked.

Suzanne replied, with sincerity. "Yes. I wish your father was here and that you and Chris were at peace with each other."

Anita knelt down in front of her mother and hugged her. "Mom, Chris and I are fine. Really. As for dad, well, he'll show up at the strangest time whether in spirit or in actual body form. He always did."

Chris evaluated the scene, and laughed. "Sorry, Suzanne. I can see right through your little scheme. So, Anita, please tell your mother our news so she'll stay. I have a feeling she's bored, and I'd throw in homesick, too."

Anita released her hold on her mother and sat back, looking at Suzanne intently. Then she laughed, and said, "You know Chris, you're right. Her eyes have that less-than-angelic look." Anita got up and placed one hand on Chris's, and the other on her mother's. "Mom," she said, "We're going to have a baby."

Suzanne's mouth dropped and her eyes opened so wide, they almost covered her entire face. The excitement caused her eyes to spill over. Anita wasn't sure if this was a good sign, and quickly added, "This Dante mess will soon be over. When all is settled, I would like Shelan to come and join us."

Suzanne tried in vain to find her voice, and finally shrieked with delight as she hugged the couple, and managed to get a few words out. "I'm so happy," she said.

Wiping her eyebrows, Anita slumped into her chair, and said, "Thank goodness. I thought. Never mind, it isn't worth mentioning." Anita pleaded directly with her mother, saying, "Please tell no one." Looking into her mother's intense, but subtle eyes, Anita laughed and flicked her fingers at her mother. "Go tell Delia. Then we have work to do. Mom, before you go, would you like a little suicidal adventure? Never mind, forget I asked."

Suzanne was a little miffed when Chris spoke harshly to Anita, saying, "Are you out of your mind?"

Trying to sound innocent, Anita let her plans slip out, before her mother had disappeared, knowing she had already baited her. "What?' she said. "She could entertain Dante while I mysteriously slip away. But I vetoed that thought. It *was* good, though, I must say."

Before another word could be spoken, Delia came out to spy on the trio because she was becoming a big part of the family. They asked her to sit down as there was something they needed to tell her. Delia sat down so hard on the chair that it fell over, and they had to help her out of it, and back into a proper sitting position. Her face went flush, because she thought they were letting her go, but was overcome with joy when she learned they were soon going to need her more than ever because there would be a baby to tend to. Stamping her feet, and clapping her hands, Delia showed them how much she appreciated being a part of the family, and hugged them both. When she had regained her composure, Delia asked Suzanne to help her in the kitchen so they would be ready for the troops.

As soon as Suzanne got up to oblige her friend, her face became luminous. "Yes," she said, in response to Anita's earlier question. "I would like some adventure in my life. Deal me in."

Chris was appalled and said, firmly, "No. It's too dangerous. What if something went wrong? You are making it three times as hard for me, because, now I have two more lives I must protect."

Sitting down again and crossing her slender legs Suzanne replied, clearly. "That's my choice. I say deal me in, and you are not responsible for me. You are responsible for my daughter and grandchild, and so am I. This is my way of protecting what's important to me – to put an end to Dante."

Chris butted in before Anita had a chance to open her mouth. "Look, Mom," he said. "This man is a devious tycoon. What if something went wrong? Who would be here to help Anita?"

Suzanne's senses were keen and she put them to the test, as she protested. "If this means an end to a charade Douglas created, I want to be a part of it. You two have a wonderful life ahead of you, and I'm so excited about sharing it. If I get shot, killed, or whatever, I'll think of it as being a soldier helping the world to be a better place for my grandchild to grow up in. I don't see any harm in trying to do that. I'm better at being conniving than I appear. Douglas taught me a lot. So, what's the plan?"

Chris was furious and stormed off leaving the two women to stare after him as he disappeared into the woods. Anita stated that what she wanted was for her mom to get semi-acquainted with Dante, and keep him occupied so they could scope out the house and let Gappy and his men enter. Suzanne thought that sounded easy enough and couldn't wait to begin her next stage in being an adventurous woman.

In the distance they could see a vehicle quickly approaching, and Suzanne headed into the house to assist Delia. Chris emerged from his retreat, and headed in the direction of the house. The car glided in as if it had all the time in the world, and all four doors opened. Jeremy stepped out, but wasn't sporting a happy face.

Jeremy motioned for Anita and Chris to join him in a secluded area, while the others headed inside for a good home-cooked meal. Holding up a cassette tape, Jeremy talked earnestly. "I have some evidence that not only proves Carolyn and your father are alive, but that they are living in Dante's house."

Anita's face went grayish in color, and her hands began to shake. Her head started twitching, and she yelled, "No, no. That can't be right."

Chris grabbed her before she crumbled to the ground and took her into the den to settle her down. Chris then took the tape and played it. Carolyn and Douglas's voices were more than clear, and Anita was horrified that neither of them had contacted her to let her know of their whereabouts. Shivers of relief came over her, as she was pleased her search was now over, but she made no attempt to stop the tape. She had to hear it for herself, and waited for the tape to finish.

The darkened pupils of Anita's eyes were like those of a cat on the prowl: watchful, tense, and precise. Now she wanted answers. Jeremy had done his job, but it wasn't quite over, yet. He gave an account of mostly Dante's activities during the allotted time. Deep in thought, Anita shooed the two men to the dining room; she had to make a call. Jeremy's accounts of Blake's movements, according to Anita, were sketchy, but he did say he had seen him talk with Dante. When both men left the room, Anita made a call to Gappy, and explained to him that they had an additional mission: to rescue her dad and Carolyn from Dante's clutches, and it had to happen the following night. This, she thought would complete her life.

Dinner was eaten in silence. When it was over, Anita looked at Susanne, "Mom, can you be ready in half an hour? Dress like you really want to seduce the pig. Chris and I will join you shortly," she said. Anita then turned her attention to Jeremy, and asked, "Are you sure Blake didn't see you?"

"I'm not the smartest person on the block, but neither am I the stupidest," he shot back.

Not batting an eye, Anita's expression was stone cold, like that of a serial killer. "Be ready to leave in half an hour," she replied. "We have some night surveillance to do." Now turning her attention to Chris, Anita continued, "I know you don't approve, but I want my family here, with us, to explain just what happened and why." She cut her speech short and then yelled at Jeremy, who was almost out of earshot. "I need to know where the voices came from within the house."

Jeremy reentered the room and gave a quick explanation. "It's a device used to pickup noises as far away as five hundred yards. To pinpoint where the voices were coming from within the area is not that easy."

"Then I suggest you pinpoint possible places on the map they could be seeking shelter in. I want the information before the night is over. I want answers," Anita said, sharply.

Using a firm grip, Chris turned Anita around to face him, but his voice was compassionate, when he said, "Just what are you planning to do when you meet up with them, and I mean all of them?"

Anger, fear, and mistrust shot past her hardened face, but truthfully, she had no clue what it was she would find, or what answers she would receive. "I really don't know," she said.

Chris's hand relaxed and her circulation once again flowed freely. She knew he cared about her well being, when he asked her, "You really want to involve your mother? Hasn't she been through enough?"

Her face turned a crimson pink and her words were full of empathy, but Anita was justified in her own mind for involving her mother. "I know it's wrong. I've thought of that, but she is beautiful, and her beauty will distract Dante and his men. I have a plan." Anita left it at that.

Chris's head tilted upwards. His eyes became rigid, not allowing Anita to move until she'd laid it out for him. "I want details, now," he demanded. "I need to know it's not going to blow up in your face or harm anyone."

Biting her lips, Anita replied quietly, "I want to surprise them all. How could my family betray us like that? I don't even know where to begin. My plan is to find their location, and rescue them, with Gappy's help. After all, he'll be there anyway."

Chris's deep probing eyes bored holes through his wife as though he were digging an escape tunnel. "Explosives," he said, simply. "Care to explain?"

"Gappy's turf. You heard him. He wants me to get his men in so they can plant devices. I need to get them in and around the house. My mom can detain him, so I can do my part. Gappy's ready for a battle. That's all I know," Anita quipped back. Grasping Chris by the shirtsleeve, Anita led him back to the group, and announced, "Let's go. I want my family back."

Suzanne looked stunned at Anita's ungraceful approach in detailing what she knew. "Dad and Carolyn are very much alive, and living at Dante's. Why? ... I don't know – but I intend to find out."

Suzanne's mouth was ajar. She quickly recovered and forced the words from her barely parted lips. "That makes two of us," she said. "We have a job to do, let's get at it."

CHAPTER SIXTY

Arriving first at Dante's home, Anita watched as several other cars, with their lights out, approached and parked at different locations, forming a circle around the home. It reminded Anita of an old western and she giggled. Being antsy, Anita couldn't wait to get her family out of the house, and share her new life with her best friend. Reality now faced her when she was approached by Gappy. Chris and Gappy spoke briefly. Gappy's men lurked in the shadows, and before anyone knew it, they had vanished into the night without a sound.

Taking a deep breath, Suzanne and Anita got into the car and drove up to Dante's gate. A short conversation took place between Dante and his guard over the intercom, and within minutes the car had been searched, and then they were allowed onto the forbidden grounds.

The ladies didn't have to knock, as the door was already open, inviting them to enter. A butler was there to greet them, and beckoned the ladies to follow him. The entrance was so lavishly decorated, that Suzanne was in awe that a tycoon could have such good taste. The butler guided them through as he swung open the doors to the den; there stood Dante with a smile that seemed to fill the entire room. The smile started to fade as he focused on Suzanne, and he demanded, "Who is this woman? Why have you brought her here?"

Suzanne took her cue, and interrupted Anita before she could speak. "If I'm not welcome," she said, "I'll sit in the car and wait until business is over."

Dante's smile broadened again, and he retracted his statement. "I didn't mean to imply anything. I was just curious," he said, still smiling.

Anita extended her hand and shook Dante's. Then she turned towards her mother and began to apologize. "I'm sorry, Dante. This is my mother. We were out and about and I had some business to tend to. Rather than take her home, I brought her with me."

Anita could see the man drooling as his eyes feasted upon Suzanne. She chuckled to herself when he gestured for the ladies to sit and get comfortable. Doing as asked, Suzanne made sure she showed some leg, and Dante fell for the vision that was before him.

Suzanne smiled and broke the ice, by saying, "Your house is very intriguing."

Dante's chest stuck out and Anita was sure he was about to beat it with his fists like an ape in heat, when he whipped back, "Designed it myself. Even picked out the furniture. Would you like a tour?"

"I don't want to be an inconvenience to you. You and my daughter have business to discuss," Suzanne said, coyly.

Snapping his fingers, Dante was instantly surrounded by five men with guns. He then gestured that they begin the tour. Anita took notes mentally as they walked through the house, and was surprised at how different and bigger things looked when it was all lit up. She stayed quiet and let Suzanne captivate Dante. When the tour was done, and they had arrived back at the den, Dante's eyes were almost black in color, and he asked, "Anita, what was the true nature of this visit?"

Unnerved, Anita answered, "We need to go over a few things before the trial, and because we were out anyway, I thought I'd save myself a trip. Is there somewhere she can sit while we talk?"

Happy with her unflawed answer, Dante relaxed, and replied, "She can sit over there in the corner, and perhaps read a book. I'm sure we won't be long."

Sighing, Anita pursed her lips and shook her head, admitting defeat. "Dante, you saw right through me. I just wanted to show off my mother. Guess I'll have to improve my bluff. Can't win at poker with a face that tells all."

Dante's laugh was genuine, and he sat down at the desk, and watched as Suzanne took her place over by the many books he had collected. "You're right," he said to Anita. "But in this case, I guess you had two ulterior motives: show off your mom, and take care of business."

Dante studied Anita while they went over some testimony; he was surprised she really had business to conduct, and that she didn't watch the time. Every so often, he found he couldn't take his eyes off Suzanne, and he wanted her, alone.

Anita could feel his eyes roving towards her mother. She closed the file and announced, "That should do it for now. I'm sure more will come up in the next day or so." Anita was about to turn away, when she ambushed Dante with a question. "You and my dad are or were in cahoots, weren't you? Only he didn't deal with it and faked his death to avoid the repercussions. Tell me, what could he possibly have been into that he couldn't deal with or face his family?" Dante was about to open his mouth to speak, when Anita cut him off, and added, "Before you deny it, I know you two were close."

Dante's face reddened and his mouth twisted, as he spoke, "I assure you, your accusations are false," he replied.

Shaking her head, a devious smile appeared on her face, as she retorted, "No. You both used me."

Suzanne joined them and Dante walked them out the door. Optimistically, he said, "I know things will work out for the best."

Anita's ears perked up at the tone of his voice. "And if they don't, what then?" she asked. "You'll dispose of Chris? My wish is that when Karma comes back to haunt you, it will be painful – because that's how I feel, like you and father have destroyed me from the inside out."

Dante's manner changed, and an arctic front hit the room, and he replied, "You just do your job."

Shaken up by his body language, the ladies were escorted to their vehicle by a man who towered over them, creeping them both out. They were stopped at the gate and could hear Dante's diabolical voice over the intercom. "Anita, you can bring your mother here anytime," he said, laughing maliciously.

Suzanne's face radiated hatred, but she spoke with kindness, as she replied, "Thanks for the offer. I just might take you up on it." They could hear him sigh, as though he had completed his mating call.

Anita looked crossly at her mother. "Why did you say that?" she asked, demanding an answer to satisfy her curiosity.

Patting her daughter's hand Suzanne said, simply, "You may need my help tomorrow, and what better way to get in than by an invite," she laughed.

Anita left it at that; she knew it was not a good idea to argue. She also didn't want to admit that was exactly what they may have to do: pay another horrid visit to the demon.

CHAPTER SIXTY-ONE

All parties descended upon Chris's house and entered into the den where they sat around in front of a map and drew in what they had seen, and marked it accordingly. Jeremy pointed to a couple of places where Douglas and Carolyn may be taking refuge. Gappy marked a X on places he had planted bombs on the outside, and congratulated Anita on having a great distraction for Dante, so they could plant bombs on the inside and made it known she was off the hook as being a tour guide. All eyes transferred from the map to Gappy, as everyone wondered what exactly he had in mind, and why.

Gappy, not making any splashes about his reasons, looked at everyone, stating, "I will blow up his house in about an hour."

Anita took Gappy by surprise when she bolted towards him, but she restrained herself from physical violence, and threw her words like stones, instead. "You can't do that," she said. "My father and Carolyn are in there. Let me get them out first. Jeremy has a device that I'm sure can detect their exact location – you know by using that infrared think-a-ma-bob. You promised to wait." When Jeremy tried to remain out of sight, a little voice in the back of Anita's head made her blink and she accused him. "Why didn't you use it? You know where they are, don't you? You're afraid of my father. Better tell me what is going on, and it had better be the truth."

Jeremy remained distant, and said nothing. Chris stepped in, and asked, "Where's Blake? That's who you were suppose to be tailing, or are you two friends?"

Rocky had had enough of the interrogation, and piped up, "Blake's with your family, and before you ask, Jeremy did not divulge their whereabouts in the house. He merely mentioned Blake was with them."

"So why didn't anyone take a few minutes to pinpoint their exact location?" Anita asked, hotly.

Rocky, very apologetic, answered, "We ran out of time. We barely had enough time to plant the bombs Gappy wanted done. I am truly sorry, but it wasn't mentioned and didn't seem to be high on the priority list, not from Gappy, anyway."

Tapping her toe on the floor, Anita's arms flinched as she clutched her hands and released them several times. "What's going on?" she asked, only half-believing what was being said.

When no one responded, Chris was sure Anita grew horns on her head. Smoke seemed to come out of her mouth when she slammed her fist on the table. She could feel heat rising from the pit of her stomach. Her sweat glands swelled and moisture leaked from very pore in the body, as she spoke, "Tomorrow night we will rescue my family and, after that, I don't care what happens. Are we all on the same page, because I don't feel like turning back so everyone can catch up."

"What are you going to do about Jeremy?" Chris asked, calmly.

"My instinct says to lock him up, but I want him to face my father. So, tomorrow night he will be handcuffed with his mouth sealed shut. I think it's time I got a little excitement going, rather than always be the one to have my mouth hanging open in surprise. Besides, as far as I'm concerned, Jeremy is in the same category as Blake: traitors."

Jeremy opted to say nothing in his defense, and accepted his fate, but deep down he pledged to stop the mission anyway he could, and smiled knowing he knew exactly where everyone was located in the house. Anita watched his smug expression, and couldn't wait to wipe the smirk off his face with her own plan of attack. Before having him locked up for the night, she spoke directly to him, unruffled, and said, "You are nothing more than a pain in the ass." Then she watched as he was escorted away.

Gappy was about to leave when Anita's sudden movement towards him caught him off guard. "I'll ask you one time," she said. "Please let me get my family out before you blow his house to bits."

Shaking off the unwelcome hand on his shoulder, Gappy growled back, "You will have until eight p.m. Rocky will be here to help you. You will not see or hear from me again."

CHAPTER SIXTY-TWO

Not able to sleep, Anita rose early. She had the vehicle packed with all the necessary equipment and waited for Chris to join her for breakfast. Watching Anita inhale it, rather than eat it, prompted Chris to study his wife, and asked, "Why didn't you wake me?"

"Because I was so excited, and one of us should have a level head," Anita said, in one breath.

"Since when did you care about being level headed?" he shot back.

She felt like someone had kicked her in the leg. Anita replied, "Um, since now!"

"Uh huh. And what are you going to with Jeremy while we're gone?" Chris asked, hoping to get a satisfactory answer.

"He'll go with us. I don't trust him, but he'll be handcuffed, and just out of reach of anything so he can't botch things up. His mouth will be taped so he can't bother us. When my father is safely in my hands, they will be forced to face each other and, then, we'll let the games begin, and we can walk away," Anita said, earnestly.

Rocky entered the room and spoke with a sharp tongue. "Let's move out," he said. His voice caught Anita by surprise and she dropped her cup, leaping up as the hot liquid hit her legs. "Oh man, does that hurt," she yelled. "I'll be there in a minute."

The pain was unbearable. She scooted Rocky out and, when he was out of sight, she slowly peeled her pants off. Chris grabbed a cold cloth and knelt down to apply it to her leg, when Suzanne walked in. The sight she saw made her gasp. Anita and Chris looked at her and then at themselves, and burst out laughing. Anita quickly explained what had happened and her mother began to laugh, too, and said, "You two do not know what it looked like from here."

"I do now. Mom, could you run upstairs and find me a pair of pants? I don't care what they look like. And before you do that, would you give

Rocky an egg sandwich and see if Jeremy has eaten? I don't want to be accused of being an ogre."

"Yes, dear. Apply some ice on that. It will help relieve some of the burning," Suzanne said, and began her task of making a bit to eat for Rocky and Jeremy.

Having completed her tasks, Suzanne handed her daughter some fresh clothes, and Anita redressed and was ready for action. Taking refuge in a nearby van resting in a secluded area, Anita's mission was to sit and monitor the planted hidden microphones in the house and warn the others of danger, should Dante become suspicious. Chris and the other men skillfully scaled the wall and, using the infrared goggles, they began their task of seeking out Anita's loved ones. Silence filled the airwaves, not even Dante was speaking. Anita threw the headphones off to the side, miffed that she couldn't hear anyone talking. Jeremy sat in the corner and, even though there was tape over his mouth, Anita knew he was smiling. She chose to say nothing, just observe.

Circling the surroundings, Chris and his gang were unable to detect the whereabouts of Carolyn, Douglas and Blake. They were baffled and confused by Jeremy's sketchy coordinates. Rocky asked Anita if she had heard anything, and she replied that it was so quiet in the house, she could hear the clock ticking in the background. She quizzed the others as to what was taking them so long, and when they told her they were having a hard time finding them, Anita became upset and kicked Jeremy out of spite.

The search was called off, and everyone was expected to retreat, but one man slipped as he began to scale the wall and fell to the ground. Dante's guard caught this movement and, as the man managed to climb halfway up the wall, a gunshot filled the valley and the man fell to the ground. No one dared to go to his aide because it was understood it was a booby trap. All the others gathered at the van and hoped Anita had some news about the fallen comrade.

Adjusting the headphones, Anita tuned into the surrounding areas of the house and prayed someone would talk. Dante's men were clearly dumbfounded that no one attempted to recover the corpse, and Dante, himself, instructed his men to get rid of the body. His guards walked up to the lifeless body, and one held a gun on the victim, while the other kicked at it with his foot, receiving no response. One of the guards knelt down beside him to take his pulse, and as he did, the injured man took his knife and stabbed the guard twice. The other guard fired his gun at the intruder, ensuring he was now dead. When the lame guard asked for help, the other guard pointed his gun and shot him once in the heart. There was no doubt about it, Dante and his men were cutthroats, and without conscience. Anita was horrified by these events, and rubbed her belly. Chris peered at her over his shoulder, and said, "And you once rescued me. You don't know how lucky you were."

Without blinking an eye or missing a beat, Anita responded, "That's because Dante and my father were in cahoots. They needed me for their own gain."

At that precise moment, they heard voices and Anita immediately put on the headphones. She heard Dante's voice order his men to clean up the garbage that had accumulated on his lawn. He grunted because no one had come to claim the dead man, and the identity of his intruder was, therefore, unknown for the moment.

In the background, Anita could barely make out what her father was saying. "You have to get us out of here," Douglas said. "Someone knows we're alive and it's too soon. What if it's Anita?"

Dante's voice was preoccupied, yet he responded, "She's clever, but not this good. And, if it is her, then she'll have to be dealt with accordingly – but not until my court case is over."

Defending his daughter Douglas said, with authority, "You leave her alone. She's innocent and she is doing her job."

Dante replied in a grumbling tired old voice, "I'm sure she has followed the paper and money trails," he said. "Her job is to prove me innocent. Once I'm free, her fate is in my hands, and you are to stay out of this. You will be able to leave when I say so."

Anita's eyes welled up. She was speechless, and laid the headphones down. Her voice had little emotion in it, and she looked at her husband, and said, "We need to follow the money trail. Why didn't I think of that?"

Chris put his arm around his wife, giving her support, and said gently, "You probably didn't have the right information. Your father left you only a few details. Now, you get down to business and begin your research. We'll see what comes up and act if the right situation comes our way." He then turned to Jeremy and directed his words right at him. "I can't wait to see where you and Blake fit in."

Looking at her husband as though she was lost in the universe, Anita agreed and began to delve into Dante's finances. She was stunned at what she turned up, and cross-referenced her finding to verify them. She suppressed the horror, and with hostile eyes, she turned to Jeremy, and said, "You were working for Dante. Is it just you and Blake? I must say you had me fooled. No wonder you were afraid of my father being freed." Jeremy's eyes dropped to the ground and he sat still, barely breathing. All Anita could do was shake her head in disgust.

In total exasperation, Anita's voice was husky, as she demanded they get Gappy there right away. Rocky looked at her and said, flatly, "He has a detonator, and will choose when and where it goes off. Plus, he had made it very clear he does not wish to be seen anymore."

Hissing her words like a hungry snake, and flicking her tongue in and out, Anita studied the information before her. "Get him here, *now*. Seems we have some unfinished business to tend to," she said, flatly.

Rocky looked at Chris and Chris nodded his head, telling him to do as requested. Rocky disappeared to make his lengthy call, and when he returned, he said, simply, "He'll be here at seven thirty sharp, because he doesn't want to miss the fireworks."

Chris found a cup Gappy had used and lifted his fingerprint from it. Satisfied with the print, Chris scanned it into the computer and waited patiently for the results. While that was in the works, Anita was trying to piece it all together. No matter how hard she tried, she could not figure out how Carolyn fit into things. Putting on her headphones, Anita waited for Carolyn to speak, in hopes that she would clarify it for her.

Evening fast approached, and still they had no answer for their mystery. Just before Gappy was due to arrive, his true identity was revealed. Anita was very upset with the results. Gappy walked in like a man with a clear future, and the computer was shut down so he couldn't see what they had discovered. Assertively, Anita pointed to Gappy, and herself, saying, "You and me. We need to talk to Dante face-to-face."

Gappy's expression was like that of a madman, and he raised his voice, saying, "The game is over."

"No. Not quite. Let's go see Dante. When you walk away from his place, I assure you it will be for the last time. But until then, we need to talk to Dante. Chris and Jeremy will be accompanying us, I mean, why should I keep the secrets to myself."

Resistant, yet curious, Gappy went along with Anita's wishes and, at the gate they could hear the disbelief in Dante's voice. When they were greeted at the door, it looked as though Dante might have a heart attack as he saw Gappy and Jeremy standing on his doorstep with Anita and Chris. Without waiting for a proper invitation, Anita barged past Dante and headed right for the den with all the men following behind her, wanting to be there when she confronted her Father.

Once everyone was seated, Anita cleared her throat and began her theory. "Dante, I know my dad and Carolyn are here. What I want to know is what does she have to do with the hoopla I've been forced to live in and survived through?"

Dante and everyone in the room remained silent, so Anita sat back and patiently waited, making it very uncomfortable in the room. Knowing no one would let out their dirty little secrets, Anita continued, "Here's what I think. Dante, you and my father were buying girls for slavery. My guess is Carolyn set it up, and Gappy was the buyer. Blake and Jeremy were the ones who chose the women. For whatever reason, there was a falling out. I was brought in initially to be sold and no one was going to figure it out, but when I escaped and botched your plans, my dad knew I'd come back to find Carolyn. It was a matter of time. He played the hero in trying to save me, and the camp invasion was a play for my benefit. The camp my dad blew up was an attempt to get rid of Chris, but that got botched. You all used me for your own games, but I botched every one of them. The stakes were getting higher and no one could be left behind to tell. I guess I made a bad Pictionary player and couldn't see what was going on. There were too many directions in which to head. The stakes were getting even higher from what I can gather, you turned on one another – or pretended to – to throw me off. And here we are. So how's my story?"

No one stirred. Anita got up and walked around the room, and then over to Gappy. She reached into his pocket and pulled out the detonator before he had a chance to stop her. She held it high so everyone could see it. "That's right," she said, in a patronizing way. "Gappy was going to blow up the house, and surrounding buildings, and everyone inside."

Touching Chris's arm, Anita motioned for him to go with her. They walked backwards out of the room, and she made sure her words were very clear. "Don't touch me," she said. "Don't come after me, or make any attempt to move, or I swear I'll press the button. I expect to hear from all of you in the morning, with apologies and complete stories so we can get his court case out of the way. Oh, and by the way, after we are done prepping for the court case, I expect my father and Carolyn to meet with me privately. I want them to hear what I think and how I feel, face-to-face. Arrange that, will you please."

Walking out the door totally disgusted at how her family had played her in a game of chess, she waited until she reached the gate, looked up towards the heavens, and said quietly, "This is for you Jake," and she pressed the fatal button, on the deadly device.... all in a split second decision.

The End

Edwards Brothers Malloy
Oxnard, CA USA
August 29, 2014